The Major's Daughter

WITHDRAWN

Books by Regina Jennings

THE FORT RENO SERIES

Holding the Fort
The Lieutenant's Bargain
The Major's Daughter

OZARK MOUNTAIN ROMANCE SERIES

A Most Inconvenient Marriage
At Love's Bidding
For the Record

LADIES OF CALDWELL COUNTY

Sixty Acres and a Bride
Love in the Balance
Caught in the Middle

An Unforeseen Match
featured in the novella collection *A Match Made in Texas*

Her Dearly Unintended
featured in the novella collection *With This Ring?*

Bound and Determined
featured in the novella collection *Hearts Entwined*

Intrigue a la Mode
featured in the novella collection *Serving Up Love*

The Major's Daughter

REGINA JENNINGS

BETHANYHOUSE
a division of Baker Publishing Group
Minneapolis, Minnesota

© 2019 by Regina Jennings

Published by Bethany House Publishers
11400 Hampshire Avenue South
Bloomington, Minnesota 55438
www.bethanyhouse.com

Bethany House Publishers is a division of
Baker Publishing Group, Grand Rapids, Michigan

Printed in the United States of America

Library of Congress Cataloging-in-Publication Data
Names: Jennings, Regina, author.
Title: The major's daughter / Regina Jennings.
Description: Minneapolis, Minnesota : Bethany House, a division of Baker
    Publishing Group, [2019] | Series: Fort Reno series ; 3
Identifiers: LCCN 2019024674 | ISBN 9780764218958 (trade paperback) | ISBN
    9781493420285 (ebook) | ISBN 9780764234781 (cloth)
Subjects: GSAFD: Christian fiction. | Love stories.
Classification: LCC PS3560.E527 M35 2019 | DDC 813/.54—dc23
LC record available at https://lccn.loc.gov/2019024674

Scripture quotations are from the King James Version of the Bible.

This is a work of historical reconstruction; the appearances of certain historical figures are therefore inevitable. All other characters, however, are products of the author's imagination, and any resemblance to actual persons, living or dead, is coincidental.

Cover design by Dan Thornberg, Design Source Creative Services

19 20 21 22 23 24 25   7 6 5 4 3 2 1

Prologue

From the growing ruckus outside the door, President Harrison could tell the time was approaching. Men who'd arrived early had tried to keep their voices down, but their excitement couldn't be contained.

One scrawled signature, and the news would go flying across the country. Congressmen would rush to their offices, newspapermen would run to their wires, and the message would race from coast to coast.

Rush. Run. Race. That was the chaos his pen would unleash. The greatest race in history, with a starting line over three hundred miles long and the finish line wherever one found it. In less than a month, tens of thousands of people would line up on foot, on horse, in wagons, buggies, trains, and even on bicycles to race for the greatest prize ever—their share of a nearly two-million-acre bonanza, almost three thousand square miles of prairie.

President Harrison took one last sip from his cup of Darjeeling tea and set aside the tariff proposals he was studying. He motioned for his secretary to clear his desk before the impatient guests entered and the ceremony commenced.

This proclamation represented hope to so many—immigrant farmers crowded on the East Coast with no room to plant, black sharecroppers from the South who'd never found the freedom the war had promised, young men and women ready to strike out on their own and leave behind the dusty duty of their fathers' trades. With all the Indian tribes settled, the Unassigned Lands sat fertile and empty while the nation waited, breathless, for his decision.

Congress had already amended the bill. All it lacked was his signature.

They entered with a burst of energy. Handshakes all around, with whispers from the Kansas delegation about the hordes already amassing on their border. Most of the representatives crowded around his desk, but some lingered by the door, jockeying to be the first out to make the announcement. The country held its breath. Across the plains, cannons were primed for celebratory firing, and punch bowls were set out for more genteel festivities.

There were no guarantees. Many would suffer disappointment, but he was giving them a chance. That was all they wanted.

President Harrison dipped his pen into the inkwell. Let them run. It was in the air and in their blood.

With the stroke of his pen, the matter was settled, and the core of the nation was forever changed.

Chapter One

We're getting a town lot, and it's purt near guaranteed. You see, we ran into this man selling town lots in Fort Worth, so we've already put our money down for a corner spot, but we're going to run anyway. I figure, why not? Make a claim on a 160-acre homestead, and then we can decide whether we cotton to the farm or the town. There'll be plenty of losers out there to sell to when we decide which one we want. Easy money. That's what I'm saying."

In Caroline Adams's opinion, the train from Garber, Texas, didn't need steam power. It could have been propelled solely on the hot air provided by its passengers. She turned her face toward the window to squelch the impulse to challenge the braggadocian man seated behind her. Did he not understand the nature of the race? Why did he think someone in Texas could sell town lots in the Unassigned Lands when no one was permitted inside yet? And what town? Besides some depot workers, no one lived in the region. There were no roads, no houses, no neighbors. The whole idea was ludicrous.

Having grown up on the fort that protected the lands, Caroline had insight that no one else on the train possessed, but they wouldn't credit it to her. They'd think her too fine a lady to know about the untamed lands they were headed toward—just as the society people in Galveston thought she was too uncouth to know her way around a drawing room.

There was a sharp jab on her leg, and Caroline turned to see her friend Ambrosia Herald wielding her parasol.

"You have that look on your face." Amber's blue eyes twinkled. "Scowls can cause irreversible damage to your skin, and once a wrinkle appears on the surface, it will never completely disappear. It lurks there, waiting for fatigue or age to summon it and mar your complexion."

"You and your faux facts," Caroline retorted. "You're as full of malarkey as every other speculator on this train." But while Amber was jesting, the passengers on the overcrowded train believed the tall tales they were spouting.

"Do you think you'll see him?" Amber asked. "Do you think the infamous Frisco Smith will make the run?"

Caroline rubbed her nose. It had been two years since she'd seen the man in question, and his name still left her disconcerted.

Frisco Smith—roguish frontiersman and boomer—had spent more time in the guardhouse at her father's post than at the illegal homesteads he tried to establish. She shouldn't feel foolish about her youthful infatuation with him. He was, after all, uncommonly handsome and debonair. But when she'd left the isolated fort to move into society, she learned what her father had known all along. Men like Mr. Smith had nothing to offer a lady. She had to think about her future, which was exactly why she'd returned to Oklahoma Territory.

"Oh, I'm sure Mr. Smith will be about. He won't pass up a spectacle like this," Caroline said. "But you'd better prepare to see Bradley. He'll be on tenterhooks, waiting for you to get to the fort."

Bradley Willis was the younger brother of Caroline's stepmother. Four years earlier, he and Amber met when she and her father were riding a herd of camels across Indian Territory. Of course Bradley would fall in love with a spunky camel-herder. And as both girls were daughters of cavalry officers, Amber and Caroline had much in common. They'd been fast friends ever since, often spending the hot summers together at Caroline's grandmother's house in Galveston.

Amber dug the tip of her parasol into the wooden floor of the train car. "I hope Bradley is eager. He claims that he's determined to let his enlistment expire in a few weeks. If that's the case, then there's no reason the wedding won't go on as planned, as long as he hasn't changed his mind."

Caroline snorted. "He fell in love with you in August. In Oklahoma Territory, any two people who can tolerate each other in August are in love. Otherwise the heat would make them too cranky to bear. He hasn't changed his mind."

"Purcell Station ahead," the attendant called. "Last stop on the southern border of the Unassigned Lands. Thirty-minute stop, and then we're pulling toward Oklahoma Station. If you are continuing on, don't be late."

Amber stood and shook out her white-and-green tartan dress. "Come on, Caroline. Let's see the town—or at least, let's let the town see us."

Taking her reticule, Caroline stood in the aisle amid the boisterous passengers collecting their belongings. When she'd heard that the railroad had increased the number of trains to Purcell, she should have expected the town to be crowded, but nothing prepared her for what they encountered when they stepped foot on the platform.

It was like being caught in a cornfield that pushed back.

No matter which way she turned, Caroline couldn't see past the wall of humanity that milled around her. The air was stale with nervous sweat. Someone stepped on her toes. Amber was jostled against her with nothing more than a grunted apology to cover the offense. It was as if the denizens of every bank, tenement, and saloon had congregated in this small town in the Chickasaw Nation. And there was nowhere for them to go. Not enough hotels or public rooms. Which accounted for the odor.

"Have you ever seen the like?" Amber asked. "If you're looking for a beau, there's plenty to choose from."

"Among these men?" Caroline responded. "Needle in a stinky haystack." Still, the thought of who she might meet was exciting.

"If we want to get off this platform, we're going to have to push through." Amber linked her arm with Caroline's. "Ready?"

Caroline set her hat and nodded with a grin. This was better than sipping lemonade in the sweltering humidity of Galveston.

The ladies wove their way forward. Occasionally they were knocked off track by someone swimming upstream against the passengers departing the depot, but they finally found a path through the crowd and into the street.

"Watch out!" Caroline twirled Amber around just in time to keep her from being hit by a team of horses barreling through. Standing still clearly wasn't advisable. "Why don't we see what the mercantile has to offer?" Caroline said.

"I wouldn't be surprised if it was sold out," Amber said. "These people are like a horde of locusts."

There was nothing Caroline needed to buy. Unless something had changed, the shops here didn't supply the scented soaps and creams she'd grown fond of. Besides those, her stepmother would provide everything she required. But Caroline wanted to be a part of the enterprising crowd. She wanted to share in their excitement and judge if there was any place for her among them.

Amber pushed the door to the mercantile open halfway, then

had to wait for a hardscrabble woman to shift her basket over before they could squeeze inside. Amber spotted a basket of dried fruit and went to the counter to fill a sack.

The familiar scents of the store brought back years of memories. The smell of leather reminded Caroline of shopping for shoes with her father. The sharp nutmeg pulled up scenes of cooking at Christmas with Louisa and Daisy. All homecoming smells, but the woman staring at Caroline was a stranger. With a chapped hand, she wiped her mouth and took in every detail of Caroline's garments.

Caroline had already noticed that the farther into Indian Territory they traveled, the hungrier the women's gazes when they spotted her and Amber's new gowns. When she'd moved to Galveston, it had taken her half the season not to despise the constraining layers of the latest fashions. By the time she'd learned to appreciate their beauty, she'd found the carousel of societal expectations even more exhausting.

A girl about Caroline's age joined the staring woman. Decked in the same threadbare fabric and with similar hobnailed boots, she stood by her mother and gaped. "You don't think she's running for a homestead, do ya?" she whispered. She arched her back and stuck out her derriere to imitate Caroline's bustle.

Caroline turned to the side, pretending not to hear them, and instead perused the nearly empty shelves.

"Probably." The mother wiped a drop from her nose with the back of her hand. "Rich girls think they can do anything, but don't you worry none. That contraption on her backside will bounce her plumb out of the saddle."

Caroline fumed. That people would speak about her thus in Oklahoma Territory was unfathomable. They must be strangers come to town—that was the only excuse. Otherwise, they would know of her. And how presumptuous of them to assume she couldn't ride a horse! Nothing could be further from the truth. Perhaps most ladies wearing a pleated accordion skirt couldn't jump astride a bareback horse and outrun a cavalry unit, but Caroline wasn't most ladies.

Although she was usually quick to speak her mind, Caroline was unsure in this moment. It was possible that these women had encountered ladies dressed like her before and had reason for their scorn. How could she explain that she was different? Before she decided, the mercantile door was pushed open, and this time it was she who was bumped out of the way.

A tightly coiled cowboy stepped inside, took one look at her, and whistled. "Wooo, doggies, ain't you far from home."

Caroline found her tongue. "No, actually. I lived here. Ever since—"

"You ain't going to run, are ya?" the cowboy asked. "What would you do with a homestead, anyway? Ain't likely that you're going to break ground and put in a crop."

Of all the impertinent upstarts. Where was Amber? They'd spent enough time in this place.

Emboldened, the woman stepped forward. "Don't intend no disrespect, but he's right. This contest ain't for the likes of you. Your kind won't last long out here."

Her kind? Caroline's eyes tightened. "I'm sorry to contradict you," she said, "but you've misjudged me. I am a capable lady who knows more about Oklahoma Territory than any of you. If I chose to homestead, there'd be no challenge that I—"

"You won't believe what I found!" Amber appeared at Caroline's side. With a flourish, she produced a paperback booklet titled *The City Girl's Guide to Homesteading for Novices*. "I bought the last copy," she said.

Caroline cringed as laughter erupted in the room.

"They going to homestead by a book?" The woman braced herself against her daughter's shoulder as she laughed.

"I hope they got a plow and draft horses hidden in those pages," the cowboy guffawed.

This wasn't the awed reaction Caroline had expected on her arrival. Taking Amber by the arm, she pushed out of the store, leaving the mocking homesteaders behind.

"What was that about?" Amber asked. "Are we offended?"

"We don't have time to be offended," Caroline said. "We can't miss the train."

"We do have time for ices. See that sign? That'd help wash down some of the dust I've swallowed."

An ice did sound good, but one look at the line and Caroline shook her head. "I'd rather do some exploring. You go ahead. I'll meet you on the platform."

Amber dug through her green-fringed reticule as Caroline moved along the crowded boardwalk. The streets were awash with men. For the most part, the women wore their faded, Sunday-best dresses and stayed against the buildings, protected by the shade and out of the press of people. Many eyes watched Caroline as she made her way down the sidewalk. She tried to smile at the ladies in return, but they often looked away as if embarrassed to be caught staring. Why were they acting like that? What was wrong? But then she took another look at her dressy cotton sateen gown and realized that she stood out like a piglet in a hatchery.

Surely some wealthier people had come to invest in the new land. They couldn't all be poor. Then again, if a man had funds to secure one of the few hotel rooms in the city, his wife wouldn't be standing outside, trying to find shade.

A group of people gathered around a freshly painted board advertising maps of the Unassigned Lands for ten cents. Caroline took the top one off the stack and was immediately addressed.

"That'll be ten cents, ma'am. No free looks allowed." The

compact salesman had his sleeves rolled up to his elbows and dollar bills sticking out of his arm garter.

"That's ridiculous," Caroline said. "How do I know it's a good map if I can't open it?"

Three young men approached. They tipped their hats at her while one of them dropped a dime in the palm of the salesman, then took a map.

"Are you going to buy one or aren't you?" the map man asked her.

Another man, this one of a rougher sort, handed the salesman a dime, but when he took his map, he managed to pick up two.

"Hey, you only get one. . . ."

Caroline used the distraction to open the map in hand. She spun it around, trying to place the railroads marked on the map with where she knew them to be. And that lake? There wasn't a lake like that anywhere that she'd seen. She held the map closer and squinted at the title. The word *Oklahoma* was carefully printed over *Ontario*.

"Thief!" she gasped. "These aren't maps of Oklahoma Territory. They aren't accurate at all."

A burly man with two sons scowled. "What d'ya mean, miss?"

"I mean that this man is a huckster. These maps are useless." She raised her voice along with the map. "Don't buy these," she announced.

The peddler stuck his nose right in her face. "You'd better be mindful of name-calling. What do you know about it?"

"Everything, I suppose." Caroline brushed back a wisp of her red hair. "My father is the commander of Fort Reno, and he and his troopers will not look kindly on you taking advantage of these people."

Before the madness of this land run had brought strangers to the nations, everyone knew who Caroline was and who her father was. She had to admit it was gratifying to see the effect the information had on an outsider.

He snatched the map from her hand, and even though his tone was congenial, his expression was not. "Are these the wrong maps? My goodness, I must have pulled the wrong crate out of the wagon." He lifted the stack of papers and tucked them under his arm. "I'll just put these away." And with that, he spun on his heel and took long, quick steps away from the crowd. Judging by the way the burly man took after him, Caroline had no doubt the peddler would be giving back at least one dime.

A strong young fellow with a double cowlick nodded at Caroline. "Fine work clearing him out," he said. "If you think that's something, you should see the chap over there. He's not just selling maps, he's selling the land itself." The boy snorted. "As if he can lay claim to any property yet."

The infamous city lots that her train companions were talking of? Caroline checked her watch. She had time to right one more wrong. Honestly, with this many swindlers about, how would the new territory ever get lined out straight? Thanking the young man, she followed his gesture to another group of people gathered around a man doing business on the end of a barrel.

She couldn't see much, but looking through the crowd, she could see a paper spread over the barrel and money exchanging hands.

"That's lot ninety-six on Buchanan Street, just north of Tenth. Here's your certificate."

The lucky buyer, a young wrangler wearing chaps and a bandanna, popped out of the crowd, waving the paper over his head.

"Excuse me, may I have a moment of your time?" Caroline asked the cowboy. His eyes lit up at the sight of her. In this case, the scarcity of well-dressed women on the street worked to her advantage. "What exactly did you just purchase?"

"It's a city lot in Redhawk. It's not on a main thoroughfare, but I only paid one dollar for it."

A dollar? Caroline fumed. "And where exactly is Redhawk located?"

He shrugged good-naturedly. "On some fertile soil with a healthy creek and a railroad passing through."

"Step on up. Only thirty-eight lots left in Redhawk," the barker chanted. "You can trust me, folks. I know this land better than my own reflection."

It was too much. "You should get a refund," Caroline said before excusing herself to confront the barker. She huffed as she wedged her shoulder between two men and made herself a space, although they weren't pleased to have to make room for both her and her bustle. Caroline tugged her skirt to pull it out from under a boot. It was worth a ruined hem to disrupt this huckster's game.

With the charlatan still bent over the map, the first thing she saw was the top of a bowler hat, then a nice tailored suit. Nicer than she'd expected from a confidence man. Evidently he was successful at his deceit.

"I apologize for disenchanting your audience," she said, "but by whose authority are you selling city lots in a town that doesn't exist?"

The pen paused over the map. The customers surrounding the barrel straightened to get a better look at her. Caroline met their wary gazes. They would thank her for interfering if they understood what she was protecting them from.

The man in the bowler hat raised his head, and a pair of sparkling dark eyes met hers. His smile was as slow as honey dripping from the comb. "Miss Adams, it's a pleasure to see you again."

Frisco Smith. Caroline's hand went to her stomach. She'd thought she was prepared to see him. She was wrong.

"Mr. Smith," she stammered. "I didn't recognize you."

He folded up the map and gathered his papers into a worn traveling bag. "That's all for now, folks. As you can see, I have to attend to more pressing matters. I'll be back in half an hour, as soon as I settle some business with this kind lady."

He was laughing at her, probably remembering how she'd idolized him when she was younger. Well, she was grown up. She'd been in society—real society. Now it took more than a flowery compliment and dashing smile to turn her head.

The time he took gathering his things gave her the chance to compose herself. "Where are your buckskins?" she asked. "In that fancy suit, I took you for a city attorney."

"That's what I am."

Her eyebrows rose. "I've heard a lot of malarkey associated with this event, but that tops them all."

"Who do you know that has spent more time in court than me? And all those hours in guardhouses and jail cells? Instead of carving on a pine knot like my incarcerated neighbors, I read law." He picked up his traveling case and offered her his arm.

Another lawyer? She'd met enough of those in Galveston. With his black curls and swarthy skin, he looked more like a pirate than a solicitor, so obviously he wasn't spending all his time at a desk. She eyed the offered arm warily. She had grown. She had matured. Having an escort through a crowd was no sign of weakness. She slid her hand into the crook of his arm and allowed him to part the crowd as they headed toward the depot.

"And I suppose that was legal work you were doing just now," she said. "Selling lots off a map in a town that doesn't exist?" Her tone might be cool, but she wanted him to know that her options for entertainment were no longer limited to his incarcerations at the fort.

"Well, it is legitimate. I'm well aware of the legal constraints."

Caroline bit her lip. If anyone knew the Unassigned Lands, it was Frisco Smith. On that, he was telling the truth. He'd been a boomer for years, petitioning the United States government to open the territory for homesteading while leading forays into the forbidden land to show its benefits. Every time her father's troopers caught him, he was confined to the guardhouse at the fort until he could get a court date. If it weren't for Frisco and his allies, this land run wouldn't be happening.

"Perhaps it isn't technically illegal, but is it ethical? The nature of this contest should be kept pure. An attempt to fix the outcome—"

"I appreciate your attempt to explain my errors, but with your train departing, I don't have the time or inclination to defend myself further."

"I'm sure it's so complicated that someone like me couldn't understand," she said.

He drew his head back and studied her through narrowed eyes. "I've never questioned your intelligence, Miss Adams. I hope you don't give me reason to now."

"What do you mean by that?" Caroline asked.

"It seems you've changed a lot since I knew you."

So he had noticed. "Yes, I'm no longer the impressionable child I used to be."

They'd stopped before the depot, and Amber was making her way toward them, her parasol bobbing over the crowd.

Frisco followed her gaze to Amber. He released her arm and took her hand. "You might have been young, but you weren't ignorant," he said. "At least then you knew that fancy manners are no substitute for substance."

Caroline inhaled so sharply that she hissed. When she tried to pull her hand away, he pressed a firm kiss on the back.

His black eyes sparkled under a rakishly tilted bowler. "It was a pleasure seeing you again, Miss Adams, but I'd recommend that you get back to the fort and stay there. This here game is high stakes and could get rowdy. Better stay close to your daddy and out of the way."

Caroline yanked her hand free, dismayed that her heart had skipped a beat at his kiss. He was little more than a criminal. No fortunes, no prospects. All that gallantry that had been directed at her over the years hadn't meant a thing. Just a charlatan trying to get under the skin of a major enforcing the law.

But before Caroline could fire back with a sharp retort, Frisco tipped his hat and disappeared into the crowd with his satchel. He no longer wore the frontier garb of the interlopers, but he still had the heart of one.

But he didn't have *her* heart. For that she could be thankful.

Chapter Two

You mean all I have to do is follow this map, and it'll get me to the North Canadian River? That's where the best farmland is, right?"

"That's right, sonny. This map can't lead you wrong."

Would that man never give up? Frisco had shut down his scam twice already, and the huckster had just moved his pile of fraudulent misinformation to another corner. Frisco ran a finger beneath his starched collar. After a few days of rain, the April sunshine was welcome, but not the humidity. It made tempers short, and his had been pushed to the limit.

His satchel crushed against him as he squeezed through the crowd of suckers standing under the balcony of the bank. Cash sprouted from the confidence man's arm garters, showing that he'd been busy.

"Ladies and gentlemen," Frisco proclaimed in his best oratory voice, "the race of next week is supposed to be a fair contest. Everyone who stands on the starting line will have an equal chance to find a home, no matter their age, race, or creed. Buying a map of Ontario, Canada, will not increase your odds."

"Ontario?" A man flipped open his map and held it at arm's length as he squinted. "This says *Ontario*! I demand a refund."

"Ontario? What?" The shyster manufactured the same counterfeit shock that he had the last two times Frisco pointed out the error of his product. "Honest mistake, gentlemen. Honest mistake." He dug deep in his pocket and began distributing dimes as Frisco gathered up his stack of maps. "Hey, where are you going with those?" he demanded.

"I'm going to find a privy that's running low on paper," Frisco said. "That's all these are good for."

The peddler puffed up like a potato getting ready to split its skin. "Mr. High and Mighty. Let me guess—your father is a general at the fort, and he'll throw me in jail if I don't stop."

Frisco couldn't help the grin that broke out. So Miss Caroline hadn't changed entirely. No wonder she was suspicious when she saw him with a map selling town lots. While he had nothing in common with this crook, he could understand her confusion. That was Miss Caroline for you. Always sticking her nose where it didn't belong.

"He's not my father," Frisco said, "and he's not a general. He's a major, and he'll throw you in the guardhouse, not jail. On this, I speak from experience."

And then he left to find a burn pile so the loathsome pamphlets couldn't do more harm. For years Frisco and his mentors—men like David Payne and William Couch—had demonstrated against the government keeping good land unclaimed when there were so many willing hands ready to farm it. Years ago, all Indian Territory had been set aside for the tribes, but it was 1889. The tribal boundaries were set. Now, whether those treaties were fair or made under duress, that wasn't for Frisco to say. They were law, and there, right in the midst of all the native nations, was the jewel of the territory sitting fallow and unused. Nearly two million acres ready for the plow.

According to the Homestead Act, adults over twenty-one had the right to claim empty government land if they could hold the land for five years and make improvements on it. But for some reason the government thought the rules didn't apply to the Unassigned Lands. So Frisco and other boomers like him decided to test their resolve. In 1884, the government lost their case against Payne, and it was ruled that it was legal to settle on the Unassigned Lands, yet even the court's decision didn't change the soldiers' orders. Thus the charade continued— soldiers following their orders to arrest boomers on the land, boomers being taken to court, the court releasing them because they hadn't broken the law.

It was a parody of justice, but Frisco and the others persisted, knowing that public opinion was lining up behind them. And finally they got the news they'd been waiting for—the government was declaring the Unassigned Lands open for homesteading.

And all these people—wagons as far as the eye could see, depot crawling with newcomers, tents pitched in every empty lot—were proof that the boomers were right. Americans needed this land. They needed a new start, and they'd do anything to get it.

Flames licked the sides of a cauldron situated in the center of a group of tents. A harried woman wiped the sweat from her forehead as she stirred her laundry in the bubbling brew. Frisco tipped his hat and stuffed the maps into the blaze.

A tent flap burst open, and a young pup rushed out and began yapping at Frisco's heels.

"Chauncey, come back." A stout little fellow barreled out of the tent and caught the dog around the middle. He grunted as he lifted the long-eared pup off the ground, but it stretched as he pulled. Doggy toenails never left the ground.

"Get him back on his tether," the woman ordered. To Frisco,

she said, "Sorry, sir. It's a lot of excitement for a dog . . . and a boy."

"No harm done," Frisco replied. His nose twitched at the smell of lye soap. "You wouldn't happen to be taking in laundry, would you?"

"Yes, sir. That's exactly what I'm doing. It's a week until the run. Might as well pass the time while bringing in some coin."

"Well, I'll be. That isn't Frisco Smith, is it?" a new voice said.

Frisco spun on his heel to see a bull of a man coming out of the tent. He was clean-shaven, with a fresh haircut and eyes that nearly disappeared when he smiled. His swagger was so like the little boy's, there was no denying the connection.

"Patrick Smith!" Frisco cried. Patrick extended his hand, but Frisco pulled him forward for a hearty embrace. "I can't believe my eyes."

"And look at you!" Patrick clutched him by the forearms and stepped back to survey his suit. "You've been busy."

Frisco nodded at the boy. "So have you."

Patrick beamed as he motioned the boy to his side and ruffled his hair. "Millie, come here and meet my partner foundling in crime."

Frisco hoped she didn't notice his wince. He hated the word *foundling*. It sounded so weak, so vulnerable.

"Mrs. Smith." He removed his hat as he bowed. "I should have known Patrick wouldn't settle until he'd won the most beautiful lady for his own."

Her cheeks were already pink from the fire. She pushed back her damp blond hair and said, "This is Frisco? I thought you said he was a wild rabble-rouser."

"Don't let the clothes fool you, ma'am," Frisco said. "They don't change the man."

"Have a seat." Patrick ducked into his tent and carried out two milking stools. "I suppose you mean to run next week."

If he only knew. "Of course. And you?"

"Absolutely. I've got my sights set on a homestead but would settle for a town lot. Being the first saddler in an area is my goal. Guess I'll hop the train and head to Oklahoma Station. If all the lots are full there, I'll ride on up to Guthrie."

"Oklahoma Station is the train's third stop," Frisco said. "By the time you get past the Norman depot and Moore, the horsemen from the eastern border will have reached it. Never mind Guthrie. You're on the wrong border for that."

Patrick stretched a leg out in front of him. "It might not be a good plan, but it's all I got. My old draft horse isn't fast enough to get us anywhere. I'm better off jumping from the train and trying my luck on foot. Surely I'll find something."

No, not surely. Very unlikely, with the fifty thousand people coming in.

Frisco pulled his satchel around in front of him and unfastened the latch.

"You're still hauling that old bag around, I see," Patrick said. "Looks like you could afford a new one by now."

"It's the perfect size to carry my things," Frisco said. "I'll unpack it when I get home."

"Home? Have you got a home I don't know about?"

Frisco ignored the stab of pain the observation brought and shook his head.

"You are a mystery, Frisco Smith," Patrick said.

"And here I am, ready to explain the world to you. Let me tell you how your luck has changed." Frisco pulled his city plans out of his satchel. "I've spent the last four years traversing the Unassigned Lands looking for the best place to set up a city, and I found it. Fertile land, adequate water, nearby timber, and almost a guarantee that the railroad will be passing through in the next three years. Redhawk is going to be a prosperous city. Why don't you and Mrs. Smith settle there?"

"If there's no railroad, how am I going to get there? I may be strong, but you know I've never been fleet-footed."

"I'm going to claim it. I know the best route—the only route from the west—and instead of sitting on one hundred and sixty acres, I'm dividing it into town lots."

Patrick's dark brows lowered. "You always have a plan, and you'd think by now I would've learned not to get caught up in your grand schemes. I like the sound of it—"

"Of course you do—"

"But how much is it going to cost me?"

Frisco watched Mrs. Smith lift a heavy paddle dripping with water. Industrious even while waiting for the grand event. He turned his attention to the boy playing with his puppy and then looked back at his friend. "How about free laundering of my sundries for a month? But you can never tell any of your neighbors what a bargain I gave you."

"Only a month? You can't be profitable that way. What's your angle?"

"I'll keep the best lots for myself. In fact, I've already got a dugout built and a summer crop in on the plot. Just a few acres, mind you, but enough to give me some sustenance in the fall."

Patrick's brow furrow deepened. "You can't claim land beforehand. That's cheating."

"I'll be on the line with everyone else at high noon," Frisco said. "We all have the same opportunity to run. All I've done is sweeten the prize at the end. It'd be even better if I had an expert saddlemaker in town." He nudged the paper toward Patrick. "Far be it from me to change your plans. Go ahead and buy that train ticket, but know you have a place in Redhawk with me if you don't succeed."

"Thanks, Frisco," Patrick said. "I'll be just fine, and you will too, as long as you keep your socks dry—"

"—and your stomach full." Frisco hadn't heard the saying

since he'd lost contact with his friends, but it brought a bittersweet smile to his face.

Frisco had always been a man of vision, but his visions weren't always shared by the other boys in the orphanages. His friend Patrick had intervened repeatedly and if not saved Frisco from every beating, had at least prevented them from being worse. Frisco's offer was generous, but it would benefit him as well, for more important than the big lot in the new city was the fact that he'd be the founder. The fatherless would be a city father, the homeless would be responsible for a whole community. Having someone with Patrick's character and loyalty would prove invaluable to his dreams.

It would be a win for everyone, and Frisco could think of nothing that motivated him more.

Chapter Three

Caroline smoothed the Irish point embroidery that embellished her sleeve. She'd thought it so fine when she'd chosen it at the emporium in Galveston. Turned out it wasn't quite nice enough for the Strand, but she could wear it with pride in the territory.

Through the window of the stagecoach, she could see the white buildings of the fort looming ahead. The dairyman waved as he drove the cows in for their afternoon milking. The schedule of the fort was more familiar to her than the face of the grandfather clock in her father's parlor. What use were chimes when you had bugles calling out the hour?

How dare those people at the mercantile accuse her of being fribble? Caroline pounded her hands against her knees, earning a questioning look from Amber. She scooted toward the window, turning her shoulder away, and watched the familiar buildings pass. As if she couldn't run the race. She had as good a seat as any of the troopers who served at Fort Reno. And she was tough too. Between Cheyenne uprisings, prairie fires, and marauding outlaws, Caroline had faced dangers throughout her life. Why did people assume a woman in a pretty dress was helpless? Give her a pistol on the shooting range, and those women would eat their words.

It was that attitude that had kept her from ever feeling like she belonged among the debutantes in Galveston.

When they rounded the corner in front of the ordnance storehouse, the full parade grounds came into view. She saw more soldiers and troopers than usual. And no wonder. The next few days would be momentous. They were changing the land to the east of the fort forever. Never again would it be vacant prairie. With the shots of the guns and cannons, civilization would put down roots on the empty creek banks and open plains and would never relinquish its hold.

Coming back to the fort at twenty-one years of age, all Caroline could think of was that it wasn't her house and it wasn't her future. Every adult at Fort Reno answered to her father. Looking for freedom, she'd gone to her grandmother's in Galveston, only to find a society more rigid than the military post she'd fled. But in a week, everything here was going to be different.

The world was changing, and hopefully it would include a place for her.

The stagecoach usually stopped in front of the adjutant's office, but Caroline had informed the driver of her destination, so they were delivered right to the porch steps of the center house on Officers' Row.

As she waited for her bags to be unloaded, Caroline scanned the grounds surrounding her father's house. Would he allow her to put in a garden? On her trip home, Caroline had determined not to go without the finer items she'd used for her toilette, even if she had to produce them herself. She'd already visited a farm in Texas and had a list of herbs and flowers to plant before the summer heat became too intense.

"Caroline!" In the doorway of their home, fourteen-year-old

Daisy bounced on her toes. "She's home," she yelled over her shoulder before bounding down the steps and into Caroline's arms.

After a suffocating hug, Daisy held Caroline at arm's length. "Don't you look fine? Grandmother turned you into a real lady, didn't she? Your dress is beautiful. Did you bring me one? Or a dozen?"

"I have a shirtwaist that you—"

"Ambrosia Herald!" Daisy squealed. She released her sister to catch Amber in an embrace. "I didn't know Caroline was dragging you here. Does Uncle Bradley know? He'll be rolling in clover when he finds out. You can share my room. Let Caroline sleep with Allie Claire. She whirls like a spinning jenny."

"Where *is* Allie Claire?" Caroline turned to the house just as her stepmother, Louisa, came outside holding three-year-old Allie Claire's hand.

Louisa pulled Allie Claire forward and motioned to Caroline. "It's your big sister Caroline. Does she look like you remember?"

Allie Claire's blond hair framed her cherub face in bouncy ringlets. "Do you have a present for me?" she asked as she skipped forward.

To a three-year-old, memories weren't as important as presents. Caroline held out her arms to catch her precious half sister in a big hug. Allie Claire had the same fragile beauty that Louisa possessed but with a stubborn streak that Caroline had to acknowledge as a family trait. "Hmm . . . I wonder if I can find something in my trunk. It seems there was something for a little girl inside."

"Allie Claire, that's not polite." Louisa wrapped an arm around Caroline's waist. "I'm trying to train her up right, I promise."

"Don't worry," Caroline said. "Daisy asked too, and she's eleven years older." She gave her stepmother and former governess a quick peck on the cheek. "I'm sorry for not telling you that Amber was with me. We made the trip so quickly—"

Louisa beamed. "Nothing makes me happier than having the lovely Miss Herald visit us. And nothing will make my brother happier either."

Amber smiled. "Thank you, Mrs. Adams. As you know, this is my favorite place on earth."

"I have the feeling that might change in a few weeks when Bradley's enlistment is up." Louisa caught Allie Claire by the bow of her pinafore as she tried to run to the parade grounds. "It won't be the same without him."

Caroline bit her lip. Had Bradley shared their plans of homesteading nearby?

Evidently not, because Amber only shrugged and said, "You never know what the future holds."

Interesting. But Caroline had other issues on her mind. "Where's Father?" she asked.

"He's at the adjutant's office, lining out the plans with Lieutenant Hennessey. He didn't know you were coming today, or he'd have come home when he heard the stage. But come inside. I don't mean to keep you waiting at the doorstep. Let's get you washed up and fix something to eat."

Although not old enough to be Caroline's mother, Louisa had taken to the role with her typical enthusiasm and skill for all things dramatic. Next thing you knew, she'd be licking her thumb and scrubbing the soot off Caroline's face. But Caroline was no longer a child. She was itching for freedom, itching to make a contribution of her own.

She tried to imagine what it would be like to be the mistress of her own domain. How splendid it would be to welcome guests into a home that she'd provided, especially after a difficult journey. But as long as she was at the fort, she'd never be independent.

Her shoulders drooped as she followed her stepmother inside. She'd have to keep her eyes open for the perfect opportunity. If she didn't find it here, she didn't know where else she could turn.

Amber was at the fort. When Corporal Bradley Willis saw that parasol on the major's porch, he'd known that his sweetheart had arrived and it was only a matter of days before she was his.

Bradley brushed down his horse, swiping so fast that the brush caught and spun out of his hand. He picked it up and went slower, not wanting to cheat his mount out of proper care. It didn't matter how quickly he finished, he wouldn't be allowed to see Amber until after roll call. With fresh straw spread, the tack and gear hung up, and hay filling the trough, Bradley joined the rest of his unit as the troops assembled in the spacious room in the top story of the commissary for a briefing.

"You're just in time," Lieutenant Jack Hennessey said. "How's the line holding?"

Bradley shook his head. "You can't shake a bush without some early-comer falling out of it. It'll be a wonder if there's any land still available by the twenty-second. We marched them back across the line to wait, knowing full well that come nightfall, they'll be sneaking across again."

"What do they say when they're caught?"

"Everyone has an excuse as to why they're out there—business with the tribes, just crossing, working for the railroad. All we can do is escort them back to the line."

"Captain Woodson reports the same thing from Camp Price," Lieutenant Hennessey said. "Come by the office before stable call and file a report."

"Yes, sir." Bradley liked Hennessey, but he'd be glad when the yes, sir-ing and saluting stage of his life was behind him.

He sat by Private Gundy, who slapped his leg just to watch the dust fly.

"Just got in, huh?"

"Yep." Bradley rubbed his nose to stop the tickle. "Ain't never seen anything like it. People everywhere."

"My unit is going out tonight. Gotta wonder, if there's this many people willing to break the law from the start, what kind of territory are we starting?"

It was a fair question. Who knew there were so many people willing to sacrifice their honor for a piece of land? Sure, it was quite a prize, but Bradley's sense of fair play meant that he despised the cheaters.

The room jumped to attention when Major Adams entered. Before God and witnesses, Major Adams had married Bradley's older sister, making them brothers-in-law. Family. Kin. But on paper, Major Adams was Bradley's superior and the commander of the post. The U.S. government cared more about that paper than they cared about God and witnesses.

"At ease." Major Adams arranged his papers on a small metal stand, taking all the time afforded a man of his position. The room stilled in expectation. "Men, we are at the cusp of the most unique event ever to take place in this country, and perhaps the world. For the average man out there, this is a time of great opportunity, great advancements, and great mischief. It's our duty to anticipate trouble for an event that has no precedent, to make this fair for everyone, and to thwart those intent on cheating."

Bradley was up for the challenge. He would be on the line, holding back the crowd, ensuring the integrity of the run. He wouldn't leave a second early, but as soon as the gun fired, it was every man for himself. He already had ideas about where he wanted a claim. He'd even mailed Amber a picture he'd drawn of the land he had his eye on. He'd make the run, and in a few weeks when his enlistment was up, he and Ambrosia would be married with property. It was the best shot they had.

"Today we're announcing that any man caught in the Unassigned Lands without authorization before noon on the twenty-second is disqualified from the race and from ever holding a homestead claim in the United States." Major Adams paused while the magnitude of the decree settled on the soldiers and troopers. "No more placing them behind the border only to see them return the next day. There will be consequences. To that end, you must record every name of those you catch and submit a list daily to your officer. They will be compiled and then checked against the claims offices after the race is over."

Bradley nodded in agreement. Everyone knew that a man caught squatting on land today would be back out there before Monday. Maybe the threat of never being able to claim land would stop them.

"On the day of the race, you will be stationed ten yards in front of the line at intervals of a mile or so where there are crowds waiting. With over three hundred miles of border to cover, some of you will need to patrol the less-populated areas as well. You'll disperse from camp early to get into position. At five till noon, you should notify the runners of the time so they can make final preparations, but you must continue to hold the line. Do not let anyone cross until the fort's signal. At high noon, the fort's cannon will discharge. If you are not within earshot of the cannon, it's up to you to discharge your weapon at noon."

Major Adams paused as he met the eyes of his men. "When the cannon sounds, you must prepare yourself for an onslaught of humanity. Many of you have been charged by hostile people before, and you've had to fight for your lives. This is different. You can't shoot them. You can't reason with them. You can't help them. All you can do is get you and your horse out of their way."

Bradley leaned forward. His leg bounced with anticipation. Unleashed chaos. What could be better?

"Immediately following the starting gun, your assistance will be required in any of a thousand ways. There will be overturned carriages, thrown riders, and injured participants. We also foresee disputes over property being a rampant problem, so follow the crowd if there's nothing to prevent you. While you aren't judge and jury, you should act to settle disputes if the evidence is clear. If not, try to keep everyone alive until they can bring the matter to court."

The major leaned against the podium. "Men, as of noon on Monday, that land on the other side of the fort is going to look a lot different. As best we're able, we need to see that the honest settlers have as good a chance as the crooks, because the last thing the Cheyenne and Arapaho tribes need is a bunch of thieving scoundrels as neighbors. Do you understand?"

Bradley's *yes, sir* joined the others, and then questions were addressed. Bradley looked around the room. He knew of several men planning to make their own claims with the others. And why not? The land was worth more than they'd make in a year in the cavalry. They had fast horses, and they'd be at the line. Throw down a stake, then get back to work sorting through matters until their next leave, when they could file at the claims office. It seemed straightforward. They didn't have an advantage over any other man who'd picked his mount and waited for the gun.

It was that sense of fair play that had Bradley raising his hand. Worry flickered across the major's face. Major Adams was always on edge when he had to acknowledge Bradley in public. Bradley had too much fun at his brother-in-law's expense in private, but so far he'd managed to show proper respect before the other enlisted men. Major Adams might be family, but he was still the commander and would do what was necessary to keep Bradley in line.

"Corporal Willis, your question?"

"Yes, sir. When we request our leave to file our claims, will we be able to get half days, or should we take the whole day off? I'd imagine at the beginning the Kingfisher office will have a line as long as Methuselah's beard, but by next week—"

Major Adams lifted his hand. "I don't understand. What do you mean, *file your claims*?"

"I mean once the race starts, we'll be free to run along with everyone else. It'd only take a moment to drive a stake, then back in the saddle and off we go to look after . . ." Bradley's words slowed as Private Gundy jabbed him with his elbow. Major Adams's stern jaw looked sharp enough to split oak. What had he said wrong?

"Corporal Willis, there seems to be a misunderstanding, and in case you aren't the only one deluded, I'll address this to the whole company." The major stepped out from behind the podium and clasped his hands behind his back. "You are enlisted with the U.S. Army. You serve this government, and your time is not your own. You are not free to pursue your own interest while wearing the uniform. Do you understand?"

Although Major Adams claimed to be addressing the whole group, Bradley felt like he was speaking directly to him.

"There will be no claims made by any soldier or trooper under my command. How can enforcement be impartial when you are competing with the civilians? Furthermore, any soldier who attempts to make a claim will not only be prevented from registering it, but he will also be discharged from his post. Is there any further clarification needed?"

Bradley slouched in his chair. He and Amber had thought they had it all figured out. He'd do his duty on the starting line, then wheel around and stake the plot he'd been hankering after. Amber could hold it until he could go to the claims office. But now? What kind of future could he offer her if he didn't have a farm? He might as well stay in the cavalry.

Bradley turned his head toward the window. She was here at the fort. She'd come all this way because she believed in him. Against her better judgment, she saw potential in him. He couldn't let her down. He had to think of something.

Chapter Four

Caroline watched as Allie Claire fed her baby doll with a tiny spoon. The child moved slowly, balancing the pinto bean toward the doll's bored face. Caroline opened her mouth wide, as if the doll could be compelled to cooperate by her example. But the spoon rammed into the doll's painted nose, and the bean rolled across the parlor floor.

"Baby is hungry," Allie Claire said as she picked up the bean with chubby fingers.

"Yes," Caroline said. "But you're being a good mama and feeding her a lot."

Daisy flopped on the sofa and hung her feet over the arm. "You're sure a lot nicer to Allie Claire than you were to me. You haven't locked her in a closet yet."

"She's done nothing to deserve it. You did." Caroline pushed Daisy's feet off the sofa.

Daisy was in the process of putting them right back where they'd been when the front door opened. Amber jumped to her feet, causing all three of the Adams sisters to look at her in confusion.

"Oh." Amber dropped back to the sofa. "It's only your father."

Known to everyone else as Major Adams, Caroline's father strode into the parlor, his gear and accoutrements jangling. His eyes lit up at the sight of his daughter, but he gallantly turned to Amber first. "Welcome to Fort Reno, Miss Herald. I'm pleased that you decided to visit again. I suppose your day is drawing nigh."

"Yes, sir. Corporal Willis and I are counting the weeks. Not that he's anxious to leave the cavalry, but . . ."

"No explanation needed. Does Corporal Willis know you're here?"

"I believe he saw me from the parade grounds," Amber said.

"That's what I was afraid of." Her father turned to his wife. "I'll be sure to inform your brother that he's not to come snooping around after dark tonight. If he wants to speak to Miss Herald, he should apply for permission from me. Since her father isn't here, I'll take the role as her guardian—"

Caroline had heard enough. "Miss Herald doesn't need a guardian, Father. She's of age, and you can hardly object to Uncle Bradley's character. You married his sister."

If she knew her father, he was counting to ten before answering her. He only made it to three. "Clandestine meetings after dark can taint an otherwise spotless character. As long as she's under my roof, she's my responsibility."

"And as long as I'm under your roof too?" Caroline poked the baby doll in the stomach. "I might as well be a toy, just waiting for someone to spoon-feed me and make me play whatever game they require."

As soon as the words left her mouth, she regretted them. Her predicament wasn't her father's doing. She only wished that she wasn't constantly reminded of her status as a dependent.

"I'm pleased that you want to protect me, Major Adams," Amber said. Trust Amber to smooth over Caroline's moods. "While I can't guarantee that Bradley won't try to lure me outside—you never know what he might do—I can promise that I won't leave the house without a proper chaperone."

"Thank you, Miss Herald," Major Adams said. "I'm glad there's one reasonable young lady here." He turned toward Caroline and said with genuine fondness, "And how is my eldest daughter?"

She took a steadying breath. Her father was a good man. As much as it was in her power, she should get along peaceably with him.

"I'm fine, Father. Thank you for asking."

"Your journey?"

"Uneventful—that is, until we reached Ardmore. Ever since crossing the Red River, we've been in crowds."

"All of them heading here." Her father's eyes roved to the window. "Poor deluded people. Even if they win land in the race, they are far from lasting the five years required before it's permanently theirs."

"But just think what they will accomplish," Caroline said. "They will have contributed to a new civilization and a new economy. Not many people can say they played a part in building a society from the dirt up."

And if it were her building it, it would have different rules than the fort. For starters, capable young women wouldn't have to go to their rooms when taps sounded, and all the men wouldn't have to stand and salute whenever her father passed.

"And how do you propose to contribute to events?" her father asked.

"Daniel," her stepmother said, "Caroline just arrived. She's not even unpacked. Let's not put too many expectations on her."

"It's all right, Mother," Caroline said. "Actually, I do have an idea. Outside of Galveston, back on the mainland, we visited the most beautiful place I've ever seen. They had a whole field of lavender planted in long rows. I could've stood there forever. The farmer said it was easy to harvest and very profitable. From it, I could make all manner of soaps, lotions, and other fine things. So much more than we have at the store in Darlington."

"You want to put in a farm here at the fort?" A crease appeared on her father's forehead.

"Not a farm, just a garden."

"There are already gardens," he said.

"Those are vegetable gardens," Caroline replied. "I want to plant something else."

"And what are my soldiers going to do with good-smelling soaps and lotions? I don't see how that furthers their mission."

"It's not for the soldiers. . . ." Caroline's mouth twisted. "Never mind. Don't pay any attention to me."

"We're your family, and this is your home. You are welcome to try a garden if we can find a place for it." Louisa picked up Allie Claire. "It's good to have all my girls home again." She widened her eyes at Caroline's father. He picked up the cue.

"Absolutely!" he said. "It's good to have you back. I worried about you being so far away, but I hope you enjoyed the time with your grandparents."

A knock on the door interrupted any further discussion. "Maybe that's Lufftenant Hennessey," Allie Claire said.

Her father went to answer the door. Amber stood when she heard it open. Caroline was afraid her friend would burst like a watermelon dropped from a runaway wagon if she had to wait any longer to see her beau. Caroline recognized the sentiment. How many times had she stood like that and listened for Frisco's voice? Thankfully, she had reined in her youthful exuberance and had never confessed her affections to Frisco. Both Amber and Daisy had teased her about him, but as far as she knew, it was without his knowledge.

At least she'd been spared that indignity.

"Thank you for knocking instead of throwing rocks at the window, Corporal Willis," her father was saying.

"Yes, sir," Bradley said as Amber grabbed Caroline's hand. "I've learned my lesson on that score. Besides, Miss Herald couldn't sneak out of the house as long as you're still awake."

Amber couldn't wait any longer. Dropping Caroline's hand, she slid past the sofa to the door, where Caroline's father turned to address her.

"Miss Herald, if you have no objections, I'll loan you the use of my study." Major Adams called from the entryway, "Just remember I'm likely to walk in at the most inopportune time, Corporal Willis."

Caroline took Allie Claire from Louisa and sat on the floor. She was happy for Amber and Bradley, and she wouldn't disturb them as they made their plans together. Instead, she'd play with dolls while she tried to think of anything besides her predicament.

He had to tell Amber that their plan was not going to work. Usually only able to entertain one thought at a time, Bradley had been rehearsing the bad news so that he could present it well, but when he stepped across the threshold and saw his beloved, thoughts of the big race scattered like the stables' barn cats.

There she was, her ebony hair pulled back from her heart-shaped face. Seeing her all fancy in her green dress made him want to howl in laughter that such a beauty would have anything to do with him.

She kept her eyes down as she headed through the parlor to the major's office. Bradley nodded at his sister before easing the door closed. He let the latch click gently, having learned not to slam doors in his brother-in-law's house.

Amber had taken a seat at a small table with a chessboard

on it. Her shyness was adorable. He'd pull her out of it. Her feistiness was just below the surface, but it had been a long time since they'd met face-to-face. He'd give her a minute, if that was what she needed to warm up to him again.

"You're looking well." He leaned against Major Adams's desk.

She looked no higher than his shiny black boots. "I haven't changed out of my traveling clothes yet, but it was a pleasant day. No real heat, and it looks like it's rained recently enough to keep the dust down."

"Hmm . . ." He crossed his arms over his chest. She was making upward progress with her gaze. "You must have read my mind, because what I came to discuss was the recent rain and the state of the stagecoach trail."

A faint smile played about her lips. Bradley grinned. Higher and higher her eyes came until they met his.

"Your hair looks blonder," she said. "And now you're a corporal."

"But not for long."

The clock was ticking. Major Adams would interrupt them soon and send him back to the barracks. He'd better make the best use of their time.

"Four weeks until my enlistment is up," he said. Four weeks until they would be married, if she didn't change her mind when she heard what he had to say. "I have some bad news, Amber."

She shook her head. She stood and walked to the French doors that looked out over the parade grounds.

"It's not what you think," he said.

"Are you going to reenlist?" Her voice sounded tiny. "You might earn another promotion soon. That would be good for your career."

"That's not it at all. It's just that our plan isn't going to work. Major Adams said that troopers were disqualified from the race. We're not allowed to claim land while we're serving in our official capacity."

"If you can't run, then how are we going to get our farm? That was our start."

"Those are the rules. Even if I waited until I was off duty on Monday, all the land will be spoken for by then. We won't get anything."

He was used to looking out for himself, but now he had to make allowances for Amber too. Never before had he felt the weight of responsibility so heavily.

"Then quit," she said. "Just quit. You'd only lose a month of pay. What's that compared to getting a farm?"

"Sweetheart, I thought of that, but I'd lose more than the pay. I'd lose respect." He held out a pleading hand. "When I enrolled, I gave my word. I can't just walk away. What would your father think? Or Major Adams? I'd have to live with the shame of it every time I saw our families."

"So you're going to reenlist? When I left home, I thought I wouldn't return until I became your wife, but now . . . How many years? Another four?"

"We'll figure it out," he said. "Look, there'll probably be a lot of people who are speculating. They'll get a claim only to sell it to someone so they can make a few dollars. That someone could be us."

"But if we spend our savings on the land, we won't have anything left over for supplies. What will we eat until our crops come in? How will we furnish a house? Mother and Father gave me money for my dowry, but not enough to buy everything."

Bradley's chest rose, and he exhaled a long breath. "It's my responsibility to take care of you. I'll figure something out. In four weeks, I'll be free, and then *you'll* be shackled." He might not have all the answers, but he loved her. That would have to be enough for now. "Why worry now, Amber? I've never planned ahead, and it's worked out so far."

But that wasn't how Amber operated. In her many letters, she'd written about her homesteading plans. She'd mailed him lists of implements they would need and the quantity of seed for one hundred and sixty acres. She'd sketched floor plans for their home. She'd learned the different breeds of chickens and which would make the best layers. In their partnership, Amber laid the tracks, and Bradley was the steam power that would move them in the right direction.

"I'll figure it out," he said again. "The important thing is that you're here now. Do you know how long I've waited to see your sweet face again?"

Every time they were reunited, it was like they had to get reacquainted. And every time they were reacquainted, he fell in love with her again. She stretched her hand toward him, and he took it. That first touch sent a spark through him—one of both memory and newness.

"I think about you all the time," she said, "but when I'm face-to-face with you, I realize how poor my memory is."

He ran his thumb over her knuckles. "I hope the flaws of your memory are all in my favor."

Ambrosia stepped closer and stretched upward, begging him to slip his arm around her waist. "But they aren't. I forget how magnificent you are. Then when I see you again, I'm taken aback."

"Magnificent?" Taking her hand and her waist, he swayed in a silent waltz. "That's quite a commendation. I don't have an equal word for you, but I will say that I remember you perfectly. When I see you in my dreams, you look exactly like this, with your hair windblown and your cheeks pink. Your blue eyes are big and reading everything I've ever thought, and I'm wishing I thought better things."

"What would I be thinking right now?" she asked.

Dare he tell the truth? He couldn't lie to her. His smile faded. "You're wondering if we're going to make it. You're wondering if I can take care of us."

He knew he could. One way or another, she would have the farm she'd set her heart on. As long as she believed in him, they couldn't fail.

"That's my girl," he whispered as he saw the faith reappear in her eyes. "Enough talking."

Their lips met, and that first touch was like a sigh of relief. After months apart, the tension that sparked between them finally had a resolution, but then he kissed her again, and a stronger emotion awoke.

They could do this. Whether they had a plan or not, they would find a way. His hands walked down her back, pressing her into him. He'd endure a lot of hardships for the privilege of melting into her arms at night. Soon he wouldn't have to subject their meetings to the call of the bugle and a commander waiting outside the office door to intervene. It would be only the two of them, married in the eyes of God, working together and celebrating their love.

Bradley laid his head against her neck. She threaded her fingers through his hair as their heartbeats slowed.

"Most people start out poor and young," she said. "We'll figure it out as we go. As long as we're determined . . ."

"And I'll work so hard." He lifted his head. "If I have to take on extra work, or two jobs, or skip meals . . . As long as you believe in me . . ."

"It's getting late." Major Adams was using his commander's voice in the parlor outside the office.

Bradley scrunched his nose as he tried to smooth Amber's hair. After arranging a few locks, he shrugged and straightened his uniform.

There was a knock on the door. The good major always interrupted his fun.

"I expect Louisa will invite me to Easter dinner this Sunday," Bradley announced loudly. "Then we can talk more." He winked at Amber as she touched her lips.

"Yes, that would be splendid," she replied as he opened the door to the major.

Major Adams's gaze took in every detail, but he maintained his professional demeanor. "Corporal Willis, it's past time that you returned to the barracks. Tattoo has already sounded."

"Yes, sir." Bradley picked up his hat. "Thank you for visiting with me, Miss Herald. Renewing our acquaintance is always enjoyable."

Major Adams raised an eyebrow. "Is that any way to talk to your intended?" he asked.

"It is when my commander is standing in the room, sir." And with a salute, Bradley said good night.

Chapter Five

Situated in the shade of a cottonwood near the Darlington Indian Agency a couple of miles from the fort, Caroline swirled the paintbrush in turpentine, patted it clean on a cloth, then handed it back to Hattie Hennessey. Hattie adjusted her growing belly and looked past her canvas at the thousands of wagons and tents spreading to the horizon—settlers camping along the border of the Unassigned Lands. Hattie lived next door to the Adamses on Officers' Row and was married to Lieutenant Jack. Usually Hattie painted scenes from the Cheyenne and Arapaho villages, but with the coming of the prospective homesteaders, she'd found another moment in time to record.

Caroline wished she had something to contribute to the excitement but found herself merely a spectator. A spectator who washed brushes. At least she could do that.

"Will you send this painting to the gallery in Denver?" Caroline asked. The white canvas wagons contrasted with the bright blue sky and green prairie, but the focal point was the figure in the center. A middle-aged man wearing a suit that had seen better days stood staring out toward the empty prairie beyond the line of wagons. It was poignant. A picture of someone who'd already seen dreams crushed, looking out on what might be his last chance.

"They said it might not sell as well as my Indian portraits, but I can't pass up the opportunity." Hattie flicked a dab of yellow on her subject's stained satin vest to finish that portion of the painting. "What's it say to you?"

Caroline stepped back to get a better look. "It says that at least he had the courage to try once before, and even if he didn't succeed, he's going to try again. But there's a futility to it also. Maybe trying isn't enough. There's no guarantee that this time will be any better."

Hattie rubbed her stomach as she studied her creation. "It makes me think of how our past makes us who we are. That man probably wishes he could've avoided some of the hard knocks that came his way, but he needed them to be who he is today. Just think, had I not left home and gotten derailed by that stagecoach robbery, I wouldn't even be here. Look at what I gained from that tragedy." She gave her belly a last pat.

"Hattie," Caroline said, "if you didn't have Lieutenant Hennessey, what would you be doing right now?"

"I always planned on being a painter. Lieutenant Hennessey was an unexpected complication, but not the end to my dreams."

"Well, I can't paint."

"I've noticed," Hattie said, then straightened on her stool. "When you imagine Caroline Adams ten years from now, what is she doing?"

Caroline's eyes traveled the spotless blue of the sky. "I see myself as the mistress of my own domain. I'm providing people with a tranquil place amid chaos. And I've got a sharp eye out for trouble going on in my territory."

"You know who that sounds like?" Hattie's brows rose as she smiled. "Your father."

"I'm nothing like my father."

"He's master of his domain, keeps order amid chaos—"

This was the problem with Hattie. She was always saying things that you should have thought of yourself. Caroline tightened her shawl around her shoulders. "I'm not going to be the commander of a fort. That's impossible."

"Maybe you'll run an inn, or a boardinghouse near the railroad."

The thought hit Caroline so hard that her neck strained. It matched so perfectly with the pictures in her mind—her standing in an ornate doorway, welcoming weary travelers. And just past the luggage that was piled on the porch, she could imagine formal gardens filled with lavender, chamomile, lemon balm, rosemary, and mint. It was a lovely thought, but not something that was going to happen for her.

"Here comes a picturesque figure," Hattie said. "Maybe I should put him on a canvas for you to hang on your wall."

Still enchanted by her reverie, Caroline was surprised to see Frisco Smith approaching. Gone were his city clothes. This time he was decked out like the frontiersman she'd always found fascinating. The sleeves of his buckskin jacket dripped with fringed leather, and his soft boots were cross-laced on the outside of his britches. His wide hat shaded his face, but Caroline could have sworn she saw curiosity in his eyes.

"How long has it been since you've seen him?" Hattie asked.

"We recently renewed our acquaintance," Caroline said. "Some things don't improve with time."

"Shush," Hattie whispered as Frisco reached them.

"Mrs. Hennessey, Miss Adams." He sauntered up without so much as a tipped hat. "I expected you to stay on the post until the run was over."

Caroline's jaw clenched. Of all the people who should know better. It was like he'd forgotten who she was. "Why would we do that?" she asked. "I've traveled to the Gulf of Mexico and back. Darlington isn't that far away."

What was wrong with him? Frisco used to tease her, call her pretty, warn her father that he'd have to chase the beaux away when Caroline was grown. Now she was grown, and he treated her like a pesky gnat to be shooed. As if to prove her point, he dipped his head. "My apologies, Miss Adams. No insult meant. Just trying to make polite conversation."

Hattie's eyes narrowed as she looked from Frisco to Caroline. "Polite conversation is always admired around here. So tell me, Mr. Smith, what are you going to do with yourself once the land gets settled and trespassing is no longer called for?"

Frisco planted his feet wide and clasped his hands behind his back. "I'm pleased you asked. Despite what my criminal record might imply, I've been successfully planning my next steps for years. To begin with, I've plotted out—"

"Oh, excuse me." Hattie leaned forward on her stool. "I hate to interrupt, but that's Sergeant O'Hare with a supply wagon. Would you mind flagging him down? The heat is stronger than I bargained for." She stood and dumped out her wash jars as Frisco caught the driver's attention. She motioned Caroline close and whispered, "This is your chance. Don't waste it."

"My chance?" Caroline glowered at Hattie. "I don't want to be with him. Don't leave me—"

"Thank you, Mr. Smith. If you wouldn't mind seeing that Caroline gets home safely, I'd be in your debt." Hattie leaned on him as he helped her into the fort's supply wagon. "And I'll tell Mrs. Adams to expect a guest for dinner, Caroline. I'm sure they'll be glad to see Mr. Smith again."

No, they wouldn't, and neither would she.

Frisco loaded the easel, chair, and painting box, then watched the wagon creak away. He stood with arms crossed, the soft leather stretching across his shoulders, the fringe dancing in the wind. Then, with a jaunty spin, he faced Caroline with the same patient appraisal he'd just given the supply wagon.

Caroline's chin went up as she adjusted her shawl. For all the lessons her grandmother had given her, she'd never mastered simpering. Nothing was more against her nature.

"Mr. Smith, to what do we owe this pleasure?" That sounded a lot nicer than *Mr. Smith, are you looking for more rubes to hoodwink into buying plots for a city that doesn't exist?*

"Is it a pleasure, Miss Adams? From our meeting in Purcell, I'm under the impression that you don't approve of my activity."

"Is your happiness dependent on my approval?" she asked.

"I certainly hope not. From what I remember, you possessed a capricious nature even at a tender age." His eyes were framed by black lashes that any woman would envy.

"I can't claim to have improved over the years." She pulled her skirt free from a clump of goat's head stickers. There'd be no mistaking her conversation for flirtation. Of that she was sure.

His scruffy jaw slid to the side as he considered. "Since your friend went to heroic lengths to leave you stranded with me—"

"Not at my behest, I assure you."

"And yet here we are, and you need an escort home." He motioned her toward the road to Fort Reno. Caroline noticed that he didn't offer his arm this time. He was being rather prickly. Then again, so was she.

"Don't feel obligated," she said as they both took to the stagecoach trail.

"You threw some serious charges at me in Purcell. Aren't you going to let me explain my plans for Redhawk?"

"Redhawk?"

"The town I'm founding. It's named after the red-tailed hawk that has winged its way over this grassland for centuries. The town already has a plethora of craftsmen, financiers, and merchants pledged to settle there."

"What do you mean *pledged*?" she asked. "How can you make them live in your town?"

"They've bought lots. The lots cost between one and three dollars, depending on the location. It's a bargain, but I'm carefully picking who I want to be my neighbors."

"Location? There's nothing out here." Caroline motioned around them, causing her shawl to flap in the breeze. "What makes one acre worth more than another?"

"That is the genius of being a town father. All you do is part the grass, draw a line, and give that line the name of Main Street, and then you have property value. On Monday there's going to be people dueling over where those lines are. Instead of settling it in the heat of the moment, I'm taking the initiative and getting it mapped out beforehand."

"It's so strange to think that there are going to be towns, cities, and farms out there. I just can't picture it." They'd left the settlers' campsites behind and were out in the open with the fort ahead. Caroline found herself wanting to slow down. He was talking more sense than anyone she'd met on the way.

"I've pictured it for years." His voice had dropped. She looked up, surprised to see sincerity on his usually flippant face. "It's what I've been working toward, what I've fought for, what I've been arrested for. And it's going to happen. It's really going to happen." He rolled his shoulders as if shrugging off a weight. "It should be quite a spectacle. History before your eyes. You're lucky you're here to see all us poor saps fighting for a square of land to call our own."

Caroline turned around and looked at the masses of people camping along the border. Occasionally there'd be a break, some empty space, but then another grouping would start. Campfires, grazing horses, buggies, wagons, tents in a line that stretched into a blur. But she was just a member of the audience, watching from the safety of her daddy's protection. The comment stung.

She pushed an auburn strand of hair behind her ear. "There are a lot of people here. What makes you so sure you're going to get a claim?"

"Not just get a claim, but I'm going to get *my* claim. How long have you known me, Miss Adams?"

Caroline blinked. She knew exactly the first time Lieutenant Hennessey had escorted Frisco Smith into the guardhouse on the fort. "Six years," she said. "You were little more than a lad with curly dark hair and patched britches following David Payne. I thought maybe you were his son—"

"It has been six years," he interrupted. "Six years of preparing for this day. All those times your father had me arrested, I wasn't just sitting under a tree enjoying the sun. I was assessing the land, watching to see which rivers stayed strong even in the summer, digging wells to see how deep the groundwater was, testing the soil to see where the most likely place to produce for a farmer was. I wasn't idle."

"I never thought you were."

"When the opening became imminent, I started working in earnest. I picked out the best location for my city and the best plot in the city for myself. It's set on a riverbank and is practically guaranteed to have a railroad depot within the next three years. The land is good, water plentiful, and there are trees nearby for construction and fuel. And then do you know what I did?"

Once upon a time, Caroline would have wished that she was the cause of the fire in his eyes, but his excitement was contagious nonetheless. "What did you do?" she asked.

"I put in a garden. It's not a farm, but it'll be good supplement for one man. When everyone arrives, there'll be enough civic and law business that I won't have time for planting after the race."

"But what if someone else gets there first? Then all that work will be lost."

His devilish grin made her heart skip a beat despite her resolve. "There's no way that's going to happen." He held her gaze for a long, delicious moment, then seemed to reach his decision. "You're familiar with Cutthroat Canyon, aren't you?"

Caroline's head shot back. "Don't insult me, Mr. Smith. I ruined my first pair of white leather half boots trying to climb Holland's Point."

"Well, people running from the west border will run right into that canyon. They'll have to maneuver either through it or swing around to the south and cross the river."

"No," Caroline blurted. "There's a cut-through where the canyon narrows on the north side. You can get across without breaking stride. I've done it a hundred times. If you go that way—"

"But who will go that way? Who knows that? Only a boomer who's spent years exploring the area."

Now she saw it, and it was brilliant. "Your land is past the canyon? Of course. That's where the river turns. The land is good there, and there are trees enough." A town on the prairie heights would get nice breezes in the summer. There was a valley that led to the river. It'd probably have water. And hadn't her father talked about the railroad building a track through there?

Somehow she'd stopped walking, and somehow Frisco was standing in front of her, watching with a satisfied glint in his eyes.

"Oh, the beauty of a dream shared," he said. "Does it make it worth all the trouble you went through to arrange this private time with me?"

Caroline's face warmed, and she sputtered. "That's not true. I would've never conspired to see you alone."

"Never? Oh, there was a time. . . ." He shook his head as if disappointed in her. "There's no shame in a youthful infatuation, Miss Adams. No reason to act embarrassed around me."

"I'm not embarrassed. I haven't done anything wrong, but you . . . you should be ashamed." Her shawl was knotted in her hands.

"Me? For what?"

"For leading a young girl on. All that flattery, and you didn't mean a word you said. You were just playing with my emotions." She didn't mean to sound so adamant. It was anger, not hurt, that had her fighting back.

"Is that what you think?" He blinked rapidly, and for the first time she could tell she'd landed a jab. "You couldn't be more wrong, Miss Adams. I choose to think that I was paying tribute to an extraordinary young lady. One who had the world at her feet. One who had all the courage and mettle to accomplish anything she set her mind to." He removed his hat, ran his hand through his hair, then crammed it back on his head. She'd never seen him so agitated.

"Just stop." She turned her shoulder to him. "I'm not a child anymore. Your regard means nothing to me."

"Then you've changed." He uttered a harsh laugh. "Of course you've changed. That girl I admired, I don't know her anymore. Instead of a beautiful wild vine, all I see now is another potted plant, trimmed and pruned to look like every other one out there. One that will only survive when handled delicately."

Her ears burned. Her heart filled with every vile insult she'd heard over two decades of living at military posts, but all her tongue would pronounce was, "How dare you!"

"Did I crush a petal? My apologies."

"I'll have you know that I'm just as capable as anyone here at succeeding in the race. I don't need to prove myself—"

"Don't be a fool, Miss Adams. There are thousands of people out here who think the land is theirs for the taking."

She'd listened to enough of his insults. What had she ever done to him to deserve his scorn?

"I'll inform my father that you regretfully declined the supper invitation," she said.

"I'll assume you can find your own way from here?"

With the fort's commissary practically looming over her? If only there was a door between them that she could slam and block out his voice.

"If I don't see you before Monday, wish me luck," he said.

Had there been a trooper close enough, she would have grabbed his saber and charged Frisco. When she refused to answer, he turned and walked away.

Caroline watched him go, her sense of outrage growing. He had no right. She kicked a rock and sent it tumbling through the grass. She wished him at the bottom of the deepest river in the territory. But if everything went the way he planned, he'd be the leader of a town just outside the fort's boundary, while she'd be stuck inside her father's parlor.

Chapter Six

It was one of those perfect days on the prairie. The sun warmed the grass enough to make it smell sweet. The breeze chased away the sweat, which made you not smell sweet. Perfect in every way, but Caroline was furious. What Hattie had meant as a kindness had turned into one of the most infuriating encounters of her life. And Caroline knew a thing or two about being infuriating.

She'd walked the road past the barracks, little caring that her shawl was dragging on the ground, when she noticed a commotion in front of her house. Those weren't troopers or soldiers crowding the road by her porch but city men, some in rumpled suits that looked like they'd traveled far.

"Major Adams, what odds do you give to the success of these gamblers?" This man had a lilting accent. British? Caroline didn't think so. Maybe Irish.

As her father spoke, the men scribbled notes on pads of paper. Journalists? Must be, and why not? It was the biggest story they'd cover for years.

Her father towered above them on the porch steps, but even without the platform and his sharp blue uniform, he would have exuded authority. "That's impossible to tell. Certainly there are some who don't have the resources to last until harvest, but a man's financial decisions are not the government's responsibility."

"How do the Indians feel about getting new neighbors?" The swarthy man's mustache drooped like a rooster's tail feathers in a rainstorm.

Caroline might be the only one who noticed the weariness cross her father's normally stern face. "How do they feel about thousands of land-hungry white men taking up residence next to their nations? Do you know what happened the last time they found themselves surrounded by land-hungry white men? That's why they no longer have their homelands in Georgia and Mississippi and the Dakotas. . . . I could go on. How do you think they feel?"

The mustached man was persistent. "But some say it'll bring industry and railroads to them. They'll have more opportunity."

"It *will* bring industry and the railroads," her father said. "Whether that will benefit the tribes, it's too early to tell."

They clamored for his attention for the next question, but Caroline's attention was directed elsewhere. Amber was tiptoeing away from the house with a nervous glance over her shoulder. What was she up to?

Caroline held her skirts against her side so they wouldn't swish as she jogged around the house. Beneath the bobbing parasol, Amber scurried ahead with that peculiar gait one adopted when trying to go as fast as one could without being noticed. But Caroline had noticed.

Amber didn't hear her coming until Caroline had snatched her by the arm.

"Ow! What are you doing?" Amber growled through gritted teeth.

"What are *you* doing? This quadrant of the post holds the

barracks, the guardhouse, and the stables. To which of those are you heading?"

"To the stables," she said. "I'm going to steal a horse."

Caroline couldn't help but be impressed. Her friend had spunk. "Do you know the penalty for stealing government property?"

Amber's jaw was set. "If I knew someone who could get me a horse without breaking the law—someone like the daughter of the fort's commander—then I could avoid the penalty, right?"

Caroline noticed that she and Amber were attracting attention from the troopers drilling on the parade grounds. Since she didn't yet know if she was abetting a criminal, she lowered her voice.

"Did you and Bradley quarrel?"

"No, I'm doing this for him."

"Stealing a horse? That's not going to help his career."

"This isn't about his career—it's about our homestead. I'm going to run in the race."

Caroline's eyes widened. She didn't have to ask whether Amber was serious. She knew. And she didn't have to wonder why, because the same compulsion had tempted her since they'd stepped off the train in Purcell.

"What's Bradley say?"

"He doesn't know yet, but he told me the army isn't going to let any troopers make claims. He'd have to resign if he wanted to be eligible, but he won't. He wants to see his enlistment out. That leaves it to me."

They stopped their conversation as Sergeant Byrd paused to exchange pleasantries. Caroline made the correct answers, but her mind was reeling.

She'd known since she'd heard the rules that she could compete in the race. What was more, just like that renegade Frisco Smith, she knew the terrain. With some help from her grandmother, she would have enough funds to stay the course. It wouldn't be easy. . . .

They'd reached the long white stables that housed the cavalry's horses. "What exactly is your plan?" Caroline asked.

Amber paused at the sight of the paddocks stretching before her. "I'm going to ask Bradley to set aside a fast horse for me the morning of the race. If your father must know, I'll tell him that it's so I can observe without being trampled, but when the bugle sounds, I'll take out with everyone else and try my luck."

"If you get a homestead, then what? What makes you think you can do the farming?" Caroline had her eyes on the farthest stalls. She hadn't been to the stables since she'd returned. Just another part of her that she wanted to reclaim.

"Farming and raising horses has been the plan all along. And Bradley will join me in a few weeks. He might even be able to help put in a garden before then."

"And you already know how to build a house." The summer Caroline had met Amber, she and her mother had just finished overseeing the construction of their home in Garber, Texas. It was all Amber could talk about—besides Bradley and the camels her father was transporting.

Hardtack nickered at the sound of Caroline's voice. He lifted his chestnut head over the gate and blew his musty breath at her. Caroline held out her palm for his velvety, whiskery love. The fort commander's family was granted free livery care and feed for their personal mounts. Hardtack belonged to her. She wouldn't have to steal a horse, although she'd probably have to sneak out with the same care as if she had.

"Have they been taking care of you?" she murmured, causing the horse's ear to twitch.

"Of course we have."

Caroline turned to see Bradley come around the corner, carrying a shovel. "I've kept him groomed. Louisa tried riding him, but he was too spirited for her, so Daisy exercises him. What are y'all doing out here? Going on a ride?"

Caroline kept a hand on Hardtack's neck. "I'm going to run in the race," she said. "And to do that, I'll need my horse in top form."

"You're going to run?" Amber came at her in a flurry of green ruffles and a swaying parasol. "You are not. You're mocking me, but I can do it. I've traveled across this territory on camel—"

"Hold on a minute." Bradley held his shovel out, creating a barrier between the women. "What are you talking about, Amber? You aren't running."

Amber spun with flashing eyes. "Yes, I am. If you can't get the claim, I'm going to. We're a team. We're in this together. I'm not going to sit by and miss our opportunity."

"It's too dangerous," he said.

Caroline snorted. "My uncle Bradley discouraging reckless-ness? What irony."

"And you?" He pointed at Caroline. "Your father would kill me—literally and legally—if I let you take part in this."

"I'm not asking your permission," Caroline said. "This is my horse, and it's no business of yours if and when I decide to ride him." Already her mind was whirling. She couldn't homestead, not like Amber and Bradley wanted to. But what would it take to have a place of her own? A roof to offer shelter to travelers? A place by the railroad?

Amber twisted a black curl around her finger. "Actually, I might ask your help. I don't have a horse."

"Absolutely not," Bradley said.

"You can ride Daisy's," Caroline said. "Gunpowder is fast enough. We'll take her out and run her so you can get used to her."

Bradley rammed the shovel into the ground and leaned against its handle. His eyes darted back and forth between the two women as he shooed away a fly. "I'm trying to put my finger on exactly why this is a bad idea. Anyone with half a grain of sense would say you don't have a chance."

"When have you ever cared what anyone thinks?" Caroline asked. "We're thinking for ourselves."

"Are we?" Amber asked. "Seems to me that you're grabbing the reins of my buggy."

Amber had a point. Until five minutes ago, Caroline had been ridiculing Amber and Bradley, but now the fever had caught her too. A new start. A new challenge. Concocting a society from scratch. Frisco's insults might have lit the match, but the fuel had been there all along.

"I have my own plans," Caroline said. "I need some land near the railroad. We'll get adjoining properties and look out for each other."

"We'd be neighbors?" Amber's face lit up. "Think of it, Bradley. What could be more perfect? When Major and Mrs. Adams come to visit his daughter, your sister can walk to the next field and visit us."

"It's a crazy thing when the two of you start to make sense," Bradley protested, but that reckless look he tried to tamp down was blooming.

"We could run for land that's close to the fort," Caroline said. "Amber only has to hold it for a few weeks until you can join her. That way neither of us would be alone out there."

"The only change is that I'll be racing instead of you," Amber said to Bradley. "Women are allowed to file, just the same as men, so legally that won't make any difference."

"Maybe you could talk me into it, Amber. You're over twenty-one and a free agent, but Miss Adams there comes with complications that I'd rather not tangle with." He pointed at Caroline. "If something happened to you, Louisa would never forgive me. Thinking about your father's reaction makes me want to start digging my own grave. Besides, there's no way you can really prove a homestead on your own. So why don't you help us get ready? That'll be your part in this."

Amber stepped sideways toward Bradley. Amber and Bradley had each other. Caroline was on her own. She needed another angle.

"I know a guaranteed way to get land," Caroline said. "There's a crossing that's practically hidden. Only a few know it exists. Once we get past that, we'll have our pick of the best land in the area, but Amber won't find it on her own. For her to have a chance against all the other runners, she needs me. If you tell my father, then Amber will be running without a guide." She reached a hand over her shoulder to pat the horse who was huffing hot air into her ear as he nibbled on her hat. "And running without a horse."

Closer in age to brother and sister than uncle and niece, Bradley and Caroline had tested each other's limits repeatedly and knew when further argument was useless. So far the contests between them had ended peacefully, but there was always the chance that both of them might dig in their heels. The day that happened would be disastrous.

But today Caroline held all the cards, and she knew it.

Bradley swung the shovel up on his shoulder. "I'm not saying it's a good idea," he said, "so when the time comes, you best tell your pa that I had nothing to do with it." And then, to contradict his claim of no involvement, he added, "Leave it to me, and I'll fix everything."

And just like that, Caroline was going to get a shot at her dreams.

Bradley had never been prouder of Amber than he was at that moment. It irked him that he couldn't do it on his own, but that was what he needed a partner for, right? And in a few weeks, he'd be free of his obligations and able to make her his partner for life.

The discussion between the three of them moved rapidly, jumping from challenge to challenge as they each blurted out their ideas, preparations both made and unmade, and problems they saw ahead. Bradley already had provisions set aside at Evans's store, but one didn't race with a horse laden with supplies. One of the girls would have to come back for them. Caroline would wire her grandmother and ask if she'd be willing to forward some money from the dowry fund she'd set aside for Caroline. Hopefully the reply wouldn't alert Major Adams to their plans.

Bradley had to admit he'd worried about leaving Amber alone on the homestead while he finished his enlistment. It'd be nice knowing that Caroline was nearby. And wherever Caroline was . . . well, even if Major Adams didn't approve of what she'd done, you could bet your last dollar that there'd be a patrol going through there to check on her every hour or so.

"You might as well saddle up Hardtack and Gunpowder," said Caroline. "We need to test them. We'll put on riding clothes and come back."

"Wait a minute," Bradley said. "I have stable call, and all these stalls have to be cleaned out before noon. If you can't saddle your own horses, how are you going to make this work?"

Caroline's nose wrinkled, and she looked like she was fighting the urge to stick her tongue out at him. "Fine," she said. "We'll do it when we get back. C'mon, Amber."

But Amber's sparkling blue eyes were on him. She twisted her closed parasol. "Go on without me, Caroline."

Caroline rubbed her hand on Hardtack's nose one last time. "We can't let Father catch either of us walking across the parade grounds unaccompanied. I'll wait for you at the door." She gave them both a stern look. "Don't make me wait long." Then she turned to leave the building.

Amber dipped her head and giggled. "You'd think she was the oldest."

How could she look so fresh and clean in the stables? He planted the end of the shovel in the dirt floor and let the handle fall against the gate of the stall.

"We need to get her married off, or else she's going to pester us something awful. Can you imagine her next door with no one to boss around? She'd never leave us alone." And being left alone with Amber was something he was looking forward to.

"She's a good friend, Bradley. I'm determined to help her any way I can."

"I'm a good friend too, and the best way to help her is to get her hitched." He stepped closer.

Her forehead wrinkled. "You've been shoveling out the stables, love. My dress can't get dirty because I won't have time to launder it, and once I get the homestead, I'll be so busy—"

"Shhh," he said. "It's just my hands that are dirty."

"And your fatigue clothes."

He looked down at his shirt, which was splashed with something wet. When had that happened? But Bradley always had an answer.

"My lips are perfectly clean." He stopped just a foot in front of her. "If you don't believe me, try them for yourself."

She cast a quick look at the doorway, then leaned forward and pressed her lips against his. It was nice, but it wasn't enough. He still had months of missing her to make up for. He didn't realize that his hand had risen until he felt the sharp tip of her parasol in his ribs.

"What?" he asked.

She stared pointedly at the space between them, the space

he was doing his best to span. "That's enough," she said. "I've got to go." With a shove, she marched him back.

Bradley held up his hands. "No reason to skewer me. I'll take the hint." Although her smile showed clearly that there was no offense taken.

"Excuse me, Corporal Willis, but I have many tasks I must attend to." With a wink, she sashayed away with a look over her shoulder to make sure he was still watching.

"Ambrosia. Food of the gods," he said. And he could never get enough.

Chapter Seven

FORT RENO, INDIAN TERRITORY
APRIL 22, 1889

The dew was heavy, and the hem of Caroline's split skirt would soon be soaked, but there was no helping it. She shouldered her knapsack as she and Amber tiptoed off the dark porch.

Today was the day. It was still six hours before the cannons sounded, but they had to be off the post long before noon if they didn't want their adventure halted before it had begun.

The girls had barely reached the parade grounds when the front door to their house was flung open. With a blanket wrapped over her nightgown and her hair tied up in curling rags, Daisy ran barefoot across the porch and into the road to catch them.

"Where are you going?" With her raised voice, Daisy was showing a shocking lack of regard for the sleeping families on Officers' Row. "Sneaking away early?"

"Sorry," Amber whispered to Caroline. "She must have caught me going back for my mallet."

"And why do you need a mallet?" Daisy asked. "It's still dark."

"What's it matter?" Caroline retorted. "If Father trusts me as far away as Galveston, then shouldn't I be safe on the post?"

"You're up to no good, sneaking out before dawn with a bag packed. Why would you run away? You just got here. . . ." Daisy's eyes bulged. "You're running in the race, aren't you? That's it. You want to get a claim." The wind flapped her curling rags like crazed moths. "Father wouldn't like this. He wouldn't like it at all."

"But you aren't going to tell him. Not until the day is over." Caroline had always had her bluff in on her younger sister, but her advantage was slipping. "After I've got the claim secured, then you can tell him, but not until then."

"He's going to notice that you're gone this morning. What am I supposed to say?"

"He knows that I'm going to watch. Everyone is going to watch. He'll suppose that we got an early start. That's all."

Daisy looked back at the front door as she weighed her options. "I don't like it. I was looking forward to you being home. But maybe when you build your house, you could build me my own room for when I come visit."

Building a house? Yes, that would be Caroline's first task after gathering firewood, digging a well, putting in a garden. . . . What in the world had she signed up for? How did she think she could do all that? But she would. If it meant independence, she'd give it her best. "If that's all it takes, then yes."

"And I get to wear your new clothes whenever I want."

"They don't fit you. You're too short," Caroline said.

"Maybe it's better that I tell Father. What if you got hurt? I wouldn't want that on my conscience."

"Fine. You can wear my clothes, even though you'll trample the hems. Just go back to bed and don't wake anyone," Caroline said. "And if I come back later today with nothing to show for it, then forget you knew anything about this."

"They couldn't torture it out of me." Daisy stifled a yawn. Then she brightened. "If you die, can I still have your new clothes?"

"Yes," Caroline gruffed. "But bury me in something nice. Don't keep everything for yourself."

"Yes, ma'am." Daisy saluted, then turned back to the house.

Amber let out a sigh of relief. "I can't believe we're going to get away with this. I'd thought for sure that the money wire from your grandmother was going to get us caught."

But somehow Lieutenant Hennessey hadn't found time to mention the fund transfer to her father, and the shopkeeper in Darlington hadn't thought to notify the major that his daughter had come in at the eleventh hour to purchase one of everything he had left in his ravaged store, and Agent Williams hadn't remembered to take note of the fact that Caroline and Amber had asked to stash a few bags of supplies in the commissary until they could come back with a wagon for them. So many chances for their plans to be discovered, but with the whole countryside in an uproar, the army had more to worry about than the activities of Major Adams's daughter and her friend.

They hurried around the parade grounds. The soldiers and troopers were finishing with mess. There'd be no drill or fatigue duties on a busy day like today, so the girls needed to get off the post before a hundred questioning eyes were starting out on patrol. They walked past a handful of Troop C's men, who tipped their hats as the girls made their way to the family end of the stables.

Amber looked over every stall. "Bradley said he'd meet us."

"Bradley said he'd *try* to meet us, but his officer probably had other ideas." They reached the end stalls to find Hardtack and Gunpowder saddled, bridled, and waiting. "See, he didn't forget. He's looking out for you."

"Why am I so worried?" Amber asked. "You'd think I'd trust him by now."

But there was a lot at stake for them. A lot at stake for Caroline too, but this wasn't the time for timidity. If she was going to play a role in this new venture, she'd better be ready to fight for her spot.

The sun was up, and the air was filled with hope. Frisco gathered his paperwork and stuffed it into his rugged traveling case between the wad of cash from his investors and the rumpled handkerchief that was his only keepsake from his birth family. As a boy he'd carried this case—probably discarded by its original owner when it'd gotten a few scuffs—from the foundlings' home, to the boys' home, to the young men's workhouse, and then to the streets when he'd grown tired of being bound by others' expectations.

For years he'd carted this case around, never completely unpacking it, as he petitioned for a chance at land—something that people with Frisco's beginnings rarely got. Throughout it all, he waited for the day he could unpack the case permanently in a home of his own.

While constructing his shelter on the hidden homestead, he'd been tempted. He'd stocked the shelves, dug a well, and put in a garden. Why couldn't he finally empty his case? But the homestead didn't belong to him. Not until he'd raced from the line and claimed it fair and square. Frisco played with the law like a banjo player picked strings, but he didn't break the rules. He might get the rules to read in ways no one had before, but the written word was supreme. If it said he had to be on the line at noon to claim a homestead, that was where he'd be, and heaven help those who thought the rules didn't apply to them.

He closed the case and grabbed his leather coat from the hook on the wall as he said farewell to the boardinghouse in Silver City. Never again would he need a hotel room this close to Redhawk. By shortly after noon, the boy who'd never had a father would be a town father. Today was his day.

Paying the proprietor on his way out, Frisco went to the livery to get his horse.

Never before had there been so many people buzzing about the little settlement of Silver City. As he left town and rode west along the southern border, the crowds thinned out, but there was still an unbroken stretch of people camping along the line, not taking their eyes off the land to their north that would soon be claimed either by them or their lucky neighbors. Already men were ground-tying their horses against the riverbank that marked the southern border of the territory. Most of the wives and children were tidying up their camps a safe distance away.

Always drawn to the working of a crowd, Frisco reined his horse where a group of men stood, contemplating the river boundary.

"It's Mr. Smith." The man had an eastern European accent. Czech, if Frisco remembered correctly. "I almost didn't recognize you decked out like that."

How far he'd come. A year ago, no one would've recognized him in a suit. Now they thought his frontier clothes were re-markable. "It's not a day for fine clothes," Frisco said. "We'll have to get our hands dirty before there's reason to put on fancy duds."

"This is the man you need to talk to," said the Czech to one of his companions. "He's one of the brokers behind this deal."

"I don't know that I'd call myself a broker. Maybe an or-ganizer—"

"This here is what we're trying to figure." The second man was short and well built. His right forearm looked like he'd spent a lot of time roping. "It's going be rough going, crossing that river," he said. "That's a steep bank. Me and the fellas here figure we're going to cross it and wait for noon on the other side."

"But the border is on this side of the river," Frisco said. "Can't take out until you hear the signal."

"Are you the law?" chimed a third, taller man. He pushed aside his threadbare coat to reveal a rusty revolver holstered at his belt. "There ain't no law here to know one way or t'other. Besides, on our honor, we wouldn't take out until noon. Just would rather get the river behind us before the start."

Frisco had no patience for such maneuvers. These Johnny-come-latelies showed up in Indian Territory and decided that the contest was too difficult, so they wanted special arrangements. If it weren't for men like Frisco and their petitions, this race wouldn't be happening in the first place. And men like these fellas felt entitled to having it easy.

"How long have you been camped here?" Frisco asked.

"For a week and a half," the rancher replied. "Why?"

"Y'all know each other? I mean, you've been camped here long enough."

"Sure do. We know each other now."

Frisco nodded, then pointed to a robust man whose disdain for the discussion was evident. "You there, what do you think of their plans?"

The man stepped forward, pushing his barrel chest right into the heart of the group. "I think it's a pity that these men gathered with a chaplain yesterday and prayed for God's blessing, and today they're planning how to sneak across early. Maybe they aren't trusting God enough to get them across a river?"

Frisco had found his man. "Listen, all of you." He made sure to include those on the perimeter of the crowd. They were the ones who hadn't thrown their lot in with the rest. "Make a list. Take names. Pay attention to who is standing by you when the signal flies and who has already flown the coop. You might not have the law with you today, but are we Americans or not? Are we capable of governing ourselves, or do we need someone to come impose the rules on us? By the end of the day, some of y'all might be councilmen or mayors. Soon there'll be judges and juries ready to start hearing cases, and you all are witnesses. If you have any honor, you'll stay on this side of the river until the signal, and you'll report those who don't. Maybe they won't take the piece of land you were after, but they'll get someone's, and it's not right. It's up to us to be fair."

The looks thrown his way weren't charitable. He might have ruined their advantage, but he hoped he'd helped save the integrity of the contest.

Seeing that the tone of the discussion had changed, Frisco continued his journey along the line. He had a piece to travel before he got to the place he needed to start from, and he didn't want to wind his horse getting there.

He knew when he'd reached the corner of the territory. The line of people ended and started afresh on the north side of the South Canadian River. This was the western border and where Frisco needed to be.

The men at Silver City hadn't been wrong—the river was hard to cross, and Frisco sincerely hoped the wagons didn't attempt it. The chances of getting stuck were great, and quicksand was a likely threat to those in a hurry and not paying mind. At this corner, it was lawful to cross the river as long as they remained against the western border, and many had decided, like Frisco, to run from that direction, where the river crossing was already behind them. He kept out of the press of people, though, and let his horse trot north until he came to the place he'd chosen. He eyed his way ahead—the dips and undulations of the land as familiar to him as the beaten leather satchel tied to his horse. He might as well take a breather and dismount. Unlike the settlers around him, he had no goods to pack up and no family to calm before the cannon sounded.

The line was defined by stakes driven every tenth of a mile or so, but you didn't need to see the stakes because the people had already taken their spots two hours early. A trooper in cavalry blue trotted his bay horse along the line, pausing to visit with the jovial contestants but also keeping an eye toward the supposedly unmanned land to their east.

How many were already out there? Frisco ground his boot heel into the red soil. Some might say that he had an unfair advantage, but knowledge was power. Some people had it and others didn't. Some people had faster horses. Some people could run like the wind. You used every lawful advantage at your disposal, and that was the key. He was waiting on the line, and he expected everyone else to do the same.

"You might not want to wait here, youngster." The speaker's grizzled beard spread over his patched and threadbare shirt. "There ain't going to be anything left from this side."

"What do you mean?"

"We woke up this morning to find nearly everyone had pulled out and disappeared last night." His skin was sun-marred by dark splotches scattered over his face. "By the time the guns go off, they'll be at the claims office with the paperwork ready to file."

Frisco pulled out his watch. Even though it wasn't real gold, it looked out of place with his frontiersman's garb. An hour and a half. He didn't want to get too far from his starting position, but neither could he stomach the thought that someone who'd followed the rules would be cheated by someone who hadn't. If there was something he could do to help . . .

He marched to the invisible line and crossed it, stepping

out in front of the waiting people. Frisco caught his breath as he scanned both directions. With his view unobstructed by his fellow runners, he could see the line to the north. Sometimes it disappeared into a dip, but then it reappeared farther on, a dark smudge against the green pastureland broken up by red dirt. He tried to make out Darlington and Fort Reno, but he couldn't be sure where he was looking. All he knew was that other people were looking at *him* and getting pretty riled.

"Get back behind the line."

"Where do you think you're going?"

Frisco raised his hand in acknowledgment, certain that the runners weren't the only ones who'd seen him. And sure enough, troopers from both sides were barreling toward him.

Frisco had a lot of experience with being arrested. He'd probably been arrested by the very troopers who were on their way, so he stood with his feet planted and both his hands up, trying to cause them as little concern as possible.

"You only have an hour to wait, Frisco Smith." It was Corporal Bradley Willis, the brother of the major's wife. The one engaged to Miss Adams's pretty friend. "You couldn't go that long without a visit to the guardhouse?"

Frisco felt a spike of fear. Had he made a mistake? He'd forgotten the decree that anyone caught in the lands prematurely was forbidden from claiming a lot. He was only trying to be helpful.

"I apologize for the inconvenience," he said. "I wanted to draw your attention to the situation here. According to the settlers, a large group left overnight. They're hiding out there in the gullies, waiting for noon, when they'll pop up and grab a homestead."

Bradley's mouth twisted as his horse pawed the ground. Frisco admired the way he sat a horse. It was as if the two beasts were connected by the same thoughts. From what he knew of Corporal Willis, the horse might be the wiser of the two.

"We've got deputies out there," Willis said, "but they're greenhorns. I don't set much stock by them. On the other hand, I'm assigned to the line. I can't go thrashing through the scrub looking for sooners. Especially when there's a man breaking the law right in front of me."

Frisco took two giant steps backward. Then, looking over his shoulder, he took one more, just to make sure he was safe. Without urging, Bradley's horse moved forward as if it were interested in the conversation too.

"If I may make a suggestion," Frisco said. "They've had the same problem on the south border as well. The best course of action might be to gather a list of names of those who moonlighted away. As an added precaution, you could take down a list of people still here at noon to protect them from fraudulent accusations should they try to claim land that was taken illegally."

Bradley narrowed his eyes. "Do you have paper?"

"Do I?" Frisco looked back to where his horse was still standing next to the gray-headed man. "Yes, of course." He always traveled light, but his map of Redhawk, his money, and the list of his settlers' names stayed with him. He'd stashed his law books in his dugout house, but he had paper.

"Then I give you permission to do what you suggested. Take down the names of everyone here and those who are suspected of soonerism."

"Today? Right now? In case it escaped your notice, Corporal, there's a big race fixing to happen. I'll do what I can, but—"

"Right. Do what you can. That's all any of us are doing today. As for me, I've got to be on the line a mile north of here. There are a couple of ladies who think they're going to make the run, and I'd like to be there to see that they get a clean start. When you're able, get that list in to the authorities. If what you say is true, there'll be a lot of people grateful for your help."

And a lot of people who would want to murder him. Frisco looked again at the path he'd chosen. This wasn't the way he'd pictured the biggest day of his life.

~~~

"Bradley says to let the men get the jump when the gun goes off." Amber pulled her gloves tight. "That's the most dangerous time. We're better off coming up from behind than getting trampled."

Caroline tugged on her saddle roll to make sure her stake and mallet were secure. Also included was enough food to last her three days. It'd be a hungry three days, but she didn't dare leave her claim until things had settled down.

"For once Bradley's speaking sense," Caroline said. "Our horses are fast enough to keep up, and we're sure of our route." The air was filled with voices speaking in unfamiliar accents and tongues. Not one familiar face, though, which meant they were strangers to the area. No one here who knew the land better than she . . . and Frisco.

That was one familiar face she didn't want to see. She tightened her saddle roll for the third time and climbed into the saddle. She surveyed the people on both sides of her. Would some of them become her neighbors? What history would they share? What history would they make?

"What are you doing here?" It was Bradley, who'd spotted them as he patrolled the line. "I thought you were going to be farther north."

"According to Caroline, this is the spot." Amber rode forward to meet him at the boundary.

Caroline nodded. "And there are not as many people waiting here."

"That's because a lot of them have already flown the coop," Bradley said. "But don't you worry. If we catch them, their land will be up for the taking. Now, you girls should get in position. Step back a bit from the front, remember. You don't want your horses to get spooked or be trampled by a wagon."

Amber reached out her hand, even though the invisible barrier separated her from her man. "Wish me luck," she said.

"I wish *us* luck," he said.

The mood of the crowd, which had been jovial for the last few days, was growing serious. The time of reckoning was upon them. Bradley had backed away from the line and was passing on some communication with the line of troopers that stretched the span of the border. Women were gathering their children together and moving away from the front.

"I'm nervous," Amber said. She stretched her legs before her, testing her stirrups.

"It's just a horse ride," said Caroline, but she was feeling light-headed herself. She tested her grip on the reins and felt the sweat slicking her palms inside her gloves.

How long would they have to wait?

A call went out from the front of the line. "Five-minute warning."

At the sound, a horse darted forward. A few others followed even as Bradley spun and spurred his horse to corral them back.

One man who'd gotten a jump looked over his shoulder at the unmoving crowd. He reined hard to pull his mare back to the line. "I thought I was on my way to victory," he said sheepishly as he rejoined the group.

"I just hope you ran far enough to tire your horse," a young cowpuncher responded.

The laughter helped break the tension, but in a heartbeat it was back. A fly buzzed beneath the brim of Caroline's hat. She shooed it away, then tested her chin strap to make sure it wouldn't slip. Hardtack shuddered beneath her. He'd picked up on her nerves and was ready to break loose. She'd have a hard time holding him back, even for a spare moment. A bead of sweat ran down her spine and soaked into her waistband.

Bradley sat astride his horse in front of them, as still as a statue with his timepiece in his hand. The wind snapped the canvas on the wagon next to them. Bradley pulled his revolver out of its holster. Everyone leaned forward. A man walked between Caroline and Amber with a spike in one hand and a hammer in the other and waited.

Bradley lifted his gun over his head. No one breathed. His eyes flickered to Amber . . . and then he pulled the trigger.

Chapter Eight

"You didn't get my name." A man waved Frisco over. What in the world? The man wore a clerk's sleeve protectors and short pants and was sitting astride a bicycle. While he didn't want to give up his place in the line, he did want his name on the list of those who'd waited. Frisco pulled the rumpled paper out of his shirt pocket and produced a pencil.

"Name?"

"Phineas Stargazer."

"You've got to be kidding me."

"I had it legally changed. It used to be John Stargazer—"

The crowd tensed. A call sounded that ricocheted in Frisco's chest. Had he missed it? But no one moved. The words *five-minute warning* sounded around him as the racers reassured themselves that they only had to wait a little longer. Frisco scratched down the name and folded the list into his pocket as he turned to run back to his horse.

"Don't forget me." A man rolled a sleek black buggy in his way. "I have witnesses that I've been here, but having my name on that list won't hurt nothing either."

Why had Corporal Willis given him this task? Time was running out. Frisco didn't bother folding the paper after taking down the name but shoved the list beneath his belt, running to where he'd left his horse.

Only his horse wasn't there.

He pushed his hat back on his head and spun in a circle. The milling crowd had grown still, everyone straining toward the boundary line. His horse had been right there. Where could it have gone? He spun again and realized he was being watched by a woman sitting on a milking stool. She popped a piece of horehound candy into her mouth and crunched it slowly, never taking her eyes off him.

Something about her told Frisco that her interest wasn't coincidence. Nearly frantic, he ran to her dying campfire. "Where's my horse? You know, don't you?"

"Did you lose something?" She slurped to keep from drooling around the candy. "What a pity. You was so interested in writing down names of men who left a few hours early that you weren't paying attention. Seems like if you make those men lose their property, you might oughta look after yourn."

Frisco looked over his shoulder. Corporal Willis was reaching for his pistol. "If you cause me to miss this race, ma'am, I fear the consequences I'll bring against you. Where's my horse?"

His pain delighted her. She smiled and, with an indolent hand, waved behind the line where the families were waiting. "You might oughta look over there. Seems like there was a horse belonging to a do-gooder—"

Frisco didn't wait for the insults but ran past the campsites to where his horse was tied to an abandoned wagon wheel. He fought to get the reins unknotted, the seconds ticking away. If he knew the name of that woman or her husband, he'd make sure to personally represent anyone who wanted the land they'd illegally claimed.

The gunshot sounded like a *ping* compared to the roar that followed it. Frisco froze as the wall of horses, runners, and wagons fell away from him. Dust flew and the ground shook. He tasted the dirt they were kicking up as they sped away, growing smaller by the second.

He reached for his knife and slashed the reins short. Jumping on the back of his horse, he didn't have to spur it. With nostrils wide and ears back, it leapt after the racers ahead.

Frisco yelled a warning as his horse raced toward the line of onlookers left behind. They parted just as he broke past them. Leaning forward, it was all Frisco could do to keep the shortened reins in his hands. Good thing he didn't have a lengthy ride before him.

He streaked past a few men running on foot. The bicyclist had already crashed in a tangle of wire and metal. The wagons in front of Frisco bounced frightfully. He dodged as a barrel of spirits fell out of the back of one and busted on the ground. His horse easily overtook the wagons, which were only then reaching their full speed. A few more strides, and it was only the horse riders ahead.

Riding low, Frisco was making up for his late start. The draft horses and mules were no match for his mustang. It didn't hurt that his horse knew every hillock and ditch along the way. Together they anticipated the gentle slopes and washouts, but she still wasn't the fastest horse running, and that was where his preparation came in handy.

As the riders in front of him approached the steep banks of the canyon, they slowed. Frisco had studied the red cliffs enough to know that no one would try to rush down them. Their frustration was evident as two, then three, began pacing along the edge of the drop-off. They were losing their advantage, and they didn't like it. He, of all people, understood. Finally, one spurred to the north to follow the creek until a suitable crossing could be found. The others, not wanting to miss their chance, raced after him. Frisco turned to the south. As long as he was the first person through the pass . . .

A hat appeared at the edge of the gully, and then a man pulled himself over the ledge. With a sharp stake in hand, he ran a few feet, then drove the stake into the ground. He mopped his brow with a handkerchief and waited on the approaching runners. He obviously didn't see Frisco watching from behind.

Of all the low-down . . . why did Frisco have to care so much? With a groan, he tugged his short reins and directed his horse toward the sooner. He'd have to be quick. It wouldn't take long for riders to find their way across.

"What's your name?" Frisco called.

"Eldon Fender," the man replied. "And you can move on because this is my land."

"There's no way you made it here on foot," Frisco said. He fumbled with his stub pencil and jotted down another name on his sooner list. "But thanks for the information. It'll be useful at the land office."

Two riders were reaching the creek, and behind them came the bulk of the crowd. He really had to go. He couldn't leave it to chance that it would take them long to cross.

But then, just like a rotten apple, another man dropped out of a tree a ways farther. Was there a moonlighter under every branch and rock? With apologies to his horse, Frisco headed toward him.

Getting this right could mean the world to someone who'd obeyed the law. Were the tables turned, Frisco would want someone to do the same for him. He turned to look over his shoulder again, and the two riders had disappeared. In their wake was a cornucopia of conveyances. If they'd found the way through, there was nothing to keep others from following. As quickly as he could, Frisco jotted down the name on the homemade flag attached to the man's stake, then spurred his horse toward the crossing.

"I promise, this is the last time," he said. "We're almost home."

Almost home. And he had more than the horse to answer to. Sixty-four families were counting on him to have Redhawk established by nightfall.

Caroline didn't wince at the sound of the gunshot, but the roar of the crowd startled Hardtack. When his rear end dropped, she had a split second to keep him from bolting. She braced herself with the reins pulled tight, but it was no use. The first runners had gone, and her horse was going to be running sideways if she didn't give him his head. At the thunder of the fort's cannon, Hardtack took out.

"I guess we're going," she yelled to Amber.

"Do it!" Amber yelled back.

Caroline slackened the reins, and with a *whoosh* they were hurtling ahead. The wagons on either side of them were just beginning to rock forward as they passed. She only had time to see the man with the stake step across the line and drive it into the ground before he was a blur behind her. The thundering hooves pulled her focus ahead. A fall could be deadly. She had to control her horse's speed so she didn't lose Amber.

Even with the slight delay, the girls were still among the first runners. As the line was left behind them, they spaced out. It occurred to Caroline that as the first ones streaking across the territory, she could stop at any point and claim land, but better acreage lay ahead. So much lay ahead.

Every nerve in her body sang as she rushed headlong into the wind. If only she could bottle this feeling—but too much, and she'd never survive. Her heart would give out and her lungs would explode, but it was glorious. The men who raced along with them began to peel off to the north. Seemed like she wasn't the only one who knew that an obstacle lay ahead, but she might be the only one who knew a way through.

She looked over her shoulder. Amber had fallen behind, but she was coming with the single-minded purpose that Caroline expected from her. They were nearing the embankment. Once she crossed, others might try to overtake her in the pass, but on the opposite side there should be land for all. At first, anyway.

The embankment was a dark smudge ahead, the only spot with trees and shadows on the sun-drenched prairie that day. Then Caroline saw something that made her blood boil. A man climbed out of the gully to the south. Where had he come from? Cheater! How many were there? With hours of a head start—maybe days—there was no guarantee that there was any land available on the other side of the canyon. Fear crept up her throat. It wasn't right. Someone should do something.

And then someone did.

A racer arced out of his path to confront the man. Caroline cheered even though they couldn't hear her from that distance. Thank goodness for the deputy, or whoever he was. Having been privy to the efforts of the marshals and the military in this area for years, Caroline had no use for lawbreakers. She hoped settlement would run criminals out of the territory entirely. She didn't want them living among the honest contestants.

"Almost there," she yelled to Amber.

Reining in Hardtack, Caroline picked her way down the embankment that would take miles off their route. A campfire smoldered, proof that someone else had been squatting illegally. There was no telling how many lawbreakers had used the gully to avoid the patrols.

Barely slowing down, Amber crashed through the undergrowth down the steep embankment. "I'm here," she panted. "Let's go."

Good thing Amber was on the slower horse. With her determination, Caroline doubted her friend would've waited for her.

Together they splashed across the shallow river and climbed up the other side. Caroline caught her breath. The land spread out before them untouched. They were the first, but others would be coming, and quickly. And as close as they were to the southern border, they'd soon face challengers from there too.

"This way." She spurred Hardtack and rode straight for the most desirable area. It wasn't quite flat but had a river curving through it and trees. She and Amber raced until the river was just ahead, and then Caroline stopped. She might be close to Frisco's land, but he'd be so busy with his town, he wouldn't have time to bother her.

"We're here," she said to Amber. "Pick your spot."

Amber bit her lip. "I want access to the river, but Bradley wants more pasture. I'll head this way."

"I'll stay here," Caroline said. "And remember, our claims are a quarter of a square mile. Find the surveyor's cornerstone before you drive your stake."

Amber nodded, then with a cavalry-worthy yell, flapped her reins and took off.

Caroline slid out of the saddle and fumbled with the ties on the bedroll. She had to get her stake and mallet. Once she drove the stake, the land was hers. Then she'd poke around along the riverbank and make sure no one else was there— but if they were, they couldn't have been there fairly. While her father might be mad that she'd decided to run without consulting him, using his name would be enough to scare off most troublemakers.

The stake was rough, but her gloves protected her. The

ground gave slightly under her feet. Good fertile ground that the rains had made ready for spring planting. She held the stake upright and, with a firm pounding, had it driven. Caroline stepped back and unfurled the flag that announced her name as the rightful owner.

Was that all it took? Was it hers? She turned slowly and looked over her land. She'd done it. All on her own she'd accomplished this, but it was just the beginning. Now the real work began.

Taking Hardtack by the reins, Caroline began to search for the corners of her land, three of them marked by stones. She'd heard that many planned to start plowing immediately. Even turning over dirt would help prove that they were making improvements on the claim and make it harder to take away. She didn't have a shovel, but at least she could gather some wood and start a cook fire.

Something looked odd in the grass over yonder. Caroline strode there, surprised to find that her legs were still a bit shaky from the exhilarating ride. Even Hardtack seemed winded, although she'd ridden him much farther before. When she made it over the rise, she saw that the ground had been turned. Neatly laid rows, and they hadn't been the work of one night. There were already tender sprouts coming up. Caroline looked over her shoulder. She was alone, but someone had been there and had been there illegally.

It couldn't be Frisco's place. He wouldn't have let her get there before him—of that Caroline was certain—but someone would show up soon.

She wiped the sweat from her forehead. Last night when she'd swiped the mallet from the carpenter's shack on the fort, she had known this would require a toughness from her that she'd never needed before. This wasn't playing chess with her stepmother; it was real life. There were real consequences, and she couldn't count on someone else fighting her battles for her. Whoever had planted that plot had done so illegally. They had taken a risk by working land they didn't own. It wasn't her place to reward their speculation. She'd raced for this farm, and she would defend it as soon as the other runners found their way around the gully.

It didn't take long.

Instead of coming from the north, the lone rider must've come through the same pass she'd taken. He was riding like a prairie fire was chasing him, and he was headed straight for her stake. He must not have seen her over the rise. Caroline ran across the field as he jumped off his horse, pulled her stake out of the ground, and tossed it aside.

She hadn't run so fast since she'd chased her little sister years ago. She'd nearly reached him when he took his own spike from his saddle, but then he looked up, and she skidded to a stop. Frisco Smith? Her eyes widened. He stood there panting with a stake in his hand, looking at her like she was a ghost.

How had she beat him? But she couldn't show weakness. She moistened her lips. "I was here first," she rasped. "This is my land."

His mouth twitched. He blinked. His hand tightened on the spike, and his jaw clenched. "Miss Adams? You're breaking the law. You'd best get back to the fort before your father finds out."

Her father? Caroline had done this to prove herself, and all anyone wanted to talk about was her father. She swooped down and snatched her stake, straightening the flag for him to read. "I put this in the ground. This is my claim."

"No." He put his foot over the hole the pulled spike had left behind. "This is my land. This is where I was going. You can go somewhere else."

His land. She blinked into the wind. She'd wondered about the garden, but with all the possible spots along the river, she hadn't been sure. Well, she'd beaten him. She didn't know how, but she had, and she couldn't bow out now. She wouldn't get another chance.

"Go somewhere else," she said. "You have the whole valley."

He shook his head. "This is my land. I've worked it already. I have the map—"

"The map doesn't mean anything."

Horsemen came over the ridge. They'd worked their way around. Soon the whole area would be crawling with people looking for a place.

"Be reasonable." His words were fast and harsh. His face had turned an odd shade of green beneath his swarthy complexion. "You can't prove a homestead. You can't farm. You don't want this. I don't know what you're trying to prove, but it's time you grow up. This isn't a game, and you can't have it just because your pa is the major."

Had he always thought so poorly of her? Caroline blinked dry eyes. It would've been nice if they could have remembered a shared past fondly, but ever since she'd arrived in the territory, he'd done his best to insult her.

"You've mentioned my father twice now," she said. "You don't suppose he'll let you run me off my lawfully obtained homestead, do you?"

A horseman rode up, then seeing them, streaked on down the valley. The white canvas top of a wagon appeared, bouncing over the horizon.

"They're coming," Caroline said. "You're running out of time. Do you want to wager that the court will give you this plot?"

Frisco's jaw worked. A part of Caroline's heart shriveled at the anger in his eyes. But she was strong. She didn't need his permission. She was doing this on her own.

"Good luck, Miss Adams." He jumped on his horse with his stake in hand. "You're going to need it," he said as he spurred the horse and shot out after the others.

Chapter Nine

He'd guarded his tongue, but his temper was raging. His horse seemed confused to be running away from the place they'd been working over the last months. Frisco was confused too. It was unfathomable. After all his planning, all his preparation, he'd been beaten by a novice. With every stride, he debated turning around and trying to reason with the stubborn woman, but there was no time for negotiation. Already the crowd was hot on his heels, fighting for whatever land the moonlighters hadn't illegally claimed.

He roared across the river, only to find a rested horse grazing next to a cook fire that had been burning all night. Another sooner to add to his list. He pressed on, but a man riding ahead of him slid off his horse and drove his spike. He spun and squared off to Frisco with a challenge in his eye.

Frisco was no fool. He'd lost that claim fair and square. He headed south. At a distance he saw racers coming to meet him. They'd gotten across the southern border. Everything was going too fast. If he didn't find a place soon . . .

He turned north. "Come on, girl," he begged the horse. "Give me just a little more."

When he broke out of the trees on the riverbank, he paused. Ahead was a whole campsite—tents, wagons, cots, fires. There had to be nearly fifty men there. Was it a campsite . . . or a town site?

"Come on up." A man pulled his pocket watch out by its gold chain and flipped the cover open. "We still have town lots available, but you'd better hurry."

Frisco's heart sank. Town lots? He was supposed to be securing a town for others, not joining this one. But today was not the day for indecision.

"Yes," he said. "What's the best lot you have left?"

"Twenty-five after noon, and you ask that question? The main street is marked with green stakes. There are a few lots left on the far north of Main Street. Branch off to the east if you want to be more centrally located. You could take out and look there."

This was what he'd come to? Settling for a back lot in someone else's town when he'd planned to be the founder of his own? But procrastinating would mean he'd get nothing.

He followed the green markers past men hurriedly scrambling to pitch their tents. He got off his horse and walked into a lot.

"Hey, this one's taken," a man called from a group of people in the next lot.

"Sorry. How about that one?" Frisco asked.

The man turned to his companions. They leaned their heads together, then reached a decision. "Take that one, friend. We're glad to have you."

This wasn't the end. He wasn't giving up on his dream, but he couldn't let the unexpected paralyze him. Frisco pulled his horse behind him to a piece of pasture already set about by people. Redhawk had its own Main Street, and it was on the banks of a river. It had more shade. It had more timber. Now that timber all belonged to Caroline Adams.

And what was she going to do with it? Nothing. Frisco's blood boiled. Likely some smooth-talking huckster would sugar her up, and next thing you knew, he'd have her hand and her land. Frisco's jaw clenched as he drove his stake into the ground. He'd always admired Miss Adams's determination and intelligence, but he'd never thought she'd misapply it so grievously. The more he thought through the day's events, the less sense it made that she'd beaten him to the land. Had she used her connections at the fort to get her across the line before noon? He'd thought she had more character than that, but maybe she'd changed more than he'd realized.

Wagons had begun to pull in over the horizon from the west. Horses lathered in sweat were driven by men with desperation all over their faces. Frisco watched as they were directed to lots here and there. Overall it was organized, considering that everyone had descended at the same time. At least that was what he assumed. Surely if someone had come early, the first racers there would have denounced them. Instead, everyone was working in cooperation.

Hammer strikes rang out across the field. No, no longer a field—a town. What had been a field was now a town.

But it wasn't his town.

He would get his land back. He would. Otherwise he'd have to face his investors and tell them that he'd failed. By May 22, he was to meet them in Purcell and lead them to their new homes, if they hadn't found him first. One month. He had to have a city for them, or he had to return their money—all one hundred and seventeen dollars of it. He had the money in his traveling case, but that didn't sway his determination. He mustn't fail them.

In the meantime, his plans had temporarily changed. Frisco had stocked his property with food and provisions, but he'd raced with nothing. Now nothing was all he had left. He'd have to use some of his funds to buy a tent, but how did he go about procuring what he needed while still standing guard at his claim?

His neighbor seemed to recognize his dilemma. The man had a sunny face, a broad smile, and the swagger of a conqueror. "It's safe to leave the horse," he said. "No one is going to take it. Look around. There'd be a hundred witnesses if they did."

He had a point. With no buildings to hide behind, nothing obstructed the view. Just a bunch of people unloading knapsacks and wagons and trying to make a camp before the spring day came to an end.

"Do you know whereabouts I could get a tent?" Frisco asked. As soon as he took care of business here, he'd go back and deal with Miss Adams. He had no intention of giving up his land, but that didn't mean he wanted to sleep uncovered tonight.

"No, sir. There's not exactly a town map or city directory."

A pity, because Frisco had one for his town.

"Thanks," he said.

His horse's reins were too short to ground-tie her. Instead Frisco unsaddled her, then piled his gear next to his stake. Borrowing a rope from his neighbor, he tied the horse to the saddle on the ground and prayed that everyone would be as honest as they were claiming. Then he took off down a swath of grass designated as a street. Already there were hand-painted signs propped up against saddles that advertised services. *Barber, carpenter, physician.* He'd have to put out his own sign advertising his services as a lawyer. Plenty of legal advice would be needed once they started to sort through all the questions concerning the run.

"You can't have this land. It's a street," an angry voice exclaimed over the melee.

Frisco looked to the side to see a covered wagon with an elderly man at the reins. "I don't aim to live here," the man said. "I'm just selling my goods."

True enough, his wagon rode low and heavy. The canvas was painted with the words *Wilton's Mercantile*. With a snap, the canvas side of the wagon broke loose as a young lady rolled it up to display her wares. She wore a flashy silk dress and a flashier smile. Frisco smiled in recognition. What did you know? He might be a stranger here, but he was among friends.

"C'mon over and see what the peddler has brought," she sang. "If you don't get it now, we'll be gone, and you'll have naught."

The man who'd stood in their way stepped back. "As long as you're not planning to stay."

"No, sir," said the old gent. "My granddaughter and I will sell what we can, then move on. We'd rather take our quick profit than stick around and civilize this forsaken corner."

"What have you got?" The man looked cool and collected in his cassimere suit. Like he'd just stepped out of an office, not like he'd just run a race.

"Oh, a little bit of everything." The young woman smiled encouragingly. When she caught Frisco's eye, she didn't falter. Sophie's show must go on. "What are you looking for?" she asked the clerk.

"That depends on your prices," he answered.

She bared her teeth. "It's half past noon, and it's unlikely you've had anything to eat. Grab one of my delicious sandwiches for twenty cents and fill your stomach."

"That's robbery," he said. "I'll have you know I'm a deputy, and I don't appreciate you gouging people like that."

He was a deputy? Frisco took in his getup from his derby hat to his leather boots with the opera toe. He didn't look like any lawman Frisco had ever met in the territory, but he'd heard they were hiring them by the dozen to have on hand for the race.

Sophie's smile dripped with innocence. "You're a deputy now? Ain't that something? Last I heard, you dealt in property.

Well, overpriced sandwiches aren't a crime, but it would be a crime to go to bed hungry tonight. Isn't that right, Ike?"

Either the man's neck had seen too much sun or Sophie was getting his goat. Leave it to Sophie Smith to know every man in the crowd. She'd always been one of those people who came out on top.

"Just one sandwich," the deputy said at last. After taking it, he decided to keep the peace like he'd been hired to do. "This will be the best dinner I've had in a month. We're fortunate to have you here in Plainview." He dropped his coins on the side of the wagon that served as her counter.

"Yes, sir," she said. "We'll rest easy knowing that lawmen like you are protecting the territory." She bit her ruby lip until he strode away, then turned to Frisco. "Frisco Smith, you old goat. Get up here and give me a kiss." Bending at the waist, she flung herself across the countertop to hug Frisco's neck.

Nearly choking on her scented powder, Frisco dutifully smacked her painted cheek, then helped push her up to regain her footing in the wagon.

"Sophie Smith—or is it Sophie Wilton?" he asked. "You've acquired a grandpa since I last saw you."

"He's my husband, but we sell more merchandise with me being single." She beamed. "Let me get a look at you. My, what a fine-looking man you've become. You don't have any need for a wife, do you? Most days Wilton would be glad to be rid of me."

Frisco tamped down the pity that threatened to arise. Sophie wouldn't know what to do with it. Instead he shrugged. "All I've got to offer a woman is a piece of empty ground back there. Looks like you're running a better deal with Mr. Wilton."

"It's a fine life on the road, and from the looks of it, you've done yourself flush as well. Still a will-o'-the-wisp looking for adventure? You'll never settle down, Frisco Smith. No use driving a stake today when the road will always beckon."

"Maybe you're right." Although he knew she wasn't. To the outsider it might look like he was always hunting for adventure, but really he was hunting for home. And he'd thought he'd found it, until Caroline stole it from him. "But even on the road I need somewhere to sleep. You wouldn't happen to have a tent in there, would you?"

The wagon squawked as Wilton joined her in the back. "Did you ask for a tent, young man? We wouldn't come to this hullabaloo without tents. My granddaughter has just the thing for you." Then he leaned closer and whispered, "You've got to try her sandwiches."

The thought of the stocked shelves of food back at his homestead made Frisco's jaw clench. The frantic pace of the day hadn't allowed him to think through all he had lost on his property. But he hadn't lost it. He couldn't. People were counting on him. He'd get it back from Caroline immediately.

The exchange was made, and Frisco walked off with a tent, food, and well-wishes from another friend from his past at the foundling house. He shouldn't be surprised to see so many of them here. If anyone was in need of a fresh start, it was those who'd had to overcome a poor beginning.

He had just put up the tent when he heard a ruckus down the road—if the grassy pathway could be called a road yet. A man with a megaphone was announcing some upcoming elections.

"If you have any interest in selecting a governing body, then meet at the barber pole. We'll elect a council today so that the town of Plainview can commence organizing."

Plainview? That was what the deputy had called it too. Redhawk was a better name—majestic, noble, brave. Frisco couldn't settle in a place called Plainview—it lacked allure—yet he might learn something from watching the election proceedings. After all, he'd have elections in Redhawk once he got his land back.

A row of men stood before a wall of pallets that had been nailed together. Were they the candidates? How were they chosen already? The whole affair seemed fishy, but Frisco would bite his tongue and observe before rushing to judgment.

A short, spare man with a pointed beard waved his hand over his head. "Gentlemen, gentlemen. We're going to elect your city council today. That council will choose a mayor so we can begin organizing. Now, these fine men here have consented to be the candidates."

Frisco's eyes narrowed. Consented to being candidates? That wasn't how he'd planned it for his town. Limiting the choices before everyone had a chance to take stock? Before he could stop himself, he called out, "Why those men? Who picked them?"

The pointy white beard jutted straight toward him. "These are all fine men, but if you want to be considered for a post . . ." He turned to get approval from the men behind him. There was some shuffling of feet, some furtive glances with weak nods. "Yes, if you'd like to join the candidates . . ."

Frisco crossed his arms, feeling the buckskin when he should have felt a suit. So much for biting his tongue. "I don't have any reason to do that. Just asking a question."

"Is that you, Frisco?" Mr. Cotton from Purcell sauntered up. "Y'all should listen to him. He's the boss man around here."

"Tom," Frisco said, "I only have a claim here. This isn't Redhawk. Soon I'll get—"

"Frisco Smith?" A man stepped out of the lineup of candidates. It was the same man Sophie had embarrassed. "I've heard of you. Did you used to frequent Wichita, booming for this day?"

Frisco turned from Tom's confusion to answer. "That was me, but I have no dog in this fight. I'm just here as a spectator."

"We could use a man of your talents. C'mon up." The man put a hand on Frisco's shoulder and nearly shouted in his ear. "Folks, this is Frisco Smith, a solicitor from Kansas who petitioned for the opening of these lands to homesteaders. If he wants to join the candidates, he's welcome—"

"And uninterested." Frisco removed the man's hand. "As I said, I'm a spectator, and I don't know any of you, so I couldn't speak to your qualifications or lack thereof. I only asked who'd chosen the candidates. It seems that every landowner should be included in the process."

Murmurs were starting in the crowd, and Frisco had worked a crowd enough to know that the tide was turning. Why did he care? It wasn't his town or any of his business, but he recognized a fix when he saw it. Had these men had their way, the vote would've been over and done with before the others had time to wonder why they'd voted the way they had.

"Old Bill Matthews here is an honest man." A rancher was thrust forward. He stood looking humbly at his feet as his friend kept talking. "If any of you are from up Sedalia way, you've heard of his family. He'd make a fine representative."

"I can vouch for him," another voice said over the din.

And just like that, the natural inclination of Americans to govern themselves had been reasserted. Frisco had accomplished that much at least, but it didn't ease his frustration. Tom Cotton hadn't purchased a Redhawk lot from him, but it wouldn't be long before he ran into someone who had. He had to have an answer.

Back at his lot, he sat on the ground, leaning against his traveling bag and eating his sandwich from Sophie. The elections were completed. Men were going back to their plots to prepare for evening, but all he could think about was what was happening on his land. What if Caroline lost it? What if some bully came around and ran her off before morning? His stomach turned. She didn't know what she was doing. She wasn't prepared for what lay ahead.

But neither were most of the settlers in Plainview. You

couldn't survive eating the grass beneath you. They had to have money to spend, and everything would cost a premium until regular commerce was established. Two men had immediately begun digging a well on their property and now were charging five cents per cup of water. People were paying too. It was either that or walk to the river, and that was likely to cost, if the man who owned that plot ever thought of charging passage. Even firewood came at a price, but Frisco wasn't ready to hand over more valuable coins for it. Not yet, because a plan was forming.

He couldn't fathom what Miss Adams proposed to do with one hundred and sixty acres of prairie. He couldn't fathom how she'd even claimed it before he got there, but if she insisted on taking part in this venture, here was something he had to offer—a nice town lot in the booming metropolis of Plainview. He would wait a few days, make sure all the drifters had cleared out, and then offer her a trade. Wouldn't she rather be in town? It made more sense. Her stubbornness would be the only reason for her to reject the offer.

"Mr. Smith?"

Frisco shaded his eyes against the strength of the sun as he tried to see who was talking to him.

"I'm Ike McFarland, a deputy here. I wanted to thank you for your insight back there at the election."

It was the deputy who looked like a clerk. Frisco stood and, after a moment's hesitation, offered his hand. "Pleased to make your acquaintance, Deputy McFarland. I hope I didn't stir up a cyclone."

"Not at all. Some of the boys just got a little ahead of themselves, but they're satisfied with the outcome. The council includes a few people we hadn't counted on, but it's a good mix."

"We? Who is we?" Frisco asked.

"I heard you had designs for your own town. What are you doing here?"

"When I got to my plot, someone was already there."

"Really?" Ike looked over his shoulder. "As a deputy, it's my duty to turn in evidence against those who were here without authorization. Where's your land? We could help you get it back, and you could go on with your plans."

"I have a list full of names," Frisco said. "Since this morning I've been making a record of those who waited at the line and those who left before dawn. During the run itself, I noted lots that were peopled before it was physically possible for someone to be there." He fixed the deputy in his gaze. If there was anything he was suspicious about, it was this town, but the deputy didn't falter.

"Good man. That's exactly the kind of record we need to compile to sort this mess out. Do you have that list with you?"

Frisco rested his hand on his traveling case. He had to turn it in to someone, but he'd rather it go to an official of the land office than this green deputy. "Give me some time to make some notes," he said. "I'll get it submitted."

"Good enough." With a tip of his derby, McFarland walked away from Frisco's tent.

Frisco filled his lungs, already tasting the cook fires that had been started around him. He didn't need a fire tonight. First thing tomorrow he was going to pay a visit to Miss Adams. But first he needed to make a copy of the list he was going to hand in.

He reached inside his traveling case and pulled out a blank sheet of paper. Fishing out his crumpled list, he carefully replicated it, marking the location and time of the names—both those who were waiting at the line and those who had disappeared before the gun. He worked chronologically down the paper until he reached the minute the guns sounded and he started meeting sooners who'd crossed early.

The cheaters didn't deserve a homestead. There was no way they could have beaten the honest people at the line. If justice truly was blind, it should be meted out without preference or malice. Frisco wasn't swearing that he had firm evidence against each of them, merely the suspicion that they'd circumvented the rules. Suspected sooners—that was who was on this list. They would have their day in court. They should have to answer for their actions, even if they had a well-connected father.

But what if he was wrong? What if Caroline had miraculously bested him? She knew the way through the pass, and he'd gotten a late start. Well, she'd have no problem arguing her case if she was honest. If she wasn't telling the truth, then it would give him another chance at winning back what had been taken from him.

Frisco only hesitated a second before writing *Miss Caroline Adams* at the bottom of the paper. He blew on the page to set the ink, then went to find an official who would present the list to the land office.

Chapter Ten

The way Caroline had to guard her property made her feel like a one-legged man trying to stamp out prairie fires. She couldn't be everywhere at once, but for the most part the stragglers were coming from the south, so she found herself patrolling that border to turn them around before they got any ideas. Here she was, the possessor of a tract of land that she'd yet to explore, and the mystery excited her.

She'd been up and down the east bank of the river, which looked steep enough to prevent flooding but gentle enough to travel easily. The land was capped with a majestic apex near the center of the property, the natural place in Caroline's opinion to build a house, but would it be the best place for a boardinghouse? Where exactly would the railroad come through? She needed to see if there were maps at the fort before she picked the perfect spot. Would the railroad company buy part of her land for a depot? Perhaps that would give her the funds to start construction.

On the northern riverbed, she found ragged ravines. Caroline was the child who'd never gone to sleep without first looking under the bed and behind the curtains—a tendency made stronger by her ornery sister's pranks—and unexplored areas were bothersome to her peace of mind. Before nightfall, she'd have to hop down in each ravine and see what it held. Only a girl who'd grown up on the prairie would feel such anxiety when her view was obstructed, but Caroline wasn't one to shirk from the question. She'd explore as soon as she was convinced no one else was coming.

Honestly, she hadn't had much trouble convincing the men to keep moving. The fact that there was already a garden in helped settle the debate of whether she'd been the first one there or not. Several had less than kind words for her, assuming that she'd cheated and had been hiding there early, but she knew the charges were false and that she had witnesses to vouch for her. She hoped that Amber was able to settle her disputes as easily.

Caroline rode Hardtack slowly around the two-mile perimeter of her farm. She found a nice well dug near what she was already considering the homestead site. Wedged between the canyon and the river, she'd yet to meet any neighbors. So far, everyone coming from the south had still been looking for land, which meant all the plots around her were spoken for.

How had Frisco fared? Did he find a place to put his town? Had he settled in the vicinity? It would have been convenient to have a town nearby, especially if Frisco was in charge of it. If he wasn't still angry with her, that was. He'd been irate when he'd left, but what was she supposed to do? Of course she would stand her ground. Hadn't he said how he'd admired her strength and resolve? Hadn't he accused her of forgetting who she was?

Surely he'd get over it. It had been a trying day. Once things settled down . . .

Getting off Hardtack, Caroline stood at the cornerstone of her homestead and looked over the green expanse stretching before her. Amber had taken out this way. Had she been able to claim this plot, or did she have to go farther to find available land?

Caroline stood on her tiptoes at the invisible line and shaded her eyes. Someone was coming over the gentle rise. It was Amber, waving both hands over her head. Dragging Hardtack behind her, Caroline ran toward her friend, meeting her and grabbing her hands.

"Did you get it? Is this yours?" Caroline asked.

Amber nodded. Her eyes shone. "Can you believe it? We'll be neighbors."

Living next door to her best friend, being there for her and Bradley as they started a new life together . . . Caroline couldn't think of a better outcome. She'd done it. She'd secured herself a place in this new land.

Another horseman appeared on the horizon. No longer were they running. Instead, the weary animal, slick with foam, plodded across the grassland. One after another they wandered by with the same story. They'd raced far and fast, but there was nowhere left for them. Was she interested in selling her claim? They'd pay cash money. Caroline had even been offered a marriage proposal. He'd treat her good, build the house, and do the planting if she'd be willing to be partners on the land. She'd attracted masculine attention over her years, but nothing quite so mercenary.

Amber waved her hand at the man as he approached, motioning him off her property. With a drop of his shoulders, he turned the horse and rode off, disappearing with the curve of the land.

"It's so sad," Amber said. "Have you had many on your place?"

"A few." Caroline's jaw tightened. The first had been the hardest to drive off. After that, it had gotten easier. But she couldn't be gone for long.

She looked over her shoulder. Their celebration could wait, because another contestant had arrived. A Conestoga wagon rolled over the crest on Amber's side of the field.

"Excuse me," Amber called out. "This property is already spoken for."

The driver straightened on the bench, even as his wife seemed to shrink next to him. "We are claiming it, fair and square." He looked at the cornerstone on the ground. "We were here on this side first." He wasn't being belligerent, just stating what he thought were the facts.

A girl of about eight years poked her head out of the hole in the canvas, then seeing Amber and Caroline, she darted back into the wagon. The woman pushed aside her hair with a hand already stained with dirt.

Amber's hand reached up to fiddle with the top button of her blouse. Caroline knew that sign. Uncertainty. She stepped to Amber's side. She understood the sorrow, but Amber and Bradley needed the land, and there was no way for both them and this family to claim it.

Without her prompting, Amber reached the same conclusion. "I'm sorry," she said, "but I've had my stake in for hours. This is my neighbor, and she can verify my claim."

The man didn't move, only studied her as if he was waiting for her to slip up and expose herself in a lie. When that didn't happen, he shook his reins. "C'mon, Nellie. We're not home yet. We have to find somewhere else."

Caroline's throat tightened as she watched the woman wipe her eyes.

"I'm sorry," Amber said. "My fiancé and I are going to live here and farm. Otherwise I'd let you have it. . . ."

The man didn't say a word. Only slapped the reins on the back of his draft team and bounced over the rough ground, hopefully to somewhere unclaimed.

Caroline linked arms with Amber. Was every victory marred by sorrow for the vanquished? She thought again of Frisco riding away from the land he'd wanted to claim. How did one find the resolve to continue? Caroline stiffened, pulling Amber upright with her. Caroline was the daughter of a major in the cavalry. Her father had faced darker questions and hadn't wavered in his resolve. Endure through today, and then another test would begin.

A rider was coming quickly toward them. With this many people still wandering and looking for land, staying away from her plot was foolhardy. Caroline shouldn't linger. She had to get back to her property or risk finding it under another man's boots, but she hated to leave Amber to face another challenger alone.

Thankfully, it was Bradley.

"Bradley, we got it! We got it. We got the land!" Amber cheered.

Caroline stepped aside as Bradley slung himself out of the saddle and snatched Amber up in an embrace.

"You, Caroline? You got a plot too?" he asked.

"Yes, I should go back—"

"Wait," Bradley said. "There's a nice German family on your west. Name of Schneider. They're willing to let both of you bunk down with them once it gets dark. Do that. If I hear of either of you sleeping out here unprotected . . ."

"Schneider?" Amber nodded. "I'll find them as soon as you're gone."

"Thanks, Bradley," Caroline said. "That's a comfort."

He managed to tear his eyes away from Amber to grin at Caroline. "We're in this together. To the homesteaders!" He gave a coyote-like yelp before turning again to Amber, leaving Caroline to go back to her property.

She rode a quick jaunt around the high ground again and then, finding no challengers, decided to explore the lower banks of the river. It would be better if it were done before dark. Not that she expected to sleep much by some strangers' family fire, but she'd sleep better knowing that no one was hiding down there.

Coming along the rough side of the property, Caroline dismounted and walked Hardtack down the slope. The red earth crumbled away from the bank, which was dotted with bright emerald spots of spring grass. The ravine didn't go far, but it was deep enough that she couldn't see the high ground from its floor. In fact, only a narrow view of the river was visible through its opening. It might be a good place to hide supplies, unless the river rose.

Perhaps tomorrow she or Amber could ride over to Darlington to retrieve the supplies they'd purchased. Before then, she could set up a fire pit and gather some wood. Deadwood was plentiful along the riverbank, so she didn't have to wait until she had an axe to get started.

Hardtack's tail swished. She needed to find something to do with him too. A horse standing in the open after nightfall was an easy target. Down below the riverbank looked like the most promising place to hide him. If she could tie him into one of the washouts that wasn't visible from the high ground . . .

Caroline rounded the bank and stopped in her tracks. Was that a door? She blinked, then shaded her eyes, but the scene didn't change. It was a door, but where did it lead? Into the ground?

She rested a hand on the sandstone ledge and looked behind her. She was still within her boundaries. This was her land, but she hadn't expected to find a door built into the side of the hill. Now that she looked at it, she could tell the roof was made of tin sheets and covered with sod. Sod bricks finished out the wall on either side of the door, which was held closed with a latch on the outside. No lock that she could see.

Down in the shade, the damp earth gave her a chill as she knocked. A corner of the door had been chewed away by something. A pack rat? She wasn't surprised when no one answered. Somehow, she could sense that she was all alone. Someone had built this dugout and hadn't returned. Someone . . . like Frisco.

Caroline's mind reeled. He'd spent days out here before the race, planting crops and digging a well. That was what he'd told her. He hadn't mentioned a house. She lifted the latch and pushed the door open. Standing to the side to let in the sunlight, she surveyed the little room.

The raw stone walls looked to be sandstone and unlikely to crumble. In fact, they were unlikely to give even if hit with a pickax. An army-issued blanket covered the cot against one wall, and a simple wooden stool sat against the other. A shelf over the bed held a lantern, a hand mirror, and a stack of books. A pipe stretched up from a small stove through the roof for a chimney.

Tying Hardtack to the door, Caroline entered and lit the lamp. The books were law books. Frisco's, definitely. Besides that, the rest of the floor space was covered in crates and barrels. She picked up a turnip, and her stomach growled. Bags of flour and sugar told her that there'd be something for her to cook. He'd planned well.

And she'd taken it.

Choking doubts assailed her. The items in here represented a substantial investment. While Frisco might find another plot of land, he wouldn't find another piece that had a house, a garden, and a well on it. Even if she owned the land, all of this was his property. And yet something told her that he'd gladly let her cart off all his supplies if she'd give the one hundred and sixty acres back.

But where would that leave her? If she gave the land to Frisco, she'd have to drag herself back to the fort and into her bedroom next to Daisy's. And where would she go from there? Back to her grandmother's? There was nowhere that belonged to her, nowhere that she belonged.

Frisco had all the advantages. He was a man with a career, a reputation, and enough nerve to try anything. He'd known the risks of investing before the land belonged to him. He'd had an unfair advantage, and if he wasn't able to capitalize on it, he shouldn't complain. She'd beat him here fair and square. Besides, if she handed it over to him, what would he think? It would only confirm his opinion that she was another weak and simpering lady.

She would keep the land, and he'd hate her for it. Caroline rubbed her forehead. She hadn't wanted Frisco for an enemy. Was it worth it? What she had to do was focus on the future and how she imagined this territory would look in five years. By then she'd have accomplishment, respect, and property free and clear. It would be her world because she would have built it. Until then, if she had to live in a house built by his hands, she couldn't be blamed. He'd left it on her property.

Were those raisins on the floor? Caroline bent and squinted in the poor light. While the blankets on the cot were mussed, everything else was in place. Had a rat gotten inside? There was a scratching noise from beneath the cot. Caroline lifted her skirt and hurried out the door. From the sound of it, that was one big rat.

She gripped the plank of wood that formed the doorframe and peeked around the edge. A black nose and two eyes watched her from beneath the cot. She reached into the room and picked up a poker leaning against the potbellied stove. Her father would laugh at her for arming herself against a rodent, but this was no ordinary-sized vermin.

There was an odd high-pitched cry from the animal. With one eye closed, she aimed the poker, ready for her chance. But suddenly a black-and-white mammal bounded out from under the cot.

Caroline lowered the poker. It wasn't a rat, or a dog. It was a tiny black-and-white goat, bleating at her with its pink tongue flapping.

"Oh, you're precious." She propped the poker in the corner and knelt to get a better look. The little thing walked right up to her and bleated, like it was reciting all the hardships it had endured being there alone. Had Frisco left it locked up? But then she looked again at the door. The gap was big enough for the goat to wiggle through. And on second thought, those weren't raisins on the floor.

"Caroline!"

Hardtack neighed at the familiar voice. Caroline steeled her spine as she scooped up the bleating kid. She'd only forgotten about Frisco for a moment and was already faced with another unpleasant but inevitable confrontation.

Chapter Eleven

Do you know the trouble you've caused? I have men who should be officiating the run, but instead they're out searching for you. I cannot allow such a misuse of my resources on today of all days." Her father kept an eye on the ravine she'd just climbed out of, as if concerned they might be rushed by hiding outlaws, which wasn't that unreasonable an assumption. "I expect the troopers to do their best work today, but my own daughter is behaving irresponsibly. Is that a goat?"

Caroline took a deep breath. She'd answer the easiest question first. "Yes. I think it is."

The kid hung out its tongue and bleated at the major. At least one of them could fight back.

"What are you doing out here?" he asked. "Who did you run away with?"

"No one. This is my land. I won it."

A token of surprise flashed across his face as he looked the place over. "I'd imagine not many know how to cross the canyon."

"Exactly. And I can ride as fast as any of them."

He was reasoning it out. If Caroline had to guess, she knew

her logical father was debating between frustration at the inconvenience she'd caused and pride at what she'd accomplished. Anything she could do to tip the balance . . . "This is good land, Father. The best. It has water and timber available. The soil looks rich, and it's not too far from the fort."

"Anywhere outside of my threshold means danger for my daughters," he said.

"But I can't live with you and Louisa forever. Why shouldn't I take the same chance everyone else is taking to better my lot in life? I'm over twenty-one—"

"Barely."

"But by law, anyone twenty-one years of age is eligible. It doesn't say anything about having to have their father's permission."

It was no mystery where she'd gotten her stubbornness. He rested his hand on the hilt of his saber. "So you won the race, but that's not all there is to it. What are you going to do with this land? Farm it?"

"I'm going to build a boardinghouse, right in the vicinity of the railroad. It'll be the finest place to stay in the territory. It'll have gardens surrounding it. I'll grow lavender or something else precious that ladies will like. That'll be easier to manage than corn and wheat. And I won't be alone. Amber and Bradley will be right next door."

"I should've known Bradley Willis had something to do with this. Did he leave his post?"

"No. Amber and I raced on our own, but when his commission is up in a few weeks, we'll have him around for protection."

From the droll tilt of his head, her father didn't think much of Bradley Willis as a protector. "Until you have your inn built, where are you going to stay? Sleep here on the grass? This territory was dangerous enough before. Now every down-on-his-luck drifter has permission to be here. You aren't going to be outside after dark, and don't pretend like a tent will protect you."

Caroline's eyes darted down the bank. She wished Frisco hadn't invested so much into land that now belonged to her, but he had. There was no way to give him back the house and keep the land. And as long as it was there, she might as well make use of it.

"Follow me," she said. Setting the goat on the ground, she traipsed down the bank with her father on her heels. He paused when they got down into the shadowy ravine. "C'mon," she said. "This isn't a battlefield you need to analyze before you enter."

"With you, everything is a battlefield," he said but continued to the door of the dugout. "What is this? Who built it?"

She lifted one shoulder. "Look, there's a latch. I can pull the latchstring in at night, and then I'd be behind a locked door. Besides, no one will ever find this house."

Her father pounded on the door, testing it for strength before opening it. Funny how small the room felt with him in it.

His forehead furrowed when he saw the supplies. "No, young lady. Someone is coming back for this stuff. Someone is going to be furious that you're here. You've made an enemy."

"If they broke the law by being here early, then what recourse do they have?"

"I'm not worried about them taking you to court, Caroline. I'm worried about you being attacked, or disappearing, or any number of things an outlaw might do to a lady when she's crossed him."

He was right. Had it been a random house that she'd found, she wouldn't have dared stay. She'd be fearful of the owner returning. As it was, she might not want to face Frisco again, but she wasn't afraid of him. Not in that way.

"I know whose belongings these are," she said. "He protested, but then he moved on and has found another property, I'm sure."

"You know this outlaw?"

Caroline couldn't meet her father's gaze. She studied the dirt floor, patted firm by the tall moccasins of the man who'd so impressed her years ago.

But the man who loved her—her father—was no fool. Going to the shelf, he took the top law book off the stack. Opening the cover, he ran his finger down the page, then snapped the book closed.

"Frisco Smith, who else? Between him and Bradley Willis . . . Why did God see fit to give me impressionable daughters among so many renegades?"

"I am not impressionable." Caroline took the book from him and returned it to the shelf. "Frisco wanted me to leave. He cajoled, he threatened, and he tried to intimidate me, but I stood firm. I didn't let him take anything." Maybe because she didn't know this all was here, but it was still true.

"He threatened you?"

"Not like that. He tried to convince me that the land office would award him the land because he'd done improvements on it, but I wasn't fooled. Improvements done before the race don't count."

"That's right. It was his own foolish wager, putting this stuff here when we were trying to keep him out of the area. He deserves to be taught a lesson. And he's got quite a stash. Enough to support a person for a couple of months." The major turned a full circle.

Caroline held her breath. It seemed that the tide was turning. Her father couldn't help but like the fact that Caroline had gotten the better of Frisco after years of playing cat and mouse with him.

"I don't approve of you being here by yourself."

"I'm not the only single woman homesteading," she said. "And with Bradley and Amber next door . . . "

"You do have a secure place to live for now. And I could post a sentry here. I have to post them somewhere. This would be as good a place as any."

Still under her father's watchful eyes? If Caroline thought she was running away from home, she hadn't run far enough. But she smiled. "At least until those who missed out have stopped roaming and looking for a place. Once they're gone, it should quiet down."

"Don't count on it." Major Adams reached up to pull an earthworm out of the dirt wall. He watched it squirm between his fingers. "If I know Frisco Smith, he's not going to give you any peace until you return his things."

"I'm not afraid of him."

"But you should be afraid of starting on a course if you aren't determined to see it completed. Are you sure you have the tenacity to succeed here?"

"Yes, sir." Caroline almost saluted. If she could convince her father of her success, then surely she could convince herself.

⌒⌒⌒

Frisco pushed the moth-eaten Indian blanket off his face and squinted into the light filtering through his cheap tent. How could the night have been so short? For hours after sunset, people had wandered about, shouting greetings when reunited with friends, hunting down missing livestock that had gotten loose from hastily constructed pens, sitting around campfires, and comparing the breathtaking stories of their runs. They weren't ready for the eventful day to end, while Frisco wished it had never happened.

How he wished he was back at the boardinghouse in Silver City awaiting the race. How he wished he could do it again and not get tied up chasing down moonlighters. Not leave his horse at the mercy of that horrid woman. Not get beat to the piece of land that was going to be his forever home. Instead he was on the ground with a moldy blanket while someone else slept in the house he'd built with his own hands.

That someone else was a girl who'd been nothing but trouble her whole life. He should've known better. He'd let down his guard, and she'd taken advantage of him. While her father had always treated him courteously when he was arrested, he had a motive—to plumb Frisco's knowledge of the territory and what was going on in the recesses of the Unassigned Lands. Miss Adams had treated him the same way. Smiled politely, listened intently, and then taken the information gleaned and used it for her own purposes without any consideration for how it affected him.

The apple didn't fall far from the tree.

And now it was morning, although the hammers had been ringing for hours. Roosters remembered their dawn duty even in their new environs, while someone belted a maudlin song that begged a young lady named Barbara Allen for mercy. What was he doing lying around? Just losing ground.

Frisco tossed off the blanket and reached for his boots.

"Yah, boys! Forward! Forward!"

Frisco got through his tent flap in time to see massive flatbed wagons laden with lumber rolling past. Dressed in a leather vest with Indian beading and boots laced up to his knees, the driver snapped a black bullwhip over the backs of his eight-oxen team. They surged forward, their massive muscles bulging against their yokes. Frisco had never seen the like, until he looked down the street behind them. Four more identical wagons and teams stomped forward. No sooner had they gotten past than the wheels stopped turning. Two middle-aged Chickasaw men with white sleeves rolled up for business hopped off the back of the wagon bed and began selling.

People came from every direction. Everyone, like Frisco, had the same dirt-worn clothes they'd worn yesterday, but they had cash, they had land, and they needed the freshly sawn boards that some genius had hauled to town. Men called out amounts, getting larger and larger. Losers stepped back while the moneyed bidders closed in on the wagons. Soon all five wagons were spoken for. The drivers woke their whips and, with a bellow, the oxen followed the winning bidders to their lots.

All that happened before Frisco had tasted his first cup of coffee.

"There are more coming behind us," the Chickasaw man called. "Our sawmills are running nonstop. Get your foundations dug."

"Breakfast for sale." A barefoot boy with patches at his knees jogged by. "Eggs, potatoes, corn bread, coffee. One plate, thirty-five cents."

"Surgeon and dentist!" a man shouted, declaring his skills. "Anyone ailing or hurt, come see Doctor Carr at the corner of Main and Fourth Street. I've got the cure for what ails you."

"Livery services," a woman with a baby on her hip advertised. "Feed and water for your horses for only five cents a day. Professional farrier looking for work."

It was a lot to absorb. Whatever Frisco had imagined, this hadn't been it, but these people were wasting no time. The town was getting built. From an empty prairie, they were going to have a city in a matter of hours. They'd gone to bed worried about procuring sleeping mats, fires, and vittles, and they'd woken to the morning ready for commerce and construction. The pace dizzied him.

His horse's tail swatted at a cloud of gnats rising from the dew-drenched grass. He'd check into that livery. After what had happened before the race, he didn't like leaving his horse tied to his tent with no corral or protection.

But first, breakfast. Frisco dropped his wide-brimmed hat

on his head and took out after the boy who'd offered the best deal on morning sustenance.

Chasing down breakfast gave him an appreciation for how the town was being laid out. It also frustrated him to know that his own Redhawk property was idle. He should be getting word out to his subscribers to come meet him. He should be directing them to their lots. If some were successful in the race and had found farms then they wouldn't get their money back, but otherwise he would have to refund anyone who was relying on him—and from the crowd of people still milling around looking for unattended property, he imagined there were many whose only chance for a plot was on his shoulders.

The only thing he knew for sure was that all his subscribers wouldn't fit on his town plot here in Plainview.

The eggs and corn bread were dished out on a tin plate. He stood by the back of the wagon and ate with an odd assortment of others in various costumes and stages of dress. Frisco supposed that if you slept outside, bathed in the river, and relieved yourself behind a tree—of which there were but a few—then maybe appearing before your neighbor without your shirt buttoned to the collar wasn't a serious offense.

"Excuse me." The man addressing him had soulful eyes and a posture that looked used to waiting. "I don't mean to interrupt your breakfast, but did someone say you're an attorney?"

Frisco scraped a last bite from his dish, then shook it upside down to dump the crumbs before giving it back to the woman in the wagon. "Yes, sir, I'm an attorney, but I haven't set up a practice yet."

"You haven't?" The man's forehead wrinkled. "What are you waiting for?"

Good question. He wanted to be a town father, but this town had more fathers than a litter of twenty kittens. What if he couldn't get his land from Miss Adams? He'd staked a claim here as a contingency but hadn't thought beyond that. And if he had to refund the money of everyone who'd purchased a lot in Redhawk, he was going to be light in the pocketbook.

After taking another look at the man, Frisco nodded. "How can I help you?"

"I thought I had a claim," he said. "My wife and I came in a light buggy and made good time, but when we got here, it seemed like every good plot was already spoken for. We took one out of the way and began setting up, but then some fellow showed up and said that he had both sides of the street. Mind you, there was nothing on it showing that this plot was connected with the one opposite of it, and I didn't think that was legal, claiming two town lots."

"It's not." Frisco could say with certainty because he himself had monitored the wording of the bill as it had been debated in Congress. He'd considered every nuance when the law was passed. Most definitely, two claims by the same homesteader wasn't allowed. "Have you left the property?" he asked.

"No, sir. I hate to leave my wife there alone, but one of us is staying put until we have a claim filed."

"The nearest claims office is in Kingfisher."

"And I hear you'll wait in line for days before they call your number. But now it's gotten more complicated." The man took a clean handkerchief out of his overall pocket and folded it over and over. "A second man came and is squatting on our plot. The neighbor and he say that it's his plot. That the neighbor was holding it for him."

Frisco's mouth twisted. Legal work would be the easiest labor out here if every case was this clear. "He's living there with you? That's ludicrous. The land is yours. I'll be happy to present your challenge to the land office."

"I don't have a lot of cash money to pay you, but maybe I could pay you in kind."

"What do you do?"

He produced a hammer out of his waistband. "Carpenter."

Finally some good news. "If you don't have cash money now, you will by nightfall. All that lumber being hauled in needs someone to work it."

"That's what me and the missus are counting on, but I don't want to lose my land while I'm working."

"Come back to my place, and let me take some notes," Frisco said. "We'll get your story on paper, and then I'll have a talk with your neighbor. How's that sound, Mr. . . . ."

"Mr. Nesbitt. And it sounds dandy."

Soon Frisco and Mr. Nesbitt were sitting outside Frisco's tent on barrels borrowed from a neighbor, scratching down the basics of his story along with the location of his land. It seemed a simple case of bullying and nepotism. Something Frisco could address, set aright, and move on. And with each friendship he made, he'd feel more secure in leaving his scant belongings behind while he traveled out to visit Miss Adams and reclaim his land.

Speaking of Miss Adams . . .

Frisco bolted off his barrel when he saw the fiery red hair. "Miss Adams! Get over here. I want to talk to you," he bellowed.

He hadn't meant to sound so commanding, but it did the trick. Miss Adams turned her horse from the public thoroughfare and rode onto his plot. She was a sight to see on horseback, but Frisco was determined not to be swayed by how her simple riding habit and split skirt accentuated her lithe curves. Or how her robin's-egg blue hat accentuated her complexion. Or how her ease and beauty accentuated his frustration at being her victim.

She dismounted and led her horse to his tent. "Mr. Smith, am I ever relieved to find you settled here. What a splendid location you've found. Right in the middle of a booming town, just like you wanted." She was breathless, hopeful, and oh, so wrong.

"This is not my town," Frisco said.

"It might not be where you planned your town, but it certainly is your town."

"It is not my town. These are not my investors. These roads are not the roads I planned. This is not Redhawk."

She drew back at his outburst, but her face smoothed into an unreadable mask. Then she noticed Mr. Nesbitt. "You have a guest. I apologize for interrupting. Good day."

"This isn't a guest. It's Mr. Nesbitt. He was just leaving."

"I was just leaving," Mr. Nesbitt said as he stood. "About this matter—?"

"I'll be by directly to speak to the man on your land. If he fails to yield, I'll apply to the Register and Receiver at the land office. You should have resolution soon after." He didn't mean to rush Mr. Nesbitt off, but if he was dealing with claim jumpers, Miss Adams was a priority.

Mr. Nesbitt tipped his hat to Miss Adams as he passed. He was a real gentleman, because his eyes didn't linger. Frisco wasn't always so gentlemanly with a beautiful woman, unless the woman had usurped his success.

"What did he want?" Miss Adams tilted her head as she inspected his tent.

Frisco stepped back and pulled the flap closed to protect the interior from her prying. "He's a client. I'm an attorney, remember?"

"I'd almost forgotten. I have something for you." She walked back to her horse, then returned with a bag. "I guess these belong to you."

The morning sun emphasized the smoothness of her skin, but he couldn't forget the conniving of her heart. He opened the bag to find his law books. "There's a lot that belongs to me that you should return. Why did you decide to give this back and not the other stuff?"

She twisted her fingers together. "You can have the rest of it back too. As soon as I can get a wagon, I'll cart it to you."

"Don't you dare. Those supplies are exactly where they are supposed to be—in my house. There's no reason to move anything, because you and me are going to trade."

Her head lifted. Her direct gaze caught him. "What do you have to trade?"

"This plot, right here in the city. Just think of it, Miss Adams. You could resume the spectacular life you left behind in Galveston instead of resigning yourself to the drudgery of a farm."

"You think I want to mimic the life I lived in Galveston?" She blinked wearily, then turned her face away to look over their surroundings. "Let's see, we have an assortment of tents, wagons, crates. I'm sure it'll rival the beautiful architecture on the Strand soon. And then there's the Gulf. Where exactly will the shore be when they are finished?"

"It's better than being on a homestead all by yourself. What are you going to do with that farm, anyway?"

"I'm going to build a luxurious sanctuary where people can rest after traveling across the territory. My inn will have extensive gardens surrounding a spacious porch. Who knows? I might dabble in making scented soaps or perfumes for income while I wait for the railroad to come through with the travelers."

"There aren't going to be any travelers coming through for years, and you won't be satisfied living out there alone."

"How do you know what will satisfy me, Mr. Smith?"

He was losing control of this conversation. "I'm a very good judge of character," he said, "especially people I've known as long as I've known you."

"You know my family, but you don't really know me, and in this instance, you're mistaken. I loathed my time in Galveston. I was nothing but an ornament dragged out for inspection at every social function. If I wished to resume that life, which I don't, I would do it somewhere more interesting than . . . what's the name of this town?"

He shrugged. "Does it matter?"

"I suppose not. I'm rejecting your offer. Life in this sorry excuse for a town does not interest me. At least on the homestead I have shelter. There's nothing here. Where would I keep my things?"

"Back at the fort where you belong?" He tossed the bag of books into his tent.

"I'm done with the fort too. It's time I struck out and made my own way."

"And how better to begin than by stealing a man's house, property, and goods?"

"Then file a grievance," she said. "If what I did was wrong, the land office will evict me."

He really hoped it wouldn't come to that. "Don't you feel some remorse?" he asked.

Beneath the flawless sheen of her skin, her face went rigid. "I might pity the man who didn't succeed yesterday, but that doesn't mean I would give him my prize."

Frisco bristled. He didn't like being a commonplace loser in her books. Winning his land was going to be more difficult than he'd thought.

Chapter Twelve

What had she expected? That he'd graciously thank her for taking all his possessions from him? It was unlucky that things had turned out the way they did, but she knew no remedy. This was the first time in two years that she'd felt hope for her future. The first time she'd seen a challenge that would mature her into the woman she could be. He couldn't ask her to give up on something that important.

"Why are you here?" Frisco asked. "Did you come just to bring my law books back?"

"Since you asked so kindly," she said, "I'm on my way to the land office in Kingfisher to file."

"It's a waste of time," Frisco said. "You'll get a number and then wait for days before it's your turn."

"Are you trying to keep me from finalizing the process?"

"The process won't be finalized for five years—five very long years."

She straightened the cuff on her riding habit. "If the land office isn't expedient, I could do some shopping today to supplement the supplies we bought in Darlington. Would you happen to know where the mercantile is?"

"What do you need to shop for?" he asked. "Don't you have everything of mine?"

"I need a better lamp. Yours smokes something frightful. And the dishes? I nearly cut my lip on that chipped mug."

It was the first time she'd seen him smile since the run. He smiled until his eyes wandered to her lips, and then he growled.

"Toughen up, buttercup." He crossed his arms over his chest. "If you can't take a scratch from a mug . . . Besides, I don't want you filling my house with superfluous junk. You're going to have to cart it all out when I get an official decision from the land office."

He'd have better luck appealing to her sympathy, because if he thought he could intimidate her, she was disappointed in his intellect. Compared with the task of proving her claim, Caroline didn't lack confidence in her ability to win an argument.

"And who would be making that decision? Oh yes, it's Mr. Robberts and Mr. Admires. I've been meaning to invite them over for dinner."

"You mean you'll ask your pa to invite them to dinner? Of course. When you don't get what you want, all you have to do is—"

"I did this on my own." Caroline jabbed him in the chest. "My father didn't even know."

"You jumped in on your own, but you can't swim. If someone doesn't come to your rescue soon, you're going under." The last words were said in a tantalizing whisper. His eyebrows bounced once for emphasis.

Caroline stepped backward. There were two things she really enjoyed. She liked getting her way, and she liked to claim that she was independent and didn't need her family. What if she had to choose? Was it possible that Frisco was right? Could she succeed without falling back on her father's influence?

The conversation in her head was even worse than the one before her.

"Which way to the mercantile?" she asked. She didn't mean to sound cross, but she was tired of the guilt.

Frisco watched her with dark eyes. It was the longest she'd ever seen him stand still. Finally, he dipped his head toward the road. "There aren't any established stores yet, but if you see something you like, make an offer. For the right amount, everything is for sale."

She looked at the piles of home goods next to wagons and jumbles of belongings next to cook fires. It didn't seem right, walking up to a man and offering to buy his lantern off him.

"If that's what I have to do." Caroline tugged on her glove, tightening it against her fingers. "Thank you for your help, such as it was."

"You aren't going without me," Frisco said. "You have my land, and I'm not going to let you wander among the greatest collection of swindlers and confidence men ever assembled until it's safely in my name."

"I'm not going to lose your land."

"Yes, you are. Sooner or later, and it better be to me." His mouth twitched. Annoying how easily he amused himself. "Tie up your horse with mine while I get my traveling case."

She didn't comment on the short reins on Frisco's horse. She figured there'd be stories aplenty from what they'd been through, and she'd be blamed for all of his. But he caught her puzzled gaze when he returned.

"When the race started, I was occupied with collecting the names of moonlighters. Some didn't appreciate my attempt at enforcing fair play. They decided to teach me a lesson."

126

"What lesson did you learn?" she asked.

"Not to trust a woman when there's a prize at stake."

He could stand there and glare all day, but she had errands to run. She tethered Hardtack and started forward, but Frisco pulled her back.

"We can't cut across everyone's property," he said. "We have to walk on the street. Civilization has arrived."

Caroline looked at the green field dotted with lumber, tents, and animals. "How can you tell where the streets are? It all looks the same to me."

"The streets are marked by those little stakes. See them? They all look alike."

"Who put them there? The first person to arrive?"

"I don't know who the first person was here," he said. "It does seem like a lot of work to get done before everyone else came thrashing through the town."

"Maybe they started early," Caroline said. "Maybe they were boomers, and they came in weeks ago and prepared the town site."

But her jab seemed only to pique his curiosity. "That's probably what happened," he said. "As long as they were back on the line by noon and ran with everyone else . . . but this close to my homestead? It seems I would've seen them here in the days before the run."

"Where does the road go from here?" Caroline asked, because the way was blocked by a group of men settled around a campfire.

"What are y'all doing?" Frisco asked them. "This here is a right-of-way. You can't set up camp in the road."

"Sure, governor." The man slurred his words as his head bobbled. "Just waiting around in case somebody decides to pull up stakes and go back where they came from."

Caroline watched as Frisco weighed his response. He seemed,

like her, to want to run them off, but for some reason he escorted her around them.

"Why didn't you tell them to leave?" she asked. "They're going to cause trouble for someone."

"It's not my town, and I have my doubts as to the legality of its founding," he said. "Now, if those men had squatted on my place by the river . . ."

"Right is right and rules are rules," Caroline responded. "You don't need a title to remind people of the law."

"Miss Righteousness herself. I hope you sleep easy at night, in a house you didn't build, on a bed you didn't buy."

The sun was gathering its strength. The wind blew constantly, and the people moved restlessly, as if driven by its gusts. They passed one lot crowded with men in lines, with a few women and children sprinkled in. Caroline craned her neck to see what the draw was. All she could see were three hastily constructed shacks and a sign that said 5 *cents per visit.*

"What are they doing?" she asked. "This is the most popular spot in town."

Frisco pulled her along. "Don't linger. It's the privy."

Then the smell hit her. Caroline wrinkled her nose. "People are paying to use the privy? That's nonsense."

"No, that's enterprise. The owner of that lot saw a need, and he filled it. Dig three holes, put up some walls, and he has a business."

"But who would want to build a house on a lot full of cesspools?"

"By the time everyone has their own privy built, he'll have enough money to build himself a nice house. Just shovel dirt over the holes—"

"And don't ever drink from his well."

Frisco grunted. "Good advice. But by then, you'll have left my land, and I won't have to worry about whose water I'm drinking."

His jabs might be justified, but they were tiresome. She'd thought that returning some of his belongings might help him forgive her, but it seemed that her presence only increased her offense.

They were reaching the center of the town. A bricklayer slapped mortar on a brick and splatted it on a wall about knee-high.

Frisco slowed. "What have we got here?"

The bricklayer pulled a kerchief out of his pocket. "First National Bank of Plainview, already taking deposits. Do you have any funds you'd like us to protect for you?"

"What makes you a national bank?" Frisco asked.

"There are people from a lot of different nations here, and I'm holding money from several of them."

"A bricklayer and banker?" Caroline didn't like the tilt of the man's mouth. "That strikes me as questionable."

"The name's Sorenson. I'll work hard for your trust, and I'll work hard for your money," the bricklayer said. "Don't hold it against a man that he's willing to work with his hands. If you're going to make something of yourself here, you'd better be willing to do the same."

"I'll consider my options," Frisco said, "but thanks for the information."

Caroline lifted an eyebrow. "You have money that's weighing you down?"

He swung his traveling case high. "And it's cumbersome to haul around. I won't have it for long if we can't reach an agreement. Still, if Mr. Sorenson has a safe place . . ."

"Yes, sir." Sorenson cleaned his hands on a work apron hanging around his waist. "See that wagon there? It's reinforced with iron bars and locked at all times."

"Mr. Smith!"

Caroline turned to see a man approaching. He was nicely

dressed but rumpled, like everyone else in the territory that morning. His eyebrows had a strong curve to them that made him look like he was expecting you to say something astonishing. It was a pleasant expression. He removed his derby hat to show thick blond hair, freshly cut.

"I beg your pardon, I didn't realize you were accompanied by a lady," he said to Frisco.

Did Frisco notice how impressed this man seemed to be with her? Did he feel a tad foolish for the way he'd treated her since her return to Oklahoma Territory?

"This is Deputy McFarland," Frisco said, "and this is Miss Adams, the daughter of Major Adams at the fort." For once it was Frisco dropping her father's name. Maybe he wasn't immune to jealousy after all.

"Pleased to meet you," Deputy McFarland said. "Does this mean that our fair city can claim you as a resident?"

"Not exactly. I live just outside of town, but I suspect this is my nearest municipality." If she was putting more warmth into her answers than normal, it was for Frisco's benefit.

"You certainly seem to associate with the right sort of people. Mr. Smith has already made a smashing impression here in town."

"Already? He said nothing about it to me."

"We have more pleasant things to talk about," Frisco said. The way he smiled at her, you would have thought they'd just finished a very private conversation.

Caroline blinked up at the man who minutes ago had been haranguing her. This was more like the dashing renegade she remembered. For some reason, he'd decided to be charming in front of Deputy McFarland. What did it mean?

"I'm glad you came along," Frisco said to the deputy. "I was considering using the services of our First National Bank. Do you have any previous dealings with them?"

"Deputy Sorenson? He's of the finest character and has my trust. We've served as deputies together since the beginning of this affair."

"You mean since President Harrison signed the bill? One month ago?" Frisco's eyebrow raised.

"Was it only a month? Seems like an eternity," said Deputy McFarland. "All the same, I had some business I wanted to talk over with you. We're going to have elections for mayor at noon, and we're trying to get the word out. Three candidates have been chosen by the council. I know your objections to the council deciding that, but the council was duly elected by the populace. Things will be easier to manage once we're all settled in, but until then, we need some sort of order established."

"Where does one go to vote?" Frisco asked.

"See those three wagons lined up over there? One candidate will stand in each wagon, and you get in line for the one who has secured your vote. Put your tally mark down, and the man with the most tallies wins. Simple enough for a first election. Once that's settled, we'll hold a celebration to install our new mayor. It'll be a dance later this week." He smiled at Caroline. "We'd be honored if you'd attend. Having the major's daughter here for our first official town celebration would lend it an air of legitimacy."

A dance? Despite her objections to being displayed like an ornament, that sounded better than sketching house and garden plans in her underground room with the goat. While Caroline could wish they desired her company for her own attributes instead of her father's, celebrating the establishment of a local government was a worthy cause. Her father had often stressed the importance of the girls attending official ceremonies to show their support for the troops. This was no different.

"Certainly," she said. "I'd be delighted."

"And you too, Mr. Smith. You should become more involved in our municipal business. Plainview would benefit from your skills. Can we count on seeing you at the dance?"

Frisco's teeth flashed in that hair-trigger smile. "Absolutely. I can't allow Miss Adams to attend unescorted. We'll both be . . . where exactly is the dance?"

"On the lot to the east of the First National Bank. By then we'll have some lanterns hung. It'll look quite festive. Don't forget to vote today!"

Frisco bid the deputy farewell under Caroline's bemused scrutiny.

"They aren't wasting any time getting themselves entrenched," Frisco said as the deputy moved on to another settler. "What are the chances that all these deputies happened to have the fastest horses in the race?"

"The horses' speed wasn't the only consideration," she said.

"Someone had to have seen them before the race. They must have been lined up by the fort. Where are the witnesses?"

"What I just witnessed was you intimating that our relationship is of a closer nature than I've ever acknowledged. Besides, I remember accepting Deputy McFarland's invitation to the dance, not yours," Caroline said.

Frisco scratched his cheek. "I'll meet you at the dugout that evening, if you're still residing there by then."

"Dancing with a man who has sworn to take my property doesn't appeal to me."

"Do you mind walking, or should I borrow a buggy?" His eyes darted down her form. "Unless you've procured a sidesaddle, going on horseback won't be optimal in a ball gown."

"On the other hand, perhaps dancing with my opponent might be the easiest way to convince him to end this harassment."

"You're not that good of a dancer, Miss Adams." His rakish grin gave Caroline a chill that reminded her of her infatuation with him back before she knew better.

"I expect my time will be precious at this dance, with so few women in town."

"It's likely to be lopsided for some time," Frisco said, "but I suspect every day there'll be more and more women showing up to join their menfolk. Not every lady is brazen enough to compete in this men's contest."

"Men's contest? It's a contest, that's all. Some people won and some lost."

"But the contest isn't over, Miss Adams. We'll see who wins in the end."

She only needed a lamp, and then she headed back to await the arrival of her supplies from Darlington. When Frisco thought of how crowded the little dugout would be with her loot, and how empty his tent was, he was tempted to utter unchivalrous statements again, but look where that had gotten him last time. Perhaps if he had not been so free with his opinion before the race, she would've felt more charitable toward him afterward.

His fault for speaking his mind, but she had disappointed him. There were few women like Caroline Adams in the world. Purposely deconstructing the very things that made her unique was an outrage, and he felt honor bound to protest. But perhaps he could've done it in a less offensive manner.

After Miss Adams had retrieved her horse, Frisco decided he might as well send his to the livery. He had no protection for it at his plot, but stabling a horse cost money, even when there wasn't a stable built yet. He couldn't spend freely—not when most of the money he had was being held in trust for his townspeople. He had one month before he had to produce the land or return their money, and until then he needed it kept in a safe place.

After leaving his horse in the green pasture of the livery, Frisco returned to Mr. Sorenson and handed over the pile of bills that represented the future of sixty-four men and their families. He was astute enough to request a deposit slip, which the thorough Mr. Sorenson had already commissioned and had professionally printed. Frisco stared at the address printed on the paper. *East Main Street, Plainview, Oklahoma Territory*. Either the printer had worked quickly or Mr. Sorenson had predicted the exact plot of land he'd win. Frisco slipped the deposit receipt into his traveling case.

Mr. Sorenson had been a deputy with McFarland. He would have known the address if they had conspired together to form a town before the race, just as Frisco had attempted. There was no rule against that, as long as they were at the line when the cannon fired, but as deputies, the temptation to go early would have been great.

Frisco checked himself. He couldn't let his failure sprout jealousy against those who'd been successful. Unless it was Miss Adams. Then he felt no guilt in his coveting.

He went to find some food for himself. Even though his grumbling stomach reminded him that breakfast had been hours ago, everything in this place came by standing in a line. But if Frisco had to judge from the wooden frames going up all around him, things would change in a hurry.

In the meantime, he had to figure out the best way to persuade Miss Caroline Adams. For years Frisco had frequented the fort as a prisoner, but for the most part, Major Adams understood the dance. He and his troopers treated the boomers with respect, and in return the boomers didn't resist arrest. Doing so would have been unethical and would have created negative coverage from the press. Instead, Frisco tried to be as helpful as he could to the troopers by giving them information on the real criminals he'd spotted in the territory or rumors of unrest he'd heard. It made for an interesting relationship with Major Adams, and because Frisco couldn't help but win over a crowd, Miss Adams somehow got caught up in it.

Five years older than she and decades wiser from his life on the street, he couldn't miss the adoration in her young eyes. He also couldn't miss the warning in her father's. So Frisco did what he did best. He charmed while walking a tightrope. He couldn't have pretended that the young lady wasn't beautiful. He abhorred dishonesty. And she'd been at just the age to begin appreciating attention from beaux, although no trooper on the fort could express his admiration while under her father's command. That was why Frisco thought it his duty. Every young lady should know that she was beautiful. He didn't want it to go unremarked. So he told her frequently, or at least he told her father frequently in her hearing. If it made Major Adams uneasy, then so much the better.

But a few years had changed everything. No longer was she an undiscovered beauty. She was out in the world and had learned to wield her charms, which in his eyes was a disaster. While the willful child of the prairies had intrigued him, her time in Galveston had smoothed out all of her interesting merits. They had nothing in common now. She certainly didn't need him to bolster her confidence. The thought was laughable. But what did she need? What could he offer her in exchange for his land?

He took a cold sandwich from Mr. Wilton and handed over an inordinate amount of coin for something so paltry. Surprisingly, it was even better than the sandwich the day before, probably on account of his hunger more than the quality.

Chewing, Frisco headed to the center of town, where the

election was being held. True to McFarland's word, the three candidates sat on stools in the wagons. Frisco had missed the speeches, but when he recognized two as being part of the founders' group, he went to join the line behind the wagon of Bill Matthews, the man from Sedalia he'd helped get placed as a candidate.

What would it take to get Caroline off his property? Once upon a time, he could have tempted her. Now she claimed that she was impervious to his charms, but was she? What would it take to convince Miss Adams that he was a serious suitor?

Living on the streets with easy relationships and scant regrets, Frisco had never seriously considered what courtship of a lady like Caroline would entail. For the most part, he'd avoided the hoity-toity set, preferring to spend his time with practical women, strong women, women who rode in the rain, women who spoke their minds, and women who'd call you down from across the street just to say howdy.

Like Caroline used to.

But if he needed to swallow his ire to sway her, then that was what he'd do. And it wouldn't hurt to listen more closely to her plans. While he couldn't bring a railroad through Plainview, he could try to create her dream on his town lot. It would make his offer of a trade more attractive. And in the meantime, he needed to keep her away from the likes of Deputy McFarland and any other man who might be tempted by the combination of a beautiful woman and a promising homestead.

"Are you in the line for Matthews?" a young man asked.

"Yes, I think this is the end," Frisco replied.

"My name's Ernest Pickens. My brother is in the next line." He waved, and a similarly dressed man at the back of the other line waved back. "We can't agree on anything. Can't imagine how we're going to run a bakery together."

Frisco looked from the man standing next to him to the man

in the other line. They were more than similarly dressed. They had to be twins. "A bakery? Please fire your ovens up immediately. The restaurateurs need the competition," Frisco said.

"Yes, sir! We've got our brick oven about completed. Needs seasoning, but then we're running. Come by, and I'll give you your first dinner roll free."

He took his place behind Frisco. Wait in line to be counted, and then they'd see who won. Sounded simple enough. Frisco looked ahead, and his was easily the longest line. It'd take longer to go through, but that was the cost of democracy.

After some instructions, the line started moving. A scribe in the wagon made a tally mark as each man went by. A handful of men joined Frisco's line, but he was surprised to see the baker's brother with more people behind him than in front.

"Mr. Bledsoe's supporters must live on the outskirts," said Frisco. "They are tardy about getting in line."

The baker looked behind them. "Now they have more folks. If Evan's fella wins, I'll never hear the end of it."

Bledsoe clearly was going to win. While the other lines were almost through, his line kept growing. Frisco watched as the voters were counted at the front. Was that register going slower than the others? Then he noticed something. After they'd voted, a couple of men meandered toward the back of the line. For a second they stood, as if only in the vicinity, but then after a furtive look around, they stepped one behind the other and rejoined the line.

Frisco grabbed the sleeve of the baker and spun him to face the other line. "Did you see that? Those fellas just got in line to vote twice." And they weren't the only ones. About half the men going through worked their way around for a second time . . . or was it a third or fourth?

"Well, I'll be. You're right. That fella was in front of Evan, and now he's in line behind. I wonder—"

"Whoa, whoa, whoa," Frisco hollered as he stepped out of line and waved his hands over his head. The vote counters in the wagons strained to see him over the crowd. "We have an irregularity occurring."

Deputy McFarland and another deputy came busting through the lines to get to him. A few of the other town fathers had gathered next to the third group. It looked like a reunion of all the men who'd gotten involved with the last election trouble. Maybe Frisco should be happy that he wasn't responsible for messes like this.

"I'm Deputy Juarez," the man said. He had a black, flat-brimmed Spanish-style hat with a pull string that hugged his chin. "Is there a reason you're interrupting our residents just as they are exercising their civil rights?"

Frisco took a step back to size him up. He recognized back-alley bullies, but he also knew that some of them grew up and continued their ways beneath the safety of a badge. Frisco had won a fight or two, but his strength had always been in persuasion. He scanned the crowd, drawing every eye as witness. "I watched that line and saw men getting back in line after casting their vote. Some are voting twice."

Evan Pickens stretched his long torso out to look behind him. "Well, I'll be." The two brothers shared expressions, even if they didn't share political views. "Those fellas were in front of me. I saw them both go through and vote. And y'all too." He gestured at another handful of men who were trying to leave the line without being noticed.

"Don't look at me!" Sitting in the wagon, Mr. Bledsoe lifted his hands in surrender. "I didn't tell them to do that."

McFarland and Juarez exchanged glances. McFarland didn't let it take any wind out of his sails. "Then we'll have to start over. Throw away your tally marks, and in an hour we'll vote again. This time sign your name next to your vote, and each wagon will have a deputy in it to watch that the same man doesn't go through twice."

"We're twins," Evan Pickens called out. He pointed across the way at his brother and then at himself. "Just 'cause we favor each other doesn't mean we don't each get to vote."

"Duly noted," McFarland said. "Thank you for the clarification."

"Excuse me." The first candidate, known to Frisco only as Mr. Feldstein, stood in the back of his wagon. "I've had some time to think it over, and I'm withdrawing my name from the race. I'm throwing my support to Mr. Bledsoe. He'll do a fine job, so go on and vote for him."

Frisco studied the lines. That meant that Mr. Bledsoe would win even without the cheating. Not surprising. Bill Matthews was a Johnny-come-lately, supported only by some of the common people and none of the deputies. By banding together, the deputies had managed to get their man in position.

"Once again you have proven yourself invaluable to Plainview, young man." McFarland motioned Frisco away from the wagons as people began to rearrange themselves into two lines. "We're lucky to have you here. When will you be ready to start reading law?"

The question surprised Frisco. What did McFarland know about that?

"I've already started. Saw my first client today." If he was wary, he had good reason. So far, every bit of official business done in Plainview had been tainted.

"Excellent. Once we're up and running, the city would like to utilize your skills. I have the feeling we'll need someone who has an eye for the law looking over our ordinances. That's not to mention getting all the property disputes settled."

Frisco nodded. That sounded promising. Perhaps the irregularities were only disorganization. "For something as straightforward as a race, there was a lot of corruption," he said. "It'll take years to get it all straightened out."

"Nothing like a guaranteed income," McFarland laughed. "Not that you would wish conflict on people," he hastily amended, "but you might as well profit when it's there."

It was the profession Frisco had chosen, but he didn't like McFarland's assumption. And yet he was the deputy in town and was looking for honest men to help him in a difficult situation. Frisco would be a fool not to offer his services.

"Don't forget the dance on Friday night." McFarland slapped him on the back. "And be sure you bring that feisty redhead."

Frisco ran a finger under his collar. Dancing with Miss Adams when everything was at stake? Who would blink first? But if he was going to see clients in earnest, he needed somewhere better than a tent to store his records. One good Oklahoma Territory thunderstorm and his files would be carried by the wind, page by page, all the way to Arkansas. He might ask around and see if more shipments of sawn lumber were coming in from the Chickasaw. Or maybe Sophie would have a strongbox for sale that would hold records until he could build something more permanent.

Forgetting where the roads were, he cut across a lot to return to her wagon but stopped when he came across a furniture builder. The man had a row of chairs sitting alongside his wagon. Chairs? That was definitely something Frisco would need for customers.

Three rockers, two ladder-backs, and one spinning office chair were displayed. He sat in the office chair and swung back and forth, testing the spring.

"That'll be a dime." A copper-topped man had appeared from behind the wagon.

"A dime for this chair? Sold." Frisco reached for his pocket.

"No, you dolt. Not for the chair. It's a dime to sit in the chair for an hour." He brushed sawdust off his sleeve.

"Why would I pay you to sit in a chair? That's ridiculous." The chair's spring squawked as Frisco leaned back in it.

"Someone got tired of having nowhere to sit besides the grass and asked if I'd lease it to him. These chairs have already paid more than I was ever going to sell them for."

Of all the tomfoolery . . . "But are they for sale?" Frisco asked. "I don't have any interest in leasing one, but—"

"I've been looking everywhere for you."

Frisco turned to see Patrick Smith, dirty and dusty but none the worse for wear. Frisco grinned, but then his smile hardened when he remembered why his friend would be searching him out.

"So this is Redhawk?" Patrick said. "You really did it? If I remember the map correctly, my plot is going to be on the north side."

"This isn't—" Frisco rocked forward in the chair. "Did you get your farm, Patrick?"

Patrick dropped his traveling bag and took a rocking chair next to Frisco. "The train was a bad idea. The one I was on was the fourth one to leave the station. By the time it set out, three other trains and all the horsemen had already had their pick. We did pass through one section that looked unclaimed, but the train didn't slow down. People started jumping out the doors. I couldn't because I was stuck in the middle of the car, but I did get to a window. Scared me to death thinking about what would happen to Millie and Jonathan if I didn't clear the tracks, but I did it anyway. Hit the ground, rolled, and then ran."

"By the tracks? How far did you have to go?"

"Till right here. Never did find land that didn't already have someone on it telling me to keep moving. But I didn't despair. That deal I struck with you was the best investment I've ever made."

Frisco looked at his shoes, dirt still resting on the tops of them. "This isn't Redhawk, Patrick. I didn't get my land either."

"What do you mean? I thought you had it all figured out."

"I made a mistake. Several mistakes. When I got there, someone had beat me to it, but I haven't given up. I'm going to get it."

"So you have nothing? We have nothing?" His rocking chair stilled. His head drooped.

Frisco's throat tightened. He didn't have what he wanted, but he had something, which was more than Patrick and his family had.

"I have one city lot," he said. "One. I have hopes of regaining my town site. I don't think the current homesteader can prove out."

"How long will that take?"

Frisco drew in a long breath. "It's a particularly stubborn person. I couldn't say."

Patrick might have been brave on the train, but the fear was starting to show on his face. "We sold out of Kansas. We sold everything, loaded up, and came this way. How can I go back and tell Millie that we have nothing?"

"You can stay on my lot," he said. "Be right here in town. There's good money to be had for a saddlemaker and laundress. You can start by fixing me up with new reins. And while every lot may be claimed right now, once the dust settles, a lot of people will pack up and go home. With my position in the city, I'll be the first to know when someone quits a claim."

"What do you mean, 'position in the city'? I thought you were going to get your Redhawk land back."

"Keep your options open," Frisco said, while trying not to wince. "Didn't you teach me that?"

"Show me where this place of yours is," Patrick said. "Maybe I can get Millie and Jonathan back before dark."

"Let's go."

"Excuse me." The chair owner stepped between them. "That's rentals of two chairs that you owe me for. Twenty cents, please."

Patrick turned on the man, ready to make him answer for his insolence just as he'd done for many of Frisco's foes.

Frisco sighed and put his hand in his pocket. "Twenty cents," he said as he dropped the coins into the man's hand and started back to his property.

It was only a square of empty field. Not much to offer a family, but it was everything to those who sought it. And at this rate, it might be all he ever had.

Chapter Thirteen

S he could do this. She could.

Amber hooked the heel of her boot on the plow and bounced on it. The reins had gone slack as the horse waited for her command. Convinced she had the clod busted, she called to the horse, and it stepped forward. Success. The plowshare—that was what the instruction booklet had called the blade—sliced through another six inches of red soil, then popped up. Another clod? Amber wiped the sweat from her eyes. She wouldn't give up. She had to get the field plowed. She threw her weight against the handles to drive the blade back into the ground. Another call to the horse. Another six inches before the blade hopped out again.

This would take forever.

She'd been proud that she'd succeeded in the race, proud that she'd made it to Darlington and back with her supplies, and thrilled when she'd managed to set up a tent on her own land with the help of the Schneiders, but now it was time to settle down and start this farm, and she'd met with nothing but discouragement. The two lines she'd managed to scratch in the dirt snaked back and forth, overlapping each other and separating. The handbook she'd bought described the correct method, but it didn't explain how to instantly make oneself stronger and heavier to control the plow.

Three steps, then stopping the horse to drive the plowshare back into the ground. Three steps, maybe four if she was lucky. She might get half a line done before it was time for dinner. Or maybe she wouldn't stop for dinner. It didn't seem worth the hassle and cleanup. She didn't have anything hot to eat anyway.

She gasped and dropped the handle of the plow. Pulling off her glove, she turned her hand over to see watery blood trickling from a broken blister. She hadn't thought to include bandages in her supplies. The homesteaders' handbook hadn't listed them as a necessity.

Maybe she'd take time for dinner after all. Keeping one hand clenched, she tried to unhook the trace from the collar to give the horse a break, but her fingers were too weak. Biting her lip, she straightened her hand and pried her numb fingers open. If she were just a little stronger, a little tougher, how much easier this would be. But even then, there was so much to do.

The horse could wait until after she'd eaten. Wearily, she walked to the tent and, taking a knife, cut off a piece of a rag she'd brought along. She wrapped it around her hand. With a wince, she tugged it tight, but tying it with one hand proved more difficult than she'd imagined. Biting on one end of the rag, she made a loop, but before she could thread it, she heard someone outside.

"Amber? Are you in there?"

Her hand dropped to her lap, and she felt giddy with relief. "I'm here," she called.

Bradley's outline moved across the tent's canvas before he came through the door. Her heart swelled at the dashing figure he cut in his cavalry uniform and his shiny black boots. There was no one she'd rather see at that moment.

He stood over her, his hands on his waist. "You can't quit already," he said. "You've barely got started. If we don't get the seeds planted before summer hits, then we won't have anything to show for our first year. Nothing to eat. There's not time to sit around and daydream."

Amber blinked. "Excuse me?"

"And you're doing the furrows the wrong way. You have to put them in against the slant of the land, or the topsoil will disappear with the runoff. Thankfully, you're only getting started. By the end of the day you should have—"

She jumped to her feet. "You haven't asked how I am, how I'm doing, or if I'm hurt. You just come in telling me what to do and telling me that I've done it wrong. But where have you been? Sitting on a horse and parading around when you could've been helping me?" She looked for something to throw at him as her indignation grew, but she was too tired to give it much effort.

"Oh, simmer down," he said. "I'm doing everything I'm assigned to do, including hauling Caroline's personal things to her by request of Major Adams. He gave me leave for the rest of the day, so here I am. Now you don't have to worry about anything."

Her hand fell on her pillow. If she couldn't find anything heavier, it'd have to do. He was smiling so big that he didn't see it coming. Amber swung and walloped him upside the head.

"That's what you should've said in the first place." She drew back to hit him again, but he intercepted her and pulled her into his arms.

"I've always been slow about my lessons, honey. But once I learn them, I learn them good."

He cradled her head against his chest. Her burden felt lighter, although her hand stung just as sharply.

"First I'm going to tend to that hand." He smoothed her hair off her damp forehead. "Then I'm going to get behind the plow

146

while you fix us some dinner. I should have an acre or so done before I need to get back to stable call. You know, it would help if you had a real pulling horse and not Daisy's favorite racer."

"Major Adams is being kind enough to let me borrow her for now. If you want to buy us something stronger . . ." She stepped back to look him in the face. "How's Caroline?"

"I haven't been there yet. We can take her things to her this afternoon. The old major was beside himself when he realized she was gone. Poor Lieutenant Hennessey. He had his hands full keeping the major calm until they located her."

"Daisy didn't tell?"

Bradley's eyebrows shot up. "Daisy knew? No, she didn't tell. That's a first." He straightened his back, and his smile spread. "I think we've done it. We're going to make it."

"We're a long way from making it," Amber said. "Just getting the crops in is more than I can do alone. Even if the crops make it, who knows if it'll be enough to live on or not?"

"If we come up short, I'll find work. The fort employs civilians to haul wood. Or I can hire on with the muleskinners and bring supplies to the fort. Louisa knows some fellas out of Kansas—"

"Then you'd be gone." Amber took his hand. "I don't want to be here alone any more than necessary."

"Just think of Caroline at that claim all by herself."

"She's fine," Amber said. "As long as she has a locked door to sleep behind, she can tackle any other problem."

"A locked door? She has a house?" Bradley shook his head. "That's Caroline for you. Always lands on her feet. Was it an old Seminole place?"

"No, actually, Frisco Smith built it. He'd come out early to fix things up. Just took it for granted that he'd be here first." She chuckled. "He was wrong. Never underestimate the power of a determined woman."

Bradley's smile faded. "This is someone else's land? You took someone's else's land?"

"Not me. Caroline. Frisco had been hiding out on the land next to ours, and Caroline got the spot he prepared. The well is dug. The house is built, stocked even. All that work, and then it's gone. Sometimes the luck just isn't with you."

"That doesn't seem fair." Bradley released her hand after finishing the knot in her bandage. "We'll have to talk some sense into that girl."

Amber shrugged. "It's legal, but don't go too hard on her. Changing course doesn't come easy for her."

"She decided to try her hand at this easily enough. Now she can undecide."

A spark of worry flared in Amber at Bradley's set jaw. Funny how simple a stubborn person thought it was to make another stubborn person change their mind.

The rope burned Caroline's palms as she pulled it, hand over hand, to raise the bucket out of the well. Frisco had given her a start with the garden, but it hadn't rained in the four days she'd lived there, and the ground looked dry. That meant hauling paltry bucket after bucket out of the ground, then dragging it over to splash against the thirsty soil. After sloshing half the water against her legs, a bucket only covered three feet of ground. At this rate, Caroline would have to make how many trips? She closed her eyes to rest them from the piercing blue of the sky. Not knowing would be better. She should just put her head down and keep working.

The air was so crisp that it felt like she could bend it and it would snap like a fresh stalk of celery. It gave her energy to continue despite the soreness in her muscles and the sores on her hands. She'd keep working, but the sounds from town tantalized her. When the wind was right, she heard voices, animals, and incessant hammers. Occasionally there was music and laughter. None of that was happening where she was, but this was where she needed to be. In town, she'd just be a spectator. On her homestead, she had a future, and that future was becoming clearer every hour.

With the paper and pen that her father had sent with her nightly sentinel—who was completely unnecessary, thank you—she'd sketched out where her house and gardens would lie. She was enamored with designing a garden that would be beautiful and would produce marketable herbs. Already Caroline had a list of starters and seeds that she'd need to order from the seed catalog. She could afford that improvement. The house was another matter.

Before she could borrow money on her business idea, she had to have proof of what she proposed. Setting aside her lofty ambitions, she'd sketched a modest floor plan for the first stage, but lines on a piece of paper didn't accomplish much. Who would build it? How did she get started? After Amber's father had retired from the army, she and her mother had designed and overseen the building of their first privately owned home, so Caroline had asked her friend's advice with the first drafts. When she was ready to build, Lieutenant Bigelow, who oversaw the construction on the fort, would be able to advise her, but he wouldn't know who she could hire. He had the soldiers at his beck and call. Caroline had nothing.

"Bucky, you stay away from the shoots," she called.

The black-and-white goat waggled its beard as it chewed on the tender plants. With a grunt, Caroline emptied the water on the kid's head. It pranced off, stiff-legged and dripping, but not deterred. It would return as soon as she turned her back. Dropping her bucket, she ran after the goat, catching it by its rope collar.

"There's plenty of grass around here," she said as she pulled Bucky to her tether. "If you can't stay out of the garden, it's back on the rope for you." When she knelt, she felt every sore muscle in her back. After securing the rope, Caroline paused to stretch, bending this way and that to relieve the parts of her that had worked so hard, but she couldn't dally. The day would only grow hotter.

Instead of using her arms, this time Caroline tossed the well rope over her shoulder and walked away from the well, letting her legs do the lifting. See, she could learn. While Amber's book was full of helpful information, it didn't include things like how to haul water out of a rough, unfinished well, so it was good that Caroline could think for herself.

Was that a government wagon coming across the field? If the fort was giving away wagons, Caroline should be first in line. Then, with some barrels, her chore would be so much easier.

She had time for one last trip to the garden before the wagon was close enough for her to see that it was Amber and Bradley paying a call.

Noticing the bundles in the back of the wagon, Caroline grinned as she gave way to orneriness. "Are you pulling up stakes already? That didn't take long."

Bradley rolled his eyes. "Nobody's quitting—at least on our end."

His peevish tone took Caroline aback. What was stuck in his craw? "I didn't mean to insult you. I can't say that quitting hasn't crossed my mind over the last few days."

"Well, you should quit, Caroline. You should." Bradley threw the brake and helped Amber down from the wagon.

Caroline dropped her bucket and wiped her hands on her skirt. "What's wrong with you?" If anyone should have been in high spirits, it was Bradley.

"This isn't a task for a lady like yourself. Look at you, covered in sweat and dirt. Wouldn't you rather be back at the fort with Daisy and Allie Claire?"

Caroline's mouth tightened. "I'm not quitting." She picked up the bucket and headed toward the well.

"Of course you're not." Amber ran to catch up with her. "Bradley doesn't mean anything. He's just out of sorts."

"And why would that be?" Bradley called from behind them. "Maybe because she's claiming land she has no right to?"

That stopped Caroline in her tracks. "Horsefeathers." She spun around to face him. "You saw us at the starting line. You know I ran a fair race."

"This is Frisco's land." Bradley stomped forward. "You of all people should know how important this is to him. He had people counting on him. A lot of people. I can't believe you have no concern for him."

Amber stepped between them. "Caroline doesn't need our permission to live here. It doesn't affect us."

"Absolutely it affects us. We're her friends—I'm her family. Do you want to be associated with someone who stabs a man in the back like that?" Bradley asked.

Caroline dropped her bucket. "Stab him in the back? I did no such thing."

"Actually, I've always thought you were a little sweet on him—"

Caroline didn't let Amber finish. "Frisco is doing just fine. He's got a city lot just over the ridge."

"With a well and a house and a crop planted?" Bradley's eyes flashed. "With supplies that he bought and stocked? Room for the people he's contracted with? I'd rather you say that you didn't care what happened to him than pretend that he's better off because of your betrayal. And what did you do it for? As a lark?"

"I'm doing it for the same reason you are—for a future. I have a plan."

"And what about next year? I doubt Frisco Smith will come and plant you a garden again. In fact, I wouldn't be surprised if he shows up in a few months and collects his crops. It's his right, you know. And you couldn't do anything to stop him."

"It figures you would take Frisco's side. You're both ne'er-do-wells, always looking for some shortcut to riches." Caroline's fingernails dug into her palms.

"How is it that I'm taking a shortcut? You're living in Frisco's house and drawing water out of his well. You even took his goat." Bradley's shoulders twitched. "What did I do, besides expect you to act minimally decent to a friend of ours? Evidently that was too much to ask."

"I don't need etiquette lessons from the likes of you," Caroline yelled back. "I've been in high society."

"Another way of saying that you've leeched off others' profits. For the last four years, I've served in the cavalry. You've served lemonade."

Amber propped her fists against her hips. "That's enough, you two. Caroline, it's not too late to make this right. Why don't you give Frisco his land back? Then, if you still want to share in the adventure, you can come stay with me."

Caroline thudded her boot against the overturned bucket. "In a few weeks, you'll be married. Then you won't want me there any longer, will you?"

"No, she won't," Bradley said. "You should go back to the fort. You have a father, Louisa, and two sisters. Frisco has no one. It isn't right."

"You do realize that if I hadn't shown you the pass through the canyon, you wouldn't have your land either? You need to think about that before you start judging me." Caroline picked up the bucket and hurled it into the well. "I'm staying. I have my father's approval. I don't need yours."

She waited for Amber to make another attempt at reconciliation but was only met with silence. When Bradley stalked away, Amber dropped her chin and turned to follow him.

"That's it?" Caroline asked. "You're going to let him talk to me like that?"

"Don't make me choose between you." Amber's gaze was unflinching. "You both need to simmer down. Until then, I have a farm to tend."

Amber's answer stung. With a grunt, Caroline pulled the rope until the bucket reached the edge. It was so unfair. For every plot that was claimed, there were three people who didn't get one. What if someone else had claimed Frisco's land? Would Bradley think poorly of them, or would he chalk it up to bad luck and move on?

She should help them unload the bundles from the back of the wagon, but Bradley wasn't waiting on her. Without any preamble, he'd pushed a trunk to the edge of the wagon and let it fall. Despite Amber's protests, he tossed Caroline's bags on top of the trunk before lifting Amber into the wagon and driving away.

Chapter Fourteen

Caroline watched as her best friend's profile grew smaller and smaller on the horizon until the wagon dipped behind the rise and disappeared from sight. Part of her wanted to chase after them and apologize, but the other part insisted that she stand her ground. She was within her rights. One didn't give up this kind of fortune to appease a sore loser.

It was probably inevitable. Amber had Bradley, and Bradley was as unreliable as damp gunpowder. So what if they had a falling out? But Caroline couldn't reason away the heaviness that grew with Amber's absence.

Taking the bucket, Caroline poured the last of the water on her hands to wash up before carrying her belongings inside. She scrubbed and scrubbed. It didn't matter how much water she had, she still felt like her hands were dirty. She crossed the green pasture to her bags and started moving them inside.

If she'd thought the water bucket was heavy, it was nothing compared to her trunk. Caroline rolled it end over end until she reached the riverbank. Then she opened it and carried down her clothes until it was empty and light enough for her to drag down the bank.

The trunk made the space feel even smaller, but it was a nicer seat than the low stool that Frisco had left. In typical motherly fashion, Louisa had sent Caroline an extra blanket, sheets, and her favorite feather pillow. She repacked her personal items into the trunk and then looked around for a place to hang her gowns. She could get some hooks, but the walls were dirt. Even if the hooks would stick, her gowns would get filthy brushing up against the wall. She closed the door and breathed a sigh of relief when she saw some hooks on the back of the door. The unexpected convenience delighted her, but then contemplating Frisco's handiwork increased her guilt.

Under the riverbank, the air hung still and heavy. No voices from town, no music, no noise from construction could reach her through the dirt walls. She was on her own. Someday, when the railroad came through and her property was a haven for travelers, when the community was established, then she'd be appreciated and counted as one of them—a pioneer, a founder. Until then, she had to prove her intentions and show that she was just as valuable to the success of this territory as anyone else.

But it was too quiet in the little room.

Frisco's bookshelf had been emptied of his law books, but there were a few that she hadn't carried back to him yet. One was his Bible. Caroline had never thought of him as a saint, but a lot had changed since she'd known him at the fort. The Bible had a solid wooden cover, worn around the edges. She let it fall open and stuck her nose into the seam. The smell of ink must have faded years ago along with the print, but she could still make out the words.

The pages rustled as she searched for the desired passage. Something about the conquest of Canaan. Something about God's promises to the children of Israel. That was what she was after. In Joshua, she found what she was looking for: *And I have given you a land for which ye did not labour, and cities which ye built not, and ye dwell in them; of the vineyards and oliveyards which ye planted not do ye eat.*

She sat up straighter as she nodded. While she didn't purport to claim the promises of the Israelites, this was the proof she was looking for. God didn't expect a person to give up everything just because someone asked. On the contrary, sometimes He was in the business of rewarding one with land that wasn't theirs at the get-go.

Chew on that, Bradley Willis.

She flipped through more pages until something caught her eye. Notes had been scribbled in the margins. Bright ink underlined faded words. Frisco's writing? Her heart sped up. What deep secrets might Frisco reveal in the pages of his Bible?

"Hello?"

Caroline snapped the book closed and reached for the door. Inching it open a crack, she took a peek. It was him. She slammed the door closed and fell against it, crushing layers of calico.

"Hello?" he called again. "Miss Adams? May I come in?"

Why was he here? Did he know that her best friend and her uncle had taken his side? Had he come to reclaim his property? Was he going to haul her trunk back up the bank and kick her out?

She opened the door another crack. His forehead wrinkled in concern as his eyes did a sweep of her from head to toe.

"Is everything all right?"

Could he tell that she didn't want him here? Evidently not, because he leaned his tailored suit against the door and slowly pushed it open despite her resistance.

"I've been working hard," she said. "You caught me out of breath."

His gaze moved around the room, seeming to note every

change, from her trunk to her bedclothes folded on top of his cot. Then he looked down her form again with such slow deliberation that Caroline felt her face warm.

"Where have you been working? The river?"

Her water-splashed skirt stuck to her calves. She looked like she'd wrestled a pig, and he was dressed to the nines in a fine suit. "I was watering the crops."

"Did they look dry?"

"How am I supposed to know?"

"You're the homesteader."

Her knees wobbled, but she wouldn't back down. "Yes, I am, and I should get out there and work until it's done."

"Don't take too long," he said. "You don't want to be late."

"Late to what?" Caroline hadn't seen a clock in a week. Did time even exist anymore?

"To the dance. I'm here to take you to town."

The dance. It was Friday? She'd been so busy trying to convince people that she deserved his property that she'd forgotten that she had an engagement with him that very evening. And here she was, exhausted and dirty, barely able to stay on her feet.

"I haven't changed my mind about the property," she said.

"We'll see what you say after spending the evening in my company."

"I hope you can handle disappointment like a gentleman."

His teeth flashed in a reckless smile. "There's a first for everything." Then, taking another look at her, he said, "You didn't return all of my books, I see."

She pushed the Bible toward him. "Here. I'm surprised to find it in your collection."

"Law books weren't the only thing I read while in jail." He waved her offering away. "Keep it for now. Maybe reading it will do you some good. How much time do you require before you're ready?"

Caroline tucked the book under her arm. "I've got chores to complete before I can get clean. Can you come back?"

"No need. I'll finish the chores while you get ready." He began unbuttoning his suit coat.

She'd thought she was prepared for an avalanche of charm, but she hadn't considered how appealing his offer of help made him.

He pulled off his coat and swung the door closed to look for a hook to hang it on. The room darkened instantly. Caroline swallowed. She'd never been in a room alone with Frisco. He was still a man who had once held her under his spell, and despite the conflict, he hadn't lost all of his allure.

"I suppose I should ask permission before hanging my coat over your gowns," he said.

"I can put them on the bed."

"Don't bother." He hooked his coat over her sapphire skirt. "I'd forgotten how much I liked this place." They were still in the dark. The earthen walls seemed to swallow up every sound as soon as it was uttered, making each more precious. "The dirt here has such a clean scent."

Good, because she was covered in it. But he was acting so noble that she felt he deserved some credit. "You did a fine job building this place," she said. "Without it I wouldn't have dared to stay here alone."

"I orchestrated my own demise." He unbuttoned his cuff and rolled up his sleeve.

"Come now," Caroline said. "You seem happy in town."

"I'd be happier in my own town."

"Why are you going to help me if you want me to fail?"

Frisco looked up from fiddling with his sleeve. His eyes narrowed, twitching like he was surprised to see something that he hadn't seen before. "I'd never cheer for the failure of someone as valiant as you, my dear Miss Adams. But I will pray that you find your success on someone else's property."

Caroline brushed her hair back with bruised fingers. He thought she was valiant? Had his opinion of her improved, or was he trying to chip away at her resolve? "Thank you for your prayers, Mr. Smith, however misguided they are. Are you really going to help me water the garden?"

"Not the garden, no. Those plants don't need water yet, and by the time they do, it'll probably rain. In fact, with rain more than likely, I'm going to shore up the roof to make sure no tin blows off. I want to protect my property. Can't have all my belongings getting wet."

"If you want your things, then please take them." She picked up a washrag from her linens. "Otherwise I might charge you for the storage of your goods."

"Patience, woman," he said. "I've acquired a client, and he has undertaken building me a house to pay his fees."

"I see." She couldn't keep herself from looking at the house plans she'd sketched and pinned to the wall.

Frisco followed her gaze. "What's this?" He rested his forearm on the wall as he leaned in to see in the dim light. "Is this the house you want?"

"Yes. Surrounded by lavender and mint."

"One hundred and sixty acres is a lot of herbs."

"I'll expand slowly."

"But this house looks reasonable."

"You're the first person to tell me so." She really should start getting ready, but Bucky was short on conversation. Having someone to talk to was a rare treat. "And your house," she said, "once it's completed, you'll haul your things out of here?"

"On the contrary, once the house is completed, I'll have something to offer you in trade. Until then, I want to make sure this roof is secure. Now, let me get to work before it's too late. I was hoping to take a beautiful lady to the dance tonight." He winked, then left, closing the door behind him.

"I am beautiful," she yelled at the tin roof above her head. She waited, listening for his laugh. There it was. How she'd listened for that ringing laugh back when she lived at the fort. That sound meant an exciting guest at her father's dinner table. It meant that she'd be treated like a grown-up. It meant a glimpse of someone who lived life freely, not regimented by the call of the bugle and drum.

Caroline wadded the rag in her hand. As dismal as the day had been, Frisco, her supposed enemy, had redeemed it. Even if he didn't mean a word he said, he was taking her to a dance, and she was going to have fun. Bradley could take his opinions, throw them in the pond, and see how they floated, for all she cared. And Amber—well, she'd worry about Amber later. Caroline would find a way to win her over.

She took the rag to the river to scrub her hands and arms to remove the dirt and the grubby feeling of a conflict with friends. Funny how the prospect of good company could restore one's spirits. Frisco whistled some Irish jig above her as he stacked rocks along the edges of the tin roof that lay even with the ground at the top of the bank.

She rubbed the rough rag up and down her neck, knowing that her sensitive skin would turn as red as a turkey's wattle. The curse of her coloring. She rolled her sleeves as high as she could to wash her arms, since her evening gown would bare them. A crash sounded behind her as Frisco dropped another rock on the edge of the sheet of tin. Was he trying to destroy the dugout?

"Careful," she said. "You don't want to get dirty."

"I have another shirt in the house," he answered. "Unless you threw it out."

"What kind of beast do you take me for?"

"Maybe I shouldn't answer that question." He stood on the roof, one foot planted atop a rock, and watched as she finished at the river. "This really is the prettiest spot in the territory. I chose well."

"Just wait until I get my house and gardens in," she said. "Now, mind your own business while I change my dress."

"I'll stay up here."

Back inside, Caroline thought about lighting a lamp but then decided that dressing in the dark might be safer. Another stone thudded, and dirt salted the room. She'd better hurry, or she was going to need another cleaning in the river. She shimmied out of her skirt and reached for the blue one on the back of the door. Her fingers fell on Frisco's coat. Curious, she gathered it to her face. It smelled of leather. She'd seen the beaten bag he carried. Undoubtedly this coat had been in there, since the rest of his belongings were with her. The summer fabric crumpled between her fingers. She'd always wanted Frisco's attention. Now, for good or ill, she had it. She took her skirt off the hook and hung the coat back in its place.

After four days alone in this place, Caroline didn't want to miss out on a moment of company. Checking twice that her bodice covered her waistband, she sat on the bed and unlaced her boots, tossed her socks aside for some finer stockings, and slid on her newest slippers. She picked up her hand mirror, but the light was too dim. Taking her mirror and brush, she went outside to the riverbank.

"You about ready?" Frisco asked from the roof of the dugout.

"Not quite."

With sure hands, she pulled the pins holding up her twisted braid. It fell heavily down her back. Should she keep her preparations to a minimum and not give him more reason to think her frivolous? She pulled the auburn rope over her shoulder and unraveled the braid. It was then she realized that Frisco hadn't resumed his whistling. In fact, it was suspiciously quiet behind her.

She whisked her brush through the ends of her hair to clear the snarls before she worked her way up through the thick strands. She wouldn't hurry. Her grandmother had always said that her hair was one of her better features, so she'd take her time. Frisco could think what he wanted.

When her hair reached its silky best, she put down her brush. Her curiosity piqued, she picked up the mirror to take a look over her shoulder. What was he doing? His reflection was grinning back at her.

"That color is so beautiful, it's gonna make the evening sky jealous," he said.

She lowered the mirror. His comment was like the exaggerated compliments he used to pay her in front of her father. Something to irritate the major and flatter a silly young girl.

Well, she wasn't a silly young girl, and the thought that he didn't know the difference irritated her. Dropping the mirror, she gathered a section of her hair to start a braid. Frisco might not take her seriously, but she still had a reputation to uphold. She couldn't show up at a society event with no more preparation than a normal workday, of which she'd had very few in her life.

"If you're done inside, I'd like to take a look at the walls and make sure they aren't in danger of crumbling," Frisco said.

With a hairpin in her mouth and both hands lifted to her head, she nodded.

Once he was gone, it took her no time at all to finish. The reflection in the mirror pleased her except for a spot of dirt that she'd missed. She licked her finger and rubbed at it, only to find it was a new freckle. She wrinkled her nose, which did nothing to balance the unsophistication of the freckle. Was there any powder in the things Louisa had sent from the fort? Caroline lifted her chin and smoothed her coif. She'd have to see.

The dance wouldn't be as elaborate as the ones in Galveston, and for that she was glad. She couldn't look forward to seeing old friends, though, because the town hadn't existed a week ago. Frisco was the only person she knew there. Guiltily she thought of how much Amber would have enjoyed going to town instead of spending another night in her tent, but Amber wouldn't want to go with her after Caroline's fight with Bradley. No use in asking.

Caroline met Frisco at the door of the dugout. He stepped aside so she could put her brush and mirror away. She noticed her socks hadn't been picked up and kicked them under the bed, even though he'd already walked over them while she was outside.

"Should I take a wrap?" she asked.

He looked at her white arms. "If you get chilly, you can have my coat."

"Oh, there's my powder. Excuse me."

Frisco stood at the door, watching the river roll past until she'd hidden the freckle.

"There," she said. "As long as the goat is safe to leave behind, then I suppose I'm ready."

"The goat is the safest one among us."

The walk to Plainview was less than a mile. They discussed whether they were trespassing as they crossed someone else's claim on their way to town but settled for staying away from the tent on the property. As there were no fences, they couldn't be sure where a road should have been. Frisco claimed that surveyors would come out to mark roads, but the waiting list was long. A breeze had picked up and swept away the afternoon heat.

"What would your father say about us going to a dance together?" Frisco asked.

"It doesn't matter, does it? If you're still flattering me to annoy him, then you're wasting your time."

"Why? Has your father's opinion of me changed?"

Her sleeve felt like it was slipping off her shoulder. She

tugged it up. "If you wanted to know what he thinks, maybe you should've invited him to the dance."

"If I thought he'd get me my land, I would've."

"And here I thought you asked me to accompany you just so Deputy McFarland wouldn't have the pleasure."

"I admit I do feel a sense of possessiveness toward you. It's entirely unwarranted and inappropriate, but I'm not one to hide from the truth." His eyes gleamed speculatively as he waited for her response.

"I . . . you . . ." Caroline rubbed her gloves on her bare arms. "Don't be ridiculous. This outing was ill-advised from the start. You'll gain nothing from me tonight. You might as well find another lady who will look on you more favorably."

"On the contrary, you are exactly who I need at my side to-night. While my accomplishments are impressive considering my age, my upbringing has left me rough around the edges. I can't pretend to belong to the same set as many of the men who have found themselves in power already, but it's a new town—a new territory. No one has any history here." He bent suddenly and plucked an Indian blanket flower out of the tall grass. "While there's no established aristocracy here, if there were one, it'd be the family of the commander who resides just inside the border of the reservation to our west."

Caroline took the offered flower, then stopped to rip the stem off short and push it into her hair arrangement. "Once again, you imagine that my family relations give you leave to toy with my emotions."

"My apologies. I didn't realize your emotions were engaged. I can take you back to the dugout. . . ."

"I have my own invitation to the dance," she said and took out over the grasslands. "I'm going with or without you."

"With. You are most assuredly going *with* me," he said.

And this time Caroline didn't argue.

Chapter Fifteen

Was he toying with her emotions? Frisco hadn't thought that grown-up Caroline would give him a second glance. Years ago, when she was an obstinate, opinionated young lady, she seemed to enjoy the annoyance he caused her father. All those times she'd followed Frisco to the door as Lieutenant Hennessey was escorting him back to the guardhouse, he'd known she was intrigued by him and didn't care a jot if her father disapproved. But she was beyond his reach now. Surely she'd had better opportunities in the time they'd been separated.

To be fair, she was still obstinate and opinionated. That set of her jaw when she refused to leave his land probably wasn't appreciated in the fine dining rooms of the seaside gentry. And then there was her propensity to ride bareback astride a horse if she was of a mind. He hoped she hadn't broken that habit as well.

But in the newborn town of Plainview, she was high society and the perfect prop for his show. Perhaps the only reason she had agreed to go with him was guilt. If attending a dance would assuage her conscience, he'd accept—and then figure out how to prick it again.

The progress made in town in four days was remarkable. Nearly half the lots had some roughhewn framework up. Several buildings had roofs and the beginnings of walls. A few structures were completed. The people were wasting no time, as he could attest from the hammers ringing throughout the night.

"This is really going to be a city," Caroline said. Dressed in her sapphire finery, she didn't look like someone who'd be impressed with the new construction, but Frisco loved that she was.

"That's been the plan all along," he said, "but even I'm surprised how quickly it's happening."

"All except for the bank." Caroline pointed to the row of bricks on the low wall that was visible across the empty lots. "They haven't made much progress. I would think getting the walls up would be a priority for them."

"Their priority is taking in money. With so much business starting, they don't have time for construction. I find myself in the same predicament. I'm busy from morning to evening speaking with clients. No time to look after putting a building on the lot. Thankfully I've got Patrick to supervise Mr. Nesbitt as the work goes up." And now that he'd seen her house plans, he knew exactly what his house would look like.

Wagon ruts and footpaths were finally defining the streets between the city lots. On either side, piles of lumber and rolls of tar paper hulked. By consensus, any unwanted scraps of building supplies were left near the street, where women and children picked over them, hoping to find the right-sized material for a smaller project.

"It's exciting," Frisco said, "to see what's in the imagination of all these people. The town is being formed as we watch." He pointed to a crane being guided with a counterweight to hoist a bell up high. Before the houses were even finished, they were starting on a church.

"Who's Patrick? What's he doing for you?" Caroline asked.

With his hands clasped behind his back, Frisco jerked his head to the side. "Follow me." Maybe it was a mistake to show her the beginnings of the house, but he wanted her to see what he saw. To understand that she could be part of a community from the start, and that it would be infinitely more rewarding than going it alone.

Patrick's family had just gathered for supper. Millie dished out boiled turnips from a cast-iron pot hanging over a fire while Patrick handed a plate to Jonathan, who sat next to his dog. Frisco had turned to leave the street when Caroline stopped him with a hand on his arm.

"I don't want to disturb them."

"Nonsense. They'll be glad to meet you."

"Why?"

Frisco was surprised by the uncertainty on her face. "Because you are someone who is worth knowing."

"Because of my family?" Her lips tightened, and her chin rose.

"Lay down the hatchet," he said. "Come on."

He took her by the elbow and led her toward the family. Patrick stood, removed his hat, and smiled wide. Millie, on the other hand, took one look at Caroline and stepped back, keeping the fire between them.

"Miss Adams, may I present to you Mr. Patrick Smith, Mrs. Smith, and their son, Jonathan."

"Don't forget Chauncey," Jonathan said.

"And Chauncey," Frisco added. Chauncey wagged his tail furiously. "Smith family, this is Miss Adams."

"Pleased to meet you," Caroline said. "I know the last name is common, but are you and Frisco related?"

Patrick guffawed. "As family as you'll get from any of us. We were both in the same home, and they named all of us foundlings Smith. Going by their logic, I have more brothers than Father Abraham has sons."

"Foundlings?" Caroline turned to Frisco.

Frisco shot Patrick a warning glance. Not here and not with her. "Patrick was planning to live in Redhawk—my town by the river," he said. "Since that didn't happen, he and his family are staying here for a spell."

"I'm helping a carpenter build him a house," Patrick answered. "He can't keep meeting with clients in a tent."

"If you decided to move to town, the house would be yours," Frisco said to Caroline. If she didn't feel any compassion for him, maybe she'd pity this family. "Think of it, Miss Adams. Instead of lonely evenings by the river, you could live in this exciting metropolis."

She lowered her eyes. Frisco hadn't meant to make her uncomfortable in front of his friends, but if she would only consider . . .

"It was a pleasure to meet you," she said.

And that must be his cue. Millie remained bent over the kettle, stirring it aimlessly. Caroline stayed on his far side, nearly hidden as well. But the conversation had run its course.

"I'll be back after dark," Frisco said. "There's a social we're expected to attend, so don't wait up for me."

"Aye, aye, captain," Patrick said.

The sun lingered over the tops of the tents and house frames that spread for a half mile. The air had cooled and turned crisp. Caroline would want his jacket before the evening was over, and Frisco would be happy to loan it to her, if she'd take it. Had he pushed her too hard? If her silence was the product of guilt, then he might have miscalculated. She wouldn't become enamored with someone who made her feel ashamed.

The lot next to the bank's brick wall had been set aside for the city offices, but tonight it was a dance floor. Chairs had been placed around the edges of the lot—Frisco wondered if the chairs were leased—and a rope stretched across the side bordering the street to make a barrier. Having been on the wrong side of that barrier for most of his life, Frisco teetered between pride and annoyance. Yes, he was finally included, but so many worthy men weren't. Well, one had to start somewhere. He'd use his influence for the best.

Before they found the gateway through the rope, they were stopped by a man wearing a striped shirt and knickers.

"How about a commemorative photograph with the lady?" he asked. "Years from now you can boast to your children that you were at the first ball of Plainview."

"We're not married," Caroline said. "He's only escorting—"

"But a photograph would be a novelty," said Frisco. "Don't you want a memory of tonight?"

In all his life, Frisco had only had two photographs taken of him. Once when he was a toddler and they were trying to place him with a family, and the second time when he'd posed with a group of boomers for a Kansas paper sympathetic to their plight. Yet people of his class—or at least the class he aspired to be a member of—had pictures of themselves in their homes. Framed proof of their significance.

Caroline's gaze traveled toward the music and the dancing couples. She smiled. "You're right. Why not, indeed?"

"If I may impose, is my cravat straight? Any red dirt from my work on the roof?"

Caroline did a slow appraisal of him. She gently brushed off one shoulder and then, grasping his neckcloth with both hands, gave it a slight tug sideways. "You look dashing, Mr. Smith."

"I was aiming for respectable."

"You are respectable, but that doesn't mean you must look it, right?" She met and held his gaze.

She was no longer protected by her tender age. Did she think she was safely out of his reach? That she could flirt with impunity and nothing would come of it?

A reckless desire ran through him. He grinned. "Let's get a photo and be a part of history."

A painted canvas was pegged to the side of the photographer's wagon, and an oriental carpet was spread on the grass beneath. He had two braziers lighting up the mountain scene painted on the canvas. Caroline stood next to the Grecian column, and Frisco stood tall and straight next to her.

"Angle toward each other," the photographer directed. "Yes, that's it."

"I've never posed for a picture with anyone outside of my family," Caroline said, trying not to move her lips.

"I've never posed with any family," Frisco replied. He tilted his hat up so the flash wouldn't shade his eyes.

"All right now, on the count of three I'll pull the cord," the photographer said. "Be ready. It's bright when it blows."

Caroline was prepared. Shoulders back, chin lifted, and hands folded sedately, she knew the proper pose, but her lips curled with a hint of a confident smile. He wasn't as sure how he was supposed to look, but he turned to the camera's glass eye and prayed that he didn't look too out of place next to this beautiful woman.

The flash was blinding. Frisco squeezed his eyes closed, but a purple cloud filled his vision.

"One more picture," the photographer called.

With a grimace, Frisco resumed his station, and this time the flash wasn't as painful. When the photographer thanked them, he knew they should leave, but all he could make out were the braziers burning on either side of them.

He felt Caroline's hand on his arm. "I've never had that done at night," she laughed. "Can you see?"

"Not a thing." He took her arm. "Blind leading the blind?"

She leaned on him, bumping against his arm as she missed a step. "He said the picture will help us remember the event, but we're going to be incapable of actually seeing it, much less dancing."

The big blob of color in his vision was fading, as was her melancholy. They'd stumbled somewhere out of the way, but Frisco kept up a hand so they wouldn't trip over the boundary rope. He couldn't help but join her laughter when he thought of how ridiculous he must look. Making a good impression was his first aim, and here he was, blinded and helpless.

But they were having fun.

"It's getting better," Caroline said. "I can see people, just not their faces."

"I hope we're not introduced to anyone before the faces come back." But through the purple blot, he could see the hint of devilment in her eyes. "There, I think I'm ready now."

"I'll follow your lead." Although she didn't release his arm, she straightened for a more formal entrance.

It was no more than a grassy lot, but the participants walked about with the pride of a ballroom, or at least that was what Frisco figured, since he'd never been to a ballroom. A trimmed and combed gent stopped fiddling with his cuff links when they approached.

"Your names?" he asked.

"Mr. Frisco Smith and Miss Adams," Frisco said.

"I don't know—"

Caroline leaned forward. "By invitation of Deputy McFarland."

"Oh, Mr. McFarland told you to come?" He lifted the rope that stretched between two chairs. "C'mon in, then."

Frisco had to admit, Caroline's artfully timed interjection was more successful than the challenge he'd been fixing to issue. But once inside, Frisco knew how to meet the right people. Or at least he thought he did. Mr. Feldstein made introductions nicely enough, but he might as well be leaning for the weight of the chip on his shoulder. Anthony Bledsoe, the new mayor, kept looking at the top of Frisco's head as if trying to measure who was taller—Bledsoe was—and Melvin Sorenson asked him twice where he got his suit made and if he knew a good tailor in the territory.

But word had already gotten around about Miss Adams. Instead of offensive challenges, she was met with deferential questions about her father's health and what it was like to grow up surrounded by the reservations.

Caroline answered graciously but adroitly turned the conversation to current matters. "What did you say your profession was, Mr. Feldstein? Oh my, another federal deputy? How did you go from blacksmithing to law enforcement? Mr. Sorenson, you don't have a horse? However did you get here in time to claim a lot on foot? The Premiers of Plainview, that's what people are calling you? How quaint. Yes, Mr. Bledsoe, please introduce me to your wife. I'm quite an admirer of the arts. Perhaps we could arrange a musical evening soon."

Caroline set them at ease, while Frisco only ruffled feathers. It was no wonder that he and Caroline parted ways early in the evening, but after a discussion on the levying of fines for gambling in the street grew dull, Frisco approached her with an offering of raspberry punch in his hand.

Caroline rose from the bench of ladies when she saw him coming. The burning braziers behind her shadowed her face, but her red hair caught every fiery hue. No wonder heads turned when she walked by. Not everyone knew her pedigree, but her beauty was evident.

She cradled the cup in her hands. "Has your time been beneficial?"

Terrific. He'd gone from valuing her for her connections to evaluating her on her appearance. But he couldn't have his head turned. He had to remember how much he stood to lose. A true relationship with her was off-limits.

"Do you want to dance?" he asked. Frisco had always had a hard time observing limits.

"That's why I came." Caroline set her drink down on a nearby barrel. "The festivities are nearly over, and I haven't accomplished anything."

Oh, but she had. She'd gotten him past the first awkward introductions and established him as someone with connections and class. With Miss Adams at his side, he was respected and envied. The association would get him into the circles he longed to move in years before he could have earned the right on his own. He owed her a dance or two.

If only he knew how to dance.

"Shall we wait until the next song begins?" he asked. He needed a few minutes to figure this out. He watched as the couples moved gracefully over the ground, alternating steps but doubling up on the third. The primary objective seemed to be to show off the lady's dress and avoid collisions with other couples. Frisco might get the steps wrong, but if the song was slow enough, he could figure it out as he went.

His attention shifted from the dancers' feet to the dancers themselves. So these elegant people were the upper echelons of Plainview? How fascinating that they'd been thrown together and were now finding their place. Many claimed to have been leaders from their hometowns, proving that even though the city was new, there was no such thing as an even playing field in life. Whether by experience, talent, funds, or desire, these people were destined to guide the city through its infancy until it was ready to stand proud in the new land. And if robbed of his own plot, Frisco would be a leader here.

"Y'all grab your favorite girl, because we're going to stop with the sleepy music and play something to wake you up." The speaker was Bill Matthews, the councilman-come-lately. "We have the best caller west of St. Louis here tonight. The band will kick it up, and we'll get to toe-tappin'."

Hearing the fiddle player break into a lively tune, the spectators on the other side of the rope crowded forward, while the finely dressed ladies and gentlemen moved away from the center. Frisco took Caroline's hand to lead her away. He knew a jig or two and could do some stomping with the best of them, but Caroline, like the other fine ladies, wouldn't approve. It was a pity. The music was good, the air festive . . .

"You promised me a dance," Caroline said.

"It's a barn dance. Do you know—"

"How to do-si-do and promenade? Those enlisted men danced every week, and they don't like to waltz with each other." She narrowed her eyes. "Or maybe *you* don't know how. . . ."

Frisco took off his hat and tossed it onto the barrel. "Try me."

Matthews and his wife had taken the floor. His daughter had found a partner, and the Sorensons joined them. Four couples.

"Maybe I shouldn't have suggested this," Matthews said, "but it seemed a more fitting kind of dance for the people I represent on the council."

"You did the right thing," Caroline assured him as they formed a circle. "This will be great fun."

And it was. Frisco and Caroline stood across from each other. Her shoulders bounced as if hammered by the rhythm of the music. The light reflected off the sheen of her dress as her skirt snapped in the wind. Mr. Matthews and his wife skipped to the middle and joined hands. Frisco could only catch glimpses of Caroline as the couple spun between them. The finery Caroline wore didn't seem to fit the folksy outdoor music, but her vivaciousness couldn't be contained indoors.

Matthews and his wife parted, and Frisco and Caroline danced toward each other. They spun so quickly that if his hands had slipped, they both would have fallen on the ground.

He held fast. They didn't fall. Her smile remained clear while the people behind them blurred into bright colors.

He'd once seen her riding bareback, streaking toward the fort with her hair flying out behind her. It had surprised him, because she'd always seemed jaded, on her guard lest her dignity be questioned. But that glimpse showed him an unbridled side of her that he hadn't suspected. And here, her mouth open, head thrown back, stomping her heels against the soft grass field as they paired off for another promenade, he saw the same woman who longed to live life to the fullest instead of being constrained by convention. The kind of woman who would make a death-defying run in a race and then hold on to the land she'd won by her fingernails, even if it was certainly hopeless that she would ever succeed.

Frisco caught her around the waist and held her to his side for their next revolution. Despite the scented powder she wore, her fair complexion glowed pink from the exertion. The fiddler increased the tempo. Mr. and Mrs. Sorenson were huffing to keep up with the steps. Mrs. Matthews finally stepped out of the set with a hand against her bosom, leaning on her husband's arm.

Caroline didn't falter. Frisco lengthened his stride so they covered more ground with each rotation. Without pause, she matched him, their bodies moving in tandem. Her skirts flew as he spun her, then switched sides to spin counter to the clock. Her nimble feet didn't lag as the crowd shouted their encouragement. Her eyes flashed. Her hair dampened against her neck. His own suit felt confining.

This time her feet left the ground as Frisco turned her. She had both hands on his shoulders, her face below his, and then she was gone for another quick sashay as the set rounded to a close.

They'd somehow found their original positions opposite each other. The woman standing across from him looked nothing like the one he'd taken a photograph with earlier. Her dress had been impressive then, but now . . . now no one would even notice what she wore. Her clothing was inconsequential compared to her beauty. Just like the bright light of the flash pan had temporarily blinded him, his own breath dulled his hearing. Gradually he became aware of the crowd cheering them on. Remembering their audience, Frisco bowed gallantly to his lady. Caroline swept her gown to the side and curtsied, then came toward him with her hand extended.

She was still winded. So was he, but not so tired that he couldn't take her hand.

"That was fun," he said. "We need to do this every night."

"I agree. Forget the cares of the world—"

"Mr. Smith, that was quite a show," Deputy McFarland said. Mayor Bledsoe and the banker had joined them as well. "You and Miss Adams are adept at winning the admiration of the crowd, and that's a useful skill."

The crowd? At that moment, Frisco wanted to be alone with Caroline more than anything.

"Mr. Smith has always been a persuasive leader." If heightened color could give an opinion more credibility, Caroline's word was as good as gold. "He has a sense for what the common man wants, and he knows how to get it for them." Breathless praise, perhaps only because she was catching her breath.

"That's what I was just telling Mr. Bledsoe." McFarland pulled a handkerchief from the pocket of his uncrumpled suit and dabbed at invisible perspiration on his forehead. "We are certainly glad you've decided to get involved in Plainview. The both of you are an asset."

Frisco darted a sideways look at her. None of his campaigning had ever been so successful, or so enjoyable.

For the last week at her homestead, she'd felt so alone, so isolated, but tonight had been a night of dreams. The spirit she'd tried to hide in Galveston and the skills that were useless at the fort had come to her aid when she'd needed them.

Leaving the glow of a hundred campfires behind them, Caroline and Frisco set off across the dark prairie to her home in the hill. The new moon shed no light on their way, but the clear sky gave them stars by the millions. And in her opinion, each of them twinkled.

"I can't tell if I'm exhausted or exhilarated." Caroline hopped over a rabbit warren that she'd barely seen coming.

"What's the difference?" Frisco asked.

"Whether I think I could do it some more," she said.

He grinned and took her hand. Higher and higher he swung it while they walked, until it was high enough that she could pass beneath his arm for another spin.

"Knowing how irrepressible you are, I should've guessed that you'd dance like a fury," he said after her pirouette.

"Knowing how persistent you are, I should've figured that you'd dance until they dragged you off the floor."

She stood on her tiptoes and motioned for him to pass under the arch. He scrunched down to fit, bumping against her side as he twisted through. Emerging, he threw his arm out wide and spun around to swoop her up against himself.

This was no longer a dance. Her feet were back on terra firma, and she was in his arms, held against his warmth. Wind whistling over the grass was the only music they swayed to now, rocking each other gently. The cool night air caressed her bare arms as they stretched up around his neck. An auburn curl caught the wind and teased his face.

At the dance, Caroline had thrown caution to the wind. She'd ridden the excitement wherever it had led, but it was leading somewhere definite now. Or was that what Frisco wanted her to think?

"Caroline?"

She'd heard the same tone from the swains in Galveston, but she hadn't expected Frisco to be able to mimic it so precisely.

"You're calling me Caroline now?" She tilted her head back and wrinkled her nose at him. "That's why Father always cautioned me against robust dancing. '*It leads to familiarity*,' he said." She stepped away, vaguely aware that her inhibitions were fading. But as long as she remembered the consequences of letting down her guard . . .

Frisco rubbed his cheek even as a rueful smile spread across his face. "I wish I'd had a father to teach me the same. Then I wouldn't have to protect myself from young ladies like you."

"Well, maybe you spun me around one too many times. I can't be held liable if I'm too dizzy to stand up straight."

"Then allow me to help you," he said as he offered his arm.

It was a respectable gesture, she supposed. Proof that he was as pleased with the evening as she was.

"I've never apologized for what I said to you before the race." His voice was low and even as they walked along the riverbank. "I had no right to evaluate you in the first place, and when I did, I did it poorly."

"Your words hit the mark," Caroline admitted. "I haven't been at ease since I returned. In fact, I never cottoned to Galveston either. The city was too confining. Sure, there's excitement and activity, but I couldn't enjoy it because I was too busy making sure I enjoyed it the correct way. In society, you can't react honestly."

"And that's why you came back?" he asked.

"With the whole country talking about the run, I had to come back, but everything had changed."

"Or maybe you had changed?"

"But I haven't. Not really. Yet everyone scorns me like I'm some fragile lady who's going to dry up and blow away with the first windstorm."

"No one scorned you tonight."

"At the party? Of course not, because they're the same sort, trying to impress society. Your friend Patrick's wife, though, did you see her?" Caroline's throat tightened as she watched for his reaction.

"She was cooking," he said. "Busy getting dinner served."

Caroline shook her head. "She didn't want to know me. That's the truth. I have to prove that I'm one of them."

"And settling a homestead will do that?"

She ran her finger over the button on the cuff of his sleeve. She didn't want to revive the argument. Not while the night was still golden with contentment.

They'd arrived at the house. Frisco held the door open for her. At first she feared that he was going to stay, but he motioned to the lamp.

"Get it lit first, and then I'll go."

"It's late, and you have a long walk back." She struck a match and held it to the wick. The light swelled and filled the room.

"After the ruckus we raised tonight, maybe everyone will sleep in."

"Not the roosters." Caroline placed the chimney over the flame, then went to the door.

He'd taken to studying her again, and this time his swarthy features looked perplexed. "I should curse you," he said. "What's wrong with me?"

He didn't look like he was in a cursing mood. Her senses sharpened. If he decided to take liberties, would she have the fortitude to resist? She couldn't be sure, but she was willing to find out.

With a sweeping bow, Frisco removed his hat. "I had a pleasant evening, Miss Adams. Thank you for the gift of your company."

"It was a gift I enjoyed bestowing." She dipped a small curtsy.

"You know, after all these years, it seems that I've had misconceptions about you too."

His eyebrow jogged, and his lips spread into a smile. "Do tell."

"I thought you were a dashing, reckless, romantic figure who would forever remain out of reach. A hero to be admired from afar." She lowered her eyes to the flame of the lamp, but when she raised them, his smile had vanished.

"And now what do you think?" He reached for her. Caught the tips of her fingers in his.

Even though they were in the warm shelter, a chill ran through her. "You aren't so distant after all," she said. "Be careful, Mr. Smith. I might have a game of my own."

"I expect nothing less of you, Miss Adams." With a quick squeeze of her hand, he stepped back and waggled the door handle. "You'll lock this as soon as I leave?"

"Of course."

"Good. I don't want anything to happen to my supplies."

"They're in good hands."

"For now," he said. And then, with a wink and a smile, he was gone.

Chapter Sixteen

It had been a long two days, but productive. The reins jangled as Amber urged Gunpowder across one more homestead and on to home. Gunpowder's tail swished away the flies as Amber rotated her parasol to discourage the pesky insects. Bradley hadn't liked the idea of her riding to Kingfisher alone, but it needed to be done. Until they filed their claim at the land office, they were vulnerable to anyone who wanted to swear possession of it. Someone like Caroline with a dugout completed and crops planted would have a stronger case. Honest people like Amber and Bradley needed the piece of paper to show that they'd been there all along. At least until they had something more substantial than a one-room wooden frame covered in canvas.

She brushed a fly off her face. Not that she thought Caroline was dishonest. Not really. But she was hardheaded, just like Amber's fiancé. And Amber was caught in the middle.

A hawk swooped down ahead of her and snatched up a furry rodent for dinner. One less thief to raid her supplies, Amber reckoned. At least she hoped it was a mouse and not a rabbit. They would need all the rabbits they could get if they were going to have enough to eat before their crops came in.

But they had the land. Amber had the paper in her pocket, and it was registered at the land office as well. It had been two weeks since the race. She hadn't expected the line to be so long, but it looked like many others had done as she had—waited until the first rush was over before venturing off their homesteads. And then she'd made her wait even longer. When she got up to the front of the line, a man in chaps and boots had offered her five dollars if he could take her place in line.

Amber only hesitated a second. Five dollars? She pocketed the money, then went to the back of the line and waited again. If she wasn't worried about leaving their farm unattended, she would have stayed all day waiting in line for those wages.

She knew the moment they stepped hoof on her property. What was it that made this square of grass different from all the others? Love? Less than two weeks until the wedding. Ten days, to be exact, and she'd be Mrs. Bradley Willis. Then she'd have another certificate in her pocket, telling her that her plans had come to fruition.

But here was another wrinkle.

The man saw her riding up—he must have—but instead of coming forward to greet her, he darted into her house. With grim resolution, Amber folded her parasol, tucked it into her saddle roll, and took out a pistol. She'd dealt with claim jumpers ever since the twenty-second of last month, but for the most part, they were merely argumentative. No one had wanted to ambush her in her own home.

The four posts of her house covered the same amount of space as a wagon bed. Wooden crossbeams stretched from post to post and supported the oiled canvases that Bradley had nailed into them. One canvas had a hole cut for the stovepipe, and that stovepipe was wisping out smoke. There was someone inside. She hadn't imagined it.

Staying on her horse, Amber rode around to the flap that

served as a doorway. Gunpowder's ears twitched as she tried to figure out what was happening. Amber laid the pistol on her lap but kept her hand on it.

"Come on outside," she called. "I know you're in there."

The wind blew the flap open. She caught a glimpse of a man's legs before the canvas settled down again. Her breath was short and choppy. Her knees knocked against the saddle.

"No use in hiding," she tried again. "I'm not leaving."

What could he be doing? She didn't have anything of value in there. Her parents would bring her trousseau with them for the wedding.

And then she smelled the turnips frying.

Amber flexed her hands and loosened the reins. She squinted at the flapping tarp. "Come on out," she said. "I'll let you finish your dinner, but I'd feel better if I got a look at you."

The canvas lifted. The trespasser was dirty, tired, and not much more than a boy. He held her only tin plate in one hand and rubbed the back of his neck with the other.

"I'm sorry, ma'am. When I found no one here, I thought perhaps you'd absconded. Looked to take this claim for myself. When I saw the vittles, I knew you'd be back, but I was so hungry, I couldn't help myself. Some turnips and potatoes. I didn't take anything else, I swear."

He seemed like a harmless sort, but Amber preferred the safety of her mount all the same.

"It's been a spell since you've eaten?" she asked.

"Yes, ma'am. Came for the race but didn't prove out. Since then I've been wandering, looking for work. People everywhere are hard-pressed to feed themselves, much less take on a hand."

That might be her and Bradley once his military pay ceased. She nodded in understanding. "Get finished and move on out. As you can see, I don't have anything to spare either."

He shifted his weight to one leg as he took another bite of

food. "That's a fact. If you need some work done for the meal, I'm happy to oblige."

Amber sighed. How she'd love to have him plow another row or two, but he was a stranger, and she was all alone. Better to send him on his way.

"Thanks for the offer. I have to pass for now, but you might find work in Kingfisher. I got paid to stand in line."

"No fooling? You've been more than kind. I'll set this plate back inside, and then I'll go."

The young man did exactly as he'd said with a generous amount of hat-tipping and thanks. Still astride her horse, Amber watched him depart. He'd been pleasant enough, but she didn't like the thought that people were wandering around, helping themselves to the contents of tents. Ten days. Then she would marry Bradley and wouldn't have to worry about being here alone. Not unless he had to go find work. Hopefully by then they'd live in something better than boards and canvases.

Her nose twitched. That wasn't turnips she was smelling. Amber turned to see smoke billowing out of her house. Her jaw dropped as she kicked her heels against the horse's side and raced to the shack.

She didn't remember dismounting or running toward the door. The smoke stinging her eyes was the first thing she knew. The second was that the frying pan atop the stove was ablaze.

"Never trust a man in the kitchen."

But the blaze on the stove wasn't her greatest concern. It was the piece of canvas behind the stove that had caught fire. Maybe she should have grabbed her bedclothes and pulled everything out of the shack, but instead she attacked the canvas. Picking up their new shovel, she beat at the burning canvas. She turned her face away from the flying sparks, only daring a peek when she felt the canvas give beneath her strikes.

With her lungs burning and her eyes streaming, she finally

got the burning canvas down off the frame. Stabbing it with the shovel, she dragged it away so it could burn at a harmless distance. The fire had scorched the crossbeams. They smoldered. Not safe, not yet.

She ran back inside the open shack and grabbed a bucket. She'd have to douse everything that had been touched by the flames before she could be sure there was no more danger. Later, after her daily planting was done, she'd have to wash the smoke from her belongings and off her person, but she could only do one thing at a time.

She'd been so proud of what she'd accomplished in Kingfisher today. She'd gotten her name on a piece of paper, but it had nearly cost her everything else.

Chapter Seventeen

What makes you think the city lots were claimed illegally?" Frisco held his notebook on his knee inside his tent. Over the last week he'd yet to get one of those chairs, and the tree stump he was using instead wasn't comfortable.

Mr. Lacroix kept an eye on the opening as he spoke with a lowered voice. "Don't you think it a mighty big coincidence that so many of the best lots went to deputies and railroad men? I left from ten miles south of Darlington, and my horse didn't falter once. Yet when I arrived, there was a welcoming committee already in place, telling me where to go for the empty lots." He was clean-shaven, or maybe he had Indian blood. His dark eyes strengthened Frisco's hunch.

"Maybe they had faster horses than you?" Frisco asked. It was his job to be skeptical. This was a potential legal challenge, not a rousing speech.

"They'd have to be mighty fine horses to take time off the clock. Do you know what was on their lots while they were standing there pretending to be the law? There were fires with hot coals and ashes. Dirty dishes and scrap buckets."

"Any construction?"

Mr. Lacroix shook his head. "Only tents. Nothing permanent, but their mounts weren't winded, and the horses had been there long enough to leave their marks as well. I walked up and down every street around town square. I can tell you who hadn't run at noon, and it's all the men who are calling themselves the Premiers of Plainview."

Now it was Frisco keeping one eye on the flap of the tent, worried they'd be overheard. Patrick was tooling a leather saddle away from the tents and couldn't hear over the distance, but these kinds of accusations traveled fast. Yet the same thought had nagged at Frisco as well.

"What do you want to do about it?" Frisco asked.

"I want you to file a claim on behalf of the regular man against them. I heard that you helped Nesbitt get his plot."

"That was a simple case. One man tried to hold a plot for a friend. There was no question of who was in the right there."

"And there shouldn't be any question with these men either. I want you to file a claim against a lot on Main Street in my name. I could've claimed it had there not been someone there illegally. I'm willing to challenge them and let them explain what I've said before a judge," said Lacroix.

Frisco tapped his pencil against the paper. "These are serious charges. You'd be turning this town upside down."

"Better to do it now before they're more entrenched. Just think of all the people camping in the streets that they're trying to run off. If they hadn't cheated, those people would be building their own houses right now instead of begging for paying work."

Like Patrick. How Frisco would like to see Patrick with one of the lots near the square. But could the case be proven? He thought of Ike McFarland and the other deputies. Unless Mr. Lacroix and Frisco could come up with some proof, they were spitting in the wind. Not only working to no purpose, but making enemies along the way.

"You should know, Mr. Lacroix, that the city has asked me to work on their behalf. That means I'd be reporting to many of the men you are accusing. What if I decide to investigate your case and find that your suspicions have no grounds? Knowing my association with them, are you going to trust my findings?"

"Mr. Smith, I saw you at the election when they were running the same men through the lines. You told the truth then. I imagine you'll do it again."

He would, if he knew beyond a shadow of a doubt that they were guilty. But shadows lurked in the sunniest of places, and Frisco had no desire to upset the applecart when he was trying to hitch a ride on it.

"Exactly who are you accusing?" Frisco asked.

"The first man to meet me was Deputy Bledsoe, now the mayor, and Deputy Sorenson, although Sorenson dropped the deputy title fast enough and is now calling himself a banker. Feldstein and Juarez were there too. Cool as an icehouse, directing people where they could set up camp. Made sense, seeing how they were deputies, but it doesn't seem fair that deputies could compete in the contest."

Frisco had thought he'd take notes, but he didn't want any piece of paper with those names on it. "If they were lined up with everyone else at noon, I don't reckon we have any cause to complain."

"That's a big *if*," Lacroix said.

"You didn't mention Deputy McFarland. Do you think he came early as well?"

Lacroix shrugged. "There was a mess of them already here. I don't remember him in particular."

Interesting. Perhaps he wasn't involved after all. "You've given me a lot to think over," Frisco said. Besides Mr. Lacroix's name, his pad of paper remained blank. There was no sense in slandering people until he knew for sure whether they were guilty. "As I said, because of my connection with the founders of the city, I'm not sure I'm the one for the job—"

"Would you want to live in a city run by crooks?"

"—but I will consider your case. At the very least, perhaps I can direct you to someone else who could help you."

"But you won't tell them, will you? Not until we're ready to file against their claims?"

"Our conversation is protected by confidentiality, I assure you." The last thing Frisco wanted was for the Premiers to think he was questioning their right to own property in the town they were running. Not until he knew more. "In the meantime—"

He paused at a noise outside. Over the wind, he heard his name and then Patrick's answer.

"This is Frisco's place, but he's busy. A client, he said."

Mr. Lacroix's face settled into stubborn lines. "We have company."

Could it be Caroline? He hadn't seen her since the night of the dance—a night he'd enjoyed more than he'd expected. Every morning began with him determined to see her and get her off his property once and for all, but before he could leave Plainview, he got mired down correcting the wrongs others had suffered.

Frisco closed the cover on his notebook and dropped it into his traveling case. "No worries, Mr. Lacroix. I've faced down my share of authorities. If there's something amiss, you have me on your side."

But he wasn't yet ready to stand behind the allegations.

His visitor wasn't Caroline. It was none other than Sophie Smith and her husband. She walked up to Frisco, her short skirt revealing a set of unmatched boots, and shoved a piece of crumb cake into his hands.

"We need you to do that fancy talking for us." She brushed

the crumbs off her hands and pulled Mr. Wilton closer by the sleeve. "Tell Frisco what the city told you."

Mr. Wilton's gouty knees made him look like he was in the process of lowering himself into a chair. Frisco didn't own a chair, so the peddler stood there half squatting. "The city man came. It was earlier this morning. We were still selling breakfast—"

"He said we owe a dollar for a permit," Sophie interrupted. "Said we had to have a permit to sell anything here."

Frisco let a bite of the crumb cake melt in his mouth before he answered. "What city ordinance established that?"

"Told you he'd be the one to talk to," Sophie said. She nudged her husband. "Go on. Tell him."

"There ain't no city law that I know. I don't remember voting—"

"He wanted the money in his hand," Sophie said. "Cash money. Why would we be handing over our cash money just because some bloke shows up at the wagon asking for it? What's he got to do with it?"

"Who was asking?" Frisco flicked a crumb off his shirt.

Mr. Wilton grunted as he tried to straighten his back, then settled back down into his peculiar squat. "I'd never seen him before. He said he was a new deputy but looked like a dirt farmer. Had ears the size of—"

"When he was gone, McFarland came and asked us lots of questions. He asked why we thought we had the right to squat in Plainview without land. I told him it was a free country, and he said that people pay fees, even in a free country. Then I told him we knew a lawyer and we'd be talking to you about it. After that, he said he'd leave it be for a spell, but we needed to come to an understanding, and soon."

"You've got to obey the laws, even if the laws are new," Frisco said.

"I don't like it, Frisco," Sophie replied. "I think those deputies are just wandering around, coming up with ways to shake a dollar off my limbs."

How, in all his planning and preparing, had Frisco underestimated his fellow man's propensity for bickering? Settling disputes like this could be a full-time job. No wonder McFarland was content to walk away and let Frisco deal with them.

"Deputy McFarland is a busy man," Frisco said. "I'll check the new ordinances and let you know if you owe anything. Until then—"

"Does it strike you as odd," Sophie said, "that McFarland doesn't do any deputying? Back in Topeka, he bought and sold property. He takes this post to bring the law to the people, and now he's spending all his time measuring roads, arranging elections, and having secret meetings." She looked at her husband and, seeing his crooked necktie, began to fuss over him.

"Just because you weren't invited doesn't make them secret," Frisco said. The way she tugged on her husband's collar had Frisco fearing that she would knock the old man over. "And once things like property lines and streets are settled, there'll be less unrest. People will simmer down and get comfortable. Establishing the city can't wait until all the hubbub dies down. It's got to be the priority."

Sophie had quit messing with Mr. Wilton's collar. Her eyes glazed over with the same bored looked she used to get when Frisco gave her the complete narrative of a street fight he'd seen. "If it happens again, we'll fetch you," she said.

Frisco finished the last bite of cake. "I'd be happy to check into it. In the meantime, live peaceably as much as you can."

"You're one to talk." Sophie took Mr. Wilton by the arm and helped him turn around in twenty-six slow, shuffling steps. Once they were faced the right way, she waved her arm over her head as a farewell, her loose red sleeve catching the wind and ballooning full sail.

Frisco stood with his hands on his hips and looked past them at the activity all around him. The town was as busy as an anthill. Toting, hauling, constructing, bartering—everyone was scrambling to improve their lot in life. Unfortunately, a few were also swindling, cheating, and hogwashing to improve their lots. All the virtues and vices of the human race on display. All but one: There weren't any lazy people about. Lazy people didn't want any part of it.

Would Redhawk have been the same? Frisco stepped forward to steady a stack of packages a man was carrying as he walked past. With a nod of his head, the man continued. Had Frisco gotten what he wanted, would they be this far along in their progress? Or would his planning and his city map have proved superior to the hasty settlement that had gone on here?

Was it too late to find out?

He was running out of time. How many of his investors were watching the calendar for May 22? He hoped with each passing day—each day of construction on his house in town, each day Caroline was faced with monotonous labor—that she would reconsider his offer to trade lots. But she wouldn't be likely to capitulate if he didn't remind her.

He gathered his papers and notebooks into his traveling case. That was all that was laid out, since he'd never completely unpacked his case. Not until he was home, and this tent was not home.

He'd rather leave his bag somewhere more secure than his tent, so he carried it out to Patrick.

"Are you moving out?" Patrick asked around the three nails in his mouth.

"I'm coming back, but can I put this inside your wagon until then? I don't want my notes to blow away. I might bed down at the fort if the weather turns tonight."

"The fort where the redhead is from?" Patrick grinned, dropping the nails from his mouth. His expression was reminiscent of the eleven-year-old boy who used to help Frisco sneak out at night. "I don't know what she sees in a scalawag like you."

"I didn't say she saw anything. Why? Do you think she likes me?"

"Always fishing for a compliment, aren't you? Well, I'm sure it was just indigestion or some other malady. She'll recover soon enough. In the meantime, keep your socks dry—"

"—and your stomach full. Thanks, Paddy. I'll remember that."

After a brief explanation to Millie, Frisco stowed his goods in the wagon and set out on foot. He'd rather leave his horse in the care of the livery man for this short walk. The smell of fresh grass overtook the hundreds of campfires as he passed through town and out to the fields. Funny how it had only been a couple of weeks, and already the sod in town shared man's smell.

What was he going to do with Caroline? Part of him feared that he'd crossed a line the night of the dance. He wasn't such a cad that he'd play on her sentiments for profit. Or was he? He found her intriguing. Did their dispute forbid him from admiring her?

Not wanting to incur the wrath of her father, he had to tread lightly. Not wanting his property damaged, he would work to help her maintain it. Not wanting to leave her empty-handed, he was preparing the town lot so it would be a tempting alternative. It was like threading a needle while riding in a runaway buggy.

Approaching his land from the north brought him past Caroline's friend's plot. Miss Herald had a bag of seeds tied over her shoulder and was spreading them over a newly plowed field. It would be rude not to say hello once she spotted him. Frisco veered off course as Miss Herald crossed the field to meet him.

"Good day, Miss Herald," he said. "Looks like you've been busy."

She lifted her chin, and Frisco tried not to gape. Her face was covered in soot, and her hair was mussed. Even her dress was singed.

"I don't want to be ungallant, but you've . . ."

"I'm well aware, Mr. Smith. I had a fire in my kitchen, and since my kitchen is the only room in my house, it was quite an ordeal."

"Is everything all right? Is there anything I can do?"

"Thank you, but no. It's out. I'm trying not to get behind in my planting."

"I won't keep you any longer, then. I'm just passing through."

"On your way to see your claim?" Her blue eyes narrowed beneath the brim of her straw hat. "I want you to know that we didn't intend for her to take your property. That wasn't the idea, and we've let her know it."

Frisco took a step back. Even Caroline's best friend took his side? Interesting. "I would think that Miss Adams's plans would be more suited to town than a lonely farm. Although I did see her designs for her house. They're impressive."

"Thank you. I helped her draw them up, but that was before she and Bradley crossed swords. Unless one of them blinks, it's going to be downright uncomfortable around here." Miss Herald slung her arm in an arc, sprinkling seeds everywhere.

Frisco had been ready to leave, but that statement warranted asking after. "What does Corporal Willis have to do with this?"

"He knows you've been wronged. He feels horrible about benefiting from Caroline's help while she was taking advantage of you."

Frisco twisted his mouth in thought. It would be ungallant to encourage Corporal Willis in his outrage. On the other hand, when counting allies, Bradley Willis was a good man to have on your side. Especially as Caroline's closest neighbor. Yet Frisco knew to be careful wading into family disputes. He'd learned from fighting on the streets that no matter how estranged two brothers were, you had to watch your back when fighting one if the other was present.

"Tell Bradley thanks for his concern, but I'll deal with Miss Adams in my own time. Meanwhile, if she needs something from you, please help her. I don't want her out here without any friends or family to rely on." Besides him. He'd be there for her. One didn't let a lady of one's acquaintance struggle alone if there was remedy for it.

Miss Herald eyed him shrewdly. "I won't make promises I can't keep. Just look around." She flung another handful of seeds to the wind. "I'm up to my eyebrows in work. If Caroline can't make it on her own, she might as well give your land back. Good day, Mr. Smith."

Frisco tipped his hat and moved on. Caroline seemed to have a knack for getting crossways with people. That was why he found her so interesting.

He spotted Caroline from a distance. A bright sunbonnet shaded her auburn hair as she put a foot on a shovel and hopped to drive it into the ground. She clearly hadn't given up yet, even though lifting the shovelful of rich soil was a strain. She flipped the shovel, turning over the soil, then stabbed it back into the ground with a thud. Without pause, she broke the sod again and turned over another scoop of virgin earth.

Good thing he'd worn his working clothes. Frisco needed more land broken, and she'd picked the perfect spot. On his map, this area was part of the land he was going to keep. As soon as Nesbitt finished building Frisco's house in Plainview, he'd have him come out and start on his home here at Redhawk. By winter, he'd have a snug place to sit by the fire, safe from the cold wind. It might be awkward if Caroline wasn't gone by then.

A dark wet line on her blouse ran the length of her spine. The air was heavy with humidity but missing the usual cooling breeze. But then a gust came at them, swirling her skirt around the shovel as she stepped on it again.

She startled when she saw him. He noticed her hands tighten around the shovel, but then her chin came up and she composed herself. With unusual patience, she waited for him to get close enough to deliver her pert address without undue exertion.

"Mr. Smith, how pleasant it is to see you. What brings you so far from your home?" Her face glistened with sweat. A thin wisp of hair was plastered to her neck.

"Far from home? I disagree." He kicked at a dirt clod as he inspected her work. "What exactly are you doing to my homestead?"

Ignoring his assertion, she turned over another heavy scoop of earth. "I'm putting in a garden of specialized and profitable herbs. I have to have more than the paltry square you planted."

"I appreciate your help, but don't expect any compensation. I can't afford to pay you for improvements on my land."

She grunted as she dug in again. "To tell the truth, I might as well work. Otherwise, the days go by so slow and lonely."

"Lonely? With your friend Miss Herald so near?" The shadow that crossed her face told him he'd hit the mark, but she didn't let it linger.

"Your company is appreciated, but I'm not confident in my ability to maintain a conversation while laboring. Please don't think me rude."

Her pink cheeks brought to mind the vigorous dance they'd shared. Frisco filled his lungs in a long draw. That was a memory he would enjoy for years.

"Save your breath," he said. "I can chew the fat while you work and cure your loneliness at the same time."

He found a clear spot in the grass out of reach of the sharp point of her shovel and flopped on the ground next to her canteen. He bent a stalk of grass in two and set it between his teeth.

Her shadow danced, stark and defined, over the ground as she moved. The moist heat from the earth amplified the scent of prairie grass beneath him.

He'd sat here and passed the time many a day. Catching his breath after digging the well or constructing the dugout, he'd enjoy the breeze here on the plain and imagine what life would be like once the territory was open and the land was truly his.

Having Caroline Adams working his garden was never in the plans. If it weren't for the implications of her presence, he might have enjoyed having such a determined companion. He rolled the stem between his teeth. Maybe he was enjoying it despite the implications.

"Things in town are progressing," he said. "You might be interested to know that there's a church meeting regularly on Sundays and Wednesdays. Some industrious ladies managed to put together a Sunday dinner after church, which shows promise of being a regular event."

"I've missed church," Caroline wheezed. "I'll come to the next one."

"I thought you might. You know, it'd be easier to attend if you lived closer. The house on my property has the frame up already. In another week the roof and walls should be completed. It'll still be rustic, but better than the rabbit hole you're living in now."

"No, thank you." She seemed to be moving more quickly now. "I told you, your plot in town isn't large enough for what I have planned." The furrow had reached the length she wanted, and she started on a second row running parallel. No telling how fast she could have worked if she'd had a plow. Frisco decided buying her a plow went against his self-interest.

"In case you're concerned about my well-being," he continued, "I've been retained by several citizens over various legal questions. So far about half my pay has been in barter, but

I'm finding that the work searches me out. That's unexpected. Honestly, I imagined that my only chance at success here was being the founder of Redhawk. I didn't understand how easy it is to succeed in a new territory. There are no old guards. Everyone has a shot."

He fingered the stitching on his moccasin boots, looking for loose spots that might need to be resewn. "I guess when it comes down to it, I was just looking for a way to rise to the top. I thought I needed to control every aspect of the town to do that. Now it looks like I was mistaken. When Ike McFarland asked me to represent the city, that's when I had to check myself. Me? Frisco Smith? In my experience, I'm more likely to be run out of town than be asked to serve with the city leaders. But who knows? If they find out more about me, they might send me packing after all. Until then—"

He flinched as the shovel dug into the ground near his knee. Caroline dropped to the grass next to him. She reached for the canteen, took a long drink, then settled in, sitting cross-legged in her loose work dress.

"If they find out what about you? What are you hiding?"

Frisco's throat jogged as he tried to remember exactly what he'd said. He hadn't really thought she was listening. "You can't stay here," he said. "You said yourself that you get lonely. Trade me plots. You should be in town—"

Caroline ignored the bead of sweat rolling down her cheek. She was completely focused on him, just when he didn't want her to be. "What are you afraid they're going to find out? Everyone knows you're a boomer. Everyone knows you've been arrested repeatedly. It's part of your credentials. What else is there for them to know?"

Images flashed before his eyes. The boy hiding in his bed with blankets over his head while older boys fought in the foundling house. The runaway ducking behind barrels in an alley to hide from a deputy. The youngster waiting until after dark before spreading a blanket in the livery, hoping to get a full night's sleep before he was run off.

Caroline's gaze sharpened. "What are you hiding?" She gave him time to answer, then added, "Am I safe here with you?"

"Of course," he said. "I'd never hurt you or any other woman. Your father knows my criminal history well enough. If he was worried about my character, don't you think he'd find a way to have me shipped off?"

"Your friend said something about being a foundling. What did he mean by that?"

"You know the meaning of the word."

"But I don't know all that it implies. Were you adopted?"

"No."

"Lived in an orphanage?"

Frisco had mangled the grass he was chewing. He feared her knowing his deficiencies more than anything, and at the same time he wanted her to know. He wanted her to know him. Of all the people he'd met in his life, Caroline seemed to have the sense to understand. To withhold both scorn and pity.

He began to talk. "Living in an orphanage was a nightmare. Bigger kids picking on the little ones. Feeling adrift, trying to make friends and then watching those friends get moved without any warning. But the outside world was sympathetic. Ladies' groups would make us clothes. Churches would serve us meals on holidays. As long as we stayed with the orphanage, everyone pretended to care about us."

Why was he telling her this? Him, a grown man, bellyaching about whether he was cared for. She'd think him weak. He tossed away the blade of grass and started to get up, but Caroline grabbed his arm.

"They pretended to care, but . . ."

"I'll break ground. You can rest a spell."

He stood and picked up the shovel. After weeks of meetings and paperwork, he needed to exert himself. He needed to put in a good day's work so he'd be exhausted enough to sleep. Whether he was helping Caroline or helping himself by improving the property didn't matter at this point. The waters were muddied. Just like in town, they were all trying to improve their lots. Progress for one was progress for all.

He worked furiously, trying to ignore the woman still sitting, watching him. When you were on trial, you didn't tell the prosecuting attorney all your secrets. You didn't notify them of your weaknesses. Why would he tell Caroline? With the land dispute between them, she was his opponent.

Wasn't she?

He drove the shovel into the ground. "Every few years, we got moved to another home," he said. "Sometimes it was because of our ages, sometimes it was just that they had too many kids in one institution and empty beds at another. It always meant sudden separation from friends—sometimes without a chance to say good-bye." He churned through the web of roots and grasses, and the red soil appeared, clean and heavy with promise. "We had a spinning waterwheel of acquaintances. Friends, chums, but you never knew when you'd be ripped away and sent somewhere new. It was better to keep to yourself and mind your own business."

"From what I know of you," Caroline said, "minding your own business goes against your nature."

Frisco smiled as he started on a new row. Listening to someone discuss his character outside of a courtroom was a new experience. He supposed children often heard their parents evaluate them, whether for ill or good, but he'd gone through childhood more or less unremarkable and unremarked upon.

"I did it imperfectly and learned from my mistakes. Until I could control the situation, I didn't want to risk again. That's why I ran away. And that's when everything changed." He should be burying this story instead of uncovering it by the shovelful. "I thought I'd find the same support once I was on my own. I thought the kind people who brought us clothes and fed us would want to help even more." He dug deeper. "That wasn't the case."

"They were more interested in helping the institution than an actual child?"

He shrugged. "It's easier that way. They stay clean and separated visiting an orphanage. Helping a kid on the street, well, that can be more complicated. Thankfully, a man came along—David Payne. He was gathering crowds to go into the Unassigned Lands and start settlements. I was used to getting chased away. Nothing new there. At least with Payne, I wasn't alone. And it became a part of a larger calling. It was more than a family. I was part of a movement."

"A leader," she said. "Respected and admired by many."

"But none who knew my beginning."

And now that she knew, did it change anything?

⌘

Caroline skimmed her hands over the grass, letting it tickle her aching palms, but she didn't take her eyes off Frisco. This talk was too important. From the very beginning of their acquaintance, his confidence had drawn her attention, but there had always been something more that kept her spellbound. Beneath the bravado, aside from the indomitable spirit that drew the trust of crowds, was a yearning for acceptance that twisted an unguarded place in Caroline's heart.

Although she wouldn't have been able to guess for herself, Frisco's words rang true to what she'd suspected. He'd always been alone in the world. He didn't expect acceptance, but he coveted it greatly. There was much to admire in his determination, but his story made her sad more than anything.

"This whole experiment with the land run and the settlers, all of this is because of you and the other boomers," she said. "Had you not forced the government's hand, no one would be living out here at all. Most people know your name and understand the part you played. Even if the town of Redhawk doesn't incorporate, you were invaluable to the process of forming hundreds of other towns."

Why was she talking about his accomplishments, when all she could think about was the abandoned boy?

He turned over another shovelful of dirt with a strained flourish. "Don't pay me any mind. I'm just trying to get under your skin, stir up sympathy so I can get this land back."

"I don't believe that for a second." Caroline jumped to her feet and stepped in his way. "Have you figured it out yet?"

"What?"

"That the orphanage is behind you. You survived. No institution is going to rip you away from the people you care about. You're an adult. You make decisions for yourself. You have a chance to make relationships and keep those relationships."

"That's what I was trying to do." He kept his face down, as if the dirt warranted analyzing. "I was going to make a town—a permanent town. And no one could come in and change the rules, because I was going to be the one in charge. Now, well, it might work out despite you"—his lips twitched as if to soften his words—"but I'll never have the security at Plainview that I would've had in Redhawk."

Her sense of truth—the black-and-white thinking she'd inherited from her father—told her that Frisco was wrong. His wrong thinking was going to keep him fearful and untrusting until he corrected it. But she sensed that she'd been guilty of some of the same wrong thinking. Wasn't she convinced that holding on to this land was the only way to find the community she sought? What if they were both mistaken?

"Look how far you've come already," she said. "A lawyer! Not everyone is determined enough to educate themselves to such a level. You've met opposition in life before. You'll succeed here too."

His dark eyes caught hers. Her heart sped up as he took her measure. "By *succeed*, do you mean that I'll recover what was taken from me?"

Caroline could feel her grip on the land loosening. Why couldn't she let him have it? Because she didn't know what she'd hold on to if it was gone. She cared about him, cared about his hardship, but she couldn't resign herself to a cloistered existence. Especially when every encounter with Frisco only made her more aware of what the world offered.

"If you're finished with the shovel"—she took it out of his grasp—"I'll get back to work. I need to get these starts planted before the rain."

And she needed to keep her head down lest he see the tears that threatened.

Chapter Eighteen

Yesterday, they had cut the garden in, and Caroline had promised Frisco that the lavender she'd planted would bring a good return, in addition to the aesthetics. She'd also promised that he didn't need to worry about losing people. That good relationships were possible, and that many people would think he was a man worthy of friendship and trust. He'd just kept digging, afraid to believe the words she was saying. Afraid to question whether her affirmation was crafted to dissuade him from his purpose.

He'd attempted his own mode of persuasion—or at least that was what he'd claim, because it was too embarrassing to admit he'd told Caroline his story without an ulterior motive. But in the end, nothing he'd said had made a difference, while her words had struck him through the core.

Patrick's short shout signaled Frisco to pull on the rope and haul up another barrel of dirt. A woman like Caroline didn't understand the world. True, she'd faced Indian uprisings and killer outlaws on the plains, but it was always with her father's protection. She didn't know what it was to be alone. She'd never had to fear that someone would take offense at her and ruin her life. No one had that power over her. She couldn't know what it was to be him.

Frisco dumped the dirt off to the side, then lowered the barrel back down to Patrick. He should be hitting water soon. Millie would appreciate not having to haul water from the river for her laundry business, and Frisco would enjoy not having to pay for every drink he took.

Paying for water. Who ever heard of such nonsense?

He had to admit, Caroline had lasted longer than he'd expected. Definitely longer than he'd hoped. And the more time he spent in town, the more he could see himself staying there. But where did that leave Patrick and Millie? They knew his plans, and while they were putting some money away with their industry, there wouldn't be enough for them to buy land if he failed to get his homestead back.

But how fun would it be to tell Caroline that she could have the land? That he would no longer oppose her? Would she be relieved? Would she be grateful? Would she tell him again how he was a man that she was proud to know? If it weren't for the investors counting on him . . .

"Frisco, do you have a minute?" Deputy McFarland strode up to him with his head down and his hands in his pockets. He looked down the hole at the top of Patrick's head as he passed. "Is this the place for a private conversation?"

"It's as good as anywhere," Frisco answered. Patrick wasn't one to eavesdrop or to care if he heard something eavesdropworthy.

"It has come to my attention that a man is stirring up trouble for the city. Do you know anything about this?"

"Do you mean the man calling himself a deputy and trying to collect fees from people when there are no such laws?"

McFarland scrunched his face as if hit by an unpleasant odor. "Ah, yes. The peddler told me they knew you. Well, the city council has proposed new fees, but they haven't been approved. The deputy was an overzealous greenhorn. I'll delay him until the paperwork is official, but that's not the issue I'm referencing. I'm asking about a man by the name of Lacroix."

Frisco's stomach did a little flop. "Do you have a more specific question?"

McFarland's jaw twitched, and he shot another glance at the hole in the ground. "Have you helped him put together a case against me?"

"No, not at all." That question, at least, was easy to answer. "No, he's interested in weeding out the sooners who were here early. That doesn't include you, does it?"

"You don't know exactly who he's complaining about, do you?" McFarland shifted so that his back was to the hole. "Does he have any concrete evidence?"

"I know you want to help," Frisco said, "but it'd be for the land office board to decide. When there's a hearing, you could certainly share testimony as a deputy."

McFarland brushed a gnat away from his eyes. "I'm no longer a deputy. I resigned and have gone back to my true calling, which is property and real estate. For a man who likes to see construction and development, this is a dream."

"We've got a lot in common, then," Frisco said. "It'll be something to walk the streets and be able to recall when each building went up."

"Frisco Smith? Is that you?" A solemn-looking man approached in thin linen britches and a striped coat. Where had Frisco met him? Oh yeah, at Purcell before the race. "I've been looking for you."

Uh-oh. Frisco could guess what this was about.

He turned to McFarland. "Don't concern yourself about the claim dispute, friend. The town will be better when the lawbreakers have been removed and the citizens who ran the race fairly get a shot. Thank you for bringing it to my attention, though." He turned away, hoping that McFarland would take the hint, but the former deputy remained, even as the newcomer approached.

"You may not remember me," he said.

"Yes, you're the schoolteacher from . . . Amarillo?"

"Austin. Mr. Deavers."

Frisco offered his hand and relaxed a smidgen when Mr. Deavers decided to shake it.

"The reason I'm here—"

"Is that I owe you two dollars, or was it three?" Frisco was interrupting as much as Sophie Smith did, but he'd rather make this easy on the schoolteacher. It wasn't Mr. Deavers's fault that Frisco had no property for him. And he wanted this settled as quickly as possible, especially seeing how McFarland hadn't left. Frisco reached into his pocket and pulled out a small leather sack. "There you go," he said as he counted out the coins. "I do apologize. Things didn't work out exactly as I planned. I haven't given up, but I don't expect you to wait any longer."

With his hand still outstretched and the money glinting in the sun, Mr. Deavers flipped a coin over with his thumb. "That's it, then? No more explanation? No remorse for failing to get us land?" He pointed at the framework behind Frisco. "Looks like you did well for yourself."

"What's he talking about?" McFarland asked. "Have you defrauded someone?"

The accusation cut to his bone marrow. Frisco felt himself leaning away from McFarland. "No. I just gave him his money back."

"But what about the rest of them?" Mr. Deavers asked. "There's a group gathered at Purcell Station. They're losing heart that they haven't heard from you. What do you want me to tell them? At the very least, let me take their money back to them."

McFarland crossed his arms over his chest. "Why do you have their money, Smith? What's this about?"

Frisco looked from one man to the other. "For that city I was going to build, I took payments for the lots. Unfortunately, I didn't get a homestead claim. I don't have any land to divide up with them. Not yet."

"Can you give them their money back?" McFarland asked.

"Yes, I have it. It's in the bank, right here in town." Then to Deavers, Frisco said, "The deal was that I had until the twenty-second of May. If some don't want to wait that long, they can come find me. Otherwise, tell them not to lose heart."

"There's fourteen squatting there, waiting to hear from you. Why don't you send the money with me?"

Fourteen men. Thirty dollars, perhaps, but probably more if they'd reserved better lots. It had been two weeks, and Frisco still didn't have his land. Two more weeks before his failure was irreversible.

For once his jaunty attitude was failing him. "I'm not going to give out money like that," he said. "I need to know who is getting theirs and see them get it with my own eyes. You've got your two dollars. Send the rest of them my way."

The hard glint to McFarland's eyes hadn't disappeared yet, but he nodded. "That's reasonable, Mr. Deavers. You can't ask him for more than is owed you."

Deavers took another look around. "Do you need a schoolteacher here? I'd hoped to be able to own property of my own instead of living with the families in the district, but since I left Austin, I'm still searching for a job."

"Afraid not," McFarland said. "We haven't organized a school yet, and I don't know where you'd stay if we did. Best if you kept on moving."

With a drop of his shoulders, Deavers walked away.

"I'm sorry," Frisco called after him. "I'm as disappointed as anyone." But his words surely were no comfort to a man who'd gambled and lost. He should know.

Frisco had almost forgotten McFarland waiting at his side.

"You never know when your fortunes are going to change," McFarland said. "Given a chance, I think that man would've tried to ruin your reputation over a stroke of bad luck."

"He's disappointed, and rightly so, but I don't think he aimed to ruin me." Frisco twisted his head around to release the tension in his neck. "I made it right with him. There's nothing more I can do."

"But can you do that for everyone you wronged?" McFarland asked. "Just remember, if you find yourself in a quandary, it's good to have friends who'll stick by you."

But the effect of his words was anything but friendly.

Chapter Nineteen

If she had room in her little cave, she would've brought out more dresses. If she had more dresses, she wouldn't be wearing the same two work dresses over and over. Today was the day she washed one.

Caroline folded the soap into the skirt and rubbed it against itself. Next time she was in town, she should buy a washboard. She'd never paid much attention to the washwomen at the fort, but now she wanted to hug one in thanks for all her hard work. She waded deeper into the river, her bare feet squishing in the mud, and leaned forward to rinse the skirt out in the clean water. Her clothes might not come out pristine, but getting in the water, whether to wash clothes or dishes, was the best chore she had.

Bucky stood on the bank and bleated a warning at her.

"I'm not going to drown, silly thing," she hollered back, glad for the company the goat provided. Her father had long since taken Hardtack back to the fort, declaring that the horse was liable to get stolen and brought unneeded attention to the fact that someone was living beneath the riverbank. He was probably right, but without the horse, her travels were limited to visiting town or visiting Amber. And Amber didn't want to visit.

Caroline had never been so lonely in her life. Not that she wasn't busy. From morning to night she did backbreaking work, and the splendid curves and walkways of her garden were taking shape, but it did little to dull her regrets. She wanted to fix this mess for Frisco.

She'd dunked the cotton material for another rinse when a man's voice rode toward her on the breeze. Caroline froze, waiting for the dripping water to silence so she could hear better. Was that Frisco? She couldn't tell.

She had eased back to the bank and was draping her skirt over a laundry line when Frisco and three men came walking upriver toward her.

He stopped in his tracks, his eyes quickly taking in everything from her tumbling hair to her bare feet and tied-up skirts. He spun to address the men, then shook hands with them and sent them on their way, but he didn't leave. Instead he headed down the riverbank toward her.

Whatever weighty issue he'd been discussing with them still lingered about him. Maybe the thought of seeing her was what sped his steps over the tree roots, or maybe he was only eager to put an unpleasant meeting behind him.

He was wearing his town clothes—a red satin vest with black jet buttons and a silk cravat. But despite being caught disheveled, barefoot, and washing laundry, Caroline didn't for a moment feel at a disadvantage. She was glad he'd come.

❦

The sight of her took his breath away. She stood, bare feet planted wide and rooted to the red soil like the trees around her. Her tousled red hair matched the crimson mud that caked her toes and faded as it traveled up her white legs. A pirate on the bridge of his ship couldn't look more powerful than she did.

"You're trespassing," she said. She didn't even bother tugging the hem of her skirt out of her waistband before she crossed her arms over her chest. "I thought about apologizing for my appearance, but you're the one at fault."

"Don't you dare apologize for your appearance," Frisco blurted. He tried to swallow, but the knot in his throat seemed lodged. He should leave. He should save her the embarrassment, but Caroline didn't seem embarrassed. Here in the dirt and water, she seemed more confident than ever. "Were you born here?" he asked.

Her laugh rang to the leafy branches over them. "What a question. No, we didn't move here until I'd lost my mother." She took a wet skirt off the line and wrung it out. "How about you?"

The ground immediately drank up the puddle from the twisted cloth. "I don't know. It's possible. People have speculated that I'm swarthier than a lot of the foundlings."

"If you belonged to one of the tribes, they would've kept you," Caroline said. "Where does your story start? Or at least the part you know."

Maybe he was still enthralled, and that was why he told her. "I was found on a train."

"A Frisco train?"

"No. I was found in October on Saint Francis's feast day. The Spanish sister called me Francisco. As you can imagine, it didn't take long for that to be shortened."

She smiled. "I like Frisco better."

"On that we agree." Finally he could breathe again. He squinted into the sun while she pinned the skirt to the line. "I owe you an apology. I needed to meet with those men, and the meeting was best conducted out of view of anyone in town. Naturally I felt safe bringing them here, but I didn't mean to interrupt you. If you have more washing to do, don't mind me."

He wasn't offering to leave, exactly. After the disturbing claims the men had made, Frisco wasn't in a hurry to go back to the lion's den. If she'd allow him to stay . . .

She wiggled her toes, then walked to the water, calling over her shoulder, "Sounds like you're involved in something threatening. Are those men dangerous?"

He leaned against a tree as she bent to scrub her feet in the water. The front of her skirt dipped, getting wet. "Those men aren't, but they could drag me into a sticky situation regardless."

Her hands glistened in the water. She stepped out onto a grassy spot, then pulled a towel off the line and dried her feet. What was this spell he'd fallen under? He'd always longed for this place, but now he wasn't sure which drew him more, the land or the lady.

"Can I trust you?" he asked, but he knew the answer before she replied.

With a tug she released her skirt so it again covered her legs. "You can trust me, Frisco. I imagine I couldn't hurt you any worse than I have already."

He had once trusted her with his plans, and it had cost him. But here on the land she'd stolen from him, she was the closest thing to a confidante available.

"Those men want me to represent them in court. They feel certain that the settling of Plainview was done illegally. They're accusing some of the leaders of cheating at the race."

"Not the Premiers of Plainview?" She dropped her jaw in mock surprise. "Do they have any proof?"

"No more than anyone has in these cases. Just a sense of how long it'd take to reach the site, how established they were by the time anyone else arrived. Those things are hard to prove in court, and by the time a judge hears this case, it's going to be like ripping the spine out of the town."

"I can see why you'd want to meet them here. If you proceed, you could be the most hated man in town."

"I won't proceed until I'm sure that their stories are believable. You don't start a fight this big without knowing whether you can win it."

With her head tilted down, she looked up at him through thick eyelashes. "Is the winning what makes the difference?"

"They have to convince me that it's the truth," he said. "The truth is everything, and if they can convince me, then there's a good chance we can convince a judge."

She hummed a pleased note. "You want to stay for supper?"

"What of my supplies are you cooking?"

"Fish. I have a trout line set. They were biting this morning."

"Looks like rain. Maybe I should get back to town." He watched her carefully. If she'd just ask again . . .

"Are you afraid of the rain, Mr. Smith? I do know how to cook fish. It'll be better than any sandwich you buy from a wagon."

"I had some high-quality cornmeal in that dugout."

"And I aim to make good use of it."

He swept his hat off his head and let it bounce against his leg. "You talked me into it. I'll stay. And I'll even get the fish for you."

"Good. Now that you mention it, these clothes would be better off drying inside. I'll lose them for sure with the wind picking up."

And just like that they were splitting chores like a couple bound by law and duty might.

❦

She might be at odds with him, but that didn't mean she couldn't enjoy his company. As time passed, Caroline was pleased to find herself capable of so much more than she'd imagined. She could cook, clean, chop wood, tote water, wash, and a host of other household chores that she'd never had to do before. The novelty had yet to wear off, and she rather enjoyed keeping house for herself and being responsible for her own belongings. She was proud of her accomplishments, more hopeful that she could keep the land for herself. And even her father thought her plans for a boardinghouse held merit. The future looked possible.

If it weren't for the loneliness . . .

To the east, the clear sky still glowed with evening light, but the west was growing darker, smothered by the oncoming storm. At the horizon, Caroline could see the sparks of lightning spawning from the black clouds. She tucked a damp skirt beneath her arm as she reached for the blouse. This promised to be a test of her little den. Would any of these clothes dry through the night, or were they all destined to need another washing before morning?

Caroline had expected the work to be taxing, but what surprised her was how the solitude ate at her self-confidence. She'd never thought herself to be an overly social person. She'd prized her independence, and when frustrated with her family or friends, she'd often reminded herself that she really didn't need them to survive. She'd been eager to test herself on this homestead, but it was hard to remember that you were building a civilization when you couldn't see any other buildings besides your own home.

Once inside her room, Caroline hung the clothes on the primitive footboard of her bed. If the rock walls weren't so hard, she would've cut out a closet by now, but her attempts with a shovel convinced her that it would take dynamite to expand her abode.

Caroline reached for the lamp but decided instead to stoke up the fire. The cook fire would put out light and save her kerosene for another time. Taking a bowl, she scooped a cup of cornmeal and a cup of flour into it and dashed it with salt and pepper until it tasted decent. Without eggs it wouldn't coat as well, but by now everyone in the territory was getting used to doing without. Well-seasoned meals from a fully stocked kitchen were a distant memory for Caroline. She wondered if Frisco even had a memory like that.

Setting the bowl aside, she picked up the poker and rolled the coals around to encourage new flames. As she squatted by the fire, she tried to imagine a little boy adrift in a series of orphanages and foundling houses. Her stepmother's childhood had been horrific, with a drunkard mother raising her in saloons, but at least she'd had her brother, Bradley, to cling to. Together they hadn't felt—

The door opened behind her. Caroline stood upright and extended the poker between her and the man at the door.

Frisco raised his hands, including the string of gutted fish, and looked at the sharp tip two inches from his chest.

"I guess I should've knocked," he said. "I had a habit of walking into this house before you lived here."

Hiding her fluster, she took the fish from him and coated them in the mixture. He removed his tailored coat and hat and stowed them on the back of the door. Caroline put the fish in the iron skillet and set it in the fire. Frisco drew back against the wall to watch.

"Wind is really kicking up," he said. "We're in for a doozy."

"Are you regretting your decision to stay?" She picked up a potholder to better arrange the skillet over the coals. "You might be better off in Plainview."

"Better in a tent than this underground shelter? Are you looking for my demise?"

Caroline's mouth curled into a smile. "I don't want the blame if your things back in town blow away. That's all."

"Well, you will get the blame, because they wouldn't be in

town if it wasn't for you. But I might as well get a good meal out of you before I resume our conflict."

At the word, Caroline's stomach flopped. She already had too many conflicts. She didn't need another. A few pings of rain sounded on the exposed parts of the tin roof, then a deluge.

Frisco walked the perimeter of the small room with his head tilted back, inspecting his work as she cooked. The fire, the smoke, and the moist heat coming up from the ground raised beads of sweat on her brow. Caroline unbuttoned the top two buttons of her blouse. If she'd had both hands free, she would have pinned her hair up, but the fish were nearly done.

"It's stuffy in here." Frisco cracked the door and propped it open with a kettle.

"If you can't take the heat . . ." She tilted her head to steal a look at him standing in the doorway, his figure outlined by evening light.

"I'm always jumping into one fire or another. I can't play it safe," he said. "Even when I know I'm likely to get burned."

"Maybe it's your propensity for danger that makes you so interesting," she said. The heavy skillet wavered.

Frisco stepped forward and wrapped his hand around the handle, covering hers. "Careful. Let's not drop our dinner."

His arm ran alongside hers. Her forearms looked like porcelain compared to the tanned skin emerging from his rolled sleeves. He took a step closer, not shying away from the contact between them. Her side pressed into him.

The cool breeze from the door chilled her suddenly sensitive skin. He set the skillet on the coals but didn't leave. Her breathing stilled as he lifted a handful of hair off her shoulders and held it up against the back of her head. The breeze tickled her neck where it touched her damp collar.

"If I had enough light, I might be able to pin your hair up," he said. "Then again, why would I want to do that?" With deliberate movements, he lowered her hair back down and smoothed it. "Caroline." His voice was a caress, a question. "Has there ever been a world created in which I could deserve you?"

For once her quick answers were of no use. Neither were her reminders that he was playing a game. It didn't matter what his reasons were. For years she'd longed to hear endearments from his lips. She wouldn't stop him now. The fire blurred before her eyes as she held her peace and enjoyed his touch.

"Of all the things I want to tell you," he said, "the most important is that we're burning our fish."

She jerked the pan away from the fire. Frisco stepped back as she raised the skillet with both hands around the potholder and carried it to the table. Her mind was a jumble, whirling with senses, hopes, and desires. Taking a fork, she pried the blackened fish from the skillet onto the plates. Frisco lifted the table, plates and all, and set it next to the bed, then pulled up the trunk, where he sat, studying her as if he were required to pass some judgment on her. Whatever it was, she was afraid to hear it.

Before they could eat, she heard a clamoring at the door. Bucky scrambled over the kettle they were using to prop the door open. The dripping goat cried, then hopped onto the bed next to her.

"Why, Miss Adams, are you raising my kid?" He threw back his head and laughed at his own joke.

Caroline moved her clean clothes out of the goat's way. "Yes, and she's an obnoxious pest," she said, "much like her father." But the little thing cuddled up against her side and shivered.

The rain and thunder had increased, and the trees by the river swayed and bent in the wind. Frisco pinched a chunk of trout, popped it into his mouth, and hummed his approval. As the tin roof above them groaned with the hammering it was taking, they sat wordlessly and watched the pile of food disappear. She'd cooked more than enough for two, and the peppered fish had Frisco going for the bucket of water. He offered her the dipper first. With her finger in her mouth, Caroline shook her head as she licked off the last of the flavor and reached for her cup she'd already poured.

"How do you suppose your friend next door is doing in this rain?" Frisco asked. "Her house isn't finished. I'm surprised she hasn't come seeking shelter already."

Caroline's chin dropped. "If she needs help, she'll go to the Schneider family that lives on the other side of her." She took another slow drink so as to hide behind the cup, but it was no use.

"She wouldn't come here?" He tilted his head. "I thought the two of you were as thick as thieves. What happened?"

"You've got serious issues to contend with. You don't need to be bothered by something as paltry—"

Frisco leaned over the table. "I don't have any clients more important than you. Go on. Spill the beans."

"It's nothing of consequence." She scratched Bucky's knobby head. "Bradley has Amber mad at me. She hasn't been over to talk since he decided I shouldn't be here."

"Does this have anything to do with me?" He took another bite of fish.

"Why would you ask that?"

"Because I've talked to Miss Herald."

Her eyes widened. "Did you turn my friends against me?"

"I did nothing of the sort. She volunteered the cause of your spat, and I told her I didn't want them to shun you on my account. I told her we would settle the issue between us. We didn't need outside help." The tin roof rattled over their heads.

Caroline slowed her breath. She absently petted Bucky, who was now asleep. "But we haven't settled it, have we? You still have people that you're beholden to. I still have your land."

"Time is running out," he acknowledged. "I have to have land for my investors in less than two weeks, or I'll have to return their money and admit I failed. I can't lose focus, but the closer I come to losing everything, the more I realize how I'd regret losing you."

Their gazes locked. Was he fiddling on her heartstrings, trying to elicit a sympathetic response? No, he hated duplicity. And Caroline was no less honest.

"I feel the same way," she said at last. "What do we do?"

"I'm not sure. I've never been in this spot before."

Bucky moved against her. Caroline ran her hand down the kid's spine and felt cold water.

"The roof," she said. Red rivulets of water were coursing down the wall. "The blankets are getting soaked. Let's move the bed away from the side."

"Put the goods on the bed too," Frisco said. "The shelves might catch water next. I don't think the tin roof is leaking, but water is coming through the ground above us."

As Caroline lifted the last bag of flour off the shelf, she caught a glimpse of the outdoors through the slightly open door. It had been raining steadily for some time, but they'd been so distracted by their conversation that she hadn't looked outside.

"Um, Frisco? Has the river ever gotten up that high before?" Caroline clasped her hands to her chest as she backed away from the door.

Frisco spun around. Water gurgled beneath the door, shooting up like a babbling brook. "No, it's never been . . ." Then he looked at the walls. "I'm just realizing that this little alcove is here because of the river. I was so worried about the roof holding that I forgot to account for the low-lying situation of the house. Get whatever you want to keep, and hurry. There's no guarantee that the water won't cover the whole room."

He threw on his coat and reached for his hat, although where they'd go for shelter, Caroline couldn't imagine. If they had to flee the little room built into the ground, what other refuge was available?

Chapter Twenty

The wind slammed against Caroline, knocking her steps astray. Catching her arm, Frisco braced her as they came up over the bank, where they caught the full force of the gale. Her hat jerked, but the ribbons caught beneath her chin and cut into her throat. She hugged Bucky beneath her coat as she wrestled her hat back onto her head.

"We can't make it to the fort. It's too far," she said. "Is there anywhere safe in Plainview?"

Frisco had to lean close to her ear to be heard. "I hope it'll blow over before we reach town, but if misery loves company, we'll have lots of miserable company there."

Together they jogged north toward Plainview, although the storm kept pushing them off track. The clear sky to the east was quickly disappearing as the broiling blanket of clouds rolled that way. Frisco dragged her along faster and faster, both mindful of the lightning approaching relentlessly from the west.

Caroline strained her eyes, watching for a sign of the town, which was usually in sight by this time. A white-blue streak jagged across the sky and illuminated the battered tents and tarps of the settlers. No warm campfires in this rain.

Even Frisco was taken aback. "And that's just the wind," he said. "Let's take cover before something worse blows in."

Nearly running, they crossed Bill Matthews's lot. His tent shook like someone was trying to knock it from its stakes. The wooden framework on the next lot looked secure, but its door slammed back and forth on the hinges. Where were they? Landmarks in the new town changed every day, but now it looked completely foreign to Caroline. From the corner of her eye she saw a flash of movement. That was the only warning she had before she was hit and thrown against Frisco.

Everything went dark, and sound was muffled. Her chest tightened like she'd been thrust underwater. Bucky kicked and struggled against her. Then she felt Frisco reaching across her and wrestling with her attacker. He freed her from her bindings, and she watched as an oblong oilcloth disappeared into the night, riding the wind until it buried some other victim.

"Poor Sophie," he said. "She'll need to make a new advertisement."

Too bad Caroline hadn't thought to catch the oilcloth. It would have kept some of the rain off her.

She didn't recognize Frisco's plot but figured the wagon he was leading her to was his friend Patrick's. So far, the framework of Frisco's house was still standing, but his tent was nowhere to be found. Frisco reached above his head to rattle on the drawstring of the covered wagon, which had been pulled closed against the rain. The box of the wagon bounced, and Patrick peered out at them.

Wrapping her arms around Bucky, Caroline tried to make herself small as she waited for entrance. Having grown up on the prairies, she knew what the weather could do, and unless one was hiding underground, a roof over your head might not offer enough protection. A wagon? Well, they'd better pray that God had mercy on them, or lives would be snuffed out. When the clouds came down to touch the earth, they left a red scar of dirt and nothing else.

"Get in here," Patrick said through the loosened opening. He reached his hand down. Frisco took the goat from her and stuck it beneath the wagon before taking Caroline by the waist and hoisting her up. The only light was the increasingly frequent lightning that illuminated the family huddled inside. Mrs. Smith held Jonathan on a straw tick that was wedged between two crates and a butter churn. With Patrick helping Frisco inside, Caroline had to move out of the way, but she didn't see anywhere clear that she could go.

"Come this way," Mrs. Smith said. "Follow my voice."

"I'm dripping wet," Caroline replied. "I don't want to get water on your mattress."

"By the time the night is over, we'll be lucky if anything in this territory is dry," said Patrick.

He lifted the butter churn and passed it to Frisco to set outside the wagon before they tied down the opening again. Caroline took her place where the butter churn had been, and Frisco and Patrick joined them.

"Sorry to intrude," Frisco said. "My house on the river was becoming my house *in* the river."

"Do you mean Miss Adams's house?" It was too dark to see Patrick's grin, but Caroline could hear it in his voice.

"You're welcome here," Mrs. Smith said. "We're on your property, after all." Her gracious words were nearly yelled to be heard over the wind, which had intensified since they'd entered the fragile refuge.

The wagon rocked with each forceful blast. Jonathan cried out despite Mrs. Smith's attempts to shelter him against the side of the wagon. There wasn't room for Caroline to stretch out her legs, but the safest thing seemed to be staying huddled together.

The wind grew stronger and stronger. The frame holding the canvas above them groaned as two wheels left the ground and then dropped back to the earth with a crash.

"If it gets any worse, it's going to roll," Frisco said. He took Caroline's hand. "We'll sit against the windward side. Maybe that'll help."

He and Patrick shoved things around to make room on the other side of the wagon. Mrs. Smith tossed a blanket over the crates at them, which Caroline took gratefully. With their backs against the wooden side and their knees to their chests, Caroline and Frisco sat side by side, listening to the howling wind. Caroline tried not to let her shoulders bounce against the wall when the wagon bucked, but then something hit the canvas with enough force to strike her on the head.

"Ouch." She leaned away from the side of the wagon and rubbed her scalp. "Something blew against the—"

But before she could complete her sentence, the roaring of a hundred strikes drowned out her words.

Hail. Frisco looked above them as the fury outside grew. At the next lightning strike, Caroline could no longer see the top of Patrick's head over the crates between them, and Frisco must have had the same idea.

"Get down!"

He wrapped his arm around her and pulled her down to get her head beneath the side of the wagon. Angling his shoulders across her, he tucked her head into his chest as the onslaught began in earnest.

Like hammer blows on an anvil, the hailstones pounded the canvas above them. Most bounced off the tightly drawn material, but bigger and bigger stones were hurling down. Near the front of the wagon, a crate splintered. The wind howled through a rip in the canvas. Caroline felt Frisco's fingers dig into her coat as he braced himself. Mrs. Smith screamed from the other side of the wagon. Caroline moved to help, but Frisco held her firm.

"Stay down," he urged. His body was unyielding against hers. "You're covered here."

Covered by him. Through all the chaos and discomfort, Caroline had failed to recognize that Frisco was risking his life for her. She who had taken his dream from him.

The next strike hit Frisco square in the back. Caroline felt the impact ricochet against her. The sudden puff of breath across her head told her that he'd had the air knocked out of him. It was a few moments before he had enough wind to groan.

"That's gonna leave a mark," he said. He twisted to relieve the pain but stopped and settled in again with a grunt. "Good thing I've got a full set of ribs to begin with."

But if he was hit in the head . . .

Caroline reached her arms around his neck and stretched her hands over his head.

"Get your hands back," he said. "You don't want your fingers broken."

"I don't want your head broken," she said.

Only in the flashes of lightning could she see the black pools of his eyes. "You're protecting me?" he asked. "Very few people have ever done that before." He ducked as another hailstone ripped through the wagon. "If I didn't think you'd hate me tomorrow, I'd kiss you." His words, hot on her wet neck, left her shivering.

Caroline felt as untamed and reckless as the storm. "What if there's not a tomorrow?" she said. "Would you regret losing your chance?"

Wincing, he pulled her hands down and tucked them safely against his chest while his gritty smile grew firm. "There's going to be a tomorrow. We have too many adventures ahead for it to end now."

Chapter Twenty-One

I t would take more than a chunk of ice thrown from the clouds to knock Frisco out of this contest. The raging front of the storm passed, followed by bands of rain that waxed and waned through the rest of the night. Once the dangerous hail had ceased, Frisco and Patrick did their best to patch the rips in the wagon cover and rearrange the contents of the wagon bed. As much as Frisco would have liked to return to the private alcove he and Caroline had shared, decorum dictated that she join Mrs. Smith and the boy for the rest of the night.

It was for the best. Yes, Frisco gave a passing thought to what pain Major Adams could inflict on him, but even more terrifying was the agony he was likely to find at the end of any dalliance with Caroline. He admired her. He coveted her admiration. It would crush him to lose her respect, but he knew that an ugly parting was the most likely outcome of any courtship between them.

In Frisco's experience, very few things lasted forever, and relationships were the most fragile of all. Once he had time to clear his head, he knew it was better to keep his distance and keep her regard for the long haul. Especially if their paths were likely to cross again.

The sun lifted off the soggy ground, as did the battered inhabitants of Plainview. Stunned and dripping, they emerged from overturned carriages, wet tarps, and any hollow in the ground big enough to duck beneath.

Frisco helped Mrs. Smith down from the wagon. Spotting her shattered butter churn, she covered her mouth before falling on her knees and gathering the broken pieces into her skirt.

Caroline watched from the wagon, her glorious hair an unruly flash of color that hadn't been tamed in the storm. "I owe you a new churn," she said. "You only moved it out of the wagon to make room for me."

Mrs. Smith looked at Caroline's battered and muddied work dress. "I reckon we're all in this together," she said and offered Caroline a hand down out of the wagon.

Caroline went straight for the young goat, huddled next to Jonathan's dog in the mud against the wagon wheel.

"They'll be fine," Frisco said, "but we need to take an accounting of the town." He'd leave Patrick to comfort his wife and look after their belongings. After a night of helplessly waiting, Frisco was ready to get out and do something productive.

He was pleased to see that the framework of his house was still standing. His tent was tangled around a corner post, and his cot had been overturned, but since Patrick had kept Frisco's traveling case in the wagon, his losses were minimal. On other building sites, splintered posts showed the force of the wind. Had his house been further along, with walls or a roof, they most certainly would have been blown off. Not that the frame offered any protection, but at least he wasn't out the expense and time to replace it. He wondered how his little dugout on the riverbank had fared.

"I imagine you're concerned about your belongings," he said

to Caroline. "If you want me to take you back to the home-stead—"

"No. There are hurting people here. This is where my duty lies."

"Your duty?" How did she look so noble covered in dirt? "What obligations are you under?"

She lifted her chin and wiped her hands against her dingy skirt. "I'm the major's daughter. These people rely on my family. If there are needs, then who else should be attending to them?"

There were plenty of needs, that was certain. His lot was littered with debris. Mixed in with the clothing and canvas were pieces of wet paper, their ink running so that they'd never be identifiable. Thank the Lord the wagon had held, or those could have been his papers trod upon.

Caroline knelt and scraped a pair of trousers out of the mud. She tried to shake the wet red clay out of the creases, then looked around. "I'm sure the owner will be looking for these. All they need is a good washing."

"Hang them on that crossbeam." Frisco pointed to his house frame. "We'll see if we can match the seekers with the finders."

Her faint nod of approval warmed him. "More important than the goods, we need to see if anyone is hurt." She looked around again. "The higher ground toward the center of town was probably hit the hardest. We'll survey that area and identify any casualties. If I know my father, the troopers will be here soon with the ambulance wagon. It'll save time and suffering if we can point them to the area with the most people hurt."

It was a pity the army didn't have officer positions open to the fairer sex. Caroline Adams was born to lead.

"There's the Cottons. Let's check on them." Frisco motioned her toward the neighbors who were tying together a broken tent pole.

"We're fine," Mr. Cotton said. "We managed to get the

straw tick over us, or we'd have some knots on our noggins this morning."

"You shouldn't jest," his wife reprimanded. "There'll be some who weren't so lucky."

Frisco twisted his back, trying to work out the soreness. "If you hear of anyone needing assistance, let us know. We're heading toward the center of town."

Caroline righted a milking stool that had blown over before accompanying him to the next plot. It didn't take long before they'd heard story after story of property damage, missing livestock, and various items that had blown away.

One tearful woman gathered waterlogged clothing from a busted crate and threw it in a buggy as her husband harnessed one horse to a two-horse harness. "This is the last tear I'm going to cry over this sorry land," she said. "It's been nothing but empty promises and hardships. We would've been better off staying in Arizona Territory. This weather is too unpredictable."

"Don't know that we can make it back to Arizona," her husband said. "Not with one horse."

Frisco stepped into Caroline's line of sight so she'd be spared the image of the dead animal behind the buggy. "Did you file a claim for this land?" he asked. "You might be able to put some money in your pocket to aid your trip home." And Patrick might be able to have a plot of his own.

But Patrick wasn't fast enough. Mr. Wilton was making good time despite his bent back. He still had wet maple leaves stuck to his coat from riding out the storm, but that didn't dim the hope in his eyes. "You'uns leaving? I'll take this plot from you. Ten dollars cash money, and I'll see that your dead horse gets looked after."

"Ten dollars?" the homesteader said. "Do you know how much we sank into this venture? We already have a well dug—"

His wife waved a mud-coated rolling pin at him. "Take the

money and let's go. I want to get away from here before the next storm."

Her husband dropped his gaze to the muddy puddle he was standing in, then held out his hand. Mr. Wilton pulled a drawstring bag out of his pocket. Holding it in his fist, he squeezed it until a stream of water ran out the end, then fished out some wet bills and counted the coins.

"Congratulations," Frisco said. "You and Sophie are now officially citizens of Plainview."

Or what was left of it. As the morning went on, word spread that some hadn't survived the storm. Four souls in all. Two were struck by hailstones, and one child drowned when she was swept away from where her family was sheltering by the river. The fourth man drowned facedown in a puddle, but it was suspected that he'd been drowning his sorrows all night with bootleg liquor.

Frisco and Caroline directed a man with a broken arm to the center of town and made several trips back to Frisco's plot with their arms full of goods they'd recovered. Patrick and Millie stayed there, matching people with the goods they'd lost and accepting whatever was found out of place.

Millie had also been through Frisco's bag to retrieve clothes that had gotten wet when the wagon's canvas failed. She'd hung them on a line along with her family's clothes to dry. Frisco spotted them immediately and felt it to the pit of his stomach.

"My bag. Did you empty it?" He ran his hand over the buckskin trousers hanging limply over the rope. They weren't soaked, but it wouldn't take much water to ruin his records.

Millie shook her head. "No, just these clothes that were on top, but they stopped the water. Once I touched a dry portfolio beneath, I left everything else as it was."

Then Frisco saw a white square of fabric hanging on the line.

He pulled it down. "I'm going to put this back in my case. I don't want it lost."

"Oh, Frisco," Patrick said, "nobody wants that old handkerchief of yours. That monogram doesn't even match your name."

Maybe it did. How would he know? "All the same, it's liable to blow away without a clothespin. It'll be safer back where it belongs."

"I'm surprised at the civility," Caroline said, accompanying him. "As desperate as the situation is, you'd think there'd be looting."

He refastened his traveling bag with the handkerchief safely inside and felt better about life. "Not everyone needs a company of soldiers to make them behave. Besides, we're all in the same boat. Once thieving starts, where would it end? No one can lock up their belongings until houses are built. We have to trust each other."

But he couldn't stop the questions that Lacroix had raised. Had they been too trusting? Had the town been settled fairly or not?

As Caroline had predicted, an ambulatory wagon arrived with troopers before the sun hit its zenith. The fort's surgeon set bones right there in the street. Not that there was anywhere better. There was no dry, protected spot for the hundreds of people living there. Everything had been exposed. Even the photographer's work.

Against the half-built brick wall of the bank, Frisco found a leather portfolio wrapped in twine. Breaking the twine, he pulled out a stash of photos. Water had soaked through one corner of the portfolio, leaving a wrinkly quarter circle on many of the pictures, but besides that, they were fine. Judging from the fancy dress and the painted backdrop, many of the photos had been taken the night of the dance. What a change from that night to the soaked, tired people who populated the town today. Frisco quickly thumbed through the stack, looking for what he knew must be there.

Caroline leaned over his arm. "Who do those belong to?" The sun was gaining its May strength. If she didn't get some shade soon, her fair complexion would suffer.

"Two of them belong to us," he said. And there they were. Him with his cravat and pleated shirt front, and Caroline Adams in her heart-stopping glory.

He couldn't help but gobble up the beauty on the card and then turn to study her as she assessed the picture. There was no comparison. As rare as her beauty had been that night, today she was more magnificent. Many women knew how to fool a camera to their advantage. Many could look winsome or striking for the lightning blaze of the flash powder, but this woman had a grit to her that wasn't visible on the surface. Compassionate, yes, but not with a helpless sentimentality. Instead her compassion had a will to it.

Her lips parted as she took in the handsome couple they made. The sidelong glance she gave him made him feel his sore ribs again. "That seems like so long ago," she said. "It's impossible that this is the same place."

"We were standing in front of a painted backdrop," he pointed out. "What you see here was never real."

"It was real to me."

The lump in his throat made it hard to swallow. He thought of the night before and how close he'd come to kissing her. Somewhere deep in his gut, he knew she was thinking of the same thing. "We're going to make it real," he said.

What exactly he was promising, he didn't know, but he wanted something here to be concrete and unchanging. Something that couldn't be washed away by a good drenching and a strong wind. Something between him and her.

Maybe someday he and Caroline would live on that land

together. Maybe she wouldn't have to lose it after all. As long as he could return the investors' money, there might be a solution for them.

"This is your photo." He held it out to her.

"It's safer in the portfolio. I have nowhere to keep it dry right now." With her hand on his wrist, she turned it for one last look. "It might be a while before I'm that clean or dry again." Then she wandered off to direct another injured settler toward the ambulance wagon.

Frisco pushed the photos back into the portfolio, but one got caught on the edge and wouldn't go in without extra urging. It too contained a lineup of people he knew. With their august personages in a row next to a stack of bricks, it was McFarland and the rest of the Premiers posing like men were wont to do after some worthy accomplishment. At the bottom was written, *Town Fathers of Plainview, Oklahoma Territory, April 22, 1889.* The pile of bricks that were to become the partial wall of the bank were tumbling on each other as if they'd just been dumped from a wagon.

True to their claim, they'd reached the site first. The prairie behind them was void of the tents, wagons, and horses that littered it immediately afterward. Funny that even the photographer with his wagon had managed to beat lone horsemen. Frisco squinted at the picture. If challenged, they'd undoubtedly produce this photo as proof of their right to the claim. He should tell Mr. Lacroix that this evidence could make his case harder to win. Or maybe his client would be content taking one of the lots from the people who were pulling up stakes today.

Ike McFarland stepped into his light. "A moment to be proud of."

Frisco looked from McFarland back to his image in the photo. "It is surprising that you were all acquainted before the run.

What are the chances that you'd be lucky enough to be the first dozen to arrive?"

"We left together and knew a better route. Getting around that little canyon held a lot of people back."

Frisco had counted on the same thing. And as deputies, they had access to the land before the guns fired. Plenty of time to plan their route. Of course, it hadn't worked out as well for him.

"Some people have all the luck," Frisco said.

"Unfortunately, our luck hasn't held as well as we'd like." McFarland squinted into the distance. "As our legal representative—"

"—on a contract-only basis—"

"—you need to be aware of some distressing news. Sometime last night, Mr. Sorenson disappeared."

Frisco closed the portfolio with numb fingers. "Have you set up a search? If he was down by the river—"

"No, his disappearance seems to be of a more intentional sort. His strongbox and wagon are missing too." McFarland tilted his head toward the never-completed wall, where Caroline sat next to a girl with a bandaged arm.

Gone? Sorenson had Frisco's money. Money that people were coming to collect from him. It wasn't his to lose.

"You have to have some way to track him," Frisco said. "What bank did he work at previously? What were his credentials? Someone will know his family, his acquaintances. He can't just disappear."

"Credentials? In hindsight, that would've been a wise step before allowing him to open his doors. As it happened, we were so relieved to have someone settle here with banking experience that we didn't bother asking exactly what that experience entailed."

"Didn't bother asking?" The air around Frisco turned sour. His bones felt like they'd had all the marrow bled out of them.

In ten days, that money was due. It was his honor at stake. "I asked you specifically if you could recommend Sorenson. You vouched for his character."

"You deposited with Sorenson, didn't you?" McFarland shook his head. "Goodness, that's a bad turn of luck. I apologize for my error, but I was sorely mistaken about him. How easy it is to be fooled. How are you going to meet your obligations now?"

"One hundred and seventeen dollars, gone." People moved past Frisco in a blur as he tried to comprehend the loss. "One hundred and seventeen dollars. How am I supposed to recover?"

McFarland patted Frisco on the shoulder. "Fortunately for you, you've got good friends willing to help you out if you'll let them. I imagine I could raise that sum easily among the Premiers. They'd love to see you more at ease, instead of running all over the countryside pursuing land disputes that have no merit."

Frisco's acuity returned with sharp focus. "Did you lose money, McFarland? Did Sorenson rob you too, or were you spared?"

"No, I wasn't a depositor. Otherwise, I wouldn't be in a position to help you now. Granted, nothing I can guarantee this minute, but by evening I should have a firm offer. I think we all appreciate what an asset you are to Plainview, and we don't want a turn of bad luck to ruin you. Naturally there might be some special considerations that we'd expect you to make along the way. . . ."

"You want me to drop the land disputes? That's what you're suggesting?"

McFarland's smile spread. "I wouldn't be so bold as to tell you what to do, but with that kind of investment in your career, we wouldn't want to see you waste your time representing grievances that are unfounded."

Frisco couldn't prove what he'd long suspected, but McFarland's offer strengthened his hunch.

"I'm sorry, Mr. McFarland," Frisco said, "but I'm unable to accept your generosity. I've already consulted with my clients. How would it look if I took money from you, then reversed course on my decision?" He could barely choke back his disgust, but he would rather win the argument before the land office board than here in the street. He'd wait until the time was ripe.

"Have it your way. Just remember, if you change your mind, the offer is on the table." McFarland tightened his gloves as he walked away.

Frisco's lip curled as he watched McFarland leave. He didn't know what he was going to do, but he wasn't going to take bribes. The absconding of the banker left him without a choice. It was either get the land for his investors or default on his promise. Would Caroline understand? No, he wouldn't tell her. It was his gamble. He'd protect her from the burden that he carried.

He looked around. A woman hung her dripping bed linens on a leaning clothesline. A man carried a wet bag of flour, looking for a dry place to lay it and perhaps save something before it rotted. Who else had lost their deposits? That money represented lumber, food, inventory to stock a shop once they got established—all things that Plainview needed. All things he needed. All things that the people counting on him needed and planned to buy with the money he had to refund them.

His fists clenched, grinding red mud deeper into his palms. He had imagined this so differently. He pushed up his already rolled sleeves. The storm had taken more than he'd counted on. It had taken what wasn't his to lose.

～≈≈≈≈≈～

The day was well-nigh over, and Caroline had worked harder in town than she'd ever worked on her land. Dredging up pieces of clothing, righting the contents of overturned wagons, holding terrorized children while their mothers doctored their scrapes and bruises—and all done while wearing a wet, sodden mess of a dress that weighed three times what it normally would. It should have been exhausting, but Caroline had never felt more needed. And the fact that she had toiled at Frisco's side made the day that much sweeter.

With her arms full of household goods that had been scattered, she headed back to the lot where they were gathering all the items. The sun blazed every chance it got between the scuttling clouds, but it wouldn't be enough to dry anything today. Still, it was good to see people carrying debris and sundries to the collection point as well as picking through to see if anything of their own had been recovered. Caroline found room on the tent canvas for the items she was carrying, then hung up the fabric pieces.

"Here's a something for you, honey." It was Frisco's friend Sophie, wearing a tray with a strap around her neck like the waiters on the train. She handed Caroline a cup of coffee. "You probably haven't taken a break all day."

Caroline had ignored her stomach pangs, knowing that food wasn't likely on a day like this, making the coffee an unexpected and gracious gesture.

"How did your wagon fare?" Caroline asked.

"I lost my sign, but the canvas held, so the goods stayed dry. Better than I can say for my stockings." Sophie's skirt, which only reached to a few inches above her mismatched ankle boots, hadn't been dragging through the mud, but her colorful stockings were splattered. She eyed the array of goods on the ground. "If you have stuff that goes unclaimed, give me a holler. Mr. Wilton is a right handy tinsmith. He might could tidy up some things good enough for us to resell."

"I'll talk to Frisco," Caroline said, "but I imagine he'll agree to giving you first priority."

"And from what I understand, we now own a plot of land here. Someone pulled up stakes and left, so we're here for good." Sophie grinned, and for the first time, Caroline noticed a fine scar that ran from the corner of her eye to her hairline. Frisco had claimed that he'd never had good friends, but was Sophie an exception?

Caroline gulped a mouthful of lukewarm coffee before she lost her nerve. "So how do you and Frisco know each other?"

"Don't worry, miss. Frisco and I would've never suited. True, he followed me around like a little puppy for a couple of years, but with him being my brother—"

"Frisco is your brother?" Caroline blurted.

"Not like that. He was in my family group. They grouped us together, and all us—me, him, Patrick—were named Smith and kept in the same area. The idea was that we'd stay together and have a nice growing-up like real brothers and sisters. It would've been nice, but then we got a new director, and he didn't cotton to the idea, so we were back to being on our own. We kept the names, but it was no time at all before they hauled me out of there and sent me to work for a mean old woman on a ranch. I lost track of Frisco and Patrick after that."

"They told you that you'd be together, and then . . ."

"It didn't bother me much. I knew better than to get attached, but poor Frisco. He set such a store on belonging to the group. I remember worrying about him." She shook her head, her natural ringlets bouncing. "Hogwash. He's fine. Just look at him now. I should've learned my lesson. No sense in grieving over things you can't control. Nowadays I don't worry about Frisco's heart, but I do have concerns over this mess he's got himself into. I don't know what he's going to do."

"Mess? What—"

"You know, don't you? That town he was going to start. Well, everybody done paid him money up front, one hundred and seventeen dollars' worth. But now he ain't got the town or the supplies, and those people will be wanting their money back."

"He has the money, though. He told me he has it."

"Does he?" Sophie's brows drew together. "I heard he put it in the bank, and if that's the case, then he's sunk."

"Why? What happened?"

"I'll tell you what," Sophie interrupted, "if it was me, I'd get that sorry bum off my land. I don't care who got there first, it should've been Frisco's by right. But he's too law-abiding for his own good. You'd think someone who spent the last four years illegally occupying the Unassigned Lands—"

"The law and the enforcement of the law were at odds," Caroline said. She bit at a cuticle. "He found a loophole."

"Whatever you say, miss. About the only thing that can help him now is to loophole that man off his land. Hey, maybe you could get your pa to help. Isn't he someone important?"

If Sophie thought Frisco was a rule follower, she didn't know anything about Caroline's father. And she didn't know about Caroline, or she wouldn't be saying this to her. Sophie seemed to have Caroline pinned in her large brown eyes. Maybe Sophie did know something. . . .

"Anyway," Sophie said, "I'm glad you're here to help Frisco. He warrants looking after. I've got enough on my hands."

"Yes, ma'am," Caroline said. "If I think of anything he needs . . ."

She waited until Sophie had carried her generosity to the next worker, and then she spat on the ground. When had she taken to chewing her fingernails? They were too dirty to be anywhere near her mouth. Caroline didn't feel clean at all. And as muddy as she was, the last person she wanted to run into was Ike McFarland, man about town.

"Miss Adams." He'd lost his hat. His hair curled in thick

blond waves. "Why am I not surprised to see you here, organizing the recovery of our town?"

"Actually, I was enjoying a cup of coffee." She looked around for Sophie, but she'd moved out of reach.

"I admire your humility, but word has spread about your efforts. Your leadership was much needed today. And even more in the future. I've heard tragic tidings."

"About those poor souls?"

He frowned. "Well, yes. Them, and also that our steadfast Mr. Sorenson has turned out to be a scoundrel. He left town last night before the storm and seems to have disappeared with all the money that was entrusted to him."

Caroline's stomach turned. "All the money gone?" So that was what Sophie had alluded to. Caroline scanned the area for Frisco. Did he know? "That's terrible news, Deputy McFarland. When are you leaving?"

"Leaving? I don't understand."

"To apprehend him. You're the law here. I'll ask my father if he knows where Marshals Ledbetter and Reeves are. They'll want to know what evidence you have, but don't worry—they'll find you on the trail. No use in waiting."

"I'm sorry, Miss Adams, but you misunderstand. I'm no longer a deputy. That was a temporary designation. Now I'm set on helping our community in a more tangible manner, and I'd like your assistance, if possible."

More tangible than getting Frisco's and the others' money back? A request followed a compliment just like the smell followed a pig. Caroline hadn't spent many years navigating society, but she'd learned that rule. Still sickened by the news, she managed to reply, "How can I help you, Deputy—I mean, Mr. McFarland?"

"Before the storm, we were planning a grand celebration for Saturday, and now we think the people need it more than ever.

We were organizing a bit of a parade, putting together some music, a couple of tableaux, and serving some refreshments. We want to create a sense of town spirit, something that brings us all together. Would you be interested in helping?"

"A parade when everything has blown away? I don't know how that's going to help. And I haven't even looked after my own house. I might not be a neighbor to the town after today if my shelter is gone."

"It won't take much of your time. You'd be representing the spirit of Plainview—don classical dress, read a few lines, and pose in a tableau. It'd be a lot easier than the work you're doing today. I hope you would think it worthy of your effort."

"With all the work to be done?" Caroline wiped the back of her hand across her forehead. "My time's too valuable to be spent on celebrations this week. There are a lot of people who need help."

Then Caroline spotted Frisco leaning against the framework of a house that had blown down, steadying it while some other men nailed it in place. She'd ruined his plans, and she owed him.

McFarland followed her gaze. A slow smile spread on his face. "We can talk about your friends, if you'd like. Perhaps you have a suggestion for how we could convince you to participate?"

"One hundred dollars," Caroline said. Her own mouth hung open in disbelief. She couldn't believe she'd asked for so much, but why not? She recovered her composure and tried to look like a person who might be worth one hundred dollars for an hour's performance. Then, because she'd dared so much already, she said, "One hundred and seventeen dollars."

McFarland smoothed his mustache as he raised his eyebrows. Caroline's face warmed. Had she been too obvious? But McFarland didn't scold her.

"It just so happens," he said, "that we have those funds available. It's a deal, Miss Adams. If you're willing to do the presentation, I'm confident that our men will jump at the chance to secure your support. Thank you so much. I'm sure we won't be disappointed."

One hundred and seventeen dollars, just like that? But tempering Caroline's surprise was her suspicion. Who had that kind of money? How could her appearance on a stage be worth so much to these men?

A piece of sun glimmered out from between the clouds, and Caroline blinked into the sudden light. Disasters always caught one unaware, but sometimes so did blessings. If this windfall could help Frisco, who was she to question it?

Chapter Twenty-Two

Amber shoved away from the window at the first sight of the stagecoach. Yes, she was anxious to see her parents, but she was more excited about what their arrival meant. Now that they were here, it was only a couple of days until her wedding. She ran onto the porch of Major Adams's house. Ever since the fire and storm had destroyed the beginnings of her house, she'd found warm hospitality with the Adamses, who had welcomed her to take Caroline's room.

Amber trotted down the gravel walk that hedged the parade grounds to where the stage had stopped. How was Caroline doing? Amber was surprised she hadn't come back to the fort, but undoubtedly her underground house had fared better than the partially constructed cabin that Amber and Bradley had been working on. Major Adams reported that Caroline had been spied in Plainview, helping with the relief, so she must not have needed help herself. That was Caroline—landing on her feet and in her trooper's boots.

A minister and his wife disembarked from the stagecoach first, and then her father appeared. Captain Herald stretched his full height and drew a deep breath of Oklahoma air before extending a hand to the carriage. Her mother climbed out and stamped her feet as she shook the wrinkles from her skirts. Amber's steps hurried as she passed a drilling company. Bradley wasn't among them—she already knew that—so her focus was entirely on her parents.

And once they saw her, theirs was on her too.

"Ambrosia." Her mother held out her hands. "What a lovely bride you will make. We did make it in time, didn't we? I rued every minute on that train, because the air is so detrimental to your father's constitution. He doesn't need to be inhaling all that soot, but he never complains, he—"

"I have no need to complain. Your mother does an adequate job for me." He took Ambrosia by the shoulders and kissed her cheek. "How's my daughter?"

Amber relished the affection from her father. They'd shared some adventures together, but after this week she would no longer be his responsibility. "I'm so relieved you made it. With all the excitement going on, I was afraid the train would be delayed."

"Where is Corporal Willis?" Her mother scanned the unit of blue uniforms on the parade grounds. "Oh, he won't be called Corporal Willis after tomorrow. Just Mr. Willis."

"Once we're married, you may call him Bradley," Amber said. "And his unit is in Darlington, helping with distribution. They're keeping him near the fort since his term is nearly up. Now, Major Adams is anxious to visit with you, Father." Then, remembering who was the more exacting, she added, "And wants to make your acquaintance, Mother. His house is this way."

She'd just started leading them to Officers' Row when she spotted a young woman walking along the road. It was none other than her friend Caroline.

Was Caroline still her friend? They hadn't spoken since their spat over Frisco's land. Amber had never stayed at the fort without Caroline and felt her absence keenly. Knowing that they hadn't parted on good terms burned even deeper. Amber lifted her chin and clenched her jaw. Had anyone told Caroline when the wedding was? Did she even care? Well, their friendship had too much history to be blown away this easily. Caroline and Bradley were both stubborn. Someone had to offer the olive branch, and if it was going to happen, it would have to be her.

Patting her mother on the back, Amber said, "That's Caroline coming from the adjutant's office. I need to talk to her, but then I'll catch up with you."

Her mother turned to protest as Amber walked off, but she knew her father had the situation well in hand.

"Caroline," she called.

Caroline turned. Her posture stiffened. Amber clenched her fists. She would do this. Their friendship was worth it.

She relaxed her hands and forced her arms to swing gently as she caught up. Caroline wore a pair of sturdy work boots that Amber had never seen before. Her dress showed wear and a lack of good laundering. Amber knew the signs because she'd suffered the same herself until she came back under the roof of the commander's house.

"Caroline, I'm so glad I saw you." Amber kept a respectful distance while trying to pretend there was nothing amiss. "What brings you to the fort?"

"A banker." Caroline shrugged. "I needed to check on something."

"Oh." Seeing that no other information was forthcoming, Amber said, "I hope you didn't have much damage from the storm."

"Some floodwater, but it dried." Then, after a pause, "And you?"

"The roof blew off. Most of the materials can be reused, but I've been staying here at the fort since then. I go out every day to make sure no one tries to take it, but with the house started and the claim filed, I don't have to be there all the time. I might as well wait until Bradley is there with me."

Caroline's shoulders slumped, and she started to walk away.

"Wait." Amber stepped in her way to stop her. "If you have a minute . . ." She took a deep breath. "Our wedding is this Saturday, and I hope you can come."

Caroline blinked. Her eyes lowered. "I really wanted to come," she said. "Are you sure you want me there?"

"Absolutely sure."

Caroline sighed, then looked toward the barracks. "What about Bradley? What does he think?"

"It's my wedding. He'll think whatever I want him to think." Caroline and Bradley might both have a tendency to be unreasonable, but Amber was tenacious. She specialized in getting unreasonable people to do what they needed to do.

"I knew it was going to be a small affair, so I told myself that you might not have room for me—"

"Nonsense," Amber interrupted. "We'll say our vows at the fort's chapel. Nothing fancy, but we want our family and friends there, and you're both. Besides, if I understand correctly, you and Frisco have been keeping company. You must have found a way to appease him."

At this Caroline brightened. "Oh, I have. I'm working on a way to make amends, and I think I've found it."

"A process that's probably agreeable to you both?" Amber raised an eyebrow. Caroline didn't answer, but her tight smile informed Amber that her friend's fascination with the rabble-rouser had been resurrected. Amber nodded. "Then as far as I'm concerned, it's water under the bridge."

"I appreciate the invite, and your discretion." Caroline shaded her eyes. "Are those your parents? I haven't seen them in years."

"Come on, then." Amber took her arm. "And if I'm not

mistaken, you haven't met the Hennesseys' baby yet. He's so precious. I could just sit and hold him all day."

"I bet Lieutenant Jack is besotted." Caroline squeezed her arm. "He always made us girls laugh so. I can't wait to see him with his own children. Just before the race, Hattie told me . . ."

And just like that, Amber had succeeded. True, both she and Bradley felt that Caroline hadn't been fair to Frisco, but maybe they didn't understand what was driving her. Being a friend sometimes meant holding a person accountable, and sometimes it meant trusting them to correct an offense. Amber felt like she'd done both, and now the stain of a lost friendship wouldn't cloud her perfect day.

<hr />

The wedding was on Saturday. It felt so good to know that their conflict was behind them, that Amber was dedicated to restoring their friendship. Caroline's chest felt lighter, her heart happier. She reached for Frisco's Bible. After a long day of working, she'd often searched for comfort and companionship in its pages. Sometimes her search was successful, sometimes not, but this time she knew the passage she wanted.

She flipped through the pages to the fifth chapter of Matthew. This experiment in solitude had been good for her. It had made her turn to God's Word time and time again. No longer could she blame others for her malaise or inactivity. Her own character and decisions would determine the outcome of her life, and that realization helped her see how much wisdom she still lacked.

Her pursuit had been beneficial in surprising ways. She ran her finger down the column of print until she found the passage she was seeking:

Ye have heard that it hath been said, Thou shalt love thy neighbour, and hate thine enemy. But I say unto you, Love your enemies, bless them that curse you, do good to them that hate you, and pray for them which despitefully use you, and persecute you.

She lifted her head with a smile. Frisco had been her enemy, and he was still her opponent, but she would say that she'd come a fair piece toward loving him. She thought of him constantly, of how he'd sheltered her in the storm, how he was ready to stand against the Premiers even if he had to do it alone, of ways he might want to profess his love to her at their next meeting. Yes, she was growing in holiness every day. Scripture was such a comfort.

But as she moved to close the Bible, her eyes fell on the verses just above in the same column. More edification?

And if any man will sue thee at the law, and take away thy coat, let him have thy cloak also. And whosoever shall compel thee to go a mile, go with him twain. Give to him that asketh thee. . . .

The worn wooden cover of the Bible closed with a soft thud. That was enough reading for the day. She'd already found the encouragement she needed. Amber and Bradley had come around. She stood to place the Bible back on the shelf. She wished she could tell them what she was doing for Frisco, but once they learned about the money she'd raised for him, and how she was making amends . . .

The celebration. It was also on Saturday. Caroline leaned against the table. No, it couldn't be. Not on the same day. Bucky bumped against her leg. How could she miss Amber and Bradley's wedding? But what about Frisco? She'd told McFarland that she'd help him, and he was willing to pay lavishly for it. How could she justify walking away from that opportunity? What if Amber and Bradley didn't understand? Her mind darted back and forth between the awful choices before her.

She'd asked about the banker at the fort, ensuring that the

marshals had been notified. Curiously, they hadn't heard of the crime, and at this late date, it was unlikely they'd catch Sorenson while he was still in the territory. Her deal with McFarland was Frisco's best chance at getting the money.

Not that Frisco would ask, not that he'd ever know, but could she honestly look him in the eye and tell him it was more important for her to attend a wedding than to help him absolve himself of his debt? After she'd taken his land, she was going to put a party before his financial well-being? She couldn't do that to anyone, much less Frisco.

Amber would be hurt. Caroline would have even more to apologize for after this, but that was what she'd have to do: sincerely and regretfully tell them that she'd already made a commitment, and that it was a matter of great significance to their friend. Surely they could forgive her. Surely, if they understood that without the money, Frisco wouldn't be able to meet his obligations to his investors . . .

She'd do everything she could to help him—everything except abandon her own dreams.

Chapter Twenty-Three

Frisco stood at his front door, his hands propped against his waist. The midmorning breeze cooled his skin and ruffled his hair. Even though houses were going up around him, this lot seemed to catch a good breeze. Or maybe it was the high foundation of his house that increased the airflow. Either way, whoever ended up with this place would be lucky indeed.

Inside the future parlor were Frisco's cot and books. He'd given Patrick and Millie his tent, a small comfort while they waited out the settlers who might pull up stakes and leave their land to a neighbor. The individual rooms of the main floor were framed but not completed, and the upstairs would remain open to the elements for a while, since Mr. Nesbitt the carpenter had worked off his debt. Not that it mattered. Frisco wasn't ready to claim this house as his own. He wasn't ready to unpack his traveling case. Not yet.

Over the last few days, Plainview had reached a new phase. No longer were people aimlessly scurrying around to find the basic necessities. Stores had been established, wells dug, kitchens set up, and people had routines that made life somewhat predictable. Certainly it was a buoyant, optimistic predictability, but as faces became familiar and buildings became permanent, the progress only increased in pace.

Frisco was relieved to know he wasn't knocking the legs out from under all the work that had been done. Today he was going to break the bad news to Mr. Lacroix. He'd done interviews. He'd done the research. He couldn't represent them in court. The founders' stories held. There were no inconsistencies that he could find. They'd had permission as deputies to be there early, which meant they'd scouted the place out, but on the day of the run, they seemed to have competed with everyone else. They were one another's best witnesses, and by the time everyone else had arrived, there was no one to testify against them.

Just when Frisco needed paying customers, he had to turn down this one. He'd have to get a loan or get Caroline off his land in a matter of days. Those were his two options.

He reached for his cravat, which was draped over a sawhorse, and pulled it around his collar. The wedding was today, and Bradley had made a special trip to invite Frisco. Under normal circumstances, Frisco wouldn't have bothered attending, but the mess he found himself in was anything but normal. Falling in love with Caroline Adams wasn't generally recommended, but if one was going to attempt it, he'd better be ready to face fire from both her and her father. What better place to do that than a celebration of matrimony?

He stopped by Patrick's tent to see if there was anything they needed from the fort. As always, he felt a twinge of guilt as he walked past. Patrick and Millie were bringing in work and making friends in Plainview, but every time Frisco faced him, he remembered that there were sixty-three others like him who he'd failed. People he owed.

And he was turning down paying work rather than accepting money for a lost cause.

Having said his good-byes, Frisco headed toward the livery

to collect his horse. Had he remembered the big celebration planned for the town that day, he might have skirted Main Street to save time. As it was, he ran smack-dab into everyone he'd normally want to avoid when in a hurry.

"Frisco, are you here to volunteer?" Sophie asked. She'd decked herself in patriotic bunting and liberally applied cosmetics. "It's going to be a smashing parade and speech, and then there's going to be a tableau. They're going to reenact the picture of the founders, but with Ceres, the goddess of agriculture, and Liberty granting them favor. Something like that. It's going to be beautiful."

"I've got a wedding to go to," he said.

Sophie elbowed him. "It's about time! I'm surprised you got the courage to ask her. I'm surprised she said yes. I'm surprised—"

"*I'm* not getting married. It's a friend."

"Oh." Her smile vanished, then returned three times brighter. "You've got a lot of friends around here now. Just yesterday Patrick and I were telling that Mr. McFarland how it was sure something that the three of us ended up here. It's like a family reunion of sorts."

How had Sophie and Patrick managed to emerge from the same sad place and not mind talking about it?

"I'm glad you're here officially now," Frisco said at last.

"And I'll be right here tonight. There's fireworks! You better get back before dark."

"Yes, ma'am."

Maybe Caroline was right. Maybe people didn't always disappear on you. Maybe this could be home. If he didn't give up his position as the counselor for the city, then he was well on his way to leadership.

Frisco continued his walk through town. The grass had already been worn down, leaving a marked road. The smell of hot tar drifted over from a building in progress. Now two-story buildings lined both sides of the street, throwing shade where before there had been none. Not that they were completed two-story buildings, but most had enclosed rooms for their goods, offices, or restaurant on the ground floor at least. Above him, men tightrope-walked the beams as they continued constructing upward. If he were to leave town for a week, he wouldn't recognize it when he came back. New construction was popping up every day.

City hall now had four brick walls, all about hip high, and against the brick wall stood a round table. The wind ruffled the cloth that had been laid over it to accentuate the display. Frisco looked both ways, but no one seemed to be attending the table. An empty punch bowl waited by a platter that would undoubtedly be filled with sweets later. They were preparing for the celebration. He wouldn't be surprised if Caroline planned to stay at the fort with her parents for a night after the wedding, but if not, he'd ask if she wanted to accompany him. They might even get to dance again.

A framed photo rested in a place of honor on the table. Frisco lifted the picture of the Premiers of Plainville that was already familiar to him. How many of these men had Mr. Lacroix accused of cheating? Had any of them conspired to come in before the gunshot that started the race? Standing in the shadow of their accomplishments being constructed around him, Frisco wondered if it even mattered anymore. There was no way to prove anything.

Shadows used to be scarce on the prairie. No trees, no mountains or hills. Riding alone, it had been only him and his shadow many times. And in this picture, before the buildings were constructed, the only shadows were of the men themselves, stretching out long on the undisturbed grass.

Frisco's heart skipped a beat. Their shadows . . . He held

the picture closer. There had to be some mistake. Had this picture been taken at noon or shortly after, there would be no shadows—not shadows like this, anyway. He blinked in case he was seeing something that wasn't there. But no, the shadows were of the morning, not noon. The shadows of Bledsoe, Juarez, Feldstein, and even the banker Sorenson stretched long and thin. And standing there with them was Ike McFarland.

What if Frisco was wrong? What if they were afternoon shadows? But then he looked at the empty plains behind the men. Not a person in sight. Frisco lowered the picture with steady hands. He'd been praying to know the truth—Had they broken the law? Were they there too early?—and here was the evidence he'd been lacking. Here was the proof that would take away nearly half the claims on Main Street and make them available to those who'd played by the rules.

His face blazed. All that concern McFarland had about the case, all the questions he'd asked, and Ike had known all along that they were all cheaters. Himself included.

So what was Frisco going to do about it?

He was going to do everything he could. He set the picture down and backed away from the table. It would cost him. Whether he won or failed, he'd be hated by many, but Frisco knew himself well enough to know that he couldn't ignore the crime. He couldn't watch them prosper, knowing that people like Patrick hadn't had a fair chance. He was disappointed in McFarland, disappointed that the favor he'd curried meant nothing. Frisco had thought he'd lost everything, but that wasn't true. He hadn't lost his honor. Nor would he.

What would Caroline say when she learned that he was going to take on the Premiers of Plainview and expose them as cheaters? Frisco spun on his heel and marched away. If he'd judged Caroline correctly, she wouldn't bat an eye. She'd stand bravely and denounce them with all the confidence of a woman who'd never considered what it meant to lose. He needed her like never before.

Walking through the spring prairie grass in a Roman stola, Caroline felt a heaviness she couldn't blame on the delicate fabric. Amber, her best friend, was getting married. At the fort, her father, sisters, stepmother, and most of the people she held dear were gathered. And she would not be with them.

Lifting the hem of the long, draped tunic so the soft fabric wouldn't catch burs, Caroline trudged on. She'd worked on her hair so that the copper locks curled and cascaded down one of her bare shoulders. If it weren't for her old work boots, she'd look like a Roman maiden in the fields, but she wasn't going to walk barefoot to town. Hopefully her socks wouldn't leave her feet wrinkly when it was time to take them off.

What would Frisco think of her costume? He'd tease her, she was sure, but she could guarantee that there'd be admiration in his eyes. Eventually, if they were allowed time alone, there'd be words of admiration as well. He had never failed to pay gentlemanly homage to her beauty when it was warranted. So—he thought her beautiful, but that wasn't enough for Caroline.

A complete stranger could declare her beauty without any sense of obligation or commitment. Frisco also complimented her intelligence, but again, that was nothing remarkable. Caroline was smart. A teacher's examination could verify that fact. The obvious wasn't what she wanted to hear from Frisco. She wanted something more.

She readjusted the shawl she had tied over her shoulders. She didn't want people to see her costume before the grand revealing of the tableau. She hoped she found Frisco and had the money in her hands while still wearing the dramatic costume. She liked to picture herself giving him the money while she was dressed like a Roman heroine. She also liked to imagine him saying things that went far beyond mentions of her looks and intelligence. Words of feelings and emotion. That was what she wanted to hear.

But what could she say about him? Yes, she could praise him in the common ways that people praised him. He was a handsome man, dashing and reckless in his manners. He was a natural leader, smart, wily, and determined. All were qualities that the most disinterested observer could admire. Did she prefer him because of his looks and talents? That played a role, certainly, but if that was all that was required, then any single lady could be his. What attribute of his made him the perfect one, the only one, for her?

It was his vision. His view of a future that few could imagine. But he wasn't just a dreamer. He also had the tenacity to see the task completed. He saw towns and farms where there was only grass. And when he looked at her, Caroline felt that he saw the possibilities there too. He saw what she could be, what she wanted to be. He made her want to do great things and made her believe that she could.

She'd reached town. Mrs. Bledsoe, the mayor's wife, greeted her and escorted her to a tent set up within the walls on the former bank site. Maybe Caroline was being superstitious, but it seemed bad form to place the town's center at the location of the greatest theft the town might ever know. Inside the tent, she left her wrap and handbag. She unlaced her boots, wiggling her toes. She had pretty toes. She wasn't bragging, just stating the facts. The soft cloth of the stola draped becomingly around her, and the gold rope defined her waist and crossed over her bosom. Generally white was a color she didn't favor with her pale skin, but with all the bright colors of spring, she thought it was permissible.

The crowd had gathered outside. In the four years that she'd lived with her stepmother, Caroline had learned to adore performances, and this one would be magnificent. Frisco would never forget it. She picked up her copy of the script and scanned it one last time. She'd even practiced the dramatic gestures. Louisa would be proud. Hopefully Frisco would be proud too. And hopefully Amber had received her letter and would give her grace until Caroline could explain her reasons in person.

Mrs. Bledsoe returned to escort Caroline to a chair behind the painted canvas screen that hung between the city hall and a wagon nearby. They'd constructed a stage so that the actors would be high enough for everyone to see. Caroline made herself comfortable as she listened to the band rousing up the crowd. A coronet led the song, with a tuba and drum keeping the tempo. Through a tear in the canvas, she watched as people continued to arrive. Already she knew most of them. Already they'd established a camaraderie that had been forged by the hail and lightning the night of the storm. These people, from various corners of the earth, had found a shared identity. They were Oklahomans, and however new that designation was, it didn't lessen their pride.

Mayor Bledsoe had taken the stage. Caroline's mind wandered while he droned on. Her whole family would be at the wedding. Louisa was probably crying over her baby brother. Daisy would be all over the place with excitement. Would Hattie and the baby attend? Probably not. Even if she felt fine, Caroline knew Mrs. Hennessey wouldn't want to be in society until her gowns fit her again.

Her ears perked up as the mayor announced the title of her portion. *Prosperity and Nobility Taking Root on the Prairie* was her cue. Caroline draped her red hair over her bare shoulder and joined the others on the stage.

Frisco sat in the back of the chapel on the fort. He'd ridden past it many times and been marched past it in handcuffs more than once, but he'd never been inside. It was smaller than he'd imagined. Bare. It left him wondering how the God of the open sky, the God of the vast plains, could be worshiped inside it. Then again, hadn't he met God in jail cells? Still, he itched to lean out one of the open windows, because this felt like looking at the sea through a pinhole.

But it was a place of learning and fellowship—he could respect that. And this was a wedding, and it was nice, but it would be nicer if Caroline would hurry and arrive.

He had searched the chapel for her before realizing that she was probably an attendant for the bride. Major Adams had given him a solemn nod when he spotted him in the congregation and seemed to expect some kind of answer for something. Did he already suspect that McFarland and the other founders were crooked? Frisco would be glad to have the major on his side.

Before he'd left town that morning, he had met with Mr. Lacroix to tell him that he would take his case. Frisco's confidence had spread to Lacroix immediately, and before he left, he'd added four other names to the claimants—all men without land who deserved the stolen plots as much as anyone. Frisco might not have gotten to start his own town, but he would still be responsible for helping people realize their dreams.

Bradley Willis stood up. He'd been sitting in the front row, and Frisco hadn't recognized him in his suit coat. So it was true? He'd completed his enlistment and was going to try his hand as a gentleman farmer? Well, with their homestead, he'd have a better start than many. He could have had a nice place right on the edge of town—Frisco's town—but that didn't look like it would come to pass. Caroline had managed to withstand the boredom, the monotony of chores, and the loneliness that

Frisco had thought she would succumb to. She might be there to stay.

And then he'd be in Plainview to stay.

Unless he did the unthinkable and proposed a better, more personal offer.

Everyone stood as Miss Herald and her father appeared at the back door. Frisco looked past the beaming bride, but he didn't see Caroline. Where was she? Had she run into trouble on the way? But Major Adams wouldn't be standing at the front of the church if he didn't know his daughter's whereabouts.

Frisco turned to face the front. How had that fool Bradley Willis managed to land such a good woman? From what Frisco understood, Bradley hadn't had any kind of upbringing. If it weren't for his sister intervening in their childhood, he could have been raised in the same institutions Frisco had been. Yet there he was, grinning like his face was going to split, and marrying into a fine family.

Miracles did happen. Frisco might be asking for one of his own soon. He had looked forward to spending the day with Caroline. He'd wanted to squire her around the wedding and find excuses to walk her back to town and to home, but she'd gone missing, and he could hardly get up and run out of the church to hunt her down.

The happiness of the marrying couple only made time crawl more slowly. He wished them the best, but he hadn't come here for them. With all the concerns about his decision to challenge the Premiers, with all the work that lay ahead of him, he didn't have time for this. He'd make time for Caroline—in fact, he wanted her to know what he'd found. If she understood what he'd learned and why he had to do what he was going to do, then he could face what was ahead.

If he had her on his side, he could take on any challenge.

The vows were complete. Bradley leaned back and gave a

Cheyenne war cry when the pastor announced that he could kiss his bride. The ladies tittered and the men guffawed when he dipped Miss Herald—no, Mrs. Willis—for a sound kiss.

Frisco reached for his hat. He'd share his congratulations later. The two of them wouldn't remember anything about this day besides each other anyway. But before he could skedaddle, Major Adams called his name.

"When Caroline sent her note, I assumed it had something to do with you." The major rested his hand on the hilt of his ceremonial sword—at least Frisco hoped it was a ceremonial sword.

"I thought she'd be here," Frisco said. "What did the note say?"

"That she'd been asked to help with something in town. We couldn't imagine what would be more important than this wedding. That's why we thought it might be your doing."

Getting blamed for Caroline's disappearance was the nicest thing anyone had ever said to him. "You think she'd miss the wedding for me?" His chest rose. "I wish that were the case—"

"Oh, stop your preening. She'll have to answer for her absence. Just when we thought she and Bradley had smoothed over their disagreement . . . but then I learned that someone put her name on a list of illegal participants in the run. I'm not going to say anything today—it's his wedding day—but if I find out that Willis did that, trying to put her claim in jeopardy, he'll wish he hadn't."

Gripping the pew next to him, Frisco kept his smile steady. He'd completely forgotten about the list. It had been a moment's poor decision—a decision he'd forgotten. "That list is only speculation. Miss Adams has plenty of witnesses to verify her claim."

"Of course she does, but I had to answer for it to keep her from a hearing before the Register and Receiver. Willis is lucky he's no longer under my command, but he shouldn't rest easy until I get to the bottom of this. When I'm charged with applying the law and my daughter is accused of taking advantage, it's a disgrace on the level of those deputies."

"The deputies?" Frisco held up a hand. "Wait. First, don't blame Bradley. I have irrefutable evidence that he's not to blame." What that evidence was, Frisco didn't feel compelled to share at the moment. "But what's this about the deputies?"

Mrs. Adams nudged her husband with her shoulder. "You're blocking the aisle, dear. Can you step aside?"

"My apologies." Major Adams took his wife by the arm and escorted her through the chapel while still talking to Frisco over his shoulder. "Our orders forbade any soldier from placing a claim. It would have been a conflict of interest for them to officiate while competing with civilians. My troops were prohibited, but the word is that nearly every deputy specially hired for this event took land for themselves. Just think, claiming the best plots for themselves when they should have been collecting the names of cheaters. It's not right. Why were my troopers excluded, but deputies were allowed?"

"Major Adams?" Mrs. Adams looked up at her husband. "We're at my brother's wedding. Can we find a more pleasant topic, please?"

"I apologize again, dear." Then, to Frisco, "I assume you will see my daughter soon. Tell her—"

"Tell her to have a lovely day," Mrs. Adams said. "We must congratulate the bride and groom. Please, Daniel."

Frisco pulled on his gloves as they joined the wedding party. A lovely day? He hadn't expected Major Adams to hear about Caroline's name on the list of sooners, but it sounded like the matter was settled. In any case, finding Caroline and knowing that Major Adams agreed with him against the deputies meant that it would be a lovely day indeed.

Chapter Twenty-Four

The fabric of Mr. McFarland's robe was as nice as hers, but he didn't cut as striking of a figure. According to Mayor Bledsoe's wife, he was the Greek chorus narrating the beauty of what had been accomplished here: raising a civilization from the dust in a matter of weeks, although it felt like it had happened in just hours. Caroline smirked at the thought that the impartial chorus was introducing and celebrating his own accomplishments. But not overtly. That was her job.

He finished his lines, and all eyes turned expectantly toward the rift in the curtain where she was to make her entrance. She was doing this for Frisco, she reminded herself as she gracefully came to stand next to Mr. McFarland on the stage. Only for Frisco would she be missing her best friend's wedding. Her lips curved serenely as she surveyed her audience, making sure the rustling had died down before she delivered her first lines.

"It was high noon on April the twenty-second, in the year of our Lord one thousand eight hundred and eighty-nine, when the stalwart men and women of Plainview stood on the edge of their destiny, scattered among so many other contenders. Of the hopes and prayers sent heavenward that day, many were for a new start or for financial gain. But there were a few select men whose greatest goal was a chance to create a city on a hill—a city that would be an example to all of brotherhood, duty, and industry."

Did Deputy Juarez have a tear in his eye? McFarland must be pleased that he was getting his money's worth out of her, but when she looked at him, she only saw calculated satisfaction beneath a crooked wreath of laurel. Caroline had harbored suspicions about the Premiers after learning about Frisco's clients, but if Frisco had found any evidence of misdeeds, he hadn't shared them with her. She tried to keep her face impassive. Why was McFarland paying her this much? There were several young ladies in the audience who would've done it for the honor alone. Of course, they weren't the major's daughter.

She picked up where she'd paused, weaving a colorful narrative of the race and the first stakes struck here on Main Street. Over the years, Caroline Adams had suffered under the strict rule and dogged oversight of her father. It was high time she profited from it.

But a few people in the crowd weren't appreciating her recital. Three men stood with arms crossed. They had the look of people who hadn't slept on a mattress for a good long while. The grumbling came from their direction. Caroline raised her voice while keeping her tone smooth.

"The heroism and success of the brave men and women of April twenty-second will carry Plainview forward—"

"Success?" a man in a beaten hat called. "They didn't succeed. They cheated."

Caroline darted a look at McFarland. His jaw had hardened. She continued, "In the spirit of—"

"Cheating. The spirit of cheating." This from the man next to the first interrupter. "McFarland, you weren't at the line, and neither were any of these other men, including your buddy who ran off with all our money. Those plots don't belong to you, and I'm going to prove it."

Stubbornly sticking to her script—Caroline needed that one hundred and seventeen dollars—she tried to speak over the hecklers. Even if she couldn't be heard, she would finish what she had been hired to do.

The confused crowd didn't know where to look. Besides two little girls in the front, whose shining eyes hadn't left her gleaming stola or the bronze bangles on her bare arms, more people were turning to listen to the men in the audience rather than those on the stage. Whatever McFarland had planned, this wasn't it.

"Deputies," McFarland said. From different sides of the square, two men made their reluctant way toward the troublemakers.

The loudest of protesters stepped back and raised his hands in the air. "You have no cause to arrest me. I'm only practicing my rights."

And then she saw Frisco. Caroline clapped her hands together. He would see her onstage after all. But he did not look as impressed as she'd hoped. Only sparing her a brief troubled glance, he pushed his way through the crowd, reaching the men at the same time the deputies did.

Did Frisco know them? Twisting her hands, Caroline looked again. Were they the men he'd met with by her place on the river? They probably were. That day he'd said they could be in danger—that he'd needed secrecy to meet with them. No wonder. He hadn't sounded certain of their claims at the time. Frisco had better be careful, or people would think he approved of their behavior.

He stepped between them and the deputies, and doing what he did best, managed to calm the situation. The deputies backed off. Mrs. Bledsoe motioned to the band to take the stage again. That meant Caroline's portion was complete.

But evidently McFarland wasn't ready to leave.

She startled at the loud voice next to her. He projected his words as if Frisco were a mile away. "Thank you for intervening, Mr. Smith. It's a relief to know that you and Miss Adams have the good of the community as your highest goal."

Caroline had started to dip her head in acknowledgment when she saw Frisco's sharp frown. What was wrong?

"Miss Adams doesn't know what I know, McFarland. And shame on you for dragging her into this. Next time, keep it between the men."

Caroline wasn't sure what Frisco was talking about, but she hated to be dismissed, especially on the grounds that she was a woman.

"This is as much my town as it is yours," she said. "Why can't I play a part?"

"That's right," McFarland replied. "A lady as intelligent and refined as Miss Adams doesn't need your approval."

"You don't care about her," Frisco said. "You're only using her for her family connections."

"If anyone has used her, it's you," McFarland answered.

Her throat tightened, and the golden cords that crossed over her bosom dug into her rib cage. What were they talking about? She'd done this for Frisco. She had missed a wedding for him, and here he stood, questioning her intelligence and autonomy before a crowd of her neighbors.

If she'd had a tomahawk, she would have struck him down. As it was, she stood her ground—the one thing he should know by now that she was an expert at.

Mr. McFarland had instructed the band to start the music. Her portion was finished. The men with Frisco were leaving. He paused, catching her eye. What was he trying to convey? Her feelings were too raw to care. With a lifted chin and slow, graceful movements, she exited the stage just as she'd planned.

But once behind the curtain, she grabbed her boots in one shaky hand and her shawl in the other. Perhaps she could make it to the fort in time to congratulate the happy couple. It might be the last happiness she would participate in for a while.

McFarland stood in her way with two crisp bills extended between two fingers. "Payment as requested," he said, "plus a little extra for your trouble."

Caroline took the one hundred and twenty dollars, surprised that new bills could feel so grimy. Fear, real fear, was growing inside her. What if Frisco was right? What if she didn't understand everything that was going on? Caroline could forgive being snubbed or challenged. Have a temper, let a colorful word slip—all could be overlooked. But she couldn't stand being used. Nor could she stand someone claiming that she was ignorant, which was what Frisco had done.

The bills crinkled in her hand. This was Frisco's money. That was why she'd done this. That was why she'd missed the wedding and disappointed her friend. But what had she waded into?

Without a word, she turned her back on Mr. McFarland and stuffed the money through the loose neck of her tunic. What would Amber think of her appearing at the chapel dressed like this? But it was probably too late. The wedding was over, and she couldn't make it up to them.

Caroline shoved her bare feet into the boots, then marched clumsily toward the edge of town. She felt ridiculous. She wanted to get back into her own clothes, wanted to hide in her little cave, where no one could say things about her or put words in her mouth. At first people avoided looking at her, as if they were embarrassed for her, but as she continued through the streets, the people she encountered knew nothing of her recent humiliation. She tried to meet their curious stares with a smile, but her heart wasn't in it.

She had wanted to prove that she could accomplish something

herself. She wanted to be valued for her own merit, and she'd been willing to work as hard as anyone to do it. But it turned out there were issues she was unprepared for—machinations she hadn't known to watch for—things that her father would have protected her from. And that knowledge infuriated her.

"Caroline."

She stopped, her bare feet sticking to the insides of the boots. She had nothing to say to Frisco. She stomped forward as he rushed to her side.

"What was that about?" Was he breathless or angry? "I went to the wedding, hoping to see you there. I couldn't believe you'd miss it. And then what do I find? You're helping McFarland?"

Caroline spun toward him. "Why wouldn't I help McFarland? He's your friend."

"I thought he was, but no longer."

She could feel the heat flooding her face. "Now he's not your friend? When did that happen? This is the problem, Mr. Smith. You don't value people. You don't care about friendships. You're willing to just walk away, but that's not right. I, for one, will fight to keep my friends, and I'm sorry if you aren't of the same mind." Her heart was breaking even as she said the words, because they were the truth, and they meant that Frisco could never be the man she needed him to be.

"We will not have this discussion in the middle of the road," he grumbled. He tilted his head toward his plot of land.

Caroline's eyes widened. There was a house there, and although the second story was still open to the air, it looked a great deal like the house she'd designed. She shook her head. "I want to go home," she said. "I don't want to stay in this town any longer."

"You accuse me of walking away from a friend, but you won't stay?"

The hurt in his voice caught her attention. "Are you my

friend?" she asked. The wind whipped a strand of hair into her eyes, but she wouldn't swipe at it.

"I wouldn't be so scared if I wasn't." His eyes were raw. He shoved his hands in his pockets. "You don't know what McFarland was doing."

"Because you didn't tell me. You had plenty of opportunity, but you didn't trust me to—"

The hammering on the house next door had stopped. A guy on a ladder was watching while his buddy holding the base tried to hide a smirk. Caroline glared at them, then stomped toward Frisco's house. She didn't allow Frisco time to get in front of her, just swung open the door and marched inside. Frisco followed, slamming the door behind them. He tossed a blanket off a narrow cot and gestured.

"I'd rather stand," she said. "I'm just here to clear my name, and then you don't have to bother with me anymore."

One thing she'd always admired about Frisco was his debonair flair under pressure, but now that polished veneer had turned as rough as the newly sawn boards framing his home.

Frisco was furious. Not with her. She didn't know. He was furious with McFarland for putting him in this situation and furious with himself for not being savvy enough to avoid it. But whatever happened, it wasn't Caroline's fault. After hanging his hat on a nail, he yanked off his gloves and tossed them on top of his closed traveling case. He couldn't let her take the brunt of his anger. And he shouldn't be surprised if he was going to take the brunt of hers. He leveled his shoulders as he turned.

She stood like a work of art, delicate cloth draped over her statuesque figure, soft shoulders, and neck that the ancients couldn't recreate in marble. Flaming red hair that returned the sun's burning rays. The impossibility of her beauty made him even angrier. If he was going to have a misunderstanding with a woman, why couldn't it be one who didn't captivate him so? One who couldn't devastate him?

He lowered himself onto the cot and leaned against the wall at his back. "Before you tell me what you were doing validating McFarland's claims, why don't I explain—"

"No," she said. "Ladies first."

Frisco studied the ceiling, disappointed he couldn't turn his eyes all the way toward heaven. "By all means. Defend yourself, then leave without hearing my side. That sounds reasonable."

She rearranged her costume, tugging on the folds of cloth at her neckline until Frisco grew uncomfortable and had to look away. The next thing he knew, wadded paper hit him in the side of the face.

He caught the crumpled paper in his lap. It was money. A lot of money.

"It's yours," she said. Her cheeks looked like they'd been touched with a fiery brand.

"You're paying me? Did McFarland tell you to give me this?"

"He paid me for my performance."

"One hundred and twenty dollars for getting onstage and reciting some lines when there are dozens of women who would've done it for free?" Frisco's eyes closed as he shook his head. "Caroline Adams, you have to be smarter than that. You can't take money from the likes of McFarland."

"I did it for you."

He stilled. She stood proud, but her facade was cracking. She shifted her heavy boots. Frisco's face tightened as he chose his words carefully. "What do I need the money for?"

"To pay back the people who were going to live in Redhawk. Sophie told me about it. She said they were coming after you and that banker had stolen what you had. I thought it only fair since I have your land. . . ."

He turned over the bills, flipping them between his fingers. It was a large sum, and money he needed badly. If only he didn't know how it had come to him.

"Do you know what this is?" he asked. "It's a bribe, Caroline. McFarland is using you to sway my opinion about the hearing."

"He gave the money to me. It has nothing to do with the hearing. I'm giving it to you because of the trouble I caused you with the land."

"He already offered the money to me if I'd drop the case against him. When I refused—" He handed the money back to her. "I can't accept. Even if this was your money to begin with, you won that land fair and square. You're under no obligation to make up the loss on my speculation."

"I'm not taking it back," she said. "Not after I missed the wedding to earn it."

Frisco's heart began a strange cadence. "You missed the wedding for . . . ?" He could only assume that Caroline was so duty bound that nothing else mattered. That was what he'd assume, because he feared to hope it meant anything more. "I see. This is your attempt to compensate me so that I won't trouble you over the land anymore. Otherwise, you would've felt guilty."

⁂

There were certain moments in life when one knew that the next decision would mean everything. Awareness danced across Frisco's face along with fear. Caroline could stay aloof. She could feign disinterest and pretend that her high moral character was what led her to sacrifice her friend's wedding to pay a debt. Or she could tell the truth. Frisco looked terrified of the truth. So was she, but her father had raised her to be a brave soldier.

"I didn't miss the wedding for the money," she said. "I missed it for you. I wanted to help you, because that's what friends do."

He turned the bills over in his hands. "You're a good friend,

Caroline," he said at last. "But I'm afraid our relationship has reached an impasse."

"What do you mean?"

He folded the money, then set it on top of the satchel he never unpacked. Resting his hands on his knees, he looked up at her, his dark eyes searching. "Our friendship has run its natural course. We started out as acquaintances, more knowing *of* each other than really knowing each other. You bested me at a contest that meant everything to me, and to my surprise I couldn't despise you for it. You didn't despise me when I made it my goal to push you off your land. You didn't shun my company even though we had this contentious situation between us."

"You might have had ulterior motives, but I needed your help."

"I did have ulterior motives." He wrinkled his forehead like the thought amused him. "But I found I was doing it for you, not to protect my property. We've covered a great deal of territory, from flirting over your father's table to relying on each other for support and companionship."

Companionship? Something in her chest fluttered. Had Frisco Smith just admitted that he relied on her for companionship? She met his eyes, expecting to see her uncertainty mirrored there. Instead, she'd never seen him more confident.

"I don't see anything wrong with recent developments," she said.

"But this . . ." He stood and pointed at the money on the satchel. "This means something else altogether. This means you weren't merely treating me as a friend. You were putting me before your other friends—friends you care deeply for." He joined her where she was leaning against the doorway, blocking out the light of the cloth-covered window. "And that is why we are at an impasse."

Frisco had taken his post opposite her. Caroline remembered years ago when she and Daisy were banished to their corners for misbehavior. If they moved, there were consequences. She looked at the floor between her and Frisco, from her work boots to his patent leather shoes. If the gap was breached, there would be consequences.

"I apologize," she said. "I should've never presumed to meddle in your business. If you want me to take the money back . . ." She squeezed her eyes shut. What was she doing? She couldn't retreat. Not now. "No," she said, more forcefully than she'd intended. "No, I won't take it back. It was meant for you. What you do with it is your business, but I did it for you. Think what you will, but I won't lie to you."

Her eyes opened when she felt his hand on her waist. His sure grip crushed the soft draping fabric and sent her heart racing.

"For me to follow the trajectory of our relationship," he said, "I have to respond with an equal or greater show of devotion. Do you understand?"

His fingers skimmed over her bare shoulder and traced the contours of her arm, but his eyes never left hers. Her breath hitched. What was he asking? It didn't matter. She had to know. "I understand," she said.

He'd covered the distance. The space between them was all but gone. "Do you object?"

"Only if you're acting out of duty and not true feelings."

His smile was slow. His lips . . . With a shiver, she wondered what his lips felt like and then speculated that she'd know before long.

"Everything about me is true," he said. "I wouldn't know how to lie to you, nor can I think why I'd want to. All I know is that I can't imagine any greater gift in this world than your regard."

She stood in his shadow, his nearness making her giddy. He pulled her against him, both hands on her waist now, firm against her back. Her hands were on his chest. She tried to keep some distance, some control. A last view of the sky from a ship slowly going under.

"A woman who dances with abandon like you knows what has to happen next," he said.

Oh, she knew, and she'd longed for this since she'd been old enough to understand. Finally in his arms, she felt that this was the culmination of a journey she'd started long ago. As for Frisco, how many years had he spent dreaming of her? Probably a lot fewer.

And then a blade of clarity pierced her haze. He wasn't taking her for granted, was he?

Her mouth tightened. "But you won't," she said. "You won't because—"

But Frisco wasn't asking for permission again. He took her lips, took her words, took her breath. She gripped his sleeves, but she wouldn't stop him. He was holding her with the same tenacity that he'd used to fight her, and this time she would surrender. Her grip loosened, and she rested in his embrace. Her bare arm slid around his neck as he availed himself of her willing kisses. She said his name, little more than a whimper.

He blinked as his eyes focused. "Do you want me to stop?" He was breathing hard. Shaking, even. Despite his turmoil, he looked ready to give her anything she wanted.

She touched his face. Ran her finger along the crease beside his mouth and traced his jaw until she could bury her hand in his dark curls. His groan sounded far away, but then it was upon her, humming against her chest as he kissed her again.

It had all been worth it, she decided as his hands tumbled through her hair. The work, the loneliness at the farm, the conflict—she regretted nothing that had brought her to this moment. Maybe this had been her ultimate goal all along.

The sun had moved in the sky, and yet they continued kissing, touching, looking into each other's eyes, and murmuring love that had gone too long unexpressed. It was a shock to realize that she was sitting on his lap atop his cot, but she wasn't sorry. He'd gone long enough without affection.

Her lips felt bruised. Her body was exhausted with longing. "I know we should stop," she said, "but I don't know how."

Frisco followed the neckline of her stola with his finger. His gaze landed on her lips once more, but he closed his eyes and hugged her tight for a brief second before setting her next to him on the cot.

"It's past time to get you home." He stood. Caroline giggled as he braced himself against the wall for a moment before taking a step. "I have to talk to that carpenter," he said. "This floor is wobbly."

"It wouldn't be your knees, would it?"

He grinned. "Let's see you try it."

She popped up and then, with her first step, fell into his arms. He kept her at a discreet distance, she noticed, which was not what she wanted but was perhaps wise. She smiled up at him. "Take me home, Frisco. My little house in the hill misses you."

He swept a lock of hair off her forehead. "Hmmm. As much as I regret it, I'm going to insist on a chaperone. Patrick can go with us. Not to worry you needlessly, but yours truly could be tempted beyond his strength."

"So this is what my father has been protecting me from all these years?"

"Come to think of it, I'll probably bring someone along anytime I go out to meet you. Or you should spend more time in town, where I have some accountability."

"We didn't need that before," she said. "What's changed?"

"Everything," he said. "Everything."

Chapter Twenty-Five

Every morning, Bradley stood at the edge of his field (his field!) and watched the sky come to life. For years his days had started with the call of the bugle, and he'd forgotten what it was to wake up naturally. Now he found that sleeping in didn't interest him at all. Not when he could work his land (his land!) or improve his house (his house!) or when he could spend time with his wife (his wife!). He'd never thought that anything could induce him to get out of bed early, but now Bradley was often fumbling around in the dark, looking for something he could accomplish before the sun rose.

This morning, Ambrosia was feeding the chickens that Lieutenant and Mrs. Hennessey had given them as their wedding present. Mrs. Hennessey had also painted them a stunning bridal portrait of Amber. She said they could look back years from now and remember how beautiful the bride was. The chickens were so they could have eggs and not starve in the meantime.

As for Bradley, his first task of the day was to seal the raw lumber of his house before it became vittles for termites. The sealant was best applied before the heat of the day had it drying in the pan.

But even before that, he knew of a situation that needed addressing. He took out past his property and soon came upon Caroline Adams.

With a bucket of water and a bar of fancy pink soap, she was kneeling on the ground and washing something. What was it? A goat? Bradley rolled his eyes. She had no business trying to homestead, but who was he to judge?

Getting irritated came easily for him, but holding a grudge required too much concentration. He'd rather clear the air and have it behind them. Letting his big, open grin spread on his face, he marched up to her.

"Where in the world did you get that?" he asked.

She glanced up to see who was talking to her, then quickly lowered her eyes. "It came with the property," she said while holding the young goat still and pouring water over its back.

Bradley could tell she was uncomfortable. No sense in letting it go any longer. He was a happy man and wanted the people around him to be happy too. "We missed you at the wedding," he said.

Caroline lowered the bucket and looked at him again. "I'm sorry, Bradley. I thought I could come, but then I realized I had already committed to an event in town." The goat hopped away when she took her hand off it. "It was something I was doing on Frisco's behalf."

Now, that was interesting. Bradley wished Amber was here to hear it. "Let me guess. You were at the land office, deeding the claim to him."

"I haven't been to the land office yet."

"Oh, that's right. I'd forgotten about your name being on the sooner list. But now that Major Adams got that fixed—"

Caroline's eyes flashed. "My name is on a list of illegal participants? Did you do that?"

"Good grief!" He stood on one foot and leaned forward,

balancing like an acrobat. "It wasn't me, Caroline. I came over to tell you that I'm willing to overlook what you did to Frisco, and you make another accusation. I saw you on the start line. If you think I'd perjure myself to even a score, then you don't think much of me at all."

Finally she was listening to him. Her mouth turned down. "Now that you put it that way . . . but it's the first I've heard of it. If you didn't do it, then who did?"

Bradley would have never made a good teacher. He no more than introduced a topic than he was bored with it and ready to move on to another. "Frisco told your pa that he figured he knew who did it. And your pa has already talked to the board and had it removed."

"It better not have been one of those deputies. They're already in enough trouble." Her eyes narrowed, and Bradley didn't want to imagine the punishments she was concocting for whoever had crossed her.

"The point is, it wasn't me, and it's already taken care of. What I came to tell you was that if you and Frisco are square with each other, then I have no business holding a grudge. As far as I'm concerned, this feud is settled, and we can be good neighbors." He cocked his head. "Is that the lay of it, or am I missing something?"

Caroline's arms were crossed. She tapped her fingers against her elbow. "Don't you worry about Frisco and me. I'd say we've overcome our differences." She stepped forward and extended her hand. "To neighbors and to family."

Bradley grinned as he heartily shook her hand. "And glory be when someone can be both."

<hr>

The money had been returned. Not wanting to interact with McFarland any more than necessary, Frisco had sent Patrick with the money and had received confirmation that McFarland had acknowledged it with annoyance. It would cost Frisco. Without the money, he was looking at incurring a considerable debt if Caroline didn't give in. And now he wasn't even sure he wanted her to.

He watched as Caroline dipped her pen in the inkwell, then tapped off the excess. He had the prettiest assistant imaginable. Here in Plainview, Frisco's law practice was in great demand. His plaintiffs were awaiting word on whether they'd be granted a hearing. From that hearing might come a court case, but it was Frisco's hope that once he produced his evidence, the Premiers of Plainview would for once do the decent thing and leave town, saving them all time and wasted money before the board.

Even without the fight over the lots, there was plenty for a lawyer to do. The whole territory was filled with new businesses that needed paperwork drawn up. Partnerships were being formed as neighbors met neighbors and those who could have been rivals decided to join forces.

Building a civilization wasn't for the idle. A month earlier this spot had been home only to prairie dogs, grasshoppers, and white-tailed deer. Look how much they'd accomplished since then. And the townspeople had accomplished it together. With every passing day, the thought of starting over with a new group of settlers lost more of its allure.

His office was in the front room of his nearly finished house. A Choctaw furniture maker had brought a wagonload of furniture into town, and Frisco had agreed to buy the desk without even asking what it cost. Someday he'd need a large, impressive bureau to kick his feet up on, but for now Caroline needed a space of her own where she could turn his scribbled notes into neatly penned documents. The elegant curves of the walnut desk fit her, and she seemed to enjoy having her own space there. If that was what it took to get her to come more often and stay longer, Frisco would keep sitting on his cot and meeting clients with a notebook on his lap.

Again she dipped her pen in the inkwell and darted a glance at him. "I know what I'm doing," she said. "No need to watch me."

Oh, there was need. But ever since their fiery encounter, they had observed proper boundaries. There was no room for mistakes in their relationship. Her reputation and his honor were too precious to be tarnished, and his enemies were already looking for an opportunity to discredit him.

"I've got a tough choice to make," he said. "I can't decide what looks better: you sitting serenely at a desk with your hair arranged perfectly and wearing a becoming gown, or you carrying water to my garden with mud beneath your fingernails and your hair mussed."

"My lavender starts don't take much water, but it's been dry. I'll wait until the heat passes, then I need to get back. I don't want to be out after dark—"

"Caroline, have you ever thought about living in town?" Every scratch of her pen on the paper sounded like a screech as he waited for her answer.

"You've mentioned it before," she said, "because you wanted my land, if I remember correctly." She kept her head bent over the contract she was working on.

"But if you had a choice, if you were planning your future, for a life, for a family, would you rather be closer to the center of town instead of living next to a railroad?" Dust motes danced in the light coming through the shutters. How could they float peacefully when his heart was pounding so?

"And do what in town?" she asked.

"You wouldn't have to haul water and firewood for guests, at least. Instead, you could have your beautiful gardens here while you organize social events and plan the betterment of a new society. More importantly, I think you'd enjoy assisting in a law practice . . . and perhaps being married to a prominent citizen." The sound of his breathing echoed in the quiet room, but she didn't seem to notice.

"I don't remember any prominent citizens proposing marriage to me." She dipped her pen again.

"It's bound to happen," he shot back. "Especially as word spreads about what an asset you are."

"They'll propose to me for my secretarial skills?" She tipped up her head, showing off her delicate jawline. "I always thought my one-hundred-and-sixty-acre farm was my best feature."

With a wave, Frisco dismissed that idea. "Who cares about an old farm when they can live where all the excitement is?"

Was she listening? Was she thinking about his offer? But before he dared more, he saw Junior Flatts coming toward his door. Mr. Flatts was an assistant to Mr. Robberts and Mr. Admire, the Register of Deeds and the Receiver of Public Moneys at the Kingfisher Land Office. They were the men who oversaw disputed claims.

Frisco stood and opened the door. This was the moment.

Mr. Flatts took one look at the pretty woman at the desk and said, "I hope I'm not interrupting anything, Mr. Smith."

"Come on in. Miss Adams, may I introduce you to Mr. Flatts? He's working with the land office and the courts."

"Adams?" Flatts asked in a tone as dull as his name. "Seems like the major at the fort has a daughter about your age."

"Pleased to make your acquaintance," Caroline answered. "Should I excuse myself for this conversation?"

Frisco shook his head. "I assume Mr. Flatts is here concerning the allegations against the Premiers."

"That's right. We've received your notice of contest at the Land Office. I'm here to see if your evidence merits a hearing before the Register and Receiver."

"And I'm happy to oblige."

It didn't take long for Mr. Flatts to get the gist of Frisco's argument, and when he produced the photograph he'd obtained from the photographer, Mr. Flatts's placid face twitched in surprise.

"Nice of them to create evidence like this for you."

"They thought they were strengthening their claim."

"This case is destined for a hearing, I'd say. Can you appear before the board on Thursday?"

"Thursday?" Things were happening more quickly than he'd hoped. "That would be superb."

"Thursday it is. You'll present the evidence against the men, and then your plaintiffs need to testify as to why they are the logical beneficiaries of the land. If they can prove they ran the race fairly and arrived at Plainview in a timely manner, that should be sufficient." Mr. Flatts winked at Caroline. "This man has done a lot to help preserve the integrity of our little contest. No doubt he told you about all the help he was on the day of the race."

Caroline pursed her lips. "I understand he was so busy recording the names of wrongdoers that he almost missed out on securing a property at all."

This wasn't a safe topic. Frisco went to open the door. "Well, all's well that ends well. We'll see you on Thursday."

"It won't end well for the Premiers of Plainview, and it didn't end well for a lot of the people you reported." Mr. Flatts reached into a pocket on his leather vest. "I understand this belongs to you. Mr. Robberts thanks you for your assistance. I suppose your secretary takes care of your paperwork."

No. He mustn't do that. Frisco reached out a hand, but Flatts had spun and was putting the folded list right in the worst place in the world for it to land. Frisco's throat squeezed the breath out of him. He should have told her. Why hadn't he told her?

"You'll receive a summons about the hearing the same day the defendants do. It might get unfriendly, so prepare yourself."

But Mr. Flatts's words were drowned out by the roar in Frisco's ears. Caroline unfolded the list. Her head bent forward as she held it up to read.

"Thank you, Mr. Flatts." Frisco fought the urge to shove him out the door. "I'll be looking for that summons, yes, sir. You can count on me." And he shut the door before Mr. Flatts had made it down the porch steps.

The last line—that was where he'd written her name. That was where he'd made the instant decision to question whether she'd been honest or not. The last line was exactly where her eyes were planted.

"You turned this list over to the land office?" She held the paper daintily, but the knuckles on her other hand gripped the desk with force. "It's your handwriting."

"I couldn't believe that you beat me there. It seemed impossible."

"Did you think I was lying?"

"I'd already talked to dozens of people, and they all lied through their teeth—"

"According to you."

"And I was furious. If I'd had a chance to simmer down—"

"I blamed Bradley." She lowered the paper to the desk and turned away to gaze out the glassless window.

"I apologize. I'll apologize to him too."

"I shouldn't have accused him. Bradley wouldn't do that. Not to his friend."

Frisco couldn't protest, because he knew she was right. Bradley might give you a dressing down and threaten to box you if you didn't straighten up, but he'd never report anyone to the authorities. Not like this.

Caroline turned in her chair. "How can I aid you in your cases if there's concern that you might be falsely accusing people?"

Frisco stayed by the door. Minutes earlier he'd laid his heart out to her. He'd offered her everything he had, but she hadn't answered him. Was this going to be her excuse?

"I should've told you," he said, "but I tried to forget about it myself." He took a deep breath. He had known that he'd aimed too high in shooting for Caroline. He'd known that he was bound to mess up and lose her. He just hadn't thought it would be about something so paltry. "If this changes things between us, I understand."

"What are you saying?" She stood, her green eyes vivid against her pale face. "I'm the one offended, but you're telling me to go?"

"You don't have to leave, but I really messed up. If I were in your position . . ."

The hard lines of her face melted into something more sorrowful. "Of course," she said. "If it meant jeopardizing your property, you would leave me, because the property comes first, right? I tremble to think how quickly you would've forgotten about me had I not been holding your prize. Thank you for the reminder."

She took her gloves off the corner of the desk and her bonnet from the new mantel. "I'm sorry for you, Frisco. Sorry that you don't give me more credit, but it turns out that your prophecy fulfills itself. If you insist that your mistake will come between us, then who am I to argue? Good day."

Numb, Frisco watched as she walked out the door and down the grassy road away from him. This was why he'd sought to be the owner of his town, because people did just leave, even ones who claimed to be steadfast. You couldn't count on anyone, or maybe he couldn't count on himself not to mess everything up.

But he had been right all along. For all her talk about staying true, he'd found the one thing to drive her away. He would let her go if that was what she wanted. He was an expert at saying good-bye. He'd show Caroline there was one thing he was good at.

A crying woman garnered compassion. Men would offer assistance. Women would shed a tear in sympathy. Nearly everyone felt some tenderness toward a damsel in distress. Caroline's problem was that she couldn't cry. Instead she only grew angry.

Newly named Harrison Street was empty. A dog resting on a new porch stood as she approached, but with a whine it lowered its head, tucked its tail, and hid beneath a wagon. No one would feel sorry for her. So Frisco had hurt her feelings? She wasn't supposed to have feelings anyway. But it wasn't his accusation that had hurt. Her name on that list wasn't the end of the world. The true injury was that he'd given up on their relationship so easily.

The thought of going back to her dugout added weight to her steps. She'd begun to think of it as temporary. She'd begun to see it as a place to tarry until she could find an excuse to go back to town, because now town was where she wanted to be. Plainview needed her. With a partner like Frisco, she could accomplish a lot for that western settlement.

She'd been willing to trade the dream of her boardinghouse for one with him, but not if he held so lightly to their relationship.

The gurgling river failed to calm her as she reached her property. Frisco had been clear about what he wanted. He wanted this land. He'd even admitted when helping her with the roof, with the crops, that he was protecting his investment with the hopes of recovering it someday. Was this courtship his final attempt? Instead of adoring her red hair, was it the red dirt of her fields that he found more irresistible?

Chapter Twenty-Six

I reckon the Premiers of Plainview got their summons." Mr. Lacroix unscrewed his canteen and took a short draw from it. "Leaving tonight for Kingfisher, are we?"

"Yes. I told the other plaintiffs to meet there about tomorrow noon. I managed to catch a few men who partnered with me on an earlier venture and added them to the suit as well. If we win this case, there should be enough lots freed up for people like y'all who missed out. We'll stay the night in Kingfisher, then be ready for the board hearing in the morning." Frisco shifted so he was in the shade of his porch. He spent every moment looking down the road, praying that Caroline would come, but he'd been foolish to hope. Hadn't he always told himself not to count on people?

"Think there'll be trouble on the way?" Lacroix asked.

"Be prepared. There's a lot at stake, but I know this area well. I can get you there safely." Frisco had spent enough time skirting the troopers that he knew he could travel between the two points unobserved. The woman standing in the street wasn't as successful.

She was neat, petite, and confused. She squinted at the neighbor's yard as if she were searching for something.

"Can I help you, ma'am?" Frisco called.

Lacroix took another swig from his canteen as the woman came over with tiny steps.

"Yes, sir. I'm trying to locate a man by the name of Frisco Smith."

Her severe taffeta suit fit her small frame, still strong and trim even though she had passed her prime. She clutched a modest traveling bag with tarnished brass buckles. Nice enough at one time, but, like Frisco's bag, it had seen some wear.

"You've come to the right place, ma'am. I'm Mr. Smith."

Her smile trembled. Her chin quivered. "Of course you are." She switched her bag to her other hand. "I'm Franny Hunter and I've come looking for you. Is this your place?" Her head lifted to follow the house all the way to its eaves.

Frisco looked over his shoulder, as if his house could have moved and someone else's replaced it. "Yes. If you'll excuse me, I have some business to conclude, and then I can help you."

Mr. Lacroix flipped his reins over his horse's head. "I'll see you tonight, and surely we'll have this thing done," he said. "Watch your back until then."

At least Frisco was succeeding for Lacroix, Deavers, and the others. He had to have that victory, because his relationship with Caroline had failed. But perhaps this was another client he could help.

"My office is inside," he said.

"A chair would be delightful," Mrs. Hunter said. "I've traveled far."

"From where?"

"No need for water," she said. "Just a place where we can talk. That's all I require."

He led her through the door to the unfinished parlor. Caroline's chair had been empty since she left it earlier that week. He averted his eyes so he wouldn't have to see the list that still lay on her desk, then reached for the chair to pull it next to his cot, where he always met his clients. The day he had two chairs in his house, he'd know he'd arrived.

The lady sat, her mouth closed tightly against some news that threatened to burst forth. Frisco sighed. Never had anyone been that anxious to tell him good news. What trouble did she bring?

"What can I do for you, Mrs. Hunter?"

The fine lines around her eyes tightened as she tilted her head sympathetically. "There's really no easy way to tell you this."

"Best speak it plain."

She nodded, her face looking as delicate as china. "I'm your aunt, Frisco. Or Charlie, I should call you. Your mother is ailing, and she wants to see you before she passes. She sent me. I'm supposed to bring you back to Kansas. I'm supposed to bring you home."

Caroline stood at the door of Amber and Bradley's new cabin with an apple pie. It had taken the last of the canned fruit she'd purchased from Darlington, but she knew Amber's penchant for green apples, and after missing their wedding, she didn't feel right showing up empty-handed. The flour-sack curtain billowed out of the open window as Caroline knocked on the rough-hewn door. There would probably be a parade for the first people to get real glass windows. Freighters had wasted no time in bringing every imaginable item of commerce to the territory, but glass windows hadn't made it to the area around Plainview yet.

The curtain lifted, and Amber poked her nose out. "We have company, Bradley!" she called and then dropped the curtain. The door creaked but didn't open.

"What's going on?" Caroline called through the window. "If you don't want this pie, all you have to do is say so."

"Coming!" It was Bradley this time, and the door swung open.

Caroline hesitated, but Bradley grabbed the pie tin, and since she wasn't ready to relinquish it, she was dragged inside. Compared to her dugout, their house felt fresh and clean. The smile they gave each other upon seeing the pie felt healthy and heartbreaking—for her, anyway.

With her apple pie in one hand and a knife in the other, Bradley kicked the door closed with his foot. Concentric target rings had been splashed in whitewash on the back of the door. Caroline took another look at the knife in Bradley's hand.

"Target practice in the house?" She hiked an eyebrow.

"It's my own door. Just don't open it without warning me."

Amber pulled out two plates. "Caroline and I will share a plate, since we only own two."

"No bother." Bradley picked up a spoon. "I'll eat out of the tin."

They deserved this happiness. The two of them had fought for their relationship, maintained it over years of separation and well-meaning folks telling them they could find someone better. Or at least people told Amber that. But they were determined to be together, and here they were.

Unfortunately, Caroline and Frisco had no such history. She had thought about him for years, but it hadn't stopped her from courting in Galveston. And it hadn't stopped him from deciding that he didn't need her.

"Uh-oh. Rain clouds are forming on Caroline's forehead." Bradley took the pie tin from Amber after she dished out a piece for each plate. "From my experience, if there's rain with her, there's likely to be thunder."

Amber motioned Caroline toward the sawed-off stump that

doubled for a chair. "It's about Frisco, isn't it? I thought you were getting along."

Caroline dropped to the stool. "We were, but that list that Bradley told me about—Frisco is the one who put me on it."

Instead of outrage, Bradley shrugged. "That don't mean he ain't the one for you."

"The moonlighter list?" Amber shook her head. "Maybe it was an honest mistake."

"How can he innocently accuse me of being guilty? It just throws into doubt everything that's happened between us. His first priority has always been that land. He'd do anything to get it. He failed to get it legally, so I've got to wonder if he's trying to get it romantically."

"He wouldn't dare," Amber said.

"A fellow doesn't need an excuse to court a pretty lady," Bradley said. "The land is just extra incentive. Extra nice incentive."

"You aren't helping," Amber said.

"If it was only the list," Caroline said, "I'd forgive him, but he doesn't act like he wants me to. He knows how upset I am, and he hasn't called on me."

"Did he apologize?" they asked in tandem.

Caroline rubbed the back of her neck. "Shouldn't he know that the first apology doesn't count? Especially with me being so mad?"

Amber nodded, but Bradley rolled his eyes. "He made a mistake. He said he was sorry. And now you're complaining that he isn't doing more."

"If there were true concerns—" Amber began.

"But there aren't," Bradley said. "She's just got her feelings hurt that he's not chasing her down. Why not meet him halfway? Why not go to him?"

"Because what if he doesn't want me to?" It was a vulnerable feeling, saying your fears aloud, but Caroline needed an answer.

"If he doesn't want you, then you'll have to say good-bye. If he does want you and you keep hiding in your underground house, then you won't get a chance to say good-bye, but it'll be good-bye anyway. What's the difference?"

"There's a difference," Amber insisted. "But it doesn't matter. What matters is whether you love him. Whether he's worth the risk."

Caroline's teeth ground together. Could anything be more humiliating than admitting that you loved someone when he didn't love you back?

Cowardly. That was what she was being. Caroline had always stood her ground, unafraid that people might disagree or disapprove. Amber was right. She might not succeed, but she wouldn't fail for lack of trying.

She stood, her piece of pie untouched, and walked to the door.

"That's it?" Bradley asked. "Just leaving without any thanks for the wise counsel you found here?"

"Whether it was wise remains to be seen," Caroline said. "I might come back more heartbroken than ever."

"Betcha don't." Bradley winked.

If only the world was as simple as Bradley imagined. Yet he offered clarity when she needed it.

"Enjoy your dessert." And Caroline headed to town, determined not to return until she had an answer.

Frisco's first instinct was to hustle the woman out of his house and throw rocks at her until she'd been driven out of town. His mother? Mrs. Hunter's words hit the most vulnerable part of him. His mother? He never went a day without thinking of her, without seeing a woman with a child and wondering why his mother hadn't wanted him. As he grew older, his questions had changed. Did his father want him? Did he even know about him? If his parents were still alive—and someone put him on that train—did they keep track of the years? Did they think of him as a man, or in their minds was he always a baby?

All his unexpressed and expressed frustration now had a target, but the woman sitting before him didn't look evil. Despite the shock of her statement, her mission was exactly what he'd wanted for years. He wasn't sure what was harder to control— his anger or his hope.

"You're my aunt?" He forced his breathing to slow. "How did you find me?"

"Alice Maye always knew where you were. She pretended to have found you abandoned on the train. She stayed with you until the foundling hospital was called. She checked on you a few times, knew what they'd named you, and thought you would always be there."

Frisco's skin felt clammy despite the heat coming down from the sunbaked planks over his head. "Assuming that you're telling the truth, there are some things I don't understand. For instance, if she cared so much, why did she leave me?"

"She didn't think she had a choice. She and your father were in love, but he went to work the railroads so they'd have enough money to get married. She didn't know she was expecting when he left. She . . . we come from a respectable family. Our parents hid her until the baby came, but there was no question of her keeping it. She figured when your father came back and they got married, then they'd adopt you. People would never know their foundling baby was their own."

The story was everything he'd imagined. He'd hoped that his parents hadn't rejected him, but wouldn't there be some proof? Some evidence she had to tie him to the family? He had evidence, but he wouldn't tell her. Not yet. He'd hear her out before he tested her.

"What happened?" he asked. "Why didn't they get me?"

If his parents were alive, why hadn't they saved him from the beatings he'd taken at the hands of the older kids? Why hadn't they comforted him the nights he'd cried into his pillow over a fresh separation from a brother? Why hadn't they fed him when he was hungry and alone on the streets?

"She went to visit you one day, and you weren't there. She tried to track you down, but the records were confused."

"My name. They changed my name when I was a baby." The monogram on the man's handkerchief that was his only link to his origin wasn't for any Frisco Smith, but he'd held out hope that it belonged to someone who belonged to him.

"You can't imagine how devastated she was. She came to my house and cried so bitterly. There was nothing my husband and I or our parents could do to comfort her. She was a ghost until your father came back for her. That was the only thing that brought any light to her eyes."

"He never saw me?"

Mrs. Hunter leaned forward on the edge of the chair. "He wants to now. Your mother took ill, and all she can think about is getting you home so you can meet your brothers."

Brothers? Frisco's throat clenched. He dropped his eyes to hide the hope there. How badly he wanted it to be true.

Mrs. Hunter continued, "She found someone at the home who located that missing record, and from there it was easy. You've made quite a name for yourself in Kansas and the new territory."

Frisco stood next to the traveling case. He looked down at the only consistent thing he'd had in his life. Someday he'd unpack this bag for good, and maybe that someday was now and the somewhere was Kansas. Or maybe not. Over the years, the contents had changed, but there was one piece of cloth in it that had been with him through it all.

"You called me Charlie." Frisco worked his neck to make the

words come out. "Is that my father's name?" He closed his eyes as he waited for her reply.

"No. His name is Richard Everett. He never met you, but your mother left his handkerchief with you at the orphanage. She thought . . ."

She continued speaking, but Frisco dropped his head into his hands. *R. E.* Those were the initials on the battered square of cloth. Suddenly his suspicions seemed ridiculous. What could this woman have to gain by pretending kinship with him? He'd already falsely accused Caroline. He wouldn't make that mistake twice.

"How much time does she have?" he asked.

Mrs. Hunter clasped her hands together. "I know you have a life here. I know I'm asking a lot. But if she could see you, just once, before she dies . . . If it weren't urgent, I would've sent a letter. I would've broached the subject more gently. But there's no time, Charlie. There's no time."

Everett? Charles Everett? Frisco stood taller as he felt the weight of the name. In his estimation, it sounded too staid, not debonair enough. Then again, wasn't he aiming for a more respectable life? Pieces started falling together. He'd always wanted a more respectable position. Could it be that it was in-born in him? Could it be that he'd had his position stolen from him at birth, and now he was reaching for his rightful level?

But all speculation on his origins would be complete if he accepted this woman's offer. Frisco looked at the house going up around him—the first permanent residence he'd ever owned. He swiftly riffled through his dreams, trying to evaluate them in light of the new information. He didn't know how he'd fit into this family, but didn't they deserve a chance? And his mother. If he didn't do his best to ease her conscience, if he didn't take this opportunity to meet her face-to-face, he would always regret it.

Mrs. Hunter was waiting, keeping her eyes down, giving him some room to sort through his decision.

He had to go. He couldn't accept the sorrow that would be his if he didn't.

"When would we leave?" he asked.

"There's a train through Oklahoma Station today."

At four o'clock. He knew it well. He had time, and his bag was packed. It was always packed for exactly this situation. But what would it mean to leave? Certainly he could come back if things didn't pan out in Kansas. Patrick would hold his town claim for him, and as for the homestead, he'd have to send someone with his investors' money to Purcell to refund them, but it could be arranged. If he didn't come back, he'd be glad that Caroline got to keep the homestead after all.

Caroline.

"I'll be back," Frisco said and marched out of the house and off the porch. He couldn't think with Mrs. Hunter watching him so closely. He needed space. The sun's strength started a slow, unrelenting burn on the top of his head. He let it burn, wishing it would sear away all the confusion.

Was Caroline going to be a part of his life? Could she forgive him, or was this just the natural progression of their relationship? Had it only been meant to carry him this far?

Or maybe Charles Everett would be a more likely man for her. Maybe he'd learn more about himself, more about his people, and she'd be proud to have him. The major's daughter might be a natural partner for an Everett man. He rubbed his forehead, which felt near to bursting. His aunt wasn't rich. He shouldn't get such ideas, but after coming from a foundling home, there was no direction but up.

He had to go.

He'd started back inside when he saw a lone form coming down the street. He'd just had the best news of his life, but seeing Caroline jarred him. He wished he could disappear for a few days without anyone noticing his absence. Then, if his visit was a disaster, no one could mock him for his vain hopes. He hated this feeling. This fragility. He was supposed to laugh at danger and welcome conflict, but that veneer had a weakness, and today he'd been struck right in its weakest spot.

He didn't want Caroline to see him like this, but he did want to see her. She had spotted him. She didn't wave but continued toward him. Well, he couldn't hide. Besides, how he left things here in Plainview might determine choices he made in Kansas. And no matter how much he tried to look for alternatives, he knew that leaving Caroline behind was not what he wanted.

He knew what he wanted on that account, and he'd be a fool not to settle it.

Before she'd reached him, Frisco had a plea on his lips. "It's been two days since I saw you last," he said. "I'd rather go without food."

His declaration caught her off guard. She flushed. Stammered. "I missed you too. Whatever happened between us—"

"Forgive me. It's bad enough that I jumped to conclusions about you. What's even worse is that I dragged my feet in making amends."

She put a hand to her chest as the air left her lungs. Her eyes filled with tears. "I didn't know if you'd want to see me."

"I do. I want to see you every day. But first I have to see about something else." When Caroline's eyes wandered over his shoulder, he turned. Mrs. Hunter had followed him outside. "Ma'am," he said to her, "I want to introduce you to someone. This is Miss Caroline Adams. She's my . . . she's my everything."

Mrs. Hunter lingered in the shade of the house. "Pleased to meet you."

"Caroline, Mrs. Hunter is my aunt."

Caroline's jaw dropped. She looked from Mrs. Hunter to him and back again. "I didn't think you knew any of your family."

"That changed today."

Chapter Twenty-Seven

His aunt? How could that be? Caroline stumbled through the introductions, but her mind whirled like a windmill in a spring storm. Frisco stood quietly as Mrs. Hunter briefly explained what had brought her to him. Chills ran up Caroline's spine. Having lost her own mother when she was a child, she couldn't imagine missing an opportunity to know her. She also couldn't imagine a chance to see her again. If Caroline had heard that her mother was by some miracle still alive, there'd be no power on earth that could keep her away.

Frisco's face was blank, his eyes unfocused. Caroline wanted to wrap her arms around him and pull his head to her shoulders. It was the Lord's leading through the unlikely vessels of Bradley and Amber that had convinced her to set aside her pride and come to him. She was so relieved that she had. He needed someone by his side.

"Is everything all right?" Pushing a wheelbarrow of tin pots, Sophie Wilton appeared from around the corner.

Both Frisco and Mrs. Hunter looked spooked. How could he answer? He'd just found out his mother was dying . . . a mother he'd never known.

Caroline took charge. "Everything is fine, Mrs. Wilton. You have some pots for sale, I see."

Frisco was bidding Mrs. Hunter farewell. Sophie raised an eyebrow. "Is that Martha Rosini? What's she doing here?"

Rosini? Was that Frisco's family name? A quick look told Caroline that they didn't want to be interrupted. "She's a guest of Frisco's," she said. "Do you have any copper pots?"

With a grumble Sophie rattled through her wares but didn't come up with one. Just as well. Caroline hadn't planned to purchase anything. Her sole object was to free up Frisco, and she'd succeeded. Sophie went her way, but not before Mrs. Hunter had scurried off toward the center of town, leaving just the two of them.

"You're going," she said.

"I have to."

"After the hearing in Kingfisher, you can catch the train—"

"I can't wait until tomorrow. I'm leaving today." His eyes darted everywhere, not knowing where to land.

"Today?" For the second time that day, Caroline was rendered breathless. "What about Mr. Lacroix and the others? Who will represent them?"

"Come inside," he said. "The picture is the evidence they need. If you'll take it to them—"

"Frisco, I know this is an impossible choice, but they're counting on you. They've hired you to see this through. Without you at the hearing, McFarland is liable to swing everything his way. No one can replace you."

He looked ill but determined. "I've worked so hard on this case. It's costing me to leave, but if I don't go . . ." His throat jogged as he swallowed.

"I know." She placed her hand against his cheek. He turned and planted a kiss on her palm. "What if you find everything you were looking for? Will you come back?"

"I don't know what to expect. All my life I've kept my bag packed, waiting for a real home. She talked about my parents, my brothers. What if I belong there?" He took her hand in a grip that made her wince. "But I will come back. You will see me again. You don't have to wonder about that."

"It'll make the waiting easier."

"Thank you for taking the picture to the men. I'm confident they'll prevail. If not, we'll file again and hope for a second hearing."

Which didn't sound like a good idea, but Caroline wasn't going to argue with him. She couldn't stand between him and the family he'd always mourned for.

Frisco gave her the envelope with the photograph, and he already had his bag packed. After a few instructions as to where to find the men, and one scorching kiss, they parted.

Caroline had done what she was supposed to do. The accusers squatting on their friend's lot had been full of buoyant enthusiasm until they understood her mission. Then disappointment and hostility set in.

"He's leaving town? Today? He told us we'd go to Kingfisher tonight. What's so important that he had to leave today?" Deavers asked.

Knowing how protective Frisco was of his story, Caroline could only assure them that it was very important. They weren't mollified, but there was nothing left for her to say.

Feeling low, she considered going to the fort. Her father and Louisa would welcome her. And she hadn't seen Daisy and Allie Claire in a long time. Nothing would lighten her heart like playing with her little sister, unless it was holding Hattie's new baby boy. She'd need something to help pass the time until she heard from Frisco.

"Something is bothering you to distraction. You haven't heard a thing I've said, have you?" Ike McFarland was sitting on a chair in the shade of a tarp, his legs kicked up on a barrel.

She'd already stopped, or she would have pretended that she hadn't heard him. Yet it might be important. Since Frisco wasn't here to handle the court case . . .

"Excuse me. Did I miss something?" she asked.

"I was wondering if you were going to be at the hearing tomorrow." As usual, he sounded congenial and genuinely interested. What did he know?

"It doesn't concern me," she said.

"I thought you and Frisco were courting."

"And that doesn't concern you."

He stretched his arms out to his sides before crossing them over his chest. "Don't mean to pry, ma'am. I just wanted you to know that I harbor no hard feelings toward you or Mr. Smith. As a lawyer, he's paid to represent a variety of clients. I can't fault him for taking paying work."

This wasn't a man worried about losing his property. He was confident. Too confident. Had he heard that Frisco had left town and wouldn't be at the hearing? Caroline had just left the plaintiffs. Word couldn't have spread that fast. How long had Mrs. Hunter been in town looking for Frisco? Had she talked to McFarland?

"I found you a copper pot." Sophie Wilton stepped over a pile of lumber and brandished a pot over her head like it was a torch leading the way to freedom. "I think this is just the thing you're looking for." Her short skirt and muddy stockings flashed, and McFarland grinned in derision.

Caroline had nothing further to say to him. She turned and asked Sophie to walk with her. If she was going to become the proud owner of an unwanted pot, she didn't want McFarland laughing at her expense.

"I can't believe you found one just like I described," she said.

"You have particular taste, ma'am. That's a fact. But I hunted one down and offered top dollar for it so you could have it."

Caroline bit the inside of her cheek. She had to buy it now. Maybe Louisa would want it? "Can I pay in goats?"

"I can't keep a goat in our wagon." Sophie laughed and held out the pot. "This will be a dollar fifty."

Frisco's life had been turned upside down and the court hearing interrupted, and here she was, buying pots in the street. That wasn't what she should be doing. But Frisco had hired a buggy to take him and Mrs. Hunter to Oklahoma Station to meet the train. There was nothing she could do to help him now. Nothing except keep her word to his old friend. She loosened the string on her reticule and fished inside for her money.

Sophie waited with her hand propped on a shapely hip. "What's Martha doing in town?" she asked.

"Just looking to visit with Frisco." It wasn't her story to tell, although Sophie would understand better than most. Caroline found some coins, opened her palm, and pushed them around. "I only have seventy-five cents, but I'll get you the rest after I've been home."

"Don't bother. Now that I think about it, I probably didn't pay quite that much for the pot." Sophie handed Caroline the pot, then bent to stuff the coins in her sock. "What's Frisco up to?"

Her question carried no weight, unlike the pot Caroline was swinging. "I couldn't really say." She tested her grip on the wooden handle. Were people always this interested in Frisco's whereabouts? Then again, maybe Sophie knew about the hearing. That would stir some interest. "Sophie, if you hear something about Frisco, please keep it to yourself for a bit. There's no good that could come from spreading stories right now."

Sophie drew herself up tall enough to minimize her curves. "I wouldn't do anything to hurt Frisco. Don't worry about me spreading stories."

"I'm sorry. I wasn't accusing you." Caroline squirmed under the other woman's sharp gaze.

"Does this have something to do with Martha Rosini?"

"I've said enough. I have to follow my own advice," Caroline said, although the news was burning inside her. Wouldn't Sophie understand Frisco's situation? Couldn't Sophie lend some insight into what he was going through? But Caroline was stubborn. She didn't know where this urge to ask about his aunt came from, but she wouldn't betray him. He could tell Sophie about it when he came back. "Thanks for the pot," Caroline said and turned to leave.

But she couldn't. She felt that she was on the verge of making a huge mistake. What would Frisco think to hear that she'd kept his secret for less than an hour? But something was burning to be let out. She'd have to deal with the consequences.

To her surprise, Sophie hadn't moved a muscle. "That's my girl. What's stuck in your craw?"

"Nothing is wrong. I just feel like talking to you would be wise. I don't know why."

"You don't think I have anything to add? Maybe not, or maybe something's afoot, but I can't help unless you ask."

"Do you feel that same compulsion?" Caroline asked. "Like it's important we talk?"

"That's why I'm still standing here. I've learned that God talks to some people's hearts, but He talks to my gut. And my gut says that Frisco is in trouble."

With a jerk of her head, Caroline motioned Sophie toward Frisco's house on its quiet lane and away from the hustle of Main Street. "You saw that woman," Caroline began. "Her name is Mrs. Hunter now that she's married. She's Frisco's aunt."

"That's what she said?" Sophie's mouth turned down. "What else did she say?"

"That his mother wants to see him—his mother that he's never met. She's on her deathbed, calling for him, but along with her are Frisco's father and whole family. Mrs. Hunter made this trip to bring him back into the arms of the family that never forgot him." Caroline waited to see if lightning was going to strike her, but no clouds appeared.

"Every lost child's dream." Sophie tugged the open neck of her blouse closed and grunted. "They're playing him for a fool. Look, Miss Adams, that Martha Rosini isn't Frisco's aunt. I almost didn't recognize her in those respectable clothes, but she's a riverboat gambler. Makes her money by the turn of a card. Got the best bluff of anyone I've ever met. She's lying to him."

Lying? Why would someone do that? And Frisco wasn't naïve. "The story she told had enough truth to it to convince him," Caroline said. "Frisco isn't easily fooled."

"He wanted to be convinced, and that story was concocted to hook him good. Besides, I guarantee someone let the goose slip. Said too much about Frisco to the wrong person. You have to figure out why she came. What would she gain by pretending to be kin of his? Why would someone want Frisco out of town?"

Why indeed? He had warned her that his legal work would bring him enemies, but what did this woman have to do with that? Why would she want him to go on a pointless mission to find his parents?

The timing. The hearing. Caroline's fists clenched.

"The hearing tomorrow. He's going to miss the hearing. I've got to catch him." Caroline shoved the pot into Sophie's arms. "A horse. I need a horse."

Caroline ran toward the livery. Sophie hiked her skirt and tried to keep up.

"That man, there," Sophie panted. "He's on our side."

A gaunt, redheaded man was pouring lead into a bullet mold under the shade of a covered wagon. His horse was tethered nearby.

"Can I borrow your horse?" Caroline asked. "Please. It's an emergency. I have to get to Oklahoma Station before the train leaves."

"The station? You're going after Frisco?" He looked up at the sun's placement. "My horse isn't saddled."

"It doesn't matter." Caroline reached for the halter and reins.

"C'mon, Henry," Sophie urged. "Do you want Frisco there tomorrow or not?"

"Take it, take it," he said. "I'll walk if I have to. Just hurry."

Using the wagon wheel as steps, Caroline mounted and was off. Growing up with a cavalry officer for a father had given her advantages her whole life. Being able to ride bareback with the best riders in the West was one of them. Being fearless was another.

Too bad Mrs. Hunter couldn't ride like Caroline. In his impatience to get to Oklahoma Station, Frisco felt as tired as if he'd pulled the buggy himself. Maybe he should have. It couldn't have gone any slower. But they'd arrived before the train. He had enough time to buy tickets. Enough time to wonder anew at the sudden change in his circumstances.

"Would you like to get something to eat?" Frisco asked. "I don't know if you're comfortable going in establishments like the one here, but they'll serve up a good dinner."

Mrs. Hunter shook her head in tight, short jerks. "No. I steer clear of places like that. Anywhere there's gambling repulses me."

Frisco tried to ignore the smell of liver and onions coming out of the new saloon. Another start-up town just like

Plainview. Everything growing and in flux. As he looked at the progress, it was easy to forget what he was doing there. As if it were just another day, waiting for the train. And Mrs. Hunter wasn't helpful either. He'd peppered her with questions from the time they'd rolled out of Plainview, but she'd exhausted her gift of gab.

If he were in her shoes, he'd want to know everything about his newly discovered nephew. He wouldn't have been satisfied until he'd heard a complete telling of his life from consciousness to what he ate for breakfast, but she didn't think along the same lines. She didn't ask him anything and didn't seem interested when he volunteered information.

Then again, she was his aunt, not his mother. Which brought up another question. . . .

"Do you have any children of your own?" He crossed his arms over his stomach to still the rumbling inside.

"No!" She drew back as if offended. "Of course not."

"I just wondered, you know, if I had cousins."

"Cousins?" Her brow wrinkled, then she said, "Oh yes, cousins! No, you don't have cousins. At least . . . let's see. You could have cousins from another part of the family, if you want."

Frisco noted her complexion. Had she been in the heat too long? "If I want?"

She shook her head. "There might be cousins. I don't know. I'm not well acquainted with your father's side."

He mustn't judge her. She'd done so much for him already that she was entitled to a few quirks. "Coming here to get me must've been a huge inconvenience," he said. "I can't thank you enough."

"Anything at all for my favorite nephew." She smiled and patted his hand.

Favorite? More than his brothers? Frisco's head hurt from trying to make sense of her willy-nilly pronouncements. Her sister was dying. Surely the stress had affected her, along with the heat, and the journey, and the hunger. The factors contributing to her confusion were myriad. He'd weary himself trying to get answers to everything.

He was worried enough about the court hearing he was going to miss. Surely the men wouldn't be barred from a hearing just because their representation didn't appear. They'd have the evidence in hand, and it was only a hearing with the Land Office, not an official court date. Still, Frisco had seen smaller irregularities challenged and succeed in getting a case thrown out. He shifted on the wooden bench. As much as he wanted to deny it, he'd given McFarland and the Premiers an opening. If they wanted to protest on procedural grounds, they could.

But what else could he do? After twenty-six years, his mother was asking him to come home.

The bell hanging from the awning of the ticket office began to ring. A lady in homespun rose off the ground and picked up her crate of chickens. A cowboy waiting in the shade took one long draw from his cigarette before tossing it down and snuffing it out with his bootheel. An Indian in a striped shirt, broadcloth vest, and fringed buckskin trousers checked his ticket again.

The train was coming. Whatever regrets Frisco had about his decision had to be set aside. He was sorry it was going to turn out this way, but he had no choice.

He helped Mrs. Hunter stand and took their tickets out of his vest pocket. Who knew when he'd be back? He couldn't imagine life with a family, but neither could he imagine life apart from the future he had planned in this territory. He couldn't stay gone for long. Caroline warranted looking after, and—

He had to be imagining things, because no woman would ride her horse onto the train platform. But if such a woman existed, she'd have striking red hair and a cavalry trooper walking next to her, clearing the way.

"Caroline," Frisco called. He pulled Mrs. Hunter out of the line waiting to board and headed toward Caroline. She saw him. She spoke to the trooper, and he motioned the crowd to part as she eased forward. What was the matter? From the determined line of her brow, she wasn't coming for a last-minute kiss good-bye.

She slid off the horse—she'd been riding astride without a saddle—and handed the reins to the clean-faced sergeant. He saluted like she was his superior, then led the horse off the platform, apologizing every step of the way.

Caroline wasted no time in greeting but threw both arms around Frisco's neck. Frisco crushed her against himself—whys didn't matter when embraces were offered. She must have left soon after he had. Another lady inconvenienced on his behalf today.

But Caroline's words blasted his feelings of gratitude.

"Frisco, that woman is lying to you." She smoothed his cravat. Her eyes were filled with sadness. "She isn't your aunt. Her name is . . . I can't remember her name, but Sophie knows her. She's a gambler."

"My aunt is a gambler?" He tried to look past Caroline, but she wouldn't allow it.

"She isn't your aunt, Frisco. The whole story was a lie. A very cruel lie. It isn't the truth."

He wanted to shove away from it all—from Caroline, from Mrs. Hunter, from his packed traveling case, and most of all from the pain that came roaring at him with the speed of the approaching train. The image of his sick mother was too strong, too solid for him to ignore. With numb fingers, he removed Caroline's arms from around his neck.

The crowds surged around them. Thick smoke from the train's smokestack clogged his nose and stung his eyes, but he singled out Mrs. Hunter. She looked over her shoulder at him, and her face was a mask as she joined the line to board the train. Between her fingers was a white slip of paper. Frisco lifted his hand, stunned to see that he only held one ticket.

"She's going without me," he said. "Why would she go without me?"

Caroline's hand felt cool in his. "Let's sit down, Frisco. Let's take some time to think this over."

The train was going to leave. Everything depended on him being on that train. But Caroline was saying something important. What she was telling him would change everything—just like what Mrs. Hunter had told him had changed everything. His focus fell back on Caroline. Again, those sad eyes. She knew more than he did.

"You want me to miss the train?" he said. "I was going to see my mother." He felt like a child repeating a solemn promise.

"You don't need to get on the train. That woman is leaving without you because she got caught in fraud. You'll never see her again."

He allowed Caroline to lead him to a bench, but his knees wouldn't bend. How could he sit and visit while everyone boarded? He twisted his head to release some of the tension in his neck. The train whistle sounded, and the giant wheels screeched as they began to rotate. Had Caroline not held him by the hand, he would have sprung toward the stairs and made a last, desperate leap to be on the train.

In his gut, he knew Caroline was telling the truth, but maybe there was still a chance. Maybe this woman wasn't his aunt, but there could be someone at the train station waiting for him. A man—tempered by hard work and possessing confidence earned through success—might be watching for him. If he wasn't on that train, what would they tell his dying mother? How could they explain to her that her son had decided not to come?

The tension remained until the train rumbled away down the

tracks. Finally he could breathe. Finally he could learn exactly what Caroline was trying to tell him.

"Let's walk," he said. He couldn't stand still any longer.

He headed away from the tracks toward where the new houses were going in. Families lived here. Families with a mother, father, and children. Probably with a grandma and maybe a niece or nephew to boot. Frisco sighed. "I'm ready now. Say what you were going to say."

Caroline had kept his hand in hers, like he was a naughty puppy liable to bolt at any time. "Sophie recognized that woman. She isn't any relation to you. She's a cardsharp. Someone hired her to draw you out of town. Someone who doesn't want you to show up at the hearing in Kingfisher tomorrow."

Her words burned like acid, but he had to let them penetrate. "Then how did she know what she told me? She knew I'd been found on a train. She knew that my mother had visited me when I was a baby and that I had brothers. She knew about the handkerchief that was left with me. She even had the right initials."

"The train part, I don't know. Maybe Patrick or Sophie told someone in town and the story got passed around. Or maybe they concocted it based on your name. And your handkerchief was out there hanging with the rest of your clothes. Even I noticed that the monogram didn't match. As for the rest . . . do you know for certain that your mother visited you and that you have brothers, or did she tell you that?"

Amazing how quickly the pictures had taken root in his mind and become part of his story. It had only been a few hours, but already Frisco imagined that perhaps he remembered one of those visits with his mother. Perhaps he could conjure her image if he tried hard enough.

"You're right," he said. "I hadn't heard that before. I so badly wanted to believe. . . ."

"I know." She laid her head on his arm as their steps slowed.

"Nothing has changed. I'm in the same spot I was this morning, but I feel that I've lost so much more."

"Those rotten deputies have no conscience, and that's a fact. But something has changed." Her smile was finely tuned to draw him out. "They had a plan to keep you away from the hearing. Now that plan has failed, and you will be there representing your clients. That's a step in the right direction."

Frisco threw his arm around her shoulders and hugged her to his side. The events of the day would haunt him for years, but she'd said exactly what he needed to hear.

"Let's find the buggy," he said.

"And the horse I borrowed. That sergeant said he'd keep it for me until I headed back."

"We have a long ride ahead of us," Frisco said. Which would give him a lot of time to mourn what wasn't going to happen, and a lot of time to think ahead.

Chapter Twenty-Eight

Caroline dipped a washcloth into the basin and scrubbed the cool water on her face. It was still dark outside, but Frisco would be here soon. Last night had been a painful parting. How she wished she hadn't had to send him off alone after his disappointment, but evening had fallen, and even on the frontier, propriety must be observed. He'd kissed her with a longing that went beyond romance. He wanted a home, a family to belong to. She understood and was willing to join him, but he had to believe it would last. She couldn't stake her future on someone who wasn't sure he had one.

Bucky bleated, notifying her that Frisco had arrived. Caroline got her hat, gloves, and handbag. She'd prayed all the short night for Frisco. Now was the time to show the concern she'd felt in those dark hours.

She opened the door. Even with only his outline discernible in the darkness, she could tell he'd shored up his courage. The jaunty tilt of his hat, the swinging fringe on the arms of his buckskin coat, and his swagger were so much of what had captured her imagination years ago.

Without pause, he strode to her and snatched her out of the

doorway. He spun her around and gave her a confident smack on the lips.

Safe in his arms, Caroline smiled and flicked the brim of his hat. "Frontier clothes today? I thought you would wear your city clothes for this important meeting."

"I don't want to look like the rest of those impostors. I didn't come to this territory lately. This is my past. Other people have homes and families, but I had this dream of a land and a people. I don't want to be confused with the rest of the lawyers. I'm going for the runners who gave it a fair shot. The decision should have been made at the end of the race, not before a board, and I'm here to remind them of that."

Caroline nearly burst with pride for him. "It represents you well," she said. "I hope there never comes a day when an honest working man feels underdressed in this territory."

"You, on the other hand, look stunning, as always."

"A compliment on my appearance? I thought you only gave those to irritate my father."

"If you needed more, I'd say it more often. Thankfully, you are fully aware of your beauty, and also that you have a myriad of qualities that are even more impressive."

"We should go before you turn my head and we miss the hearing altogether."

He waited for her to latch the door behind her, then led her up the bank where the buggy was waiting. Caroline wiped her side of the bench, as it had a bit of morning dew on it. Frisco waited for her to get settled before slacking the reins, and they were off.

"I owe you for yesterday," he said. "I couldn't thank you properly then—I wasn't ready—but after a night to mull it over, I realized it was better to know before I got to Kansas. If I'd been duped into missing this hearing, I would've felt stupid, not just unwanted."

"Don't say that," Caroline protested. "You aren't unwanted."

"You want me?" He bounced his eyebrows. "This poor-orphan role is working."

She punched his arm, which barely made a dent in his thick leather jacket. She'd seen his agony. She knew the hurt he was covering, but she also knew that he had overcome much in his life. If he felt like laughing about it today, then she would laugh. If he was angry tomorrow, she'd let him rant. It was his story, and he'd deal with it as he saw fit.

And he'd know how to deal with the hearing as well.

Frisco had made himself scarce since returning from Oklahoma Station. If word reached the Premiers that he had never boarded the train, they might plan more devilment for him. Instead he took circuitous routes to Caroline's homestead and now to Kingfisher, not wanting to cross paths with those who were plotting to keep him away.

Kingfisher came into view as the sun reached its zenith. Another start-up town, sprouting out of the dirt. It was bigger than Plainview, but it was a verified town site, surveyed by the government before the race with a land office already in place. Still, Frisco compared the two in his mind while Caroline sang a ditty about a little brown jug. Whether she had learned it from the troopers or her dance-hall-singing stepmother, he wouldn't ask, but her happiness was contagious.

Coming home from the train station yesterday, Frisco would have sworn that it would be impossible for him ever to feel as strong as he did this morning, but the night had been profitable. On his knees, heart open, he'd talked it out with his Lord. Who was he? He was God's child. Would knowing who his parents were change who he was? Not really. The people he had come from didn't dictate who he would be. He was on the verge of choosing a family for himself. It would be that decision that set his course from here. Not his parentage.

When they reached the plain board building where the hearings were being held, Frisco dropped Caroline off, then went to park the buggy. When he returned, she was waving him toward the open door. He recognized McFarland's voice, clipped and to the point, coming out the window. Deep grumblings came from other attendees, and then another voice he recognized spoke up, but he couldn't figure out for the life of him what Patrick was doing here.

No time to spare. Frisco pushed through the crowded room toward where the contestants stood before the official Register and Receiver.

McFarland was speaking again. "There's one name at the top of this petition for a hearing, and he is not here. These outlandish claims by Patrick Smith will not be tolerated, nor should they be entertained. They are immaterial to the facts of this case, which is that these men are here without representation."

"No, they're not." Frisco emerged from the crowd. "I'm here."

No lost family member could have looked as happy to see him as those men did at that second. And no one could have looked more disgusted than McFarland, Bledsoe, Juarez, and Feldstein. Patrick slumped in relief.

Mr. Robberts dropped his fist to the table. "Finally. Let's stop arguing about paltry stuff and get to the meat. Did these men abide by the rules, or did they use their status as deputies to start the run from somewhere closer than the line?" With a grumble, he added, "Something we're seeing a whole lot of recently."

"We have witnesses who saw us at the starting line near Darlington," McFarland said.

"Witnesses besides each other?" Mr. Admire, the Receiver, asked.

Juarez sank further in his chair. McFarland adjusted his tie. "If you give us some more time, we can produce as many as you need."

"I'm sure you can." Robberts turned to Frisco. "The burden of proof is on you, sir. It's tough to prove a negative. If you have a witness saying they spotted them in the territory before noon, then how are we to determine who is telling the truth?"

"My witness is extremely reliable." Frisco went to his clients' table. Mr. Lacroix knew what he was after and passed the envelope to him. "Mr. Robberts and Mr. Admire, I'd like to present evidence that everyone in Plainview has seen." He pulled out the notorious picture and slid it in front of them.

"What are we looking at?" Mr. Robberts asked.

McFarland scoffed. "You're producing *that* as evidence? We have a copy of the same picture in our files. That picture was taken on April twenty-second, and it clearly shows who the first arrivals at Plainview were. You won't find Mr. LaCroix or any of the others there."

Frisco placed his hands on either side of the photo and leaned on the committee's table. "You won't find them in the photo because they were waiting at the line when this photo was taken. Notice the shadows. It's hours from noon yet. And just in case there's an argument over what direction they are facing, by half after twelve, the land surrounding them was filled with settlers." He straightened as his voice rose. "The only time this photograph could've been taken was the morning of April twenty-second or earlier. It's irrefutable proof that they broke the law, and it's been on full display in town."

The spectators erupted as the officials huddled around the picture.

When Mr. Robberts raised his head, his face was grim. "It is our duty to decide whether their claims are valid or whether their property should be available for other settlers. In light of the discoveries presented by you gentlemen, we find it to be justice to expel every man in this photo from the territory, and in accordance to the law concerning illegal activity, they are barred from making a claim in the future. They have twenty-four hours to gather their belongings and quit the area."

Any quick movement and Frisco might inadvertently release a victory shout, so he stepped slowly from the table. Then, remembering the conversation he'd had with Major Adams, he returned.

"Thank you, sir, but I think this case gives the board a chance to address a larger matter as well."

He looked over the room of townspeople, both from King-fisher and the surrounding areas. How many of them were pro-testing a similar case without a photograph as evidence? How many of them had been taken advantage of by those getting paid by their own government? It was high time precedent was set.

"Mr. Robberts and Mr. Admire, the case today was decided in my clients' favor because we could prove that the defendants were in the territory before the given time and date. Truthfully, the deputies were *supposed* to be in the territory, but in order to catch moonlighters. That was their job. Instead, they were competing with the very people they were being paid to protect.

"You see, according to my sources, all soldiers were disquali-fied from competing in the race because it was a conflict of in-terest. I'm asking you to make a ruling that the same restriction applies to law enforcement and anyone else who was being paid that day—whether surveyors or railroad employees—to assist in the run. If you decide this now, many of your cases will be resolved with no further hearing."

The effect in the room was instantaneous. A few people shouted *amen* like they were at a revival, while others hissed and booed. The Register and the Receiver huddled together. This time it was Mr. Admire who answered.

"We agree with Mr. Smith that the government never intended for the men hired to monitor the race to participate. As far as we know, those rules weren't expressly written out, but that does not mean they weren't implied. While this decision will no doubt be revisited in a courthouse, we will file a brief on behalf of all the civilian participants to automatically have all federal and railroad employees stricken from the claims lists." He turned to Frisco's clients—Lacroix, Deavers, and the others. "Thank you for persisting in this claim. Had you faltered, Plainview would've had corruption ingrained from its inception. My congratulations to you and your representative. Now that we've determined that the former owners have lost their rights, our next business is to deed the plots to someone worthy, with special consideration going to those who challenged the holding. We'll take a brief break and then resume."

Frisco stepped away from the table. Caroline's smiling face was easy to spot in the crowded room. Her eyes looked watery. He was feeling soft in the head too, now that he thought about it. Before he could reach her, he was engulfed by a wave of manly celebration. They might not all get a place of their own, but a way had been opened. And there was Patrick, standing before him, twisting his hat like he was wringing it after a washing.

"Patrick, I was surprised to see you here," Frisco said. "I didn't know you'd joined the suit."

Patrick looked miserable. "I owe you an apology. Me and my big mouth. When McFarland came over the day after the storm, I thought he was being friendly. He asked me a dozen questions about how you and I met, then asked how you came to be in the foundling hospital. I even told him about your handkerchief when he saw it. When Sophie told me what he'd done, I was right beset. Ailed over it something awful. It was on account of me. I came to make things right, but I'm glad you found your way here too."

Frisco clapped him on the shoulder. "You are the closest thing to a brother I have, Patrick. You didn't mean anything by it, so don't fret. And when we start the discussion, I'll do what I can to get your name included in the parcel giveaway. You and Millie still need a place of your own."

"Wouldn't that be grand? I'm just sorry for what McFarland put you through. If someone told me that my mother was alive and hunting for me—"

Frisco squeezed his shoulder. "It's behind me. Let's just keep looking forward."

And that was exactly what he wanted to do with Caroline.

Chapter Twenty-Nine

The table was upstairs in the unfinished rooms, but his four new chairs were in the kitchen. Four chairs, and he didn't have to pay anyone if he wanted to sit on them. Frisco, Sophie, Millie, and Amber were in the chairs, gathered around a page that was growing increasingly complicated.

"She likes chicken and dumplings," Amber said. "I could make those here early. What time did you tell her to be here?"

"Eight o'clock. About this time tomorrow evening." He wiped his hands on his trouser legs.

"Getting nervous?" Sophie laughed. "Don't you worry. I'll bring some nice dishes so your table will be set properly."

"How about bird's-nest pudding?" Millie leaned forward. "I haven't made one in years, but if I can use this kitchen . . ." She and Patrick were still living in the tent, but if everything went as planned, they wouldn't be for long.

"Yes, use the kitchen. I sure couldn't cook anything in it," said Frisco.

There was a crash above their heads. The ladies startled. Frisco jumped up and ran to the ladder that led to the upstairs. "Is everyone all right?"

Patrick called down, "Right as rain. Bradley and I were trying to frame out a room on the north side. A plank slipped. Nothing hurt."

"Just my pride," Bradley corrected.

"Be careful," Frisco said. "Getting the floor down is most important. I don't want her to fall through."

Mrs. Hennessey stepped into the room with a paintbrush in hand. "I've got the mural nearly done. Would you like to see it?"

He followed her into the parlor and gaped. On the wall was a masterpiece.

"I wish I'd had you put it on a canvas," he said, "because someday we're going to have to take that wall with us."

"I don't think you'll be moving anytime soon," she replied.

In the foreground, the distinctive shapes of two scissor-tailed flycatchers were silhouetted on a bare branch. Beneath them stretched out the Oklahoma prairie and a glorious sunset. While the horizon was the focus, when Frisco stepped closer, he could see a faint grid made out on the grasslands below.

"Is that Plainview?" he asked.

She nodded. "Or at least what it'll look like soon. And look closer to the horizon. To the far west."

"It's the fort. And what's that to the south?"

"That's Redhawk, going up as planned."

He beamed. "Thank you, Mrs. Hennessey. That an artist of your stature would do this for us . . ."

"Goodness gracious, if I paint for the pleasure of art galleries, why wouldn't I paint for my friends and family? Besides, have you ever seen Caroline paint? You don't want that. Now, Louisa sent these curtains. We need to get them hung."

It was all coming together. Would Caroline be surprised? He hoped not. He hoped she'd been impatiently waiting for him to ask her the question they'd both taken for granted since the trial. They had talked about the future. She'd agreed to give the bulk of her land to the prospectors who had purchased lots in Redhawk, although for the time being she was keeping her dugout home. And on his end, he'd made arrangements with his investors, and they had started moving in last week. Like Plainview, Redhawk was changing every day.

As for him, he was free and clear of the responsibility. A few days was all it took for him to direct them to the plots they'd reserved, and then he'd left them to their own devices. They didn't need his help after all. Although he wouldn't be surprised if someday the towns of Redhawk and Plainview might merge, given their proximity.

He was ready to move on to the next chapter. At any given moment he was liable to race to Caroline's homestead and blurt out his proposal, but she deserved something finer.

He was still imagining her delight when a banging on the front door brought him to his senses.

"Frisco, it's Caroline. Are you in there?"

He could've been at the fort and heard her, as loud as she was hollering. Mrs. Hennessey grimaced and shrugged. He had to answer it.

Caroline stood with one hand on her hip and the other holding a shawl in a knotted bunch. "I'm leaving," she announced.

"You just got here." Frisco looked over his shoulder to see Amber, Millie, and Sophie coming in from the kitchen. But Caroline was on a roll.

"No, I'm leaving the territory. I'm leaving my homestead, or what's left of it. It'd be nice if I could get some money for it, as otherwise I'm leaving empty-handed and I don't know how I'll manage, but if you don't know anyone in the market . . ."

Without a word, Hattie began gathering her brushes. Amber put out her hands to keep Sophie and Millie from coming any closer. Frisco crossed his arms over his chest. So this was the way she wanted it? Just like in dancing, she'd get too impatient and take out leading if you didn't move quick enough.

"Thank you, ladies, for your help," he said.

Caroline hadn't seen the others until then. She covered her mouth with both hands. "I'm sorry, Amber. I would've told you once it was all settled, but you have Bradley. I'm out there all alone."

Frisco stepped out of the way just in time to avoid Amber, who ran forward and hugged Caroline. "I'm not altogether convinced you're going anywhere," Amber said loudly enough for everyone to hear. "Now, listen to what he has to say." She kissed Caroline on the cheek, which seemed to calm her.

Caroline didn't move an inch as Sophie and Millie helped gather Mrs. Hennessey's things. Her brow creased as Frisco called Patrick and Bradley down. Patrick walked quickly by, like he was trying not to be seen, while Bradley sauntered slowly with plenty of brow wagging and smirks.

They all filed outside past a confused and embarrassed Caroline. She waited until Frisco closed the door.

"Is there anyone else here?" she asked.

"Who else could be here? That's pretty much everyone we know."

"If you're busy . . ."

"Not anymore. Come. I want to show you something." He pointed to the sturdy ladder. "You've been spending so much time underground, I thought you might want to level out."

"There's nothing upstairs," she said, but she put her foot on the first rung just the same. Halfway up, when her head cleared the opening, she stopped and looked down at him. "What do you have a table upstairs for? You don't even have the walls finished."

"Be careful where you step. We're still working on the floor." And it was getting dark. He followed her up, feeling edgy as he stepped off the ladder. This was it, then. This was him starting his life on another new venture, but on this one, he wouldn't be going alone.

Suddenly shy, she turned away and looked past the open framework of the wall and across the expanse of the little town they'd built together on the prairie. Plainview had new leadership now via a more gradual, natural process than the first one. A process that allowed people of talent and integrity a voice instead of defaulting to those who'd manipulated the outcome. Frisco was proud of all he'd accomplished, but there was so much more they could do. And he didn't want to do it alone.

"So, you're leaving?" He stood by her side and surveyed the grid of new streets dividing the plots.

"I'm sorry I interfered in the first place. I thought that being dependent on my family was the worst thing that could happen to me. As it happens, that isn't true."

"You found something worse?" He brushed his hand across her neck, straightening her collar. Her shiver delighted him.

"We agreed on the land, and your people have started to arrive, but I don't want to stay there with them. Not this close."

"It'd make me very happy to give the dugout to Patrick along with a few acres by the river."

"Patrick, Millie, and Jonathan?" Her smile was bittersweet. "That would make me happy too, but you came up with that fairly quickly. Has that been the plan all along?"

"You don't know all my plans."

"I used to. We used to work together. I helped you get your law practice started, but since the hearing, you haven't asked for my help."

"I wanted you to stay away."

"And that's what I came to tell you. You're getting what you want." Her indignation encouraged him. If he'd had any doubt about her druthers, they were gone now.

He found her wrist, then slid his hand along hers, lacing his fingers with hers. "I love you, Caroline."

She kept her face forward and squeezed his hand. "I love you too. That's why leaving is so hard."

"You aren't a farmer," he said. "And you aren't an innkeeper. You belong in a town, but you won't be happy in Galveston. It's too settled, too civilized. My Caroline's talents would be wasted there. You need a rowdy upstart of a town that's just looking for some ornery women to tame it."

"I thought I'd found the perfect place," she said, "but it'd be too hard to be here with you, but without you."

"Didn't I invite you to come for dinner?" he asked.

"That was days ago. I haven't heard a word since."

"Because I was busy getting the house in order for you. Sophie, Millie, and Amber planned the menu for the meal. Mrs. Adams and Mrs. Hennessey were decorating. Bradley and Patrick put the flooring in, and then I hauled this table up here myself—no small feat on a ladder. All to prepare for a very special meal for a very special woman."

Caroline looked around. She sucked her lips inside her mouth and then smacked them. "I came a day early, didn't I?" Her eyelashes fluttered. She pulled her hand away from his. "I'm sorry. I'll come back tomorrow. We can forget—"

"No, it's too late. Sometimes you only get one chance to do it right." He caught her hand again and dropped to one knee. Had he had another day, he would've gotten a rug placed for comfort, but the time was now. He'd almost waited too long as it was. "Miss Adams, in light of my fervent love for you and my promise to always adore and cherish you, I'm asking if you would do me the honor of becoming my wife."

Her face glowed. "Are you sure? You know what you're getting into, don't you?"

"Absolutely sure. And if we decide this isn't the place for us, then we have the whole world at our disposal."

Her mouth quirked. "I think you're obligated to stay a few years at least, Mr. Mayor."

Mr. Mayor . . . it was still hard for him to believe. But when nearly all the city council and officials were found to have cheated, there were a lot of vacancies. But she still hadn't said yes, and that was more important than any election. If she was going to be stubborn, he'd have to be more persuasive.

He hoped she was going to be stubborn.

Standing, he pulled her close. She wrapped her arms around his waist and laid her head against his chest, both of them looking out at the sun going down over the roofs of Plainview and the verdant prairies beyond it.

"If I say yes, we live here?" she said.

"That's the plan."

"And the goat?"

"I forbid it from stepping hoof on the property. It goes to Patrick's family."

"Then I accept." She snuggled closer. "But let's not tell everyone just yet. I'll come back tomorrow. I want to see this meal you had planned."

"Not possible. They'll take one look at my face and know you said yes. Besides, I'm going to be bragging about it to everyone I meet. For the rest of our lives, I'll be bragging about how I claimed the major's daughter. In fact, I'm going to Patrick's tent right now so I can start spreading the word."

"Isn't there something you'd like to do before you go to him?" She smiled up at him and tilted her head just so.

"Actually, there is."

Frisco hesitated just long enough to imprint the moment forever in his soul. The moment that his imperfect planning resulted in the life he'd always wanted. If his kisses were achingly slow, it was because he couldn't get over the enormity of what had happened. He'd been dreaming about this for days, but there was one other thing he'd waited even longer for.

After Caroline and he had spent a respectable amount of time alone, after they'd found Patrick and accepted his congratulations, and after Frisco had escorted her back to the dugout—perhaps for the last time—he came back and found his traveling case.

He paused after he opened the latches. The bag hadn't been completely emptied since he was a child, and then someone else had packed it for him. He'd learned to keep his things ready for the unexpected, ready for heartache, and ready to be uprooted, but no longer.

He lifted out his clothes, fishing in each corner to catch them all, and left them in a pile on the bed. Turning the bag over, he shook it out, just to make sure it was absolutely empty.

Amazing how light the case felt now. How easy to haul, but he wouldn't need to haul it anywhere, because he'd found where he wanted to be.

He was home.

A Note from the Author

Dear Reader,

For me, the most difficult part of writing is the world-building. Before the plot can start rolling, the story must be anchored in a place. Decisions are made on the layout of the town, the floorplans of significant buildings, and the location of physical landmarks. I start with a blank page, and from that I have to create a community for my characters to inhabit.

The participants of the 1889 Land Run had the same task before them, but instead of looking at a blank sheet of paper from the safety of their office, they had a blank prairie. Instead of typing words, they had to pick up their hammers and shovels and construct homes and towns. And instead of there being one author at the keyboard, proceeding in an orderly fashion, there were instantly thousands of "creatives," all working with their own idea of what the result should be.

As expected, the explosion method of city planning was not ideal. Conflict was rife from before the cannons sounded until today, when some city grids don't match up because two founders started at different points and neither would compromise.

Instead of discovering one quirky historical tidbit to expand on and fictionalize for this story, I had to limit the number of facts I included because many of them were unbelievable, although true.

The boomers' illegal homesteading, people selling plots of land in cities that didn't exist, jumping from moving trains, the voting methods and fraud, a photograph of founding fathers being used against them in court, and even the pay-as-you-go outhouses—all of that happened. I couldn't begin to fit all the madness of that time into this story, so I encourage you to read up on it yourself. Two books I recommend are *The Oklahoma Land Rush of 1889* by Stan Hoig and *The Birth of Guthrie* by Lloyd H. McGuire Jr.

One place where I did take historical license is that the term *sooner* wasn't used during the 1889 race. Best I can tell, it was first used in court on October 1, 1890. Before that, the men who snuck across the starting line early were called *moonlighters* or *moonshiners*, but as both of those words have other meanings now, and *sooner* has been embraced as uniquely Oklahoman, I let it appear a year early.

Thank you for allowing me to share Frisco and Caroline's story, along with some of my state's history. If you'd like to hear about new projects, you can find me and news about my books at www.reginajennings.com or on Facebook. Please stay in touch. I love hearing from my readers.

God bless, and thanks for reading!

—Regina

Regina Jennings is a graduate of Oklahoma Baptist University with a degree in English and a minor in history. She's the winner of the National Readers' Choice Award, a two-time Golden Quill finalist, and a finalist for the Oklahoma Book of the Year Award. Regina has worked at the *Mustang News* and at First Baptist Church of Mustang, along with time at the Oklahoma National Stockyards and various livestock shows. She lives outside of Oklahoma City with her husband and four children and can be found online at www.reginajennings.com.

Sign Up for Regina's Newsletter!

Keep up to date with Regina's news on book releases and events by signing up for her email list at www.reginajennings.com.

More from Regina Jennings

Confirmed bachelor Lieutenant Jack Hennessey is stunned to run into Hattie Walker, the girl who shattered his heart...and she's just as surprised to find her rescuer is the neighbor she once knew. But his attempts to save her from a dangerous situation go awry, and the two end up in a mess that puts her dreams in peril—and tests his resolve to remain single.

The Lieutenant's Bargain
The Fort Reno Series #2

You May Also Like . . .

Growing up in Colorado, Josephine Madson has been fascinated by, but has shied away from, the outside world—one she's been raised to believe killed her parents. When Dave Warden, a rancher, shows up at their secret home with his wounded father, will Josephine and her sisters risk stepping into the world to help, or remain separated but safe on Hope Mountain?

Aiming for Love by Mary Connealy
BRIDES OF HOPE MOUNTAIN #1
maryconnealy.com

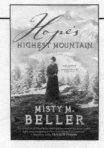

On her way to deliver vaccines to a mining town in the Montana Territory, Ingrid Chastain never anticipated a terrible accident would leave her alone and badly injured in the wilderness. When rescue comes in the form of a mysterious mountain man, she's hesitant to trust him, but the journey ahead will change their lives more than they could have known.

Hope's Highest Mountain by Misty M. Beller
HEARTS OF MONTANA #1
mistymbeller.com

Gray Delacroix has dedicated his life to building a successful global spice empire, but it has come at a cost. Tasked with gaining access to the private Delacroix plant collection, Smithsonian botanist Annabelle Larkin unwittingly steps into a web of dangerous political intrigue and will be forced to choose between her heart and her loyalty to her country.

The Spice King by Elizabeth Camden
HOPE AND GLORY #1
elizabethcamden.com

❧ BETHANYHOUSE

More from Bethany House

As part of a bargain with her wealthy grandmother, Poppy Garrison accepts an unusual proposition to participate in the New York social Season. Forced to travel to America to help his cousin find an heiress to wed, bachelor Reginald Blackburn is asked to give Poppy etiquette lessons, and he swiftly discovers he may be in for much more than he bargained for.

Diamond in the Rough by Jen Turano
AMERICAN HEIRESSES #2
jenturano.com

To help support her family and make use of her artistic skill, Mellie finds employment at a daguerreotype shop, where she creates silhouette portraits. When romance begins to blossom with one of her charming customers, her life seems to have fallen perfectly into place—but when the unexpected happens, will she find happiness despite her hidden secrets?

A Perfect Silhouette by Judith Miller
judithmccoymiller.com

After being railroaded by the city council, Abby needs a man's name on her bakery's deed, and a man she can control—not the stoic lumberman Zacharias, who always seems to exude silent confidence. She can't even control her pulse when she's around him. But as trust grows between them, she finds she wants more than his rescue. She wants his heart.

More Than Words Can Say by Karen Witemeyer
karenwitemeyer.com

◈ BETHANYHOUSE